The Ripper

"Are you in *law enforcement*, Mr. . . . ?" she asked.

"Depends on what laws you're referring to. I follow my own."

A glint turned her head down to his side. His hand now held a long, sharp knife, its silver mixing with the gaslight's yellow. By the time Elizabeth B. Rowley looked back up, his right hand was at her throat. Any sound she might've made, any objection she might have raised, was stifled by his grip.

He lifted steadily until first the heels, then the balls of her feet no longer touched the floor.

"And please, let's not get all tangled up in formalities," he said. "Call me Jack."

For Shelby—because he's always had that look

SPEAK
Published by the Penguin Group
Penguin Group (USA) Inc., 345 Hudson Street, New York, New York 10014, U.S.A.
Penguin Group (Canada), 90 Eglinton Avenue East, Suite 700, Toronto, Ontario M4P 2Y3, Canada
(a division of Pearson Penguin Canada Inc.)
Penguin Books Ltd, 80 Strand, London WC2R 0RL, England
Penguin Ireland, 25 St Stephen's Green, Dublin 2, Ireland (a division of Penguin Books Ltd)
Penguin Group (Australia), 707 Collins Street, Melbourne, Victoria 3008, Australia
(a division of Pearson Australia Group Pty Ltd)
Penguin Books India Pvt Ltd, 11 Community Centre, Panchsheel Park, New Delhi–110 017, India
Penguin Group (NZ), 67 Apollo Drive, Rosedale, Auckland 0632, New Zealand
(a division of Pearson New Zealand Ltd)
Penguin Books, Rosebank Office Park, 181 Jan Smuts Avenue, Parktown North 2193, South Africa
Penguin China, B7 Jiaming Center, 27 East Third Ring Road North,
Chaoyang District, Beijing 100020, China

Penguin Books Ltd, Registered Offices: 80 Strand, London WC2R 0RL, England

First published in the United States of America by Philomel Books,
a division of Penguin Young Readers Group, 2012
Published by Speak, an imprint of Penguin Group (USA) Inc., 2013

1 3 5 7 9 10 8 6 4 2

Copyright © Penguin Group (USA) Inc., 2012
All rights reserved

Edited by Michael Green
Design by Semadar Megged
Text set in 12-point Bembo

THE LIBRARY OF CONGRESS HAS CATALOGED THE PHILOMEL EDITION AS FOLLOWS:
Petrucha, Stefan.
Ripper / Stefan Petrucha.
p.   cm.
Summary: Adopted by famous Pinkerton Agency Detective Hawking in 1895 New York, fourteen-year-
old Carver Young hopes to find his birth father, but when he becomes involved in the pursuit of
notorious killer Jack the Ripper, Carver discovers that finding the truth can be worse than ignorance.
[1. Mystery and detective stories. 2. Jack, the Ripper—Fiction. 3. Orphans—Fiction.
4. Fathers and sons—Fiction. 5. Pinkerton's National Detective Agency—Fiction.
6. New York (N.Y.)—History—1865–1898—Fiction.]
I. Title.
PZ7.P44727Rip 2012
[Fic]—dc23
2011017516

Speak ISBN 978-0-14-242418-6

Printed in the United States of America

RIPPER

STEFAN PETRUCHA

speak
An Imprint of Penguin Group (USA) Inc.

1

MAY 23, 1895

THE LENOX LIBRARY

"LET ME show you a secret."

Elizabeth B. Rowley liked the man's confidence. She usually mingled with balding walrus types or younger men, who were as awkward as the monkeys in the Central Park Zoo. This one was different . . . *wolfish*. She liked the way he'd removed her from the boring herd. While silk-stockinged men and fine ladies with grand hats and gowns swarmed about the high-ceilinged main hall, here they were among over-flowing bookshelves, containing who knows what secrets.

"Won't we be missed?" she asked. "I wouldn't want to be rude."

He smiled. "By all means, don't let me lead you astray. I'm sure the party is far more interesting."

Beyond the stacks, Astors, Guggenheims, Rocke-fellers and other prominent families talked of this and that. Business culture. The weather in May. The new police commissioner, Roosevelt, and if he would make any difference in a police force so corrupt, one could hardly distinguish it from the street gangs.

"Where is your secret? Close by, I should hope, Mr. . . . ?"

"Just downstairs. It's a bit dark, I'm afraid."

"Then I shall count on you to guide me." She slipped her hand into the crook of his arm, impressed with how thick his muscles felt. He was tall, too.

He led her farther from the tedious crowd, deeper into the stacks, until they reached an old door that wobbled sadly on its hinges. Beyond it lay a steep staircase. Though lit by an electric bulb, it emptied into darkness.

He walked down first. Her hand was still in the crook of his arm until they neared the bottom. There, he moved ahead, vanishing. She managed the last two steps alone and stuck her head into a wide space thick with the smell of books.

"They couldn't afford to electrify the entire building," his bodiless voice said.

"Pity," she answered. She found his silhouette, watched as he twisted the valve of a rickety old gas lamp mounted in the wall. As a gentle hiss of gas emerged, he fished in his pockets.

"Not for me," he said, withdrawing a safety match. "I've always loathed Mr. Edison's bulbs. Too harsh." He scraped the match against the plaster wall, causing a spark, curls of smoke and finally a small, hot flower. When he touched it to the lamp, a yellow flame appeared, bobbing at the nozzle. "This is so much gentler."

Rows of tomb-like shelves appeared in the light. They seemed to extend forever. As the light quivered, the shadows pulsed. "Makes the dark livelier, too. Like a heartbeat."

Before she could think of a clever response, he led her down the central aisle. He stopped a quarter of the way down and ran his finger along the mottled spines. Worried she'd been silent for too long, she struggled for something interesting to say.

"Are you in publishing? An author?"

"Me? No, no. I've written a few . . . letters, but that's all."

He withdrew a thick book.

She edged closer, feeling the warmth of his coat. "Is this your secret? Aren't you going to introduce me?"

"How silly of me. Elizabeth Rowley, meet *The Crimes of Jack the Ripper,* published 1891."

She swallowed a nervous laugh. "Oh my! Talk about lurid dime novels! Isn't that the Whitechapel killer who butchered those poor women in London seven years ago?"

"Poor in more ways than one," he said, flipping through the pages. "They lived in the worst circumstances, barely scrounging enough to eat. He never touched a wealthy woman."

"Of course not. He wouldn't dare."

He turned to her. "They didn't catch him, so it's hard to tell *what* he might dare, don't you think?"

"What is it about such a horrible murderer that interests you?"

"It's just this *particular* book," he said. "It's terribly done, full of factual errors and grammar that would make a schoolboy blush. That's why there aren't many copies. It does, however, have the distinction of also being the *only* book about Saucy Jack with . . . this."

He handed it to her, open to a photographic plate. Even in the light of the distant flame she could make out the words written in a crude hand.

25 Sept. 1888

Dear Boss,

I keep on hearing the police have caught me but they wont fix me just yet. I have laughed when they look so clever and talk about being on the right track. That joke about Leather Apron gave me real fits. I am down on whores and I shant quit ripping them till I do get buckled. Grand work the last job was. I gave the lady no time to squeal. How can they catch me now. I love my work and want to start again. You will soon hear of me with my funny little games. I saved some of the proper red stuff in a ginger beer bottle over the last job to write with but it went thick like glue and I cant use it. Red ink is fit enough I hope ha. ha. The next job I do I shall clip the ladys ears off and send to the police officers just for jolly wouldnt you. Keep this letter back till I do a bit more work, then give it out straight. My knife's so nice and sharp I want to get to work right away if I get a chance. Good luck.

Yours Truly,
Jack the Ripper

"I'd read about this, but never saw the actual note," she said.

He took the book back. "Not many here have. This is the only copy someone in New York could easily get ahold of without contacting Scotland Yard in London."

With a sharp snap, he tore the page out and slipped it into his pocket. "Now . . . there are none."

Her eyes went wide. The destruction was daring, but he must have his reasons. As he slipped the book back into place, her mind searched for an explanation.

"Are you in *law enforcement,* Mr. . . . ?"

"Depends on what laws you're referring to. I follow my own."

A glint turned her head down to his side. His hand now held a long, sharp knife, its silver mixing with the gaslight's yellow. By the time Elizabeth B. Rowley looked back up, his right hand was at her throat. Any sound she might've made, any objection she might have raised, was stifled by his grip.

He lifted steadily until first the heels, then the balls of her feet no longer touched the floor.

"And please, let's not get all tangled up in formalities," he said. "Call me Jack."

2

SURROUNDED by unsettling sounds, Carver Young struggled to keep his hands still. He had to focus. *Had* to. He could do this. He wasn't some infant, afraid of the dark. If anything, he *loved* the dark. But the cracks in the attic let the wind run wild. Old papers fluttered like hesitant birds. Musty clothes rustled as if touched by spirits. And then the cleaver, wedged in the ceiling right above him, wobbled.

It was too much. He stumbled back, making the floorboards creak.

No! If someone downstairs hears me . . .

Cursing himself, he crept back under the blade. It's not going to fall. It's been there for years. No reason it should fall now. Taking a breath, he studied the lock again. The keyhole was thin, the pins that held the cylinder tough to reach. Of course *this* would be the only lock in Ellis Orphanage that ever gave him trouble.

It wasn't his first crime, but it was the only one that could change his life. Breaking into the kitchen or nabbing some school supplies could be forgiven, chalked up to what Miss Petty called "youthful indiscretion." This time, though, he could be thrown in jail.

Wouldn't Finn and his gang have a great laugh at that? Scrawny Carver locked in the Tombs, trapped among murderers and robbers, while Finn, a *real* thief, stayed free. But wouldn't Sherlock Holmes or Nick Neverseen do the same thing? Bend the law to get at the truth?

The cleaver creaked again as if eager to punish someone. Until Carver saw it for himself, he thought it was a lie the little ones used to scare each other. The story went that a nameless boy was caught stealing cookies by Curly, the cook. Drunk as a skunk, mad as the devil, Curly grabbed a cleaver and chased the boy up to the attic. But when he raised it to strike, the poor sap went to his knees bawling. The cook relented and hurled it up instead.

Maybe it was left as a warning, like the skull and crossbones on a pirate's treasure. No, it was more like that old Greek legend, the Sword of Damocles. How'd it go? Damocles envied a king, so the king offered to switch places. "King" Damocles was thrilled, until he looked up and saw a sword over his head, hanging by a thread. He got the point. Fear was the price of power.

Was that why Carver's hands shook?

Beyond the door were the private files for all the orphans at Ellis, those who'd left, those who, like him, had been here over a decade. Carver knew nothing about his own parents, not their names, not how they looked, not how they lived or even if they had died. His last name, Young, was something Miss Petty made up because he was an infant when he arrived. Ever since he'd started picking locks, he'd thought about coming up here and finding out if there was anything Miss Petty *hadn't* told him. She was always so hesitant about discussing his past. Now, with the headmistress gone for the day, he had the time he needed.

Or so he thought. After an hour of trying, the lock would not yield to his collection of bent nails. They were either too thick or the wrong shape, and he had no way to bend them now.

He stepped back and looked around for anything else he could use. The long, wide space was cramped with helter-skelter boxes, clothing racks and trunks, a graveyard of mementoes. A bit of color in the gloom caught his eye. Among some chewed, weathered alphabet blocks sat what was once his favorite toy, an old windup cowboy mounted on his horse.

It'd come from Europe, a rich person's toy, donated because it was old and broken. Miss Petty marveled when Carver, only five at the time, fixed it. Cowboy Man, he called it. Now fourteen, he picked it up. The windup key turned freely. It was broken again, but maybe it could help him one last time.

Using his thickest nail, he pried off the side of the horse. It looked like someone had poured milk inside it years ago, but the pieces were all intact. He could fix it again, but he didn't need a toy. Instead, he pulled out the wire that moved the horse's legs back and forth. It was thin enough, but rust came off between his fingers. It would probably snap. Still, it was worth a try.

He bent it carefully and, once satisfied with the shape, slipped it into the keyhole. Slowly, he turned it. Something *clicked*. The cylinder turned. The door swung inward. He had it!

Snickering at the cleaver, he moved into a room full of gray file cabinets. It was too dim to read their labels, but he guessed the bottom-right drawer would hold *X-Y-Z*. When he pulled it open, the dry metal squeaked loudly. It didn't seem right this should be illegal. The only thing he wanted was *his,* anyway.

He pulled all the files out and carried them into a scant beam of sunlight. As he sifted through the awkward pile, a breeze snatched a bit of paper from the last. Afraid he'd drop the pile if he bent to pick it up, he put his foot on it and left it there as he worked.

No *X*'s, but a few *W*'s, *Welles, Winfrey, Winters.* There it was, at the bottom: *Young, Carver.*

He set the pile on an old steamer trunk and weighed it down with a birdcage. Excited, he opened his file. Nothing. It was empty except for an annex card, the same sort he'd seen in Miss Petty's office, listing the orphan's name and any belongings that had arrived with them. Spaces for the parents had been left blank. It didn't even mention the woman Miss Petty told him had brought him to Ellis as an infant.

The card had only one entry, in the headmistress's small, neat handwriting. It was dated 1889. A letter had been received from England. From his parents? It didn't say.

Carver looked down. The folded paper was still lying under his foot. Dropping his file, he snatched up the small, imperfect rectangle. It was a letter. The paper was thick. The fountain pen ink blotched in spots. The handwriting was harsh, almost garbled.

18 July, 1889

Shan't quit, but have to stop for now, boss. Don't think I've done and gone. I'm not buckled yet and the knife's still nice and sharp for more grand work. But it's my Blood this time, and it still flows. Thought she died too quick to have our one and only, but no. He'd be eight now and I hear he has a cut ear on the shoulder for me to find him by. Same colour, to. A liking for the same job, too, I'll bet, once he gets to play my games. But that will have to wait. Try not to miss me.

Yours truly,

He read it again, then again. The fourth time, pieces began to make sense.

Thought she died too quick to have our one and only, but no, he'd be eight now.

I hear he has a cut ear on the shoulder . . .

The writer thought his son died in childbirth, along with his wife. Carver was eight in 1889 *and* he had an ear-shaped birthmark. The letter was written by *his father*!

Carver's father had tried to come for him . . . What if he was still alive? What if his father was out there still, trying to find him?

3

AFTER STEALING a few apples from the larder, Carver sat on his too-small bed in the boys' dorm. Before bedtime, the lonely hall was empty, everyone working or playing, making it the perfect place to be alone with his prize.

He was so engrossed, studying the letter line by line, memorizing every curl of the ink, that he almost didn't notice Miss Petty had appeared at the doorway. He'd barely shoved the letter in his pocket when the long thin woman crooked a finger at him and sullenly commanded, "Come with me."

Had she found out? Already? He'd been so careful.

He followed in silence as the matriarch marched him downstairs to the narrow hall between the dining room and kitchen that held her office. She was always stiff, but not like this. She must be furious. This was it, then; he'd gone too far.

He was about to apologize, to explain, when he saw that her office was already occupied. Finn Walker and Delia Stephens were sitting on a child-size bench, looking terribly uncomfortable.

At the sight of Carver, Finn narrowed his eyes and grunted in his already-deep voice, "If he said I did something, he's lying again." Big as he was, Miss Petty silenced him with a glance.

Finn was in trouble more than Carver, but what was Delia doing here? The dark-haired, round-faced girl had been at Ellis nearly as long as he and Finn, but her behavior was impeccable. Her thin cotton dress was too light for the weather, and she was flushed and sweating, as if she'd been yanked from the laundry room in the middle of her chores.

What was going on?

"Sit," Miss Petty said.

To keep some distance from Finn, Carver wedged himself between Delia and a wall.

After shutting the door, Miss Petty rounded on them. Instead of a royal ear-lashing, though, she cleared her throat and spoke in a quivering voice. "The building's been sold. We'll be purchasing a larger facility further north, with a field and gymnasium. The money left over will fund us for many years."

Finn blurted out exactly what Carver was feeling. "I don't want to leave the city!"

"Hush," Delia said. "Can't you see she's not finished? There's something else."

A tremble ran through the headmistress's upper lip, but she wiped it away like an error on the chalkboard. "The board has also decided we can no longer house residents past age thirteen. I made a final appeal that our oldest residents, you three, be allowed to remain, but was summarily rejected. I'm afraid you'll all have to make other arrangements."

Looking at their openmouthed expressions, Miss Petty rose and stepped closer to them and, in a rare gesture of affection, cupped Delia's chin in her hand. "I'd gladly offer you a position in our new kitchen, but in your case, I'm confident it will not come to that."

A more severe expression had been reserved for the boys. "As for you two, I continue to regret I could not be both mother *and* father. You each need the latter *badly*. However, if my word means anything, I strongly suggest that if you don't intend to wind up on the street, you put all mischief out of your minds and focus on making the best-possible impression on next week's Prospective Parents Day."

"But—" Carver and Finn said simultaneously.

She cut them off. "I promise nothing, but do as I ask and there may yet be a surprise for both of you. Since his father had been such a friend to Ellis, I've managed to persuade our new police commissioner to attend, bringing a great deal of attention to the event. If there is a chance for you to avoid the life of a street rat, it will be there."

Finn looked puzzled, but Carver grew excited. "Roosevelt? He's working on the library murder! They say her body was . . ."

Miss Petty closed her eyes. "Mr. Young, please. I'm delighted that you're reading, but if you broadened your focus a bit, you might have something less unsavory to discuss."

"Sorry."

She grimaced. "I'm sure. Now, leave me please. I still have arrangements to make and you all have some serious thinking to do."

But as they filed out, the only thing on Carver's mind was that he might meet a real-live detective who could help him find his father.

4

THEY HEADED down the hall, Delia and Finn somber, but Carver's mind ablaze.

"The rumor is she was butchered," he said cheerfully.

Delia rolled her eyes. "I read the papers."

"Everyone dancing and talking. She was screaming right below their feet and they couldn't hear her."

Suddenly, Finn shoved Carver into the wall. He pressed his beefy right forearm into the smaller boy's chest and brought his face close. "Shut up!"

Sick of the years of bullying, Carver refused to flinch. "Or else what? You're going to beat me up right outside Miss Petty's office? Even you aren't that stupid."

But Finn didn't release him. "Don't think I've forgotten what you did to me."

"I'm stunned, Finn, really. I mean, I'm still surprised you can *talk*."

14

Finn pushed harder, squeezing the air from Carver's lungs. "I did *not* steal that locket!"

Delia eyed them both with distaste. "Let go of him, Phineas. Haven't we trouble enough?"

The bully grunted, then lowered his arm. Carver's ribs ached. He wanted to wince from the pain but forced himself to remain expressionless. He was, after all, in the right.

A week ago, ten-year-old Madeline's locket, all she had of her dead mother, was stolen. Miss Petty announced that if it were on her desk by morning, there'd be no questions asked. But that wasn't good enough for Carver. He hid in the storage closet next door waiting, until Finn, without so much as a guilty look, appeared and put Madeline's locket on the desk.

Bad enough Finn and his gang had the run of the place, bad enough his good looks helped him get away with it. But steal a poor kid's locket for a smidgen of gold? Carver had had enough. He snuck the locket back to the boys' dorm, then waited for the deep snoring that told him Finn was asleep. Then he crept up and laid the locket on his barrel chest.

In the morning, they all woke to Tommy, one of the younger boys, shouting, "Finn has the locket!"

As the others sleepily surrounded him, a wide-eyed Finn stared at the chain dangling from his index finger. It was perfect, until Carver ruined it by grinning too widely. When Finn spotted him, even if he couldn't figure out what had happened, he knew Carver had something to do with it.

Like a steam locomotive, he came for him, shoving the bed back two feet as he rose. But before the lumbering hulk could reach him, Miss Petty arrived. Finn was dragged out by his ear, face as bright red as his hair. Detective Young had solved his first crime. A just punishment would be meted out.

Only it wasn't. Whatever went on behind the closed office door, Finn seemed none the worse for wear. Carver could only wonder what happened, or why Finn had yet to take vengeance. The whole thing had been very confusing. Even now, as Finn stormed off, instead of thanking him, Delia glared at Carver with disapproval.

Carver felt flustered. "He stole Madeline's locket. I saw him try to put it back!"

"Phineas has never been a thief," she said, her eyes narrowing.

"He's been everything *else*, hasn't he? For *years!*"

"But not a thief," she calmly repeated. "It's not in his character. Unlike someone else I know, who never seems to run out of apples."

Carver stiffened. "Oh, I get it. You're sweet on him, just like the rest of the girls."

Her face shivered. "Just because I don't think he's a criminal doesn't mean I want to marry him. And even if he is guilty, Mister Ace Detective, was that the smartest play you could have made? He could've beaten you to a pulp." She sighed. "I suppose you think you were doing the right thing, and Miss Petty says that when a jackass flies, we shouldn't question how high it flies but that it flies at all."

Carver felt suddenly small. "You think I'm a jackass?"

She shook her head. "You *are* different, though. The fact you stood up to Finn at all shows that." She examined him, as if trying to suss the change, then pointed at his bulging pockets. "Not a great hiding place for apples. Can I have one?"

Grunting, he pulled one out for each of them. She took a bite. "You'll probably want to stop swiping things from the kitchen until Prospective Parents Day."

He shrugged. "It's a waste for me. I'm fourteen, too big to be anyone's baby, too . . . *scrawny* to be a good apprentice."

She didn't disagree. "Miss Petty says I've never been adopted because I'm too smart. Men don't want anyone putting ideas in their wives' heads. It's also why she never suggested me for an Orphan Train. I think I'd go insane working on a farm."

"I was too *scrawny* for the Midwest." He used the word again, still hoping she'd disagree. "Just as well. I like it here. Tallest building, longest bridge . . . What else do you need?"

She nodded. "That's why I took matters into my own hands. I've been corresponding with Jerrik and Anne Ribe. They both work for the *New York Times*. He's a reporter; she works in the leisure department. They'll be there to meet me on Prospective Parents Day."

Carver let loose a loud whistle. "The *New York Times*? That's almost as good as the *Herald,* isn't it? Good for you, Delia, really."

She smiled wryly. "There have been a few women reporters, but they say the best I should hope for is to work for something boring like *Ladies' Home Journal*."

"They'd be crazy not to give you *some* kind of chance. That'd be grand, wouldn't it? Covering murders, exposing crime."

"Something like that," she said. She gave him a mischievous look. "Matter of fact, I've been practicing on you. Did you find anything in the attic today?"

She took another bite of her apple.

5

"WHAT?" Carver said. "How . . . ?"

"It's not complicated. I was delivering fresh linen and heard all that creaking. I thought you were a rat until I stepped in and saw you working at that lock. You were so intent, I could've been an elephant and you wouldn't have noticed. You have to admit you have a funny sense of law and order, turning in Finn, bending the rules for yourself."

Carver stiffened. "At least you know where your mother is; you even see her once a month. She just can't afford to take care of you. I was dropped at the doorstep in a basket like in a fairy tale. I love mystery stories, but I'm the biggest mystery I know. What's wrong with trying to find out about my parents?"

Her expression softened. "Nothing, but I really don't think Miss Petty would hide anything."

Without thinking, he answered, "Well, she did."

"Oh? So what did you find?" she said. Seeing his hesitation, she punched his shoulder. "I won't tell,

Carver. We've known each other our whole lives." She paused, then added, "Well . . . not if you show me whatever it is."

Carver was dying to share it with someone. Why not Delia? "Fine, but not here."

Taking her elbow, he walked her up to an empty second-floor classroom. It was evening now, the only light from an electric streetlamp. As usual, the darkness comforted him. It was cooler here, too. Carver briefly worried Delia would be cold in her thin dress, but when a cool breeze from a cracked windowpane hit her sweaty face, she smiled with pleasure.

He had started thinking how pretty she'd grown when she looked at him sharply. "Well?"

With an exaggerated sigh, he withdrew the letter. She stared at it, aghast. "From your parents? Are they alive? Why would Miss Petty keep it from you?"

He waved her closer. "Read it and you'll know everything I do."

Together the pair solemnly studied the paper. Having memorized the words, Carver tried to see past them, to feel his father's presence, the man who'd held the pen, thought the thoughts. The effort made him nervous, and he couldn't say why.

He pointed out a word. "He misspells *color*."

"That's how they spell it in London," Delia said. Her brow furrowed deeper and deeper as she read, until it looked like river waves. "It . . . seems like it was written by a crazy person."

Carver felt strangely defensive. "Or maybe it doesn't make exact sense on purpose, like a clue. It talks about a mark, right? It means my birthmark."

She scanned his face and arms. "Where?"

Eager to prove his point, he pulled his shirt half-off and turned his bare back to her.

"Not quite so scrawny anymore, are you? You're getting some muscle."

He tried not to blush. "See it? On my right shoulder?"

She leaned closer. "When was the last time you took a bath? I can't see anything except dirt."

He felt her fingers against his skin. The sensation was pleasant until she rubbed hard.

"It doesn't come off! It's a birthmark!"

"Sorry. It does look like an ear. Carver . . . that really *is* a letter from your father, isn't it?"

He pulled his shirt back on. "So what do I do about it? I can't tell Miss Petty."

Delia shrugged. "I'd try to find some kind of official help. Someone working for the city who has access to records, like . . ."

Carver brightened. "Roosevelt! If you can write to the *Times,* why can't I write to him?"

Delia looked worried. "I was thinking of a clerk or librarian. The police commissioner? You might as well write to Sherlock Holmes."

But Carver barely heard her. "He's been a hunter, a cowboy and a sheriff. I know he'd want to help. And if we met . . . if I impressed him, maybe I could even get a job, like you and the *Times.* Don't you think?"

Delia gaped at him awhile before speaking. "I'm sure he's very busy, you know, trying to eliminate all the corruption in the city, working on solving that murder . . ."

Carver gave her a grin. "I mean, why not? What do you think?"

"Well," Delia said slowly. "I certainly think you can *try.*"

6

THAT NIGHT, Carver didn't sleep at all. Instead, in the light of an old hurricane lantern, he toiled over his letter to Roosevelt, revising it dozens of times before the sun rose. In the morning, he mailed it, and that very afternoon started checking for a response.

Days went by without an answer. After a week, he worried Delia was right—he might just as well have written to Sherlock Holmes. By the time Prospective Parents Day came around, he'd decided Roosevelt was a phony, a stuffed shirt who talked big but who couldn't be bothered with anything that really mattered.

Rather than even try to meet him, Carver stood in a corner tugging at his too-small shirt and feeling miserable. Aside from the suffocating collar, the pants itched horribly, as if the lining were coated with sand. Worse, the jacket wouldn't close enough to cover the shirt's ancient food stains.

Noticing his dour face, Miss Petty said, "Take heart, Mr. Young. Who knows? There could be a surprise in store. Everything changes, after all."

She was right about that. It had finally dawned on him that his childhood, unhappy as it was, was vanishing. For as long as he could remember, plywood boards covered with Mother Goose characters separated the dining common from the main entrance hall. Now they were gone, creating a vast, open space that took up nearly a quarter of the first floor.

The chipped wooden children's tables had been replaced with folding adult-size versions, neatly covered in linen. The usually bare windows were covered with borrowed burgundy curtains. There was light all around, too much, leaving no place for Carver to hide from all the strangers.

When Delia joined him in his lonely corner, he worried she was going to criticize him again. Instead, she seemed oddly light-hearted for the occasion.

"You look unhappy," she said in a playful tone.

Didn't she get it? He nodded toward the orphans, all milling with a crowd so well dressed that he'd only seen its like strolling down Fifth Avenue on Sundays after church. "It's like we're having a . . . a . . . what do they call it when the store burns and all the goods have to be sold cheaply?"

"A fire sale?" Delia offered.

"Everyone must go!" Carver said, trailing his hand in the air to indicate the invisible ad.

Ignoring him, Delia tugged at his tight collar. "I offered to let it out for you. Miss Petty thinks I did nicely enough for the others, even if you think I only readied them for some sort of slave trade."

It was true. She'd done wonderfully matching the children with suitable clothes, then patching and mending them all.

"And me," she said, modeling her dress. "Do I look fake?"

She didn't. He'd almost taken her for one of the visitors when he first saw her. The dress was a shade lighter than peacock blue, matched her eyes and looked new.

"I suppose not," Carver mumbled.

She tugged at his arm. "Come on, you're not going to meet anyone standing in a corner by yourself."

Carver shook his head. "No one's here for the orphans. They're here to gawk at Roosevelt."

At the drinks table a crowd had gathered around a barrel-chested man with a bushy mustache and pince-nez glasses. His teeth were big and white, his eyes small and piercing, and his rasping voice carried to every corner.

"I have the most important *and* the most corrupt department on my hands," Theodore Roosevelt said. "I know well how hard the task ahead of me is . . ."

"Nothing but a windbag," Carver said.

Delia tsked. "How long are you going to stay angry because he didn't drop every murder investigation to read your letter? You love detectives? Detectives *work* for him. You might say hello."

Carver slumped back into the wall. "Don't let me hold you back," he said.

She cleared her throat. "I have some news. It's official. I'm to be adopted by Jerrik and Anne Ribe. Not even adopted, really. Mrs. Ribe, she wants me to call her Anne. Anyways, I'll be more her live-in companion and assistant. The *New York Times*! Can you imagine? Look, they're right over there."

She pointed to a young couple among the crowd surrounding Roosevelt. They were nicely dressed but not quite as stylish as the others. The man, thin, bespectacled, with close-cropped fair hair, had a pad in his hand. He was working hard to try to get Roosevelt's attention, bobbing up and down like a ferret. The woman, her curly blond hair tied neatly in a bun, kept putting her fingers to her lips as if trying to stifle a laugh at her husband's antics. Carver liked them at once.

"That's fantastic, Delia." He forced a smile to his face.

"So, good things can happen sometimes. Yes?"

"For you! I'll be selling the papers you write," Carver said. "I'll be a street rat."

"Stop pouting!" She again pointed at Roosevelt. "Mr. Ribe says all the crime reporters keep offices right across from the police headquarters on Mulberry Street. Whenever something exciting happens, Commissioner Roosevelt leans out the window and gives them a loud cowboy yell, 'Yi-yi-yi!'"

Carver shrugged. "So?"

She swatted him. "Honestly, how can you be angry with a man who leans out the window and shouts, 'Yi-yi-yi'? Go talk to him."

"And say what?"

She sighed. "Has it even occurred to you that *he* might be the surprise Miss Petty hinted at?"

Carver furrowed his brow. "Really?"

"I'm sorry I wasn't more encouraging about your writing to him. I was right, but wrong in the way I told you. I mean to say . . . even if he isn't your surprise, sometimes you have to make your own."

She whirled and walked away.

Was it even possible Commissioner Roosevelt might want to meet him? Did he dare hope again?

Leaving the safety of his corner, Carver edged along the wall. What would he say? How would he say it? As he reached a spot directly behind the punch bowl, Jerrik Ribe finally got his question in: "What about the murder of Elizabeth Rowley? There are rumors the body was—"

"Tut-tut!" Roosevelt responded. It was a gentle, educated phrase, but uttered with such authority it sounded more like, "Shut up!"

"Hardly a tale for the children!" Roosevelt continued. He offered the orphans at his feet a wide grin, revealing the substantial gap between his teeth. Out of nowhere, he frowned. Suddenly, the stout man turned back toward Carver, his instincts as a hunter perhaps telling him he was being secretly watched. For a moment, their eyes locked.

Carver felt something powerful pulse from the stocky man. Roosevelt twisted his head curiously and then went back to the reporter. "I will say this much, in the first five months of 1895, we've investigated no fewer than eighty murders. I assure you, in each instance, we are on the case!"

"I've heard—"

Again, Roosevelt cut him off. "I've faced down rhinoceri, lions and even the former head of the New York City Police and always held my ground. Don't think I can't do the same with you. Request an interview through my assistant, Miss Minnie Kelly, and I'll grant it, but only because she speaks so highly of your wife."

Satisfied but chagrined, Ribe said, "Thank you, Commissioner."

Miss Petty handed Roosevelt a glass of punch. He sipped it, smacked his lips and said, "Dee-lightful!"

Unable to bring himself to approach, Carver slipped away. Working for the police . . . what a dream. Sure, Delia could get what she wanted, but maybe dreams weren't meant for him.

7

AS THE party wore on, everyone except Carver looked like they were having a great time. Seemingly haughty women risked getting dirt on their gowns to bring themselves closer to the children. The men scuffed the knees of their expensive tuxedos for a chat or game.

The only other person sticking to the sidelines was Finn.

If Carver's jacket was too small, Finn's was ready to burst. He looked like a trained monkey, the kind that worked with organ grinders selling bags of roasted peanuts.

But then his short second-in-command, Bulldog, trotted up to his mentor, speaking excitedly. He was twelve, but wide as Finn. His flat face made him look like his namesake. His looks had put him on the outs with the others, until Finn took him under his wing, earning his lifelong loyalty.

Carver couldn't hear what he was saying, but he

was pointing to a tall bearded man by the sandwiches. Nearly all the boys from Finn's gang were there, even Peter Bishop. A recent arrival, being part of Finn's gang made him feel more American, but he had to be goaded into breaking rules.

As Finn listened to Bulldog, his look of misery faded. Curious, Carver slipped nearer.

"It's legit!" Bulldog squeaked. "That there's Colonel George E. Waring, the man who designed the Central Park sewers himself. He's looking for us young men to sweep garbage in the summer and shovel snow in the winter. It pays real money! Fifty cents a week! Guy like you'd probably be a captain or something!"

The red-haired bully's back straightened. "You think . . . ?"

A street-cleaner, eh? It was physical work, but Finn would like that. Even more, he'd love being his own man, free on the streets. With a sigh, Carver realized that even his tormentor had found a place in life.

But no sooner did the husky youth take a step than Miss Petty appeared. "Phineas, there are some people here who'd like to meet you."

At her side stood an impeccably dressed couple. The man was narrow as a piece of cardboard, pinch-faced, and severe. The gown on his well-fed wife was so wide, the hooped hem prevented anyone from getting within three feet of her.

She raised a set of glasses with a long silver handle and surveyed Finn, as if considering having him made into a winter coat.

Miss Petty made the introductions. "This is Mr. Alexander Echols, a district attorney, and his wife, Samantha. I've told them a lot about you, and they're interested in possibly adopting you."

"Uh . . . ," Finn said. His eyes were riveted on the colonel and his friends, half a room away.

"Does he talk?" Mrs. Echols asked. "I'd rather he didn't. But he does have a handsome face."

Realizing the woman wasn't joking, Miss Petty said, "He does talk. Isn't that true, Phineas?"

"Yes . . . ," Finn said. Carver could feel him sweating.

"Ah," Mrs. Echols said. "Do you have any handsome ones that don't? We only need one that looks good in photos."

"No," Miss Petty said coolly. Though she clearly didn't like them, she took Finn's hand and drew him closer to the couple. They were rich, so of course she'd see that as a good opportunity for one of her residents. So *that* was Finn's surprise.

Across the room, Colonel Waring had a little pad of paper out. He was licking the tip of a pencil, ready to write down names. Bulldog shrugged a sheepish farewell at Finn and then rushed off to join the others.

Once Miss Petty excused herself, the Echolses spoke as if Finn weren't even there.

"His arms look fat," Mrs. Echols said with disapproval.

"Perhaps it's the clothes," Mr. Echols said with a shrug. "But it will make great press to have him along at charity events."

"It seems like so much trouble," Mrs. Echols said. "Couldn't we just borrow one?"

"I don't believe so," Mr. Echols said. "And the adoption itself will look very good. Very charitable indeed." He leaned forward and addressed Finn loudly and slowly. "We would like to take you home with us. You will be fed, clothed and educated. What do you say?"

Carver could smell the wood burning in Finn's head. The muscular red-haired boy, used to barking out orders and being obeyed, suddenly looked lost and sad.

Embarrassed for him, Carver stepped away. He thought about Delia. She was right about making your own luck. If Carver cared at all about what kind of life he'd be leading, he'd march up to Roosevelt and give it his best shot.

He moved toward the punch bowl, looking down at his feet. Should he mention his letter or just talk about how much he wanted to be a detective? He was halfway there when he looked up. Roosevelt was gone. He scanned the room, snapping his head faster and faster. The man was nowhere to be seen.

Delia was at the entrance, next to Anne Ribe and Miss Petty. Carver ran and yanked her aside. "Where's Roosevelt?"

The smile fell from her face. "He left. You never *did* speak to him, did you? It was only a minute ago; maybe you could still catch him."

Carver dove for the door. On his way out, he nearly knocked over an oddly stooped salt-and-pepper-haired man. The man growled something, but Carver ignored him. He jumped down the three steps and looked frantically up and down the street. Cool air hit the sweat around his neck.

Horse-drawn hansoms and private carriages clopped and clicked along the cobblestones. Pedestrians strolled along, but none had Roosevelt's short stature or square shoulders.

Carver had stood by for hours, feeling sorry for himself, and now his chance was lost. How could he find his father alone? For as long as he could remember, Carver felt as if something were missing. Not just his past, not just knowing who he was, but someone who could tell him, show him. A father, if not his own, then someone like him. Now where would he wind up?

He turned back to the entrance and pulled so hard at his collar, it tore. The air that swarmed over the top of his chest felt like winter.

"Don't they teach manners in this place? I said, watch where you're going, boy!"

Carver looked up. It was the gnomish older man, still in the doorway, scowling fiercely. "Are you deaf as well as stupid?"

Carver twisted his head for a better look. He seemed the sort you wouldn't want to mess with. His beard and hair were unkempt as a squirrel's nest, but his eyes were practically shining with intelligence. His left hand, pressed against the door, looked terribly strong, but his right appeared damaged, mangled. It clutched the black stick of a silver wolf's head cane with three fingers, as if the thumb and index finger were useless.

What was he? The old cape covering his hunched shoulders might have been formal once, but it was threadbare and wrinkled now. The rest of his clothes looked as if they hadn't been laundered in ages. If he weren't so sloppy, he'd look as if he belonged in a funeral home. An undertaker.

Carver was about to apologize, but the man yelled again.

"I said, *boy,* are you deaf as well as stupid?"

There was something about the nasal tenor that really grated. Aside from which Carver didn't like being called *boy* or *stupid*.

"Neither," Carver said.

The man looked more curious than offended. Still holding the door, he swayed his body closer. "Neither *what,* boy?"

Carver held his ground. "I am neither deaf nor stupid. And I hardly think I'm a boy anymore."

The stranger rolled his eyes. "Are you a *farm hog*?! When addressing your superiors, whether you mean it or not, you always say *sir*. And when you nearly knock someone over, whether you mean it or not, you apologize."

"I do apologize, *sir*," Carver said. He hoped his tone communicated how little he meant it.

But the man wasn't offended. A slight smile brought the edge of his lips into the same light as his eyes. "That you are. You are one sorry boy. Where are you going in such a rush?"

Once more, Carver looked up and down the street. "Nowhere."

The man cackled. "Just like the rest of the damn fools in this city, eh?" He stretched the cane out. It almost touched the tip of Carver's nose. "At least you know it. That's something, isn't it?"

He put the cane down. "Are you Carver Young?"

"What?"

"I thought you weren't deaf. Are you Carver Young?"

"Yes," Carver said. "And who are you . . . sir?"

Saying nothing, the man hobbled inside, leaving Carver feeling very much like a stupid boy, not knowing what to say or do.

8

CARVER stared at the door a good long time. Was that Miss Petty's surprise? Was he going to be adopted by a . . . a gnome?

What could he do? Run away and not come back. He'd be thrown out soon enough anyway. He'd joked with Delia about it, but he *could* become a newsboy, spending nights in one of their lodges. It was better than working in a funeral parlor.

How long would it take to pack?

He headed back in, pelted by body heat and party sounds. Finn was in the same spot, staring enviously as Colonel Waring chatted happily with Bulldog. Mrs. Echols grabbed his chin and turned him back.

"Pssst!"

Delia was waving her hands at him. Maybe he could visit her at the *Times* when he picked up his newspapers for delivery. He took a step in her direction, but she motioned for him to stay put and frantically pointed in the direction of the back hallway where Miss Petty's office was. Where was Miss Petty anyway? Or the undertaker? Ah. Delia was trying to tell him they were in her office.

He should just go pack, but the thought of leaving Ellis forever slowed him. Maybe he should at least try to find out what the gnome had to say.

He slipped into the hallway and gently closed the door behind him. Miss Petty's office door was wide open, its light casting the oblong shadow of two talking figures. Carver pressed himself against the wall and inched along. Two feet from the door he still couldn't hear them. He did see them, though, reflected in the Humpty Dumpty glass. He dared another foot in time to hear the stranger say, in a dismissive tone, "Of course he *writes* a fine letter, but in person the boy is not nearly as impressive as I'd hoped."

Letter? The one he'd sent to Roosevelt? What other letter would there *be*? Carver's heart began to pound.

"I'll leave my card and let you return to your guests," said the man, rising from his seat. He laid it upright against the desk lamp.

"Thank you, Mr. Hawking," Miss Petty said.

Hawking. Did he work for Roosevelt? Had Carver ruined a *second* chance by nearly barreling him over, then being snotty about it?

Any second now they'd enter the hall. He doubted that finding him spying would improve Mr. Hawking's opinion of him, but he'd never make it out in time. Why had he closed the stupid door behind him? The supply closet he often hid in was just past the office door. It wasn't far, but he'd have to cross right in front of them to reach it.

When Hawking rose and faced Miss Petty, he put his back to

the door, covering her view and giving Carver the chance he needed. He crouched, raced by and slipped into the supply closet. He kicked a mop but caught the stick before it clattered to the floor.

"So sorry to have wasted your time," Miss Petty said as they entered the hall.

Hawking grunted. "If he puts on some weight, the boy could become a bouncer. At least then his people-shoving abilities would be put to good use."

Carver bit his lip. He *had* ruined it. He might never even know what he'd ruined.

The hallway door opened and their conversation melted into the rush of the party. He waited, just to be sure, and then stepped out of the closet. He was alone. He might as well continue with his plan to run away. Then again, he no longer had a reason to run.

Was Hawking with Roosevelt? He had to know. Fingering his trusty bent nails, he approached the door to Miss Petty's office and unlocked it with ease. It wasn't the attic lock, after all. Remembering the card the man had left, he snatched it from her desk. It was printed on fine thick paper, but kind of crumpled, as if it had been curled, then flattened. On the front, in raised letters, it read:

Albert Hawking—The Pinkerton Agency

The Pinkertons?! Carver gnashed his teeth. The most famous detective agency in the world! Allan Pinkerton was the *first* private detective in the United States. For fifty years he and his agents battled kidnappers, robbers, murderers, outlaw gangs and more. He'd passed away, but his agency had offices everywhere.

Their logo, a single eye over the motto *We never sleep,* gave birth to the term private eye.

Maybe Carver could still apologize. Beg. *Weep,* if it would help.

Was there an address? A phone listing? The front of the card contained nothing more than the name and the agency. He flipped it over. There were numbers and some letters on the back:

$$40 \ 42.8 \ (\text{W})$$

$$74 \ .4 \ (\text{N})$$

They looked pressed into the paper, typewritten. That was why it was curled. Someone had run it through a typewriter roll. Hawking's hand was damaged, and he probably couldn't hold a pen or pencil. But why would he go through the trouble of typing some numbers?

Memorizing the contents, he carefully replaced the card. Rather than be seen walking into the party from Miss Petty's office, he took the long way, through the laundry area, then back around front.

By the time he reached the entrance, things were breaking up. Carver scanned the milling bodies for Hawking. It was no use—like Roosevelt, he was gone. He couldn't even spot Miss Petty. He tried to remember every name Finn had ever called him so he could use them on himself.

There was still the numbers on the card. They must mean something. If he could figure out what that was, he might still impress the man. A combination? No, there wouldn't be decimals in a combination.

As he puzzled over it, Delia came up, buzzing with questions. "Did you meet him? Did you talk? He looked . . . interesting, like he'd been hurt in a war. Was he important? What did you do?"

When he didn't answer, she noticed his dark expression. "Or should I say, what *didn't* you do? Carver, tell me you did something?"

"Oh, I did something all right. I was in such a rush to find Roosevelt, I nearly knocked over Albert Hawking of the Pinkertons. Then I insulted him to the point where he wanted nothing to do with me."

"No!"

Carver nodded. "I saw his card, but it didn't even have a city, or a country, let alone a . . . a . . ."

He stopped in mid-sentence, looked briefly at Delia, then bounded down the hall.

"Where are you going?"

"To make my own luck!"

9

CARVER hurtled up the stairs that led to the classrooms. He heard Delia follow, struggling to keep up in her long dress and awkward shoes, but couldn't slow down now. Once inside, he headed to the hanging map of the world and eagerly ran his fingers along the lines.

Delia, shoes in one hand, dress hem gathered up in the other, appeared at the door panting. "You might at least tell me."

Carver grinned. "The numbers and letters on the back of the card, latitude and longitude coordinates, degrees, minutes and seconds. The degrees put it right here in New York City."

"Put *what* right here?"

"I have *no* idea, but it's exciting, isn't it?" He looked around. "I need something that shows minutes and seconds, something more local, a map of just the city . . . but where can I . . . Wait!"

He rushed past Delia. Moving faster now that her shoes were off, she stayed right behind him all the way to the kitchen. There she gasped as he began rifling through Curly's recipes.

"He'll *kill* you if he sees you going through those."

Carver waved her off. "Once he finished cooking, Miss Petty gave him the night off. You know how he's always getting lost? That's why, along with his recipes, he also keeps . . . this!"

He held up a folded tourist map.

Pushing aside dirty utensils and bread crumbs, he unfolded the map. He ran his fingers first horizontally along the top, then vertically down the center of the island.

"It's the corner of Broadway and Warren Street, right across from City Hall Park, near Newspaper Row."

"What's there?" Delia asked.

Carver frowned. "A department store, I think. Easy enough to find out. It's less than half an hour's walk."

"Let's go, then!" Delia said.

He looked at her. "Delia, I'm sorry, but I think I should go alone."

He slid open a window and climbed onto the ledge.

She rushed up, angry. "Don't you dare think I'd slow you down!"

"No, it's not that," he said as he eyed the five-foot jump down to the alley.

"Well, what, then?"

He hemmed and hawed. "It's late. There are rough sorts around, and you're too . . . too . . ."

"Weak? Slow?"

"No!" he said. "Too darn pretty!"

He jumped, landed and took off running. By the time she thought to make him promise to tell her everything, he was gone.

As she slid the window shut, she caught her reflection in the glass. Pretty? It wasn't a word she had reason to associate with herself. Yet as she looked at herself now, she smiled. Aside from a few hairs out of place, she had to admit she did look quite nice.

The time melted along with the blocks beneath Carver's feet, the air full of smells of horses and burning coal. Worth . . . Duane . . . Chambers . . . City Hall and its adjoining park grew visible on his left. To his right, he saw the brightly colored awnings of Devlin's department store.

He stopped. The itching of his jacket mingled with goose bumps caused by the cool air. A few more steps and he reached the corner. *Warren Street* was chiseled into the stone of a building. Here he was. But this was a business and government district. The Pinkerton office was at least ten blocks farther down. Had he misread the maps or the numbers?

He crossed the cobblestone, scanning all five stories. Could there be offices above Devlin's? No.

The only noteworthy thing was an oddly dark patch of concrete on the Warren Street sidewalk, about the length and width of a staircase. It looked as if something had been sealed up ages ago. Four two-feet-tall brass tubes, curved at the top, marked the corners. Some sort of pipes, but for what?

Curious, Carver reached out to touch one. The moment his hand made contact, a piercing, nasal voice turned him around.

"There, Miss Petty, I told you he'd be here within the hour."

Carver whirled. A few yards behind him, Miss Petty and Albert Hawking stood under a hissing streetlamp. At the curb behind them was the hansom cab that had brought them.

Hawking continued speaking to Miss Petty, but his eyes were glued on Carver. "Send the paperwork and his things to the address I gave you. Meanwhile, you'll have to excuse us. I'd like to take my new pupil on a bit of a tour."

Pupil?

Carver was so gobsmacked, Miss Petty had to cough several times to get his attention. "Mr. Young?" she said. "I assume this is a suitable arrangement?"

A slack-jawed Carver nodded dumbly.

"Cat got your tongue, Mr. Young?" she prodded.

"It's perfectly all right, Miss Petty," Hawking said. "I know he can speak. I heard him earlier. Frankly, I've had enough of it for one day."

But Carver found his voice. "Yes, ma'am. It . . . the arrangement . . . would be very suitable, thank you."

She offered the widest smile he'd ever seen on her. "I thought it might be. I want you to know that even though I forbade you certain reading material in your younger years, I always felt that your mind, and your heart . . . well . . . I just hope you realize . . ."

Still overcome with shock, it took Carver several moments to realize that the stoic Miss Petty was choked with emotion. They'd known each other nearly all his life. Now they were saying good-bye. He wanted to hug her, but it seemed insane.

Hawking nudged her. "Madam, please, the bird has left the nest. Time to move along."

Collecting herself, Miss Petty said, "Of course," and stepped into the waiting cab. Hawking rapped his cane near the driver. "Take her back to Ellis, and send me the bill. You're not to accept a penny from this woman, understand?"

A click of the driver's tongue set the horses in motion. Carver could see Miss Petty's face through the window and thought he spotted a tear on her cheek. Wondering if he'd ever see her again, he felt a swell of emotion grip his throat.

By the time the cab traveled half a block, the feeling was replaced by the realization that the clue had been some sort of test, and now he was to be the pupil of a *real* detective! It was as if a cover of *New York Detective* had come to life and swallowed him. And so far, all he'd offered his benefactor were insults.

"I'm very sorry about my tone earlier, sir," Carver said, mustering his sincerity. "And anything else I said that might have offended you."

Hawking cackled. "Of course you are." He narrowed his gaze and pointed at him with the tip of the cane. "But at least you know, boy, at least you know."

10

THE HUNCHED man nodded at a spot behind Carver.

"You were doing something before you were interrupted. Go back to it."

Carver didn't understand. "Excuse me, sir?"

Hawking bristled. "Your letter to Roosevelt said you wanted to be a detective, didn't it?"

"Yes, sir, but how did you—"

"No, no, no!" he said, snapping his head back and forth. "An answer to one question will lead to another and we'll be standing here all night. If you want to be a detective, go back to what you were doing. Detect."

He waved his cane at the quartet of brass pipes marking the dark patch of concrete. "What were you looking at?"

Confused, Carver answered, "Just that the concrete was different, like something was sealed in, sir."

"In 1873, to be precise. Look again, tell me more. And don't call me sir every two seconds. I despise repetition."

Carver stared at the tubes. "The tubes . . . don't belong?"

Hawking crinkled his lips. Irritation emanated from his form in waves. "Of course they belong. Everything belongs. You just don't know what the devil they belong to! How might you find out?"

Carver had barely spoken, but already felt he was doing everything wrong. It was like talking to Delia, only worse.

"Ask?"

"Ask? Who?"

"You? Someone at Devlin's."

"Devlin's is closed. And I'm not going to tell you."

It was another test, like the writing on the card. Carver concentrated, but nothing came to him.

Hawking's steely gaze was hard at work, sizing up his new pupil. Carver wondered if he could read his mind from the way he stood or tell what he'd had for breakfast, the way Sherlock Holmes might.

"This isn't a done deal, boy. Give me less than your best and I'll send you straight back to Ellis. Stop wasting time! Use the skills that got you here!"

Feeling more intimidated than he ever had in Finn's presence, Carver knelt beside the nearest tube. It was a tube, just a brass tube. What else could it be? He poked his hand into the opening. A few inches inside, his finger felt a metallic mesh. A filter.

Maybe it was connected to something below. Was it part of the store's basement? Hawking leaned against the building, looking relieved at no longer having to support the burden of his body. There was an odd door behind him. It fit the store's design but seemed newer, different, like the concrete. It didn't have any doorknob or keyhole. A gilded metal frame curled intricately over its glass center. The glass was smoky, whatever beyond it dark.

The older man tapped the whitish hair at his temple. "Don't just think, give yourself something to think *about*. The brain's like a rat spinning on a wheel in a cage. Trapped, and it doesn't even know it. All it knows is what the senses tell it. Use them."

Carver was nervous, feeling stupid, but determined not to give up. He wrapped his hands around the tube. It was thick, polished clean. In intervals, decorative rings bulged neatly from the surface.

"It's expensive," he announced.

"Well, that's something, at least. What might it be for?"

If it was a water drain, it was upside down. Carver put his ear against the opening, but couldn't hear anything because of the surrounding noise. A chilly wind whistled along Broadway, horses clopped, wheels rolled on the cobblestone. Covering his exposed ear, he concentrated, managing to hear and feel a steady, almost mechanical movement of warmer air.

"It's a vent!" Carver blurted.

"Congratulations, you're not a complete moron," Hawking announced. "Now, how do you figure out what's down there?"

The small victory rallied Carver. A *New York Detective Library* story with Nick Neverseen came to mind. Nick was no Holmes, but while trying to find some kidnappers hiding in a mine, he'd found the mine's air shaft and . . .

"Plug up the air hole," Carver said. "Whoever's down there would have to come up."

Hawking's laugh surprised him. It was different from his cackle, sharp and resonant.

"I like that," the detective said. "But *whoever's down there* wouldn't appreciate it. Didn't think to try to pull or move it, did you? Well, why would you? The thing's set in solid concrete. Put your hand around again and this time, twist to the right."

Carver gave Hawking a puzzled look and then did as he was told. The section above the top ring pivoted easily. It moved a quarter turn, then clicked into place.

Reading his expression, Hawking said, "If that little bit of nonsense impresses you so much, you won't last the night. Push down, twist left, pull up, and twist right. Go on."

Carver moved the tube in sequence, having no idea what to expect. He remembered another story in which Allan Quatermain entered an ancient temple by pressing stones in sequence. But this was in the middle of the street in New York City, a city Carver thought he knew well.

After the final twist, a series of small metallic sounds echoed from the tube. Carver rose and stepped back, half-expecting the sidewalk to grind open. Instead, there was a final, tiny click, not from the tube, but from the ornate door behind Hawking.

It had popped open.

Carver grinned like a seven-year-old. "A combination lock?"

"Yes. The designer is fond of gadgets. Can't stand them myself." He put his hand on the edge of the door. "Shall we go in?"

Hawking hobbled in about two feet, then turned to face the street. Carver thought he was waiting for him but as he approached saw there was no place else for Hawking to go. The room was five feet square at best, barely enough space for four standing adults. There were no other doors. All three walls were covered with metallic designs similar to those on the door.

Once Carver was beyond the door frame, Hawking grabbed a

small handle and pulled the door shut. There was an oily machine smell, and the small room filled with a sound not unlike what followed the last click of the tube—the soft, steady whir of hidden gears. Stranger still, the wind hadn't stopped. Only now the breeze ran not from left to right, but from the ceiling to the floor.

Carver looked around the cramped space in wonder.

Hawking shrugged. "Haven't you ever been in an elevator?"

11

HAWKING'S shaky index finger pressed a button hidden by the wall pattern. The grinding gears became more insistent, the breeze stronger. Carver *had* been in elevators, but he could always feel the rumble, the sense of movement. Here there was none.

"It's pneumatic," Hawking explained. "The shaft is nearly airtight, the car pushed and pulled by a large fan. It's a later addition by the fellow who built this place." He sneered slightly. "It does offer a smoother ride, I suppose."

In moments, the wind died and the door clicked open, revealing a huge room, dimly lit by a series of small gas fixtures. A huge steel cylinder and cogwheel were at the room's far end. It was so tall, it ran nearly all the way to the high ceiling. The metal was covered with frescoed woodwork. Between the gaps he could see huge blades turning.

"Is that the fan?" Carver asked.

"The top," Hawking replied absently. "You'll see the rest in a moment. No more questions, you'll slow us down."

They passed a metal sign reading *Broadway Pneumatic Transit Co.* Otherwise, the place seemed abandoned. They entered a long featureless hall, then walked down several steps into a tiny room. Carver thought it was another elevator, but here Hawking simply opened a second door and, with a vague wave of his hand, said, "Welcome to the future. At least what Mr. Alfred Beach *thought* would be the future about twenty-five years ago."

Carver gasped. There were chandeliers, couches, curtains, easy chairs and settees, a piano and, in the center, a working fountain with goldfish swimming in its shallow pool. To the right, beyond a low wall, were the slowly turning gears and shaft of the vast fan in the room above. It would all seem more at home in the Astor family's finest mansion or a Jules Verne novel than hidden beneath the ground.

But the most exciting part was the shining train car sitting below twin staircases. A tall metallic cylinder with oval windows on either side of a door, it was unlike anything Carver had ever seen or read about. There was just the one car, no locomotive. Beyond it was a round tunnel, an iron tube, a perfect match for the car's shape, its entrance ringed by colored gas jet flames glowing red, white and blue.

Carver longed to study every inch of this odd and wonderful place, but Hawking pushed him forward. "I'll explain it when we get into the car. I want to sit down!"

At the stairs, the reason for his testiness became clear. After putting his cane to the first step and twisting his hips to lower his foot, his face registered intense pain. Overcoming his hesitation about touching the grisly man, Carver grabbed Hawking's arm.

The detective mumbled something that sounded like "good," then continued grunting until they entered the car.

The dim, eighteen-foot space held two rows of long cushioned seats, broken up by tables with gas lamps. It looked like a luxurious, but narrow, living room.

Hawking dragged himself to one of the lamps and settled into the cushions beside it. After a single exhale, he leaned over and twisted the valve. "The zirconia light," he said with a sigh. "Two small cylinders, one with oxygen, the other hydrogen, are under the seats, feeding this nozzle, which contains a bit of zirconium."

Lowering his head to shield his eyes, he struck a match and held it to the lamp. A brilliant pencil-thin flame erupted, casting a powerful brilliance.

Unlike the usual yellow gaslight, this was like sunlight. Carver loved it.

Hawking waved at the light as if it were a mosquito. "It's toys, boy, all toys. You'll see more and more contraptions as you get older, but if I teach you anything, you'll learn that this is *all* decoration. What counts is what's inside you and what you can see in others. Got that?"

"Yes, sir."

"No, you don't. When our time together is nearly over, you may start to understand."

He shifted his back to the glow and motioned for Carver to sit beside him.

Using his heel, Hawking kicked a lever at the base of the lamp table. In response, the car moved, but so smoothly, so quietly, it was only because he could see out the windows that Carver realized they were moving at all.

"Back in 1870," Hawking said, "Alfred Beach worked secretly, digging this tunnel to demonstrate what he thought would be a more elegant way of traveling than the elevated trains that hiss and fart and stink up the air. People rode his little *subway* as a curiosity, but he never won the contract to expand. It was sealed up, forgotten, until I helped purchase it."

It was another surprise in a day full of them. "You *own* this?"

"Don't go picturing any big inheritance. The money wasn't mine, and it's nearly all gone. It belonged to Allan Pinkerton. I know you've heard of him; otherwise my card wouldn't have piqued your curiosity."

Carver nodded. "He was amazing."

Hawking's harsh demeanor faded slightly. "You're right about that. I was there when he foiled an assassination attempt on President Lincoln. I worked undercover for him during the Civil War. After that, I helped him track some of the worst criminals the country's ever seen. Amazing? He was more a force of nature than a man. Or so I believed. In 1869 he had a stroke. The doctors said he'd be paralyzed permanently. Pinkerton insisted they were wrong. It was painful as rising from the dead, but day by day, inch by inch, he forced himself to stand, to hobble and then to walk. Inside of a year he was back on his feet, slower but still worth ten men half his age." He paused. "Wish I could say the same for myself."

"What . . . happened to you?" Carver asked.

"One life at a time, boy. While Allan Pinkerton recovered, his sons ran the business and never quite gave it back. He spent the rest of his life struggling with his blood over his own company. They saw the future in factory security, not exactly what he saw as his legacy. So, in his will, he left his two most trusted agents, myself and Septimus Tudd, a considerable amount to establish a new agency, dedicated to fighting criminals. Tudd always loved contraptions, so I let him talk me into using this place as our base."

"Why haven't I ever heard of you?"

Hawking bristled. "The New York police department has an annual budget of five million dollars. They collect another *ten* million in bribes. Pinkerton stipulated our organization remain secret to avoid corruption, even fight the police if need be."

The little car slid into a wide, open area. They were still underground, but this place was so airy, it felt as if they were outside again. High above, Carver saw an arched brick ceiling supported by steel girders. The track ended at a small platform at the edge of a plaza. On either side were two three-story structures, buildings of a sort. One was open faced, the other a windowless mass.

In the open building, Carver could see inside many of the rooms. There were offices full of file cabinets, rooms that stocked pistols, rifles and strange devices. A wide space full of wires and tubes looked like a laboratory. Unlike the elegant but abandoned spaces beneath Devlin's, these were brightly lit and bustling with activity. Of the twenty people he could see, some worked in suits with bowler hats, others in shirtsleeves. There were even several women present. A man and a woman wearing goggles and greasy overalls were hunched over mechanical equipment whose function Carver couldn't even guess at.

Three men waited at the platform. Two, tall and fairly young, flanked an older, rounder man in a bowler hat. Closer to Hawking's age, he looked something like a friendly sheepdog.

"It worked well for a while," Hawking mused. "Until the money started running out."

"Are you in charge of all this?" Carver said, ecstatic.

The car door opened. The sheepdog man stepped in front of it, blocking the way, hands on his hips. "You gave him the combination, Hawking! We hadn't agreed on that!" he said.

"No, I'm not in charge," Hawking said. "He is. That's Septimus Tudd."

12

HAWKING prepared to rise. "I didn't ask if I could use the loo, either, Septimus. If he's to be my apprentice, he'll need to get in, won't he?"

"I beg you, Albert, no more surprises," Tudd responded.

Hawking offered an even smile. "I'll try, but I won't make any promises."

The two younger men tried to hide their chuckles. "Welcome back, Mr. Hawking," the slighter one said, beaming. "It's been too long."

Hawking put his cane to the floor. "Not long enough, Emeril and . . . hmmm . . . Jackson, isn't it?"

The two nodded appreciatively.

Carver moved to help Hawking, but the old detective nudged him off. At the door, the round Tudd hooked a big hand through Hawking's arm. He pulled him close and whispered, just loud enough for Carver to hear.

"Please don't demean me in front of the agents. It's difficult enough when I can't pay their salaries."

Hawking gave a noncommittal shrug. As they stepped onto the tile-and-brick platform, Tudd made a show of leading the way, but Hawking clearly knew where they were headed. As they walked, everyone's eyes were on them. Carver thought they might be looking at him, a stranger, but realized they were much more interested in Hawking.

After a lifetime of being bullied, Carver could only imagine how it must feel to be so respected. Hawking only grimaced and quickened his lopsided stride, as if their admiration were an ordeal.

They entered an open hall that ended in a set of wide mahogany doors. Two plaques hung to the side. The first read *Office of the Director,* the second, *Septimus Tudd.* A faded rectangle along the edges of Tudd's name meant his predecessor had warranted a bigger plaque. Hawking?

Emeril and Jackson opened the doors but remained outside. Tudd, Hawking and Carver entered a large, wildly cluttered office. It held an enormous desk and three long oak meeting tables stacked with files, photographs and newspaper clippings. The dark-paneled walls were papered with maps marking streets, ferry lines and railroads.

The only decoration Carver noticed was an odd oval mirror. It looked broken, everything reflected in it distorted, as if it were from a house of mirrors. Carver snickered to remember how jealous he'd been when Delia had gotten to see one at Coney Island, having gone along to help watch the younger children.

He couldn't wait to tell her he'd visited a secret detective facility. But he couldn't tell her, could he? That was the point of it being secret, why it had such a strange and wonderful lock.

He also realized something else.

"Mr. Tudd?" Carver said, speaking for the first time. "Can I ask how you knew Mr. Hawking gave me the combination?"

The hefty man turned to him with a twinkle in his eye. "Because I saw him." He pointed to the mirror. "It's something our research department came up with. Go on, take a look. It's not as if I get to show off the operation often."

Carver stepped up. The periphery of the glass remained blurry, but in the center he could see the side of Devlin's, the elevator door, the brass tubes rising from the concrete, even the bottom half of a hansom cab and horse clicking along down Broadway.

"How . . . ?"

Tudd indicated a silvery tube rising from the back of the glass. "Mirrors, placed at careful angles in this pipe, leading up to the surface. They call it a periscope."

"That's amazing!" Carver said.

"And expensive," Hawking growled. "And you wonder where all the money's gone."

Tudd scowled. "I'll have you know the army is considering purchasing the patent."

"*Considering*, as in, they haven't given you a penny."

Tudd straightened. He suddenly looked quite formidable despite his girth. "I don't have to explain myself to someone who hasn't even been here in months! I've molded this place into the cutting-edge crime facility Allan Pinkerton envisioned! You can't begin to imagine the strides we've made. In just a few weeks, we'll take delivery of our first electric carriages."

"Electric carriages?" Carver blurted.

"Quiet, boy!" Hawking snapped. "And how much did they cost?"

Tudd stepped behind his desk. "Cost isn't the issue!"

He went on, but Carver noticed Hawking wasn't paying attention. His sharp eyes were casting about the desk, studying the photographs and newspapers. When Carver followed his new mentor's gaze, he realized they were all about the library murder. The photographs showed the crime scene. The rumors were true: the body had been mutilated. Never having seen a real dead body, let alone one so mangled, Carver felt queasy. It was exactly the sort of thing Miss Petty had prevented him from seeing or reading about.

A loud hissing, like a teakettle, erupted from Tudd's clenched teeth. He motioned Carver away from his desk. "I'm sorry, Mr. Young, but the information the agency collects is not for public consumption."

"Still chasing ghosts?" Hawking asked. He snorted.

The dismissive gesture clearly angered Tudd. "A pity we don't all share your fierce instincts!" he said.

Hawking chuckled. "If you had half my instincts, you wouldn't waste your time."

13

"IT'S A theory," Tudd said. "The police are stymied. If we solved the murder, it would give us just the right opportunity to bring the New Pinkertons out in the open."

"If that's your goal, why not just do it? Why do you need some imaginary victory to hide behind?" Hawking said.

"Aside from the fact it's against Allan's explicit wishes," Tudd said with a shrug, "we have to be in the right position. And I have to admit the thought of catching the world's most famous murderer is enticing."

"It's your ego, then?"

"No! I mean to say . . ."

As the two men argued, Carver leaned forward for another look at the desk. A police report describing Mrs. Buckley's attacker as an "impossibly powerful man" caught his attention, but Tudd snatched it away. He motioned a chagrined Carver into one of two plush chairs facing the desk.

"I could use your help, Albert," Tudd said. "If only so the men would—"

"My involvement is not open for discussion."

Tudd sighed. "Damn shame a man of your ability spends all his time among the mad."

Among the mad? What did that mean?

"So do you, in a way."

"Roosevelt?" Tudd said. "I've not met a man with his integrity since Allan himself. It's positively difficult for me to lie to him each morning when I go to work."

Carver didn't know what to ask first. "You work for Roosevelt? Is that how you saw my letter?"

"Giving away your own secrets now, eh, Tudd?" Hawking chortled. "*Intercepted* might be a better word, boy. Go on, tell him. You're Roosevelt's *clerk*."

Tudd narrowed his eyes. "I could name some undercover positions *you've* held I wouldn't brag about." He turned to Carver. "Son, nearly all our agents hold posts among the police, politicians and newspaper offices. I am one of the commissioner's assistants."

"Clerk," Hawking interjected.

"Ahem. Your correspondence . . . impressed me. Mr. Hawking needed an assistant. I also hoped bringing you here might lure him from retirement. I didn't realize he planned on giving you *my* job during your first visit."

Hawking said, "There is only *one* job I'm interested in currently, for the boy."

"Really?" Carver asked. "What would that be, sir?"

"Finding your father."

Carver's heart nearly popped into his throat.

"It's an excellent way to begin your education, a mystery you'll be motivated to solve. If you think you can handle it. You'll have to do most of the legwork, but you'll have access to these facilities—"

Tudd interrupted. "Only to an extent. I want to help, of course, but we're stretched as it is. I suppose I could have someone take a look at that letter you found. Check for fingerprints, analyze the handwriting . . ."

Carver swooned. Use this place to find his father?

Hawking leaned forward. "Mr. Tudd has a new forensic document examiner who dabbles in graphology. You know the difference?"

Carver nodded. "The examiner tries to confirm the identity of the author; a graphologist tries to figure out their personality."

"Well, then," Tudd said. "Maybe you *will* be running this place one day. Um . . . did Mr. Hawking have you bring the letter?"

"I didn't have to. I assumed he'd keep something so precious on his person. Am I right, boy?"

Carver grinned. "Yes."

Tudd put his hand out. "It won't be a priority, but no reason we can't put it in the queue."

Excited, Carver reached into his pocket, only to have his hand blocked by Hawking's cane.

"Wait," Hawking said. "If you *are* going to be my assistant, I want you to have complete access to the facilities. You can't analyze the handwriting yourself, but I want you doing everything else."

"That's not possible!" Tudd said, blustering.

"To the contrary. It is."

Tudd exhaled so hard, his mustache quivered. "May we discuss this privately?"

Not wanting to seem as if he were someone who might need "babysitting," Carver promptly stood. The two men were silent as he opened the door and stepped outside, his head ready to explode from all the questions it contained.

14

THE TWO younger agents were waiting when Carver emerged.

"The older guns wanted some words alone, eh?" Emeril said. He put his hand out for Carver to shake. "John Emeril. Been with the agency three years now."

Jackson did the same, though with a considerably stronger grip. He also had a bent nose, as if it'd been broken in a fistfight, and a slight scar on his right cheek. "Josiah Jackson. Quite a place, isn't it?"

"I felt like I'd stepped into a Jules Verne novel first time I set eyes on that subway," Emeril put in. He was unblemished, though paler, and perpetually squinting, as if reading tiny print.

"I'll say," Carver answered. After the grim Hawking and the blustery Tudd, these two were a relief.

"Subway's not the half of it," Jackson said, unbuttoning his jacket and leaning against the wall. "They're developing things that'd make Verne's head spin."

"I just wish they could invent a steady paycheck," Emeril put in.

"So you're both detectives?" Carver asked.

"That's right," Emeril said. "We don't stand outside doors all day. Matter of fact, we asked for the duty because we'd heard Mr. Hawking would be here."

"What sort of cases have you worked on?"

"Not certain we should say," Jackson said. "But nothing as exciting as you might read in a book."

"Don't tell him that!" Emeril said. "Jackson and I have handled kidnappings, blackmail and bank robberies! Not that we're allowed to discuss specifics. And he's right about one thing. It's not all running around in sewers with pistols drawn, ruining your best clothes to sneak up on a thief."

Jackson warmed to the bragging. "That's the trick, isn't it? Catching them before or during. Afterward, the damage is already done. There's a lot of research and guesswork, trying to peer into the workings of the criminal mind."

"Which Jackson usually leaves to me," Emeril said. "Of course, Mr. Hawking knows the most about the criminal brain. I hear he keeps one in his desk. Quite a fellow, old Hawking."

"You'll be training with the best," Jackson agreed.

"Why did he retire?" Carver asked.

"He didn't tell you?" Emeril said. "Don't know much about his work with the original Pinkertons, but the story goes that by the time he started up here, he was the brainy sort, like me."

"Oh? I heard he was more the brawny type," Jackson said, flexing his muscles. "Like . . . ahem."

Emeril rolled his eyes. "About eight years back he became obsessed with a street gang that specialized in kidnapping."

"Extortion, too, no?" Jackson said.

"But it was mostly kidnapping," Emeril said. "As luck would have it, or lack of luck, they kidnapped the wife of a very wealthy fellow. The crooks gave him the usual bit about not contacting the police. Given the corruption, he had no reason to think the police weren't involved themselves, so he hired us."

"Hired?" Carver asked.

Emeril shrugged. "We're not averse to taking money . . ."

". . . from those who can afford it," Jackson corrected.

"Anyway," Emeril continued, "Hawking jumped on it. No leads, no clues. He pulled the answers out of the air . . ."

"Out of his ass, you mean!"

"Does it matter from where? He got things right. Figured out where she was being held."

"A warehouse. He went down there with a vengeance. Brought five agents . . ."

After sounding terribly excited, both men grew suddenly quiet.

"And?" Carver finally asked.

"Turned out the police *were* in with the kidnappers. They also had new pistols that fired off rounds faster and more accurately than anything else at the time. Hawking hadn't bargained on stumbling in on so much firepower. The wife was killed, along with all the agents. Hawking took five bullets."

Carver exhaled. He'd imagined the operation was dramatic, just not that it'd also been a tragic failure.

Jackson spoke softly. "He went overseas for surgery, gone nearly a year. Best they could do was return some of the use of his arm. You see what he's like now. Didn't want anything to do with the work anymore, handed the reins over to Tudd . . . and Tudd's . . ."

"Not a bad man . . . Wouldn't trust him to invest my savings, but he's a solid detective."

"Though no Albert Hawking."

Carver's new mentor was beginning to make sense. Who *wouldn't* be bitter and cranky after that?

Tudd's voice, hollow and tinny, erupted from thin air. "Send Carver in."

Carver looked around, unable to figure out where the sound was coming from.

"Voice pipe," Emeril explained. "Carries sound along a tube. Been used on ships for a hundred years. Best offices have them."

As Jackson reached for the door, Emeril pulled a small rubber hose from along the wall molding and spoke into a brass funnel at the end. "On his way, Mr. Tudd."

When Carver stepped in, Hawking waved at Tudd with his gnarled right hand. "Give him your letter."

Carver paused. "What . . . ?"

"I'll tell you shortly. For now, hand your precious note over to Mr. Tudd. Maybe in a year or so, when they get to it, you'll find out you're the Prince of Wales. Go on."

Carver reached into his back pocket and pulled out the folded note. So much had happened so quickly. A short while ago this was the most precious thing in his life. Hawking, Tudd, the New Pinkertons—they still felt unreal. The note was solid, real. He wasn't sure he should hand it over but couldn't imagine why not. Even though he could close his eyes and still see every blotch of ink, he felt a pang as he relinquished it.

As he took it, Tudd, sensing its importance, gave Carver a sympathetic smile and treated it with the utmost care as he unfolded and scanned it. "A year? Not *that* long," he said. "But it will be a while, son."

"I'm . . . so grateful . . . ," Carver said, stumbling over the words.

"Mmm," Tudd said. He rummaged about his desk until he found a glass tube about three inches wide, stopped at both ends with rubber caps. He pulled one cap off, carefully rolled the letter and inserted it. After resealing the other end, he inserted it into a thicker tube behind his desk. With a sudden *thok* it was sucked in.

"A pneumatic message system courtesy of the gentleman who built the subway," Tudd explained cheerfully. "They've been using a similar system at the London Stock Exchange since 1853, but I suppose our dear Mr. Hawking would think that a waste of money as well."

"If they were going bankrupt, I would," Hawking answered. He pushed himself to his feet. "The laboratory is only a few hundred yards away, isn't it? I thought I was the one who had trouble walking."

Hawking loped toward the door, giving Carver a twitch of his chin to indicate he should follow. "Be seeing you, Septimus."

Once they were in the hall, Carver figured it was safe to start asking questions.

"What . . . ?" he began.

Hawking sliced the air with his good hand. "Not in front of the agents. Good night, Jackson, Emeril."

"Always good to see you, sir."

"Good night, Mr. Hawking."

Between the voice pipes, pneumatic subways, and spyglasses, Carver never wanted to leave, but Hawking led him back to the subway. He didn't speak again until it was gliding back along the tunnel.

"It's been settled," he said. "You're to be allowed full access."

Carver let out an amazed laugh. "That's terrific, sir. But Mr. Tudd seemed so against it. How did you get him to agree?"

Hawking shrugged. "A white lie. I told him part of the reason I wanted you to have access was because, from time to time, I'd have you run errands here for me. Giving you access would be the same as giving me access."

"But . . . you have no interest in solving any crimes?"

"Not since the incident I'm sure Jackson and Emeril told you about in all its timeworn glory. There's more they couldn't even begin to guess and you shouldn't bother asking about. My prime interest is passing along what I know with what time I have left. As for you, boy, now that you've seen all the fancy nonsense, we're going to take a real look at how to study the criminal mind."

The odd smile on Hawking's face made Carver remember the conversation from the office. "Mr. Tudd said you spent all your time among the mad."

Hawking tipped his head left, then right. "Some would call it a madhouse. I call it . . . home."

15

"**BLACKWELL** Island Ferry," Hawk-
ing announced to the cabdriver. Turning to Carver,
he warned, "Don't get used to this. It's late and I
want to get home. You'll be hoofing it most of the
time."

That, Carver didn't mind at all. Aside from hanging on the back of a streetcar or dodging past the
ticket box on the elevated trains, he'd always roamed
by foot. Two things did worry him, though: the sur-
render of his father's letter and the fact that Blackwell
Island held only a prison and an insane asylum.
Oddly, the letter bothered him more. Try as he might
to lose himself in the lazy, hypnotic clopping of the
horses, he couldn't shake the nagging feeling he
shouldn't have let it go.

At the ferry, the old detective insisted on climbing

to the open top deck. They'd made it up the narrow metal steps to the prow when the captain gunned the engine. The sudden movement nearly threw Hawking. Carver moved to catch him, but his claw-like right hand snatched the railing.

"It's a game he likes to play," Hawking said, sneering back at the captain. From behind the wheel the grizzled fellow chuckled. If only he knew, Carver thought, that he was insulting a master detective.

A fine wet spray hit Carver's face. The trail of coal smoke drew back. The smell of brine came through. It was cold, but so hard to worry about anything with the lights of New York and Brooklyn on either side, reflecting in river water that rippled black as oil.

After about a mile, the tip of Blackwell Island came into view. It was so low and flat, the grim gray stones of the Penitentiary Hospital seemed to sit on the water. The ferry neared a pier. Well, living among medical staff wouldn't be *so* bad. But when all the other passengers exited, Hawking shook his head.

"Next stop."

The boat chugged along, passing the last vaguely pleasant sight he'd see, a garden where the prisoners grew their own food. Moments later, they reached a tall, forbidding wall that severed the island. Then came a second wall, with watchtowers and armed guards. The rest of the land was dominated by a dark, monstrous structure. At its center was a domed, five-story octagonal rotunda that seemed more a place for torture than for the treatment of the mad.

The ferry stopped. "Here," Hawking announced.

Carver tried not to show how hard his heart had dropped.

As they walked, his mentor pointed at the choppy waters beyond the island's northern tip. "Hell Gate. Hundreds of ships sank there until the army used 300,000 pounds of explosives to blast the rocks. It sent a geyser of water 250 feet in the air. They felt the rumble as far off as Princeton, New Jersey."

Numbed by the realization he'd be living in an asylum, Carver nodded politely.

Hawking stopped and put both hands on his cane.

"What is it, sir?" Carver asked.

"Do you expect me to believe that a boy like you, raised in this city, wouldn't know about the largest man-made explosion in history?"

Carver was confused. "I . . . never said I didn't know."

"No, but you nodded as if you didn't. If I'd said Broadway was given its name because it was a very wide, or should I say *broad,* avenue, would you nod then, too?"

"Yes, sir? I mean . . . no, sir?"

Hawking studied him dispassionately. "In the future you will tell me exactly what you do know and ask about what you don't. I can't waste time giving you what you've got, and I don't want to skip anything you're missing."

He laid his bad hand on Carver's shoulder. It weighed heavily, like a dead thing. Too frightened to stare at it, Carver tried to focus on his mentor's somber face.

"If we're to accomplish anything, I need your mind; I need it open and I need it honest. Lie through your teeth to whoever else you like, but not one false word, not one false nod or wink, to me. Understand?"

"Yes."

Hawking narrowed his eyes. "What *year* was that blast I just told you about?"

"1885," Carver answered. After a brief pause, he added, "October 10."

The hint of a smile came to Hawking's face. He tipped his head toward the ominous building. "What do you know about that place?"

Carver shrugged. "It's Blackwell Asylum." He searched his mind for more, but the clawed hand on his shoulder made him nervous. "A woman once pretended to be crazy so she could get in there to write a story about how bad the patients had it."

"Nellie Bly," Hawking said. "*Ten Days in a Madhouse.* Read it?"

"No, Delia . . . a friend, told me about it once."

Removing his hand, Hawking led Carver toward the twin stones staircases in front of the central tower. "They also call it the Octagon. It's New York's first publicly funded mental hospital. Two wings were completed, both overcrowded within months. To save money, the guards are all inmates from the prison, so for a good part of the day, the patients are abandoned to the tender mercies of thieves and murderers. Bly's little book put everyone on their best behavior for a while, but things haven't changed all that much."

Hawking waited for Carver to open the door. When he did, he saw a spectacular curved staircase rising from a glass-brick floor to the height of the tower, a circle of columns lining each floor.

Above the closed front desk hung the motto "While I live, I hope." An unshaven guard lay on the floor near two inner doors, snoring. "Think you're an orphan? Here are the real ones."

Hawking pushed open the doors to a long, dingy hall. Shadowy figures were visible along its length. Some sat sadly on narrow benches. Others moved about as if underwater. One man walked straight into a wall headfirst, staggered back and then did the same thing again over and over. Each time he hit, Carver heard a faint, hollow thud, like a ball being bounced on the sidewalk outside Ellis Orphanage. *Thud, thud, thud.*

"That's Simpson," Hawking said. "Deep down in his heart, Simpson believes he can pass through walls. An attendant will cart him off and tie him to his bed eventually."

Next, they headed for the long curved stairs. Much as Carver helped Hawking, the climb was slow and painful, punctuated by odd wails and mournful cries from the inmates.

To Carver's horror, Hawking could name each patient from the sound they made. "That growl is Mr. Gilbert, here two years, diagnosed with *mortified pride.* The wailing? Grace Shelby, seven months for *uncontrolled passion.* The high-pitched whine is Reginald Cowyn, diagnosed with *disappointed expectations.* Disappointed expectations, ha! The thing Nelly Bly never understood is that the doctors are as mad as the patients."

Just when Carver thought it would never end, they reached the top and a plain wooden door. Out of breath as he fished for the key, Hawking looked back down the many stairs and said, "*That* is why I don't travel often."

Pushing the door with his hip, he revealed a large, dark room, eight-sided like the rest of the structure but smaller. Four of the walls had tall windows that went nearly to the floor, while the other four held bookshelves. There was a couch, a table, a few chairs and something that might be a bed.

With a graceless plop, Hawking sat at the table and lit an old hurricane lantern. Every nook and cranny overflowed with objects, like scattered thoughts stuffed into a too-small brain. There were books, charts, instruments, grotesque, unnamable things in liquid-filled jars, even a bowl of what looked like bone fragments. Newspapers, some shredded, littered the floor.

On the table, aside from the oil lamp, was a typewriter sur-rounded by crumpled balls of paper and an institutional tray bear-ing the remains of Hawking's breakfast. The food looked as unappetizing as the bones.

The hunched man pointed to the chair on the other side of the table. Carver obeyed slowly, trying not to inhale too deeply near the tray.

"What do you think?" Hawking asked.

The man had demanded honesty, so Carver said, "I liked the New Pinkertons headquarters better."

Hawking snarled and swept his cane across the table. The tray, with its plate, silverware and drinking glass, went flying, then crashed to the floor. Carver was stunned, terrified. Below, the moaning increased.

The hurricane lamp cast half of Hawking's face in shadow. "Listen and listen well—all those gilded gadgets are baubles for fools! That headquarters is beneath a sewer and rightly so. This is the only *honest* place you'll find in the city, the only place where the pieces of the mind, the things that make us what we are, don't remain mute out of fear of what might be written about them on the society page. That's why I'm here, technically a consultant on the criminally insane, but I have the run of the place. Here is where we can learn what makes a criminal, what makes a man. Think that over . . . and clean up this mess."

Hawking rose, clumped over to the thing that looked like a bed and collapsed on it.

"Take the cushions off the chairs and toss them on the floor. Tomorrow we'll see about making up a more proper bed for you."

Carver did his best locating all the pieces of broken glass and piled them on the tray, hoping the morning light would reveal a wastebasket. Then, quiet as a mouse, he grabbed a cushion, kicked a space clear and lay down.

With pained wailing, manic laughter and the occasional scream rising from the floor beneath him, Carver eventually fell asleep, thinking about what it really meant to have a dream come true.

16

CARVER'S BODY was stiff. Heat was on his face.

Clack, clack, clack. Hisssssss. Clack, clack, clack. Hisssssss.

What was that sound? As he opened his eyes, his field of vision washed white from sunlight. He winced and blinked before realizing he was still in Blackwell Asylum. On the brighter side, that meant the New Pinkertons were real, too.

He looked around. The hissing came from an iron radiator. The clacking was Hawking, his clawed right hand jabbing slowly at the typewriter keys.

"I know you're awake, boy," he said. "Take a moment to gather your thoughts, but no more. Must've gotten cold last night. The heat seldom makes it up here. Means an early winter."

His mentor seemed lighter, as if all the traveling

yesterday accounted for most of his foul mood. Still, Carver remained quiet as he slipped on the ill-fitting pants and shirt he'd worn for Prospective Parents Day. Was it really only yesterday?

"Like puzzles?" Hawking asked. "Here's one. Look at the typewriter keys—*QWERTY*. Ever wonder why they're arranged that way?"

Carver repeated what he'd heard. "The most common letters are next to each other to make the typing faster."

"No. That's what most think, and most people are fools. Christopher Latham Sholes designed the layout in 1874 to *slow* the typist, to prevent the keys from jamming. The patients are at breakfast. You can shower privately. Get cleaned up and bring us back some food from the cafeteria."

Carver made for the stairs, relieved, despite Hawking's slightly improved disposition, to be away from him. In daylight, the asylum didn't look quite so awful. There was less moaning, and the showers on the floor below were, as Hawking said, empty. He wished he had different clothes to change into, but the towels he dried himself with were clean.

The narrow second-floor dining room was packed and loud. He tried not to stare, but the swollen brows and tiny eyes of some patients were freakish. Even their laughter seemed off. The only patient he spoke to was a woman in front of him in line. When he accidentally stared at her too long, she explained she was the wife of Grover Cleveland, president of the United States. Carver had no idea how to react. He worried she might get violent if he disagreed, or, if he stood too close, he might somehow inhale her madness.

Could he ever get used to this place? He had to. Hawking and the New Pinkertons would help find his father and make him a real detective along the way. That was worth a little discomfort, no?

Back upstairs, the lukewarm tea, gray oatmeal and bread tasted so dull, Carver missed Curly's cooking. Hawking didn't mind it. With a bowl next to his typewriter, he alternated between striking keys and taking spoonfuls of mush.

When the bowl was empty, Hawking said, "Ask me what I'm working on."

"Is it about my father?"

"No, that's your job. These are notes about Hunter and Smellie, the fathers of British midwifery. Their work, hundreds of years ago, saved the lives of countless women. Does that sound noble to you?"

"Yes," Carver answered. "Sure."

"Don't be so dull. Say, good heavens, what saints! Or, frankly I care more about a wart on my ass! Better yet, ask why a detective should even be interested."

"All right. Why—"

Hawking cut him off. "Because they were murderers. They needed fresh corpses for their research, so they ordered the deaths of scores of women, some pregnant. Still noble?"

"No," Carver said. "They were criminals."

"Define *criminal*," Hawking said.

"Someone who breaks the law."

"The men who founded the United States broke British law. Benjamin Franklin said, we must all hang together, or most assuredly we shall all hang separately. Was he a criminal?"

"No . . . well, yes, but . . . those were unfair laws that had to be broken."

"So, to be a man like Franklin, you sometimes have to break the law?"

Carver hesitated. "Yes."

Hawking wiped his lips and tossed the napkin into the bowl.

"I was too harsh last night, boy. I forgot your sense of right and wrong comes from dime novels. The lines aren't as clear in the real world."

"I'm not stupid," Carver objected.

Hawking narrowed his eyes. "I didn't say you were. Put words in my mouth and I'll bite your fingers off. Even the best mind can tumble into an abyss when its expectations are thwarted."

"A what? Abyss?" Carver said.

Hawking rapped the table. "Abyss. I'll make it simple. True story. A woman was sitting in a theater enjoying a play when suddenly, a fire truck drove across stage. It was part of the play, but because she didn't expect it, she screamed. Thing is, once she started screaming, she couldn't stop. They dragged her from the theater and brought her here, where she was deemed incurably mad. Any idiot would know she wasn't, but they had no idiots on staff, only doctors, alienists. That was two years ago. It was only last week I secured her release."

"But . . . why *was* she screaming that much if she wasn't mad?"

"She thought she knew the world, and in her way of thinking, real fire trucks *don't* appear in plays. She couldn't handle living in a world where they could. That was her abyss. You'll have yours one day, I'm sure. But for now, time to clean. Your belongings will be here this afternoon."

Carver didn't completely understand, but the lesson was over. For the next several hours, he worked, piling books and papers in the shelves on one wall, models along another, instruments at a third, and so on. Grateful the room had walls to spare, he even secured a space for himself, sectioning it off with what at first looked like a tabletop, but turned out to be a room divider.

After a break to retrieve lunch, he returned to find two attendants assembling a mattress frame. Carver's belongings had also arrived. To his surprise, Hawking was leafing through his small collection of detective novels.

"Allan Quatermain, Nick Neverseen, and Holmes, Holmes, Holmes," Hawking said. "Fan of Doyle?"

Carver nodded. "I'll say."

"Ever been able to solve one of his cases based on the information in the story?"

"No, but Holmes is the genius."

"*Doyle's* the genius. It's a cheap trick. The reader never has all the information, so Holmes can make up the answers at the last minute. You'd be better served reading another Holmes, H. H. Holmes, the multi-murderer. He was nabbed last year by a Pinkerton, Frank P. Geyer. Now his confession is being serialized in the *Philadelphia Inquirer.* How's that for a fire truck crossing the stage?"

Carver knew about that killer, despite Miss Petty's efforts to keep him from the stories. Holmes had been accused of over twenty murders, many committed during the Chicago World's Fair. He'd lured his victims to what the papers called a "murder castle." The thought that he'd be writing articles repulsed Carver as much as it fascinated him.

"Do you think he'll tell the truth? Confess?"

"No, but a bit of the liar always slips into the lie. It will be a good way to get into his head, the method used by *my* favorite fictional detective."

Carver was surprised to hear Hawking *liked* anything, but the hunched man put down Sherlock Holmes and searched among his shelves. Finding a slender volume, he tossed it to Carver.

The title was *The Murders in the Rue Morgue.*

"C. Auguste Dupin, by Edgar Allan Poe—inventor of the detective story. Dupin used *ratiocination,* combining logic with imagination to become so familiar with the criminal that the detective, in a way, *becomes* him. Think you can do that, boy? Become mad to find the mad? A thief to catch a thief? And worse?"

Carver thought about it. Did he mean *really* steal? What did he mean by *worse*? *Kill* to catch a killer?

Hawking regarded him as if he could read his thoughts from the furrows on his brow. "I've had enough of watching you try to think for one day. I've patients to visit. Lie in your new bed, read that book. Tomorrow bright and early you'll return to your beloved New Pinkertons and start searching for your father. We'll soon see what you're willing to do."

17

THE MORNING wind along the East River had an icy bite, but at least Carver was free of the asylum, free of Hawking. Calling his mentor eccentric didn't do him justice. He was like a bear trap, ready to snap off your foot if you weren't watching your step. Every conversation was a test. He'd even underlined the opening of *Rue Morgue*:

As the strong man exults in his physical ability, delighting in such exercises as call his muscles into action, so glories the analyst in that moral activity which *disentangles*. He derives pleasure from even the most trivial occupations bringing his talents into play. He is fond of enigmas, of conundrums, of hieroglyphics; exhibiting in his solutions of each a degree of *acumen* which appears to the ordinary apprehension preternatural.

Whatever that meant. Carver liked the story well enough. The twist ending, involving an orangutan, was fun. But for the whole of breakfast he'd worried he'd be quizzed about it. The detective, though, was interested only in typing. When Carver was about to leave, Hawking had ripped out the sheet, stuffed it in an envelope and warned him not to read the contents until he'd reached his "gilded" destination. Carver slipped it into the same pocket where he'd last held his father's letter.

A chest-shaking whistle snapped him into the moment. The ferry was docking. He was back, back in the city he knew so well, despite what his teacher had to say about it, and on his way to a grand adventure.

On foot, with barely enough money for lunch and the return ride, Carver trotted happily along the streets, swerving close whenever a peanut or baked potato vendor appeared, enjoying both the smell and the tiny blast of warmth from their smoking carts. It *was* cold for September. But the day was clear and the view of Broadway went on forever.

Eager as he was to return to the New Pinkertons, he found the corner at Warren Street was covered by a sea of bobbing hats. Thinking it'd be a stupid mistake to let anyone see him use the secret entrance, Carver crossed to City Hall Park, hoping the crowd would thin.

After about twenty minutes, he couldn't wait any longer. He crossed back and, trying to look as innocent as possible, twisted the brass pipe in sequence. To his relief, when the door popped open and he slipped inside, no one so much as slowed to look.

He managed the elevator easily but forgot how Hawking had started the train car. After a moment's panic, he remembered a lever being kicked. Finding the same seat, he pushed his heels to the base. When nothing seemed to happen, he kicked harder, again and again. He was still kicking when a glance at the window told him the car was already gliding along.

The two young agents were at the platform. The pallid Emeril was in mid-yawn, reading a copy of *Judge's Quarterly,* a humor magazine. The meatier Jackson, jacket off, shirtsleeves rolled, bent and rose in a calisthenic routine.

"Young Sherlock at last," Emeril said as Carver emerged. "Tudd saw you on the street."

Jackson grabbed his jacket from the railing. "We wondered what took you so long."

"I didn't want anyone seeing me," Carver explained.

Jackson patted him. "Good thinking, but unnecessary. It's just a door on the side of the building."

"And a useful habit of people not to notice things," Emeril said. "No one knows we exist, so no one looks for us."

"*I* found you," Carver said.

"Hawking *led* you to us," Jackson said.

"Let's get a move on," Emeril said, pocketing his rolled-up magazine. "We're to be your guides. Tudd wanted to be here, but he's busy with his pet case. Hawking thought you should start with the athenaeum," Emeril said.

"A fancy word for *library,*" Jackson added with a wink.

At the plaza they steered him right, over a small bridge, to a second structure. It was half a block long but very plain, its face a flat brick wall with double doors in the distant center.

"How is it living with Hawking in that madhouse?" Jackson asked.

"Um . . ." Carver liked them well enough but didn't feel comfortable discussing his mentor.

"Tudd worries he may have lost a bit of his mind along with his body," Jackson said. "He seem sharp to you? All there?"

Emeril interrupted him. "Here now, he barely knows Hawking three days, and the two of us less than an hour."

"Understood," Jackson said. He jogged ahead to open the doors. "If you were impressed before, wait until you see this."

Carver was impressed all right, but mostly by the smell. The musty odor wrapped around him like a blanket of age and silence. There was no second floor, no rooms, no hallways. Reading lamps sat at dozens of occupied tables and small desks, but none challenged the dominant dark. It was like a huge cave, a cave with books.

Shelves were everywhere, most running from the floor to the ceiling, all packed. Ladders ran along each, like columns buttressing a temple of paper and wood.

Emeril spoke softly. "We've got immigration records, indexed archives of every major New York newspaper published for the last decade and, the pride of the Pinkertons, old or new, the largest rogues gallery in the country—thousands of criminal files and photographs and—"

"Sh!!"

Dead ahead, behind a massive desk, sat a bespectacled man with his finger to his lips and a harsh glare on his face.

"Beckley," Jackson whispered, even more softly. "Sign in with him and you can get started. We've got our own work, but we'll keep an eye out for you."

Emeril gave Carver a little shove toward the short, thin, angular man.

His arms and fingers perfect lines, a wordless Beckley reached for a fountain pen lying parallel to a sheet of paper. He scanned a list, came to the name *Carver Young* and put a quick line through it. Then he rose and marched along the desks. Being around Hawking made Carver feel positively stiff-backed, but Beckley's precise gait made the boy worry he was slouching.

As they walked, Carver gasped as a dark metallic hulk, hidden by the dim light, grew visible. A behemoth of gears, spindles and slats, it ran nearly the length of the wall. As they got closer, Carver could see scores of small cardboard cards, each with a series of tiny square holes, held in various parts of the machine by thin metal spears, looking like insects trapped in an iron web. Thick gears connected the thing to what looked like a steam engine.

"What is . . . ," Carver blurted.

"An analytical engine," Beckley said. "Which we do not use except on rare occasions, because, like yourself, it is too *loud*."

"What does it . . ."

"Sh!"

Chastened, Carver remained silent. At the first empty desk, equipped with pen and paper, Beckley switched on the small electric lamp, pulled out the chair, then marched back. Carver sat, nervous as the chair creaked, then folded his hands on the desk.

So, here he was, ready to begin his life as a detective, ready to search for his father. Somewhere among all these millions of books his father's name, maybe even his address, could be listed.

Only, he didn't even *know* his father's name. So . . . now what?

Minutes ticked by. Panic, far worse than not knowing how to operate the subway, gripped his chest. He shifted in his seat, each creak a cannon's boom in the church-like quiet. Carver hadn't even done anything yet and he was already failing miserably.

His gaze flitted from person to person, every one reading or writing intently. Across the room, he caught the bug-like shape of a typewriter. No one would dare use it; it was too noisy. But it did remind him of Hawking, and then of the note his teacher had given him.

It must have instructions! It'd be ridiculous to just stick him in the library, right? He pulled it out and tore the envelope open. The ripping sound earned him several stares and a second loud shush from Beckley. Wincing, he pulled out the note and read:

Put yourself in your father's shoes.

That was it? He checked both sides. That was it. *That* took him all morning to type. If Carver hadn't been in a library, he might have screamed.

He read it again. It was yet another test. Put himself in his father's shoes. But how could Carver put himself in the shoes of a man he didn't know?

The answer came: he could write down what he *did* know. That would be a start. He took the pen and made a list.

1. Had a son, me, sometime around 1881.
2. Sent letter from England to the orphanage in 1889.

That letter was his biggest clue. What had *that* told him?

3. He has bad handwriting.
4. I have the birthmark mentioned in the letter.
5. His wife is dead.
6. He works with a knife—a meat packer? Butcher?
7. Told his boss he was quitting because he found out I was alive.

His mind lingered on that last one. Quitting his job. That meant his son was important to him, didn't it?

8. Knew to send the letter to Ellis Orphanage.

As Delia suggested, that created another possibility, one Carver didn't particularly want to face.

9. He couldn't, or didn't want to, raise me.

Maybe he was just poor, like Delia's mother. But if he'd gone through the trouble of quitting his job and crossing the ocean, wouldn't he at least want to meet? Wait a minute.

10. He crossed the ocean from London.

What had Jackson said about immigration records? Wouldn't there be a record of his father's arrival? He didn't have a name, but he had a year. Maybe there was a list of immigrants from England. On to something, Carver walked to the front desk.

"Yes, Mr. Young?" Beckley softly asked.

"Can you tell me where the immigration records for 1889 are kept?"

"The passenger manifests for arriving ships. Section I, shelf forty." He pointed to a dark area behind him, then opened a well-oiled drawer and withdrew a corded lightbulb fixed with a head strap. "You'll need this. There are outlets at the end of every other shelf. Do remember it's plugged in before you attempt climbing up or down. These devices are expensive."

He nodded for Carver to lower his head, then quickly fixed the strap around his forehead. Feeling like a miner, Carver headed to the shelves.

Shelf forty of section I was at least twenty feet up, so he pulled a ladder over and, cord in hand, climbed. As he rose, it grew darker. By the time he reached what he thought was shelf forty, he couldn't see a thing. Feeling along the molding, he found a protruding, rounded outlet and pressed the plug in. The bulb buzzed and created a white cone that pointed wherever he turned his head. After allowing himself a moment's pleasure at the gadget, Carver went to work.

The records ran through many volumes per year, but there was only one for 1889. Hoping this meant there might be only a few names, he pulled it out and began climbing down. After a few feet, a tug at his head told him he'd forgotten the cord. The lamp was yanked off. The book nearly flew from his grasp. The bulb clattered against the shelf, its light dancing through the darkness. Everyone stared.

At least the bulb hadn't broken. Feeling sheepish, he caught his balance, climbed back up and unplugged the headlamp before descending again.

Once on the ground, as he opened the book, he felt a rush of excitement. Only, the page he'd opened to was blank. Puzzled, he flipped to another. Also blank. He fanned the pages. Every page was empty. Was it some kind of trick?

Annoyed, he walked back to the front desk and showed Beckley.

For the first time, the librarian's face registered a vague emotion: confusion. Tapping his chin, he whispered, "Ah, yes. This book is a placeholder. From 1855 to 1890 immigrants registered at Castle Clinton in Battery Park. When Ellis Island opened in 1892, they planned to transfer the records, but most were destroyed in a fire."

Carver's heart sank. "A fire? Did any survive?"

"Some, but those would be at Ellis Island. They're attempting to recover what they can, but with the huge immigration flow, it's not a priority."

Ellis Island. A long trip for what would likely be nothing. How would he even recognize his father's name if he saw it? Wait.

There was one way. The handwriting. His father's scrawl was pretty unique.

"The records, would they have signatures from the passengers?"

"Usually, or, if the person was illiterate, their mark."

There was hope, then. Ellis Island it was. He'd use his lunch money for the ferry.

Leaving the headlamp and book with Beckley, Carver retrieved his notes and walked toward the exit. Jackson and Emeril came bounding up, speaking only once they were outside.

"Done already?" Jackson asked.

"Do you have any idea how I'd go about seeing the records at Ellis Island?"

"Ellis Island?" Emeril said with a grin.

Jackson checked his watch. "Less than an hour. Tudd lost that bet. I'll get him. He'll want to hear what comes next."

"What's going on?" Carver asked.

"You'll see," Jackson said as he broke into a run. "And don't start without me!"

18

AS EMERIL bolted for the offices, Jackson rushed a very confused Carver toward the open faced building across the plaza.

"Did I do something wrong?" Carver asked. "Where are we going?"

"No," Jackson said as he stepped up to a door, "you did something *right*. And we're going to our technical sector."

A prim redheaded woman with striking green eyes answered. She looked nearly as perplexed as Carver felt. "So soon?"

Jackson straightened for the attractive woman. "I told you, Emma. Hawking guessed it wouldn't be more than an hour."

The woman nodded and ushered them in to a large work space full of odd machines, wires, tubes and tools. Carver had no idea what most of it was, but he did think he recognized the thing sitting on the central table—a large horn rising from the center of a black cylinder, connected to a wooden crank box. He knew about the parlors where customers paid a nickel to hear music from such a device, but still had to ask. "Is that a phonograph?"

The woman answered, "It is indeed, with some slight modifications made to improve the recording fidelity."

Before Carver could ask what she meant, an excited Mr. Tudd bounded in. He sat at the table and bid Carver do the same. "Sorry for the mystery, but we've all been very curious about this. When our eccentric Mr. Hawking visited some weeks back to discuss your letter, I persuaded him to try our new sound-recording device. Rather than sing a song or recite a poem, he insisted on recording a message . . . for you."

Carver frowned. "But we hadn't met yet."

Tudd gave him a smile. "He seemed certain you would. Further, the message was to be played only after you inquired about Ellis Island. He insisted it would take you less than an hour. I thought it would take at least that long for you to familiarize yourself with the athenaeum." He pointed a thick finger at the gramophone. "Now, the sound is recorded through the vibration of a tiny needle, or stylus, which makes marks on a clay cylinder. Edison considered using a disc, but the cylinder provides a more constant velocity. When the clay dries, the same needle runs along the grooves, re-creating the sound, which is amplified by the horn. All *you* have to do is turn the handle."

Looking boy-like in his eagerness, Tudd waved his hand at Carver, telling him to go ahead. Carver wasn't sure if they were excited about the machine or about finally hearing what Hawking had recorded. Thrilled at the thought of both, he gripped the wooden handle and turned. The cylinder rotated, the small stylus rose and fell. A voice, tinny and distant, came through the horn.

"You know the letter came from London, and, given the date, you'll want to see if there's anything left of the passenger manifest from Castle Clinton for that year. Once you're at Ellis, ask for the Counter. That's his name—Counter. He's a friend. Well, a former asylum inmate, actually, but don't worry, I don't believe he'll bite. Mention my name and he'll help you try to get you what you need."

The sound ended, but Carver kept turning, hoping there was more.

After several seconds of wordless scratches, Tudd said, "I think you can stop now."

"The Counter, eh?" Emeril said.

"Probably a raving maniac," Tudd said with a chuckle. "Like Hawking."

"That's it?" Carver asked.

Tudd shrugged. "What else do you need? It's on to the next puzzle. Go on, son. Get going. Report back if you learn anything."

All eyes on him, Carver rose and headed for the door. The idea of seeking out a former Octagon inmate wasn't comforting, but given that Hawking had made the recording weeks ago, it occurred to him for the first time that Hawking might be both brilliant *and* insane.

19

CARVER entered the subway and kicked the lever. His mind was racing. How could Hawking have known they would meet? He felt oddly like a pawn in someone else's game. *On to the next puzzle,* Tudd had said. They were testing him, just like Hawking.

A shadow made him jump. His foot sent a dark metal cylinder rolling across the car. Curious, he picked it up. It looked like a baton. It was cool to the touch, heavy, but pocket-sized, a single button on the side. Without bothering to think what it might do, Carver pressed it.

Schick!

The cylinder expanded so quickly, he jumped again. Now the thing looked like a short black cane, only it tapered to a dull copper point. Carver swung it a few times. It moved easily through the air, as though balanced.

But when his last swing scraped the metal wall, a horrific series of sparks crackled from the cane. Terrified, he dropped the thing and it hit the floor. Thin curls of smoke rose from the spot on the wall where it touched. A weapon, definitely a weapon.

Gingerly, he poked it with his finger. When nothing happened, he pressed the button again. *Schick!* It collapsed back into its original form.

He had no idea how to use such a weapon, but some instinct told him his finding it had been no accident. That same instinct told him to keep it. Something was going on. He had little doubt that, even now, the Pinkertons were watching him.

Feeling a little paranoid, he pocketed the amazing device and headed out toward Broadway. Soon he was on a southbound streetcar, careening along at over twenty miles per hour. Called the *electric underground,* the cars got power from a buried cable. But what powered the baton?

By the time he reached the South Street piers, the sight of tall-masted clippers docked beside huge, steam-powered ocean liners drove any concerns from his mind. Relaxed, he wove among dockworkers, arriving immigrants and passengers. The city was his home. *No one* could follow him if he didn't want them to.

At the tip of Manhattan Island, the Ellis Island ferry was arriving. A ship's wake made the old steam workhorse rise and fall. As it dipped, scores of arriving men, women and children, gaping at their new home, stumbled forward. When it rose, they all leaned back. They looked so bewildered. Carver's father might've stepped off the same ferry. What had *he* been thinking back then?

When the ferry pulled back out, Carver was on it. After a choppy ride, it steered into a split in the rectangular Ellis Island, pulling up practically in front of the four-spired Federal Immigration Station. A half mile beyond, a giant blue-green arm and head poked above the water—the Statue of Liberty.

Inside, the mass of humanity would've been overwhelming if the space weren't so vast. Dozens of languages mingled in a constant roar. Officials were scattered throughout, shouting the same commands over and over about which lines to stand in. Behind one counter, three uniformed men struggled to answer questions. After a long wait, Carver was at last waved by a perpetually upset, stocky man.

When Carver explained why he was there, the man pointed toward the far end of the hall. "You'll want the stairs of Separation."

Seeing his perplexed expression, the official pointed. "Stairs of Separation. Center staircase means you're approved to stay; right or left means you're being detained. Take the right. At the first landing there's a door to the basement. Don't be shy about pushing. No one in that line's in much of a hurry."

As Carver made his way, the space, if possible, grew thicker with people. He angled right, earning glares as he moved ahead of the waiting. Most said nothing, but halfway down the steps, a stout man, dark stubble covering his head, grabbed his arm.

When the man opened his mouth, as if to speak, Carver hoped he spoke English, so Carver could explain. Instead, he let loose a blast of wet, fetid air and started coughing. Carver held his breath and furiously pulled himself free.

Frightened, Carver moved quickly down the stairs, where he found the basement door. He made his way down into a clean but desolate hallway, his breathing heavy, his heart beating fast.

The first door was a thick, metal affair, the faint smell of charcoal wafting from a crack at the bottom. The knob was stuck, but with some effort he pulled it open. The mess at Hawking's was nothing compared to what greeted his eyes. The room was so cluttered, he couldn't tell how big it was. It was lined with shelves and tables, piles of paper on each, all burnt to one extent or another—the source of the smell.

The piles weren't the strangest thing. That would be the strings. Countless, multicolored, frayed and rotting, they led from the stacks toward an odd mound in a dark corner. Together, they resembled a filthy rainbow spiderweb.

The mound moved, making the strings wobble. Instinctively, Carver reached for the baton, wondering how he would respond if he was forced to use it. It was a man, unshaven, like Hawking, his clothes so unclean they were a uniform gray. He had no glasses, but his eyes were wide, as if he had trouble focusing.

"What?" he said, as if it were *hello*.

"Are you Counter?" Carver asked.

The man's face scrunched, turning the lines on it into a second web. "How old are you?"

"Fourteen. I was sent by . . ."

"Birthday? Height? Weight?"

"Sorry?"

"They're numbers, aren't they? You have to keep count, or everything . . ." He swept his arm, strings fluttering as he moved. "*Everything* gets lost."

"All right," Carver said. He rattled off his height, weight and birthday, but more questions came: Shoe size? How many teeth? Carver did his best until, eventually, the man was satisfied enough for him to explain why he was there and who sent him.

"Hawking," Counter said. "Number one in my book. What year is this record?"

"Uh . . . 1889."

"New immigrant." The man's long fingers crawled along the strings. He hooked some on bent fingers and let others drop.

"New?" Carver asked.

"Before 1870, most immigrants were Anglo-Saxon, Protestant, except the Irish, same as the people already here. After that, folks started coming from eastern and southern Europe, Catholics, Russian Jews, Asians, different ideas, *new* immigrants."

"How many people do you think came here in 1889?"

Without a beat, Counter answered, "333,207."

Carver's shoulders slumped at the huge number. The Counter chuckled. "Sounds big, don't it? That number's a lion. Let's see if we can tame him. Country of origin?"

"England. London."

Counter dropped several strings. "60,552. Not so big. Just a bobcat. Month?"

"Um . . . November." That was the date on the letter, he remembered.

"5,046. A pussycat. Man or a woman?"

"Man."

More strings fell. "3,279."

"Traveling alone or with family?"

Carver doubted his father had a family. "Alone."

"Good. That's rare. 522. Just a kitten now. Skilled or unskilled?"

The letter mentioned knives. He could be a butcher. He had a boss, too, so he definitely had a job. "Skilled."

"316. Did he have money with him? Do you know his age?" Counter tugged gently at the line as if teasing a fish with bait.

Carver shrugged. "That's all. That's all I know."

The man nodded toward the six strings in his hand. "Follow the strings."

Excited, he overcame his repulsion and took the strings. The threads were hard to follow, but whenever Carver lost track, the Counter gave each one a little tug to show him the way. The strings led to a small pile of ship manifests, some too brittle to move, others too blackened to read.

Carver stared uneasily at the pile. "How many records from that year survived?"

"108," Counter said. "Puts your chances at about one in three."

Gingerly, Carver sifted through. He easily skipped any lighter writing, or the X's of the illiterate, searching for his father's distinct, heavy scrawl. He must have been there an hour and was about to give up when one rough signature made his heart leap into his throat. The writing was unmistakable. On a charred sheet, half-burned away, the ink practically glowing, was his father's signature, his father's *name* . . . Jay Cusack.

It didn't sound English. Was it Irish? Jay Cusack. How hard could it be to find him now?

The Counter's voice pulled him back into the room. "Got what you need?"

"Yes! Thank you!"

Counter nodded, sending a ripple through the strings. "Good luck to you, then. My best to Mr. Hawking. Without him I'd still be in that asylum. And kid, whatever you're doing, make sure it counts."

20

JAY CUSACK. *Jay Cusack.* That meant he was . . . *Carver Cusack*?

Upon his return to the South Street pier, Carver rolled the name around on his tongue. Not an easy sound, but what did that matter? He still knew so little. Was Carver born here or in England? *Why* did his father think he was dead?

Realizing he was hungry, Carver had absently whirled toward a fruit vendor when he thought he saw a dark figure slip around the corner. Was he being followed? Was this whole chase just a game to the Pinkertons? It could've been the shadow of a store awning bulging from the wind, but . . .

He walked to the corner and peered down the block. The late-afternoon sun was nearly behind the buildings. But, other than the long shadows it cast on the vendors, workers and businessmen, there was nothing.

Real or not, the encounter made Carver wary, but not enough to keep him from spending the rest of the return journey trying to figure out what his next step would be. New York was huge, but even so, how many Jay Cusacks could there be?

He arrived back on Warren Street and let himself into the headquarters. If anyone from the New Pinkertons had followed him, he saw no sign of it. In fact, as the subway glided up to the platform and Carver stepped off, they seemed barely aware he was there. A push of the curved door let in the sounds of a lively discussion between Tudd and some agents.

"Still *lost*?" Tudd was saying. "That prototype was invaluable! It took a full year to develop that weapon!"

They were talking about the baton. Should Carver tell them he'd found it? Before he even had a chance, Tudd saw him, brightened, and started asking questions.

"So tell us how it went," he said. "Tell us *everything*."

Tudd was so genial, Carver's sense of guilt kicked in. When he finished reporting what he'd learned, he was about to bring up the baton, but the older man quickly asked, "The sheet, the sheet with the signature, did you bring it?"

He seemed *awfully* excited about it. Carver's sense of distrust kicked in again, but rather than ask why, he handed over the envelope.

Tudd slipped the burnt sheet out and looked at the signature. "It does, it *does* look similar."

Noticing the way he grasped the browning paper, Carver felt suddenly protective. "It's brittle. You can't put it in a tube like the other. I'll take it to your expert if you like."

"No, no," Tudd said. "I'll take it there myself, with the utmost care."

Carver stared at him. "Can I go with you? I'd like to see them side by side."

Tudd shook his head. "Sorry, son. Patience. It *has* only been a day. You've done well though."

Without another word, Tudd hurried off, Carver annoyed at being called *son*. Much as Tudd seemed friendly, he'd now taken the *second* clue to his father's identity. Carver forced himself to remember Tudd had shown him nothing but kindness, given him nothing but opportunities. At the same time he was no longer quite so eager to return the baton.

Even without the sheet, he could still look up the name. On his way to the athenaeum, Jackson and Emeril ran up. Apparently, they'd somehow already heard of his success.

"Wonderful!"

"What luck! And we could sure use some of that around here!"

"Cusack? Isn't that Polish?" Jackson ventured.

"Norman," Emeril corrected. "Still used in England, mostly Irish, French before that." Explaining to Carver, he added, "Surnames are part of my studies."

"That and everything else," Jackson said, rolling his eyes.

Despite enjoying their company, Carver didn't quite trust them anymore either. He nodded toward the door. "I've only got an hour or so before I have to head back to Blackwell. I'd like to try to find an address by then."

They laughed so hard, he had to ask. "Is it *that* funny?"

"Yes," Jackson said. "It's not as though you can use the analytical engine. And even then . . ."

Remembering the huge device, Carver asked, "What *is* that? What's it do?"

"Not much since Beckley can't abide the noise." Jackson chuckled. "He almost quit over it. Tudd knows the nuts and bolts. He's the first to get one working."

Emeril interrupted. "But to answer the question, it was invented by Charles Babbage, fellow who created the difference engine, a mechanical calculator. The analytical engine is more general purpose. Using data coded into punched cards, it can sort them and answer questions. Say you wanted a list of whoever's related to the person currently living at 375 Park Avenue. Put the question on a punch card, start the engine, in an hour or so, it spits out the answer."

Carver went wide-eyed. "Really? Could I use it to find my father?"

Jackson shook his head. "First, Beckley hates the thing. Second, it keeps breaking down. Third, the cards only cover the city's current upper class. Your dad's more likely working class, don't you think? I suppose if you eliminate your other options and *beg,* Beckley might give in. Until then, it's the old-fashioned method. Frankly, you'll be lucky to have the directories stacked on a table by the time you have to leave."

As it turned out, Jackson was wrong. Carver not only stacked all the city directories from 1889 on, he also flipped through four, listing addresses for anyone named Jay Cusack.

By the time he had to leave, he'd accumulated fifty-seven Jay Cusacks. *Fifty-seven.* Worse, halfway through the fifth book he realized he should've listed *all* the Cusacks, in case a family member knew how to reach him.

On his way out, he longingly eyed the analytical engine. As if reading his mind, Beckley shook his head and proceeded to not only suggest ten more directories, but also to check the major newspaper archives, police reports and hospital records.

Daunted, Carver felt his shoulders slump as he left. Head buzzing with all the lists he'd have to go through, when he stepped out of the elevator onto Warren Street, he barely heard a familiar voice shriek his name.

"Carver!"

He looked up. A hansom cab was at the curb, a pretty girl leaning excitedly out the window. The smart new clothes were utterly unfamiliar, but the black hair and freckled face were un-mistakable.

"Delia!" he shouted, trotting up.

"How wonderful!" she said. "I was just over at the New York Times Building. It's the most *amazing* place! I saw the archives, the news desk, *everything*!"

Of course. The *Times* was on Park Row, part of Newspaper Row, just a few blocks away.

"Great!" Carver said.

"We're heading home—West Franklin Street, number twenty-seven. Jerrik's uncle rents them a lovely Queen Anne Victorian with a grand oak right outside my window. Haven't had a chance yet, but it looks like an easy climb. What about you? Shopping Devlin's for some new clothes, I hope?"

Right. Here was Delia dressed to the nines and he, still in his threadbare Ellis Orphanage clothes. Embarrassing as that was, he *couldn't* tell her what he was doing. Not only had he just stepped out of a secret headquarters, but she was now the ward of *reporters*.

"Just . . . heading home," he said.

"So you found someone to adopt you! Was it that old detective?"

Yes, and I'm living in an insane asylum with him, he wanted to say. Instead, he half-mumbled, "No, not him."

"Oh . . . ," Delia said. She looked as if she didn't believe him. "Who, then?"

"Someone—else," Carver stammered.

"Do they have a name?" Delia asked patiently.

The awkward silence lasted until the woman sharing Delia's cab leaned forward. It was Anne Ribe. He recognized her from Prospective Parents Night. Her eyes glowed with an intelligence that, even though they weren't related, reminded Carver of Delia.

She extended a white-gloved hand. "The mysterious Carver Young! Delia's told us so much about you . . . and yet so little."

Really? That was a surprise. And Delia looked uncomfortable to hear it. Carver was taken aback but remembered to shake her hand. "Not that much to tell, really."

"Can we give you a ride? I'm sure Delia would love to catch up."

"No!" Carver said. His answer was loud enough to make Anne Ribe blink and twist her lips into a suspicious half smile. "Thank you, but I really should be walking."

"Where?" Delia asked. She pushed closer and mouthed, "What's going on?"

"Nothing!" Carver mouthed back.

A fierceness took hold of her face.

"It's not that simple," Carver added.

"Seems simple enough," she said, pulling herself back inside. She sat flat against the seat, leaving her barely visible.

"Well, nice meeting you!" Anne Ribe said. And the cab rolled off.

Carver watched it go, confused and distraught. Delia had always been a challenge, pushing him, but she'd also been part of his life forever. He thought of calling out, chasing the cab, telling her everything, but he couldn't. He had an entirely new life to deal with now.

And fifty-seven Jay Cusacks. So far.

21

LIKE THE ferry prow as it rose and collapsed on the choppy gray waters, seeing Delia had lifted Carver's spirits just high enough to send them crashing down. Returning to the dreary island didn't improve his mood, nor did seeing Simpson slam his head into the wall. *Thud, thud, thud.* Carver almost wanted to join him.

As he trudged up the long circular stairs, he hoped against hope that his mentor would ignore him so he could throw himself onto his new bed and collapse.

The typewriter was silent, but the pile of papers beside it had grown. Hawking was at the table, peering through a magnifying glass mounted on an adjustable stand. Intricate brass items had been strewn across an oily cloth. One was held in a vise, and the retired detective was hard at work using his good left hand to polish it.

He didn't bother looking up. "Your housework inspired me, boy."

"What is that?" Carver asked.

"A gadget. Call me a hypocrite, but I've a fondness for trains. Not the silent type, the cranky old steam variety. This is a piece of old railway equipment, once used for uncoupling cars and switching tracks. Should still work on our elevated system. I find the mechanics fascinating. Almost relaxing."

Hawking lifted his head, revealing his intense, steady eyes. "You look like you've had quite the day."

Carver mumbled noncommittally.

Hawking tossed the cloth into the center of the table. "Shall we play at Holmes and have me guess?"

"I thought you didn't like Holmes," Carver said.

He propped his good arm on one knee. "No, but if I'm to talk to you, I have to speak whatever simplistic tongue you best understand. Could be worse, could be nursery rhymes."

Pupils black as coal scrutinized Carver. He felt as if his mind were being prodded by a physical thing. "Shoulders slumped, face wan, expression twitchy. You're far too sad to have failed completely. I'm guessing you had some success, but it didn't mean what you thought it would."

Being easily read only added to Carver's discomfort. "Yes."

Hawking scrunched his face, as if extending his gaze deeper into an unseen crystal ball. "You heard my message, made it to Ellis Island. The Counter helped you. You found a name."

"Wow. How do you know all that?" Carver asked, surprised.

Hawking cackled. "You're so easy to fool. There's a phone in the office here. I spoke with Tudd half an hour ago. What did you find in the athenaeum that depressed you?"

"Fifty-seven Jay Cusacks," Carver explained. "And I've looked through only four directories."

Hawking rubbed his chin. "I'd have hoped the Counter would have taught you something about numbers. Maybe you weren't listening. Do you know how many people currently reside in this city?"

"Not exactly. A lot."

"A million and a half, give or take. In one day, *one day,* you narrowed the field from a million and a half to less than a hundred, and you're complaining? Have you always been the sort who sees the light at the end of the tunnel and thinks it an oncoming train? Cheer up, the worst is yet to come!"

Hawking set another brass piece in the vise. "Your dime novels show only the tiniest fraction of detective work, the brilliant crime, the tantalizing clues, the dramatic chase, the final battle atop a lofty peak with ocean waves crashing down below, and then . . . justice served! If they wrote about the real world, four-fifths of the story would consist of the hero sitting in a library for months and following false leads. But no one would pay a nickel for that, let alone a dime."

He paused to look at the new piece, giving it the same scrutiny he'd just given Carver. "Thinking, reading, walking, riding, waiting. That's most of it. There *are* chases, undercover work and . . . gun battles, but they are completely unromantic and few and far between. Still want to be a detective?"

"Yes," Carver answered.

Hawking grinned. "But not as much as you did a week ago?"

Carver shrugged. "I don't mind the work. I was just . . . surprised."

"Wait until a month passes and your list grows longer rather than shorter." He stopped to look at Carver again. "There's something else, isn't there? A girl?"

That was too much. How could he possibly know about Delia? "So there *was* someone following me?"

"Eh?" Hawking said. He shrugged. "Not that Tudd mentioned, though I wouldn't put it past him. That much I actually did read on your face. Women are a difficult subject. I won't be much help to you there, except perhaps to say if they're guilty of something or not. And *everyone's* guilty of something, so the answer's always yes."

But Carver had to talk to someone about Delia. He wasn't sure about the New Pinkertons anymore, and that left Hawking. "It's not that sort of thing. I ran into a friend from the orphanage. I wanted to tell her what was going on but couldn't."

Hawking nodded. "You were *embarrassed* to be living in a nuthouse, so you probably mumbled some sad, ill-conceived lie. A waste of good creativity. Say whatever you like about me, boy. It's not as though I care what the damnable mass of humanity thinks."

"It's not just that. It's the Pinkertons. I'm not allowed to tell anyone about them," Carver said.

"Ah. Well, you don't have to *lie* about it. *A truth that's told with bad intent beats all the lies you can invent.* That's Blake. He also said, *Sooner murder an infant in its cradle than nurse unacted desires,* but we'll leave that for another day. As for the bauble-enchanted Tudd and the Pinkertons, tell her you've been asked not to discuss the work you're doing for me. That sounds mysterious and romantic, doesn't it? Some women enjoy that sort of thing. If you prefer to gain her sympathies, tell her I beat you. Which I will, by the way, unless you head down to the kitchen and bring back some dinner."

Somehow, Carver didn't think that would impress Delia.

He turned and made his way to the kitchen.

22

IN THE weeks that followed, the list reached nearly a hundred names. Carver's days were filled with such mundane and tiring tasks that even the wonders of the secret headquarters grew dull. But, dutifully, doggedly, he made the trek from Blackwell to Manhattan, visiting address after address, finally grasping the true vastness of a city he thought he knew well.

Most addresses led to tenements, where he spoke to blind beggars and women ragpickers. One suggested Carver try Potter's Field, where the nameless poor were buried with numbers instead of names. He visited families of six or seven living in two rooms, crowded around a table making artificial flowers to sell for food.

Two Cusacks were cigar makers; one a foreman in a necktie workshop; three were butchers, raising his hopes, but none had sent a letter to Ellis Orphanage. A rare few Cusacks held more prestigious jobs—a banker, a lawyer. But whenever he traveled north among the upper-class homes, he was nearly arrested for loitering. His threadbare, increasingly ill-fitting clothes were now laundered in lye by the Octagon staff and gave off an unpleasant smell that marked him as poor. Worse, each visit to the athenaeum gave him two more Cusacks for each he'd scratched off. Beckley was no closer to even considering the use of the analytical engine, though he did see an agent oiling it once.

"Sounds about right," Jackson or Emeril would say.

Tudd was too busy to even say that. Whenever Carver asked about the handwriting analysis, Tudd only shook his head.

At night the young detective in training was so tired, he could almost ignore Hawking's trying lectures. He could not yet ignore the moaning patients.

The only vaguely exciting thing happened one evening when he returned to Blackwell early. As Carver entered the Octagon, he saw Hawking emerge from a slender door on one of the patients' floors. The door fit so neatly into the wall, it was practically invisible when closed. Where on earth could it lead?

Spotting Carver, Hawking quickly closed it, then spat, "None of your concern."

Curious as he was, Carver didn't dare ask, but he kept the door in mind, imagining it held some mystery, one that might be easier to solve than his father's identity—if he could ever work up the nerve to disobey his mentor.

By October the weather turned colder. Sky, trees and even the buildings seemed to grow grayer. When Carver learned that a street vendor named Jim Cusack worked along Newspaper Row, the short walk from Devlin's took him to the front of the New York Times Building. He stared up at the first building in the city devoted solely to a newspaper, hoping he might spy Delia at one of the windows.

Some days the only thing that kept him going was the thought that all this work was yet another test from Hawking, and if he lasted long enough, the detective would offer some great insight that would speed Carver along. But, aside from sardonic quotes, trying conversations that often made little sense and an odd book or two tossed across the room at him with great force, Hawking offered no specific guidance. His only comment on finding Carver's father was, "Sooner or later, boy, you'll either give up or you'll find something. I've no idea which it will be."

Neither did Carver.

23

ONE MORNING the temperature dipped below freezing, prompting Hawking to force an old moth-eaten overcoat on Carver. "I won't have you bringing back any diseases, boy. If you want me dead, you'll have to kill me yourself."

Any objections Carver had vanished during the ferry ride. The wind was numbing. For the first time, he abandoned the top deck and huddled with the passengers below.

The day before, Beckley had presented him with an addendum to an 1889 directory. In it, he'd found a listing for a J. Cusack on Edgar Street. He scoured a map for an hour before spotting a tiny line connecting Trinity Place and Greenwich.

It was so cold, Carver decided to splurge and take the elevated train along Greenwich. Despite the billowing steam from the compact locomotive and a sweaty, red-faced engineer, the cars were frigid.

Edgar Street looked smaller than it had on the map. It was fifty-five feet long at most. There were no doors, either, just the walls of buildings that opened elsewhere. Another dead end.

Back on Greenwich, he asked a policeman, "Were there ever any apartments on Edgar Street?"

"Boarded over and sold five years back."

Carver made his usual plea. "My father may have lived there. Jay Cusack?"

"Cusack, Cusack. Tip of my tongue, but I can't shake it loose."

Understanding, Carver dug into his pocket and produced the few coins he had. Seeing the paltry bribe, the officer rolled his eyes.

"Keep your pocket change. You'll want to talk to Katie Miller. Two blocks south, hang a left, second door on the right. Just listen for the cats."

Ignoring the odd comment, Carver followed his directions. At the head of the street, an acrid animal scent mixed with the more constant smells of horse, coal and street.

The odor grew stronger at the second door, where a muffled chorus of mewing came to his ears. It wasn't unusual to have a few pets, he told himself. He lifted the brass knocker and rapped. The mewing was joined by a whisper of slippered feet.

The door creaked open, releasing a blast of hot cat smell mixed with a sharp chemical odor. Wide-set blue eyes stared at him from a wrinkled face. If the woman's nose were hooked, she'd resemble a witch.

"Katie Miller?"

The woman blinked in response. Carver took it to mean yes. "Did you own the apartments that used to be on Edgar Street?"

"What about it?"

"Did you ever have a tenant named Jay Cusack?"

Her eyes flared. "Him? Long, long time ago. Must be six years." The mewing grew more agitated. "Quiet, dearies! You'll have your rest soon, I promise!"

She looked back at Carver. "I meant to take care of them last night, but I was too tired. What would you want with Cusack? If he owes you money, forget it. You don't want to tangle with him."

"I think he may be my father."

He'd said it so often, the words no longer filled him with anticipation.

He was surprised, though, that the woman seemed so taken aback.

"A son to that beast? You . . . do look like him, around the jaw, shape of the skull, but there's something fairer in you. Your mother?"

Beast? What did she mean? Did she really know his father? Carver tried to keep calm. "I don't know. I was raised an orphan."

"I know all about orphans," she said. "I collect them."

She opened the door and for the first time smiled at Carver. "Come in."

Inside, the smell was so strong, he had to hold his breath. Cats were everywhere, big toms, calicos, kittens, even feral alley dwellers that raised their back hairs and hissed on seeing him. Some had name tags embossed with their owners' addresses.

How were they orphans?

A couch near two closed windows was piled with the animals, but the woman tossed them off as if they were pillows. As Carver moved to sit, he nodded toward the windows.

"Could we open one, please? It's a little . . . stuffy."

"Oh, no, no, no! They'd all race off! They know when it's coming."

"It?"

"The *sleep*," Katie said, settling into a chair opposite him. "Every creature fears its end."

"You . . . kill them?"

"Out of kindness," she said calmly. "Thousands roam the streets, homeless and starving." She grabbed a big white female, plopped it on her lap and rubbed her hands along its back to warm her fingers. "There was a group of us once, the Midnight Band of Mercy, but it's been nearly two years since they convicted poor Mrs. Edwards because of that ridiculous ASPCA." She paused a moment to look at him again and crooked a gnarled finger. "You do look like him."

Trying to forget the cats, Carver asked, "Do you know where I can find him?"

"No. He didn't stay long. Big man. Dark, like there was a cloud followed him. Chasing someone, being chased, no idea." Her blue eyes grew wide. "I've seen his look in animals. Not cats so much as dogs. And what are dogs but demoted wolves? Wolfish. He was wolfish. A predator, you know? I remember him mostly because of the piano."

"He played?"

"No. He . . . threw it. It belonged to a piano teacher who died. Two of the wheels snapped off, so it was abandoned in the hall, blocking the stairs, so you'd have to squeeze around. Mr. Cusack wouldn't have it. He was always in a rush. He offered to move it, but I said he'd need at least two more men to budge the thing. But he . . . shoved it. Sent it twenty feet. Pushed it out, down the stoop, smashed it and then piled the pieces. I was afraid of him after that."

Could that be his father? Stunned, he sat back, his head hitting something warm and furry that writhed and leapt away. He felt dizzy, unsure if it was the lack of fresh air or the news that his father might be an angry, violent man.

He almost forgot to ask. "Is there anything else you remember?"

"Well, there was that package he received. I say *he,* but his name wasn't on it. He grabbed it out of my hands, said it had to do with some institution."

"Ellis Orphanage?" Carver asked, not sure what he wanted the answer to be.

"Maybe," Katie said. "I don't remember. I do remember the name on it. Raphael Trone. Wrote it down in case the police came after Mr. Cusack for stealing and they wanted a witness. No offense, but he struck me as that sort."

"A criminal?"

She shook her head. "More a man who didn't care. A crook if it suited him, a hero if that's what he felt like. Tinker, tailor, soldier, sailor, rich man, poor man, beggar man, thief."

The sound of crashing glass from deeper in the home interrupted the nursery rhyme. Kate stood, the white cat in her lap tumbling off. "Not the chloroform again! Last time they knocked that over, I was out cold for three days! I'll just be a minute."

"That's okay. I'll let myself out," Carver said.

But she wasn't listening. She called down the hall, "Time to sleep, my pretties."

Once she was out of sight, Carver shot to his feet. He was eager to get out, to find a place to think and breathe somewhere far away from the old woman and her scores of condemned animals.

His father, a violent man? He thought of the letter's reference to knives, then flashed to Hawking's warning about the "abyss." He didn't know who his father was. What had he expected?

One thing was simple at least. Before leaving, he threw open both windows. Out on the sidewalk, as he reveled in the embrace of cold, clean air, he looked back to see a rainfall of cats flowing from the house.

Like them, he ran, and kept running.

24

HAWKING looked up from a thick, dusty book with the word *Railroad* in the title and said, "Keep pacing like that, I'll have you transferred to one of the cells below!"

Even that threat couldn't keep Carver still as he rambled through the details of his encounter with Katie Miller. He changed direction with every sentence, one second facing the East River, distant buildings and stars, the next, a black wall of books.

Eventually, Hawking took his cane and slipped its length between Carver's legs, sending him sprawling to the floor. He pointed the tip at Carver's nose and issued a one-word command: "Sit."

"I *am* sitting . . . now," Carver said.

"At the table. I'll let the sass pass this time, but mind your tone when you speak to me next. Now bring what's boiling inside that boy brain of yours down to a few short questions and we'll talk when you think you're able." With that, he went back to his reading.

Heart hammering, Carver rose. The man might be brilliant, but he was just as irritating.

"What if I can't sort it out? What if it's all too much?"

Hawking flipped a page with his good hand. "Pretend it's *not* about your father. Pretend it's not about you. Pretend you're a king, the president, Nick Neverseen, Roosevelt for all I care. Tell yourself you're helping an old cowboy chum from the Dakota badlands find *his* father. You like the fellow, but not that much, and certainly not enough to go mad."

Despite its nasal, airy quality, Hawking's voice had an intensity similar to his gaze. The effect wasn't immediate, but Carver tried. Soon the whirlpool of his feelings slowed.

"All right," Carver said when he was ready.

Hawking put a bookmark on the page he was reading.

"Could my fath— . . . this man . . . could he be a violent criminal?"

"Anything's possible. Why do you think that?"

Carver motioned with his hands as if to say it was obvious. "The cat lady's description of him, wolfish, dark, strong, violent. He shoved a piano out of the building."

Hawking smirked. "Wasn't it just weeks ago you were upset at how many names you had? Didn't that teach you anything? First, how do you *know* this man is your father?"

"She said I looked like him."

"A woman surrounded by cats and chloroform and you trust whatever she says? It's a lead worth following, same as the rest of your list. But wolfish, violent and strong? Shall I send you to the dockyards tomorrow to see how many men match *that* description? What else?"

Carver was chastened, but not convinced. "My father's letter said he worked with knives."

"So you conclude he cuts up *people*?"

Carver shrugged. "No, but . . . some do. That killer H. H. Holmes did. And whoever murdered that woman in the library."

"Serves you right for peeking at Tudd's photos. Off the top of my head, I'll name eight fairly low-skilled professions that work with knives—meat packers, butchers, fishermen, garment cutters, cigar makers, bakers, cooks, barbers. If you want to reach up the social ladder, you can include doctors and surgeons; that's ten," Hawking said. "Your father and H. H. Holmes also both breathed air, probably had two eyes, two arms, two legs."

Maybe Hawking was right. "But it's the *first* thing I found out about him."

"Then you clearly need to find out more."

"But . . ."

"Do you know what your friend Sherlock would say about it?" Hawking said. "*It is a capital mistake to theorize before you have all the evidence. It biases the judgment.* Recognize it?"

Carver nodded. "It's from *A Study in Scarlet.*"

"Your memory serves you better than your wits. Do you understand what it means?"

As usual during their chats, Carver felt foolish. "Yes. You end up trying to fit the facts to the theory." That reminded him of something. "Tudd has a theory about the library killer, doesn't he? What is it?"

Hawking slammed his hand down on the table. "Tudd! I'd

rather have the cat killer running the place! All he wants is a single, magic solution. Catch the library killer and the New Pinkertons can appear as angels on high, winning fame, admiration and a swath of cases in one fell swoop. His theories are drivel! I never should have . . ."

He slowed, rubbed the claw of his right hand with his left and sighed. "I've my own plan to save our agency, boy, slower, steadier, no magic involved. Well, it might *seem* magic . . ."

Momentarily torn from his own problems, Carver asked, "What's your plan?"

"Ha. You."

"Me?"

Hawking stuck out his good hand. "Give me that list of names you're always carrying."

Recalling what happened to his father's letter and signature, Carver hesitated, but ultimately complied.

Hawking flattened it on the table. "Handwriting leaves a bit to be desired, but I'm not one to talk on that score. Ah, here we go. One Cusack who had the same eye and hair color as you do was crossed off your list because he already had a large family, but here's another in the same situation with a question mark. Why?"

Hawking spun the paper so Carver could see. He shrugged. "The first family was near starving. I couldn't imagine he'd quit his job and put them all at risk to come overseas after one missing boy. The second was a little better off and his wife kept screaming at him. That made me think if he missed his first wife, he might take a risk to find their child."

Hawking nodded. "Wonder why you've been working so long without any guidance?"

Carver nodded.

"Because you're not doing anything wrong. I don't know if I misjudged those books of yours or if there's something lurking in your blood, but you're a diamond in the rough. I intend to cut and polish you. You'll never be better than me, but I will make you better than Tudd and his gadgets."

Carver and Hawking locked eyes. Detecting a hint of admiration in those coal-black pupils, Carver found he wasn't quite so afraid of the eccentric man anymore.

Hawking slapped his hand on the table again. "But back to the issue at hand. For all your diligence, all your intuition, all your clear thinking and dazzling brilliance, there's a blaring fact you now possess that leads to a simple conclusion. It's something even Tudd would spot in a second, but you've yet to notice."

Carver furrowed his brow. "The package?"

Hawking shook his head. "No. The man to whom it was addressed."

"Raphael Trone? My father knew him, so he must know my father?"

Hawking sighed. "Perhaps, but that's not what I'm getting at. I think you're due for a little hint. Listen carefully. The less I have to tell you, the less disappointed I'll be. Raphael is clearly Italian. Trone . . . it's Spanish, maybe French. Odd combination, isn't it? Not impossible, but very, very odd."

"He's from a mixed marriage?"

"Don't be so banal. What did Mrs. Miller's tenant say about the package?"

Carver searched his memory. "Only that it was his."

Hawking said nothing. Carver stared at him until he rolled his eyes.

"Don't make me reconsider my plans for you, boy," Hawking said as he pulled his book out again.

The answer came in a flash. "It could be an alias! Jay Cusack could *be* Raphael Trone. The package *was* his."

"And," Hawking added, "I imagine tracking down a name like Raphael Trone will be much easier than Jay Cusack."

25

THE NEXT morning, the skies above Blackwell, gray and swollen, stifled the sunlight and threatened a fierce, historically early snow. Carver rushed to catch the first ferry, now pleased to be wearing Hawking's coat. It wasn't just because of the weather. Having heard his mentor's plans for him, the flea-bitten rag felt like a badge of honor. The old detective had even awarded him a small, dingy mirror, to use in case he thought he was being "tailed" again.

When Carver stepped off into the city, the captain warned there might not be a return trip until tomorrow because of the storm. He was within a block of Devlin's when the stark white flakes began to fall. Most were so heavy, they plummeted rather than drifted. Only the most stalwart of folks were determined to travel, the usual crowds absent. Even the

New Pinkerton headquarters was nearly empty. An agent he didn't know was working alone in an open laboratory section, studying an assembly guide for electric carriages.

"Where is everyone?" Carver asked her.

"At their undercover positions, called in because of the storm," she said. "It's twenty-nine degrees. Second-coldest October on record."

"Mr. Beckley in?"

"Always," she said. She was so riveted by the manual, Carver left it at that and headed for the athenaeum, eager to try the new name.

He began with the same 1889 addendum that gave him the address on Edgar Street. Luck was with him again. There was a listing, just one, for Raphael Trone, at number 27 Leonard Street, only seven blocks away. Thinking this would be his only chance to do any traveling today, Carver headed back out.

He couldn't have been inside for more than half an hour, but the difference was staggering. Sheets of white hung everywhere. Ledges and tree branches were thick with snow. Carriage drivers pulled off to the safety of side streets, and there wasn't a cable car in sight.

Carver was seven when the blizzard of 1888 knocked down electric lines, covered streets and paralyzed New York, but he still remembered being fascinated that the great big city could be brought to a standstill. Today, the city had the same magical look. The wind from the storm had even driven the smell of horse and coal from the air, and how rare a thing was that?

After a few blocks, things became less exciting and more tiring. He could no longer feel the tips of his toes and was spending less time walking and more trying to blink the cold flakes from his eyes. He kept trudging on, though, until a funny sensation made him stop and catch his bearings.

At first he thought it was a shiver caused by the wind, but as he surveyed his surroundings, the feeling stayed with him. Amazing. There'd still been some people on Broadway, but here, the sole trail stretching out in the snow behind him was his own. Ahead, not a single footprint marked the white.

He was alone but felt, just as he had on his journey to Ellis Island, as if he were being *watched*. It was ridiculous. There weren't even any New Pinkerton agents on duty today. Still, he studied the empty doorways, gazed up at the rows of blank windows, tilting his head higher and higher, until his view was washed clean by white and sky.

Nothing.

Nothing to worry about, anyway. A few more blocks, a knock on a door, and he'd head back to the athenaeum. But the feeling would not release him. Was it excitement about the new name? Fear of the violent man the cat lady described? Then why hadn't he felt it earlier?

He made his way down Leonard Street, occasionally stamping his feet to get some feeling back. There were storefronts ahead, with apartments above them. Unless number 27 had been razed, his destination was among them.

A sudden wind shift brought a faint sulfurous smell. Past the storefronts he saw what looked like the columns of an ancient temple. It was the Tombs, the city's biggest jail, so called because its design was based on an engraving of an Egyptian mausoleum. It had been built atop a drained swamp, the foul smell still there.

After Hawking's lecture, he wanted to avoid jumping to conclusions, but with a jail so close, the possibility that his father was a violent criminal returned. Then again, Carver told himself, he could have gotten a job as a guard. That made sense for an angry, powerful man. That sort of put them in the same line of work, father and son.

The storm was so thick that, even up close, Carver had to squint to read the building numbers, slowing his pace even more. At last, he found a door numbered 27. It belonged to a shop. An array of thick glass bottles and more were visible through the windows: tinctures and powders, packaged medicines, like wild cherry tonic, *good for all nervous disorders*. It was an apothecary, dark and closed.

Any apartments above would have to be reached through the store. His pressed his face to the glass and made out a staircase at the back of the aisles. Unwilling to give up just yet, he knocked on the glass. Hand heavy from the cold, he worried it might break and switched to rapping on the door's wooden frame.

After a few moments, light drifted down from the staircase. A stout man with stringy hair and spectacles, wrapped in a pale bathrobe, peered down from the higher steps.

"Closed! There's a storm! The pharmacist is out!"

"I only want to ask a question!" Carver called.

The man took another step down. "Are you sick?"

"No," Carver said, "I just—"

The man cut him off. "Come back tomorrow!" He walked back up the stairs.

Carver banged three more times, but the man would not return. Oh well. He'd have a better chance of finding out about the tenants if he didn't make a nuisance of himself. The cold had crept through the old coat to his skin. Time to start the trek back.

He turned, making an arc in the snow, then stopped short.

There was something strange about the sidewalk. His instincts had caught it before he did.

Down the block, his were no longer the only footprints. There was a second set, bigger, heavier. They ran parallel to his path but, mid-block, veered off into an alley.

He *was* being followed.

26

CARVER pressed his back to the shop and held his breath. He kept his eyes on the alley the footsteps led into, straining to hear any movement. A minute passed with nothing but the sound of the wind cupping the edges of his ears and the steady whisper of settling snow.

Turning red, he gasped and exhaled, puffing clouds of vapor.

Laughter from the other direction turned him toward the prison. Along the edge of the grim, massive building, a ramshackle gang with snow shovels was having a snowball fight. Leonard was still empty, but near the Tombs several carriages struggled to move through the snow.

At least he wasn't alone. If he shouted for help, he'd be heard.

The tingling sensation on his back snapped his

head toward the alley. A tall, thick shadow wavered at the head before slipping back inside. Feeling vaguely safer with people near and remembering the stun baton was still in his pocket, the question became, who would be following him, if not the New Pinkertons?

He doubted he could just walk up and ask. He couldn't stand here freezing forever, either, though. He thought of the mirror Hawking had given him and had an idea. When Nick Neverseen realized he was being followed once, he secretly doubled back and came up behind his pursuer.

Most alleys on a given block were connected. He could walk around the corner, wait for his tail to follow, then slip into another alley, find his way back to Leonard Street and come from behind. He might get a better look, even follow him back to wherever he came from.

He headed in the direction of the Tombs, then turned the corner. There, he quickly pressed himself close to a wall, withdrew the small mirror and held it out to give himself a view of Leonard Street. He worried the biting temperature might give his fingers frostbite, but didn't have long to wait.

As he watched the reflection, a man emerged from the alley. He was tall, wearing a top hat. A formal black cape swirled behind him. He looked almost comical, as if a nefarious villain had stepped off the cover of *Detective Library*. His hair seemed dark, but before Carver could get a clear view of his face, snowflakes covered the glass.

Time to move. Carver ran for the end of the building, kicking snow up behind him. As he'd hoped, the alley there seemed to head back to Leonard Street, but it was so narrow that even the snow had trouble gathering inside. Having little choice, he turned sideways and shimmied along the slick, coal-soot-covered bricks. His slow progress, coupled with the fact that he couldn't even put his hands in front of him, made him feel trapped.

He kept moving, until a hiss made him look down. A rat, nearly as wide as the space, rose on its haunches a few feet before him. Carver kicked at it, sending some snow flying at the creature. Startled by the wet cold, it folded over itself like a sideshow contortionist and scurried away.

After a few more yards, Carver reached a rickety fence. Beyond it was the same alley his pursuer had hidden in. If he got back out onto the street here, he'd be *behind* the top-hatted man.

His adrenaline rising at the thought of turning the tables, he grabbed the fence boards with his bare hands and pulled. Carver had some arm strength but never mastered chin-ups the way Finn did. Unable to bend his legs, he forced his frozen toes against the boards and half-pulled, half-pushed. With one shoulder over, he went sideways and dragged the rest of his body over the edge. The wood was sharp, splintery, but Hawking's coat absorbed most of the damage.

Lacking even the rat's grace, his feet hit the alley heels first, then slid out from under him, sending him crashing onto his back. He forced himself up to his shoulders, thinking he'd have to hurry to catch up with the man.

But as he looked ahead, he realized his clever plan hadn't worked. Just as Carver had seen his footprints, the top-hatted stalker must have seen Carver's. Realizing what he was up to, he'd doubled back.

And here he was.

A statue centered in the alley, he stood there, looking far bigger than he had in the mirror. His face was still obscured by shadow and snow, but the hair was definitely black, and his face bore thick muttonchops, the sort an upper-class gentleman might wear.

Not knowing whether to be embarrassed or afraid, Carver struggled to his feet. The fence had torn a gash in the old coat. As wind and snow ripped through him, he held it closed by hand.

"So you caught me," Carver said.

There was no answer. The man's wide shoulders didn't even waver to indicate whether he was breathing or not.

"Are you an agent?" Carver asked.

Nothing.

Was it a game, like the ones Hawking played? Did this man want Carver to figure it out for himself?

"Did Mr. Tudd ask you to follow me?"

The only answer came from Carver's own body. It came in the form of an abrupt, overwhelming feeling, the feeling he was in the presence of a powerful predator.

Fear pelted Carver like the icy flakes that stung his face. If the temperature had any effect on the man, he didn't show it.

Carver reached into the pocket that held his stun baton. He had no idea how to use it, but if ever there was a time to figure it out, that time was now.

Empty. It must have fallen out when the fence tore his coat.

All at once, the man blasted some air through his nose. The thick lips beneath a full mustache parted. No words came out, just a low, animal growl.

Carver thought of crying out to the workers in front of the Tombs, but they'd never reach him before the stalker did. He'd have to run, but there wasn't enough room to dodge past the figure into the street. With no going forward, Carver spun, grabbed the top of the fence, barely noticing the wooden shards that stabbed his hands, and pulled himself over. What had been difficult before was now effortless, fueled by adrenaline. Insane terror helped him scrabble into the narrow gap. Landing, he felt something hard beneath his feet. The baton.

He scooped it up, but there wasn't enough space to open it. He rushed along sideways, hitting one wall, then the other, earning scrapes and bruises.

Carver didn't hear anyone behind him but didn't dare look. The street ahead was a thin vertical strip of swirling white and vague shapes. He thought he'd never live to reach it, but it grew steadily until, with a final sideways lunge, he found himself back out on the sidewalk.

Now, the baton in hand, he dared that backward glance. For a second, the sliver of an alley was empty. Then the man's thick, powerful hands grasped the fence. In one swift move, the figure, which in memory seemed too large for the space, leapt the wooden slats and slipped into the alley as easily as a shadow. The stalker slithered toward Carver at a maddening speed.

Chest aching, out of breath, Carver found the button on the cylinder and pressed it.

Schick!

He held the copper tip toward the alley. As snowflakes landed on it, the copper sparked and sizzled.

Seeing it, the figure hesitated and then withdrew.

Carver rose, still holding out the crackling cane. The workers, still having their snowball fight, seemed hopelessly far off.

"Help!" he cried. He moved backward across the street, eyes on the receding shadow in the alley. He didn't think he could scream any louder, and no one seemed to hear.

"Help!"

At last, when he was a half block away, a few of the workers turned toward him. The stalker gone, he pressed the button, retracting the baton, and slipped it back into his pocket.

By the time he was a quarter block from the workers, they'd gathered to look and point at him. Carver was a little surprised by how young they were, no older than street rats. A short, stocky boy with a flat, animal face pulled ahead of the pack to greet Carver first.

They recognized each other at exactly the same time.

"Carver?" a squeaky voice said.

"Bulldog?" Carver rasped.

27

"IT'S A reee-yoon-yun!" Bulldog squealed, sounding as if he were using the word for the first time. The boys behind him picked up their pace. Among them Carver recognized the other members of Finn's former Ellis Orphanage gang. Once over the shock of seeing them, he remembered how they'd all gleefully signed up for sanitation jobs.

Their rivalry seemed so long ago, so childish, he couldn't imagine they wouldn't help him.

"Bulldog," he said, trying to catch his breath. "Someone's after me; I need help."

"I'll say you do," Bulldog answered with a chuckle. He hefted his iron-headed shovel. "We been waiting for this a long time."

Following his lead, the others swung and tested their shovels.

Carver was shocked. "You still want to beat me because Finn stole a locket?"

"Think we'd forget how you set him up?" Bulldog said.

"This is serious," Carver said. He took a step closer, only to be nearly knocked over by the flat end of a shovel.

"*This* is serious," Bulldog said.

Part of Carver realized how badly outnumbered he was, but the other part, fresh from his encounter with a far greater danger, was incensed. He thought of taking out the baton and shocking Bulldog into dreamland.

"Are you *really* this stupid—?" Carver began.

Whoosh! He had to leap back to avoid being hit.

"You really *want* to call me stupid?" Bulldog said. The others laughed.

"This is crazy! I'm—"

Whoosh!

"Or crazy?" spat Bulldog.

"Put that—"

Whud!

The last swing caught Carver in the stomach, knocking him on his back. Bulldog stabbed down with the shovel's edge. The blade sliced through the snow and clinked into the pavement near Carver's head. Having had enough, Carver glared up at Bulldog and tensed his leg muscles, preparing to kick.

A taller figure came up, so much taller that Bulldog didn't even have to crouch for Carver to see his face.

"Hi, Carver," said a deeper but likewise familiar voice. His flaming red hair was neatly cut, parted to the left, his freckled skin clean. The stylish black overcoat he wore was unbuttoned, revealing a suit and tie beneath. His face remained the same, cleaner maybe, but just as good-looking as ever.

"Finn," Carver said. "What's with the monkey suit? Someone leave *all* the cages at the zoo unlocked?"

"I like to hang with my friends when I can," Finn said.

"And Miss Petty's not around to save him now, huh?" Bulldog said, elbowing Finn.

Carver tried to simultaneously rise and reach into his pocket for the baton, only to have his arms grabbed by Bulldog and Peter Bishop. They hoisted him onto his feet, held his arms behind his back and thrust his face toward Finn.

Finn eyed Carver's ratty coat. "You a street rat? That where all your brains got you?"

"I'd take my coat over your monkey suit any day," Carver answered. "How often do your owners change the straw in your cage?"

Finn's eyes flared. He tugged off his coat and loosened his tie. "Thanks for making it easy."

"How easy does it have to be? You really need all this help?" Carver said.

"Nah," Finn said. "But this way's more fun."

Bulldog chuckled as Finn raised his meaty fist. Carver braced himself, but nothing happened. There was an odd hesitation in the bully's face. Was it possible Finn thought it unfair to pummel someone who couldn't move?

The others began chanting, "Finn! Finn! Finn!"

"Go ahead," Carver said. "You stupid thief."

That did it. Finn pulled back. The next thing he knew, the chanting stopped and the bully said, "Ow!"

"Phineas! What on earth do you think you're doing?"

It took Carver a moment to recognize Samantha Echols, Finn's new mother. She wore a peacock-feather hat and was wrapped in white fox fur that made her look like some sort of arctic creature. Her chubby hand twisted the cartilage of Finn's ear so severely that Carver winced in sympathy.

"Come away!" she said, pulling him by the ear. "Mr. Echols is about to meet the commissioner and there'll be photographers! Look what you've done to your clothes! You'll iron them yourself again!"

Stunned, Bulldog and Peter released Carver as the portly woman dragged the burly Finn through the snow. Even after they'd vanished into a side entrance, the boys kept staring.

"Ironing?" Bulldog muttered. "Ironing?"

With the gang lost in wonder, Carver backed up a few feet and then broke into a trot. As the snow made its way through the rips in his coat, he thought about Finn's newer, warmer clothes and how far, but how comfortably, the mighty had fallen. Why hadn't Finn punched him when he was down? For that matter, what were the Echolses doing at the Tombs in this weather?

He moved east toward Centre Street. It was away from the New Pinkertons, but he desperately wanted to avoid crossing paths with the dark figure.

He didn't think it possible, but the storm was getting worse. By the time he'd made half a block, lines of swirling white all but wiped the gang from view. Even the vast Tombs were blurry and indistinct, the swampy smell faded.

Ahead he saw even less. The line between street and building was clear, but not between street and sidewalk. Before he realized it was there, he walked straight into a hansom cab. It sat lopsided and horseless in the snow. Apparently the driver hadn't seen the curb. There was no sign of him, either.

Carver was thinking of climbing in just to catch his breath when the cabin door swung open. Whirls of brown and gray emerged from the black interior.

Was it the stalker? Carver stumbled back. As this new figure stood, though, Carver could see his shape and clothes were wrong. This figure was older, hunched . . .

"Mr. Hawking?" Carver said. Frost ringed the man's bowler hat. Flecks of snow mingled with his salt-and-pepper mustache. He looked particularly vulnerable standing in the storm. Carver was thrilled to see him.

"Fool driver said he'd be back after he saw to the horses," Hawking mumbled. He looked at Carver, only vaguely interested in the coincidence of running into him. "There's been another murder."

Body wobbling slightly in the wind, Hawking stabbed his cane in the direction of the Tombs. "And the killer was kind enough to leave the body there."

28

"I WAS followed," Carver said.

Ignoring him, Hawking attempted a few steps through the snow before waving him over to help. "After you left, Tudd called from Mulberry Street, jabbering like a mad old woman. He's still hoping to get me involved, I suppose. I stupidly said I'd take a look."

"I was followed!" Carver blurted again.

Hawking chuckled.

As he told him the story, Carver put his arm around his mentor's broad back and hoisted his bad arm across his shoulders. Leaving an odd set of tracks, they moved diagonally across Leonard toward Center Street. Part of him hoped Hawking would roll his eyes and give him some banal explanation that would make Carver feel stupid, but safer. Instead, Hawking stopped so suddenly, Carver nearly slipped and fell.

The detective twisted his head this way and that,

scanning what little was visible of the street. "I doubt just anyone would be out and about. You may well have stumbled upon the killer."

"Why?" Carver said, stunned. "Why would he follow me?"

Hawking grimaced. "Must I explain the obvious? You've heard how some like to return to the scene of the crime? A man who dumps a body at the Tombs is looking for attention at the very least. Seeing you lurking around, he'd want to make sure you hadn't seen him with the body. He was probably more afraid of you than you were of him."

He looked at Carver's fearful expression and sighed. "That last part was an exaggeration, I admit. We'd better keep moving. He could still be here and there's safety in numbers, even if it is just Tudd and our corrupt police force."

As they worked to get nearer, the front of the vast Tombs glimmered through the icy lines of the blizzard like a mirage in a sandstorm. When they turned the corner, Carver was startled by the commotion. Carriage-mounted searchlights, powered by hand-cranked generators, burned away the swirling snow, creating an eerie patch that looked like a sunny morning. A collection of wagons and carriages lay helter-skelter along street and sidewalk. That explained Bulldog and the rest of the snow shovelers. Clearing the streets near the Tombs was a priority because of the murder.

Hawking winced at the arc lighting, but Carver, fascinated by any machine, was pleased he could make out the features of the fifteen or so thick-coated men standing in a semicircle on the stairs.

"I want to stay out of sight," his mentor said, indicating a street clock across the way. The pair soon rested against its wrought-iron pedestal, taking in the scene.

Hawking cleared his throat. "Don't ask any fool questions until I've finished and you'll get your answers more efficiently. A few nights ago, after an evening on the town with her friends, Mrs. Jane Hanbury Ingraham of Park Avenue vanished. Her body was found here early this morning. Despite the strenuous objections of an extremely distraught Mr. Ingraham, Roosevelt, apparently not a complete idiot, has kept the crime scene untouched until it can be completely examined, a difficult task even for the competent in this weather." He motioned toward a familiar man in the center of the group, who was stamping his feet and gesticulating wildly. "I'd hoped to beat our silk-stockinged cowboy here, but no such luck."

Hawking put his arm back around Carver's shoulders. "We'll have to get closer to learn anything. Should be easy to stay out of sight if we keep away from those lights."

Moving as carefully as their odd configuration allowed, they edged closer. The eerie spotlights made the crime scene look like some fantastic outdoor theater play. Roosevelt, his square head, bushy mustache and pince-nez glasses, was center stage, his open overcoat flapping.

"Under our noses!" he barked. "The dastardly coward is saying he can do as he pleases whenever and wherever he likes! Can't *anyone* tell us anything yet?"

For the first time, Carver spotted Tudd, the head of the New Pinkertons, looking wan and tired. He approached the commissioner but spoke too softly for Carver to hear.

Volume was not a problem with Roosevelt. "More time? The coroner's had an hour! Mr. Ingraham is beside himself! He won't even allow us to take her near the prison morgue. Do we at least know if she was killed here or elsewhere? Speak up! No?"

Hawking whispered to Carver, enhancing his sense that they

were watching a play. "Quite dramatic, isn't he? Well, now . . .
look who else we have."

A solitary, pinch-faced man had stepped out from the building's wide doors.

"Alexander Echols," Carver said. So, that's why Finn had been
here.

"Reading the social pages when my back is turned?"

"No, they . . . he . . . adopted . . . someone. Isn't he a district
attorney?"

Hawking nodded. "Pit viper. If Echols adopted, it was window dressing. Your friend will have money, but only what passes
for affection among reptiles. I'm sure he'll appear in a lot of photos, though."

Carver wanted to say that Finn was no friend, but the timing
didn't seem appropriate.

Echols shoved his way past the patrolmen and looked down.
Immediately, his thin face twisted like a sickly pretzel. He covered his mouth and stepped back.

"Ha. A lizard with a weak stomach. What about you?" Hawking said. "Ever seen a dead body? Want to get a little closer?"

When Carver hesitated, Hawking bristled. "It's not for enter-
tainment; it's part of your training. You'll see a real horror sooner
or later. Better you vomit here in the snow than in front of some
agent who might think you weak. Besides, I have to tell Septimus
about whatever the police get wrong. Be quiet, be quick!"

They moved another ten yards. All of Carver's thoughts
coasted to a halt when the body came into view. At first it looked
like a pile of expensive clothing, dropped in a heap. But then his
mind distinguished the folds of gown and cloak from the flesh and
hair.

The harsh light rendered Jane Ingraham's skin nearly white as the snow. She looked like a statue carved in a ridiculously broken pose. As he stared longer, Carver made out a thin black line across her neck, dark stains on gown and ground. Maybe it was the distance, the snow or the lights, but as much as Carver knew he was looking at a human body, he couldn't make himself believe it was real.

"Tudd will have a field day," Hawking whispered.

"What do you mean?" Carver asked.

"Unless my eyes fail me, and they're the only organs yet to disappoint, those wounds are vaguely similar to those found on Elizabeth Rowley in May. *Vaguely* is all Tudd will need to connect them."

29

"**NOTHING** yet?" Roosevelt bellowed. "What's taking so long?"

"Amateurs," Hawking whispered to himself. "It's obvious she wasn't killed here; there isn't enough blood."

Roosevelt picked up his head and, for an instant, seemed to stare directly at them. Hawking grabbed Carver and pulled them behind a listing carriage. His shoulder hit the side, knocking off a bit of the snow.

If Roosevelt actually saw them, there was no sign of it. He was busy demanding to know how soon they'd be able to get the coroner's wagon through.

"We can't bring her into the Tombs. Her husband thinks it would be a scandal!"

"Barks like a dog, but still worried about class," Hawking mused as they hid behind the carriage. It seemed to Carver that Roosevelt might just be concerned about the grieving man's feelings. His mentor's lips twitched. "We should be fine here; I'm confident no one saw—"

"Carver!" a voice cried.

Hawking leapt a foot. A pink face surrounded by a woolen hood was pressed into the cab's window.

"Delia!" Carver said, fighting to keep his voice a whisper.

"Do you know *everyone* here, boy?" Hawking growled. "Why not hand out glasses of punch and we'll have a party?"

"It's Delia Stephens, my friend from Ellis," Carver said.

Hawking furrowed his brow. "The one the Echolses purchased to go with their new rug?"

Delia turned up her nose. "Nothing of the sort. I'm here with Mr. Jerrik Ribe of the *New York Times.*"

Saying nothing, Hawking pulled Carver away from the cab.

"You're not going to run away *again,* are you?" Delia called.

"I . . . don't know," Carver called back. He hoped not. Ever since Hawking had given him an idea what to say to her, he'd wanted to see her and try it out.

His mentor, for his part, seemed antsy. "The *Times?*" he whispered. "You didn't mention that. Well, it can still work well. Stay and chat, see what you can find out. Make notes. Roosevelt will protect you from any bogeyman still around. If the ferry's down, they have a cot at Pinkerton headquarters. But obey this—do *not* return to Leonard Street until we've had a chance to talk again."

He touched the rim of his hat toward Delia and then moved down Center Street, managing the snow far better than Carver imagined him able.

"And he was . . . ?" Delia asked from the window.

"Mr. Albert Hawking," Carver said. "He's a retired detective."

Her face lit instantly. "Oh, how *wonderful* for you!"

She opened the door and waved him in. "It's awful out there!" she said, scooting over to make space.

Carver didn't realize just how cold he was until he joined her and felt the stiffness in his bones.

"Why didn't you just say so last time? And what are you doing *here* of all places?"

Having practiced this conversation many times in his head, Carver said, "I can't tell you. I promised Mr. Hawking I wouldn't discuss his work. Last time we met, I was afraid I couldn't say anything at all, but I got that much straight at least."

"Not so retired, then, is he?" The little sparkle in her eyes told him how quickly she was thinking. "But, you know, that's exactly what Jerrik told Anne about a story *he's* working on. She said to me, don't worry, I know my husband. He'll tell me eventually. And he did, and now I know, too. If I were the betting sort, I'm betting you'll tell me eventually, too."

Annoyed by her calm self-assurance but relieved there wasn't going to be an argument, Carver decided to ask some questions himself. "Why are *you* here?"

"I'm to tell you what you can't tell me?" she said. Then she laughed. "Oh, of course, I'll tell you. I'm too lonely to hold back! I've so few friends my own age."

She spoke a mile a minute. "I'm working at the paper now, assisting Anne on the fifth floor, where all the women handle the society pages and light features. We spend all day on these silly anagram puzzles, like *titian chemist* for *a stitch in time,* you know? That one's mine. Anyway, Jerrik's big secret was that he'd been covering the library killer and trying to convince the editors to do more hard crime reporting. The *Times* is known for *not* being sensational, so it's an uphill struggle, but they *are* losing money lately, so they had to consider it. This morning, Anne stayed home because of the storm, and Jerrik and I were just picking up some things at the office when the call came. He was the only reporter there, so they gave him his chance. He couldn't very well leave me there in the storm, so after I begged and pleaded not to be sent home, here we are. Isn't it exciting? I mean . . . terrible, but exciting? So, what are you? Like a detective in training?"

Realizing the conversation had suddenly shifted back to him, Carver answered, "Something like that."

"What's it like? Where do you live?"

Before he could deliver his prepared response, she turned back to the window. "Hold on. Another wagon's pulling up. Come watch."

She pulled at him to join her. "We can both squeeze in. It'll be like listening at the vents back at Ellis."

Soon their faces were pressed against the glass. Her cheek wasn't all that much warmer in the carriage, feeling icy against his, but he found he enjoyed it.

"See the man in the Stetson hat?" she asked. "That's Jerrik. And the wagon . . . must be from the coroner's office. They've got a stretcher. Oh. They're finally going to move the body."

A rough blanket was placed over Jane Ingraham. Two men prepared to lift her onto the stretcher. Before they did, Roosevelt barked an order, muffled by the closed cab door. At once, everyone on the steps removed their hats, clasped their hands and bowed their heads for a moment of silence.

Delia, who'd removed her woolen hat, nudged Carver and glanced at his soggy cap. He pulled it off and looked solemnly downward.

The moment over, the two men lifted the stretcher and carried it to a wagon marked *City Morgue*.

By now their faces had caused the glass to fog a bit. Delia pulled her sweater sleeve up so it covered the heel of her hand and wiped the window clean.

"It's horrible, isn't it? The most horrible thing I've ever seen."

"Me too."

"But I don't feel it, you know? Maybe I will later when it's had a chance to sink in. Jerrik was afraid I'd burst into tears or become hysterical, but I didn't. I guess it would bother me more if she *looked* like a person. But with all the snow and the light, she doesn't, does she? Do you think that makes me heartless?"

Delia and Carver turned to each other at the same time, finding themselves nose to nose.

"No," Carver managed. "I don't think you're heartless."

Not heartless at all, he added in his head.

30

CARVER woke to pitch darkness, mind throbbing with the remnants of arc-lit dreams, full of snow and blood. When he'd finally returned to the New Pinkertons' headquarters, even Beckley was on his way home. The librarian had stayed long enough to help Carver find a cot, folded in the corner of a windowless, box-filled storeroom. Exhausted, Carver collapsed onto it and quickly fell asleep.

He awoke in the morning to a weak septic odor. Hawking mentioned the place was under a sewer. This little room probably shared a wall or floor with it. Sewers reminded him of the alley rat; the rat reminded him of the killer. For a moment he felt as if the caped stalker were hovering over him, seething, dark as the night.

He shook his head and rolled gingerly off the cot, careful not to upset its rickety frame, then fumbled for his clothes. Hoping he'd put them back on correctly, he found the doorknob and stepped out. In the outer hall, sunlight filtered down from unseen skylights in the high brick ceiling.

Beckley warned that everyone would be at their undercover posts, collecting details about the murder, so Carver wasn't surprised to find the place empty. He did wish he knew where they kept the food. His stomach was growling. Absently he poked around, checking doors. Most were locked, but that wasn't really an issue. He still had his set of nails.

And he was alone.

That presented interesting possibilities. He could sneak into Tudd's office, read all those files on his desk, maybe find out if—and why—they'd been tailing him. He could even unearth the man's theory about the killer and see why Hawking held it in such disdain.

Passing the laboratory area, Carver couldn't resist having a look around. All the devices he'd seen there during the day had been locked away. One metal cabinet was easy enough to pick. Heavy with hanging rifles, the door swung open, revealing a stock of weapons.

Some were familiar, but many not. Two shelves held about ten odd pistols, each mounted on even odder metal stands. The stands had six jointed legs, several gears and spring-wound motors. The guns might be loaded, so he decided to leave them alone. But his eyes shortly lighted on something that looked like a folding knife.

Thinking it less dangerous, he picked it up. When he flipped out what he thought would be the blade, instead an intricate set of thin pieces of metal jutted from the top in the shape of a key. As he turned a dial at the bottom of the handle, the "key" changed size and shape.

Was it some sort of lock pick?

Deciding to try it out, he closed the cabinet door, then inserted the weird tool into the lock. He rotated the dial until he heard a click and was thrilled to discover he could lock the door with a simple twist of his hand. Excited, he withdrew the tool and tried again.

This time, the lock didn't budge. Worse, the device seemed stuck in the door. Carver shook and yanked it, rattling the cabinet before realizing all he had to do was turn the dial back a little. It slipped out easily, pulling the door open again.

What an amazing contraption! Much better than the nails. With this, he could go anywhere. But could he just . . . take it? It was different from the stun baton. That he'd simply found. Realizing it had saved his life, he was glad he hadn't returned it. But what about this? It seemed such a small thing among the wonders of the place. Hadn't Hawking said something about Benjamin Franklin breaking laws and becoming like a thief to be able to catch one? His mentor was a great detective, after all.

He slipped it into his pocket, next to the baton. A guilty pang hit him, and he heard his own voice, full of hatred, calling Finn "Thief!"

But this wasn't a gold locket, a child's only possession. Besides, he was only borrowing it long enough to get into Tudd's office and find out what was going on.

Mind made up, he closed the door to the cabinet a little too hard. Suddenly, there was a loud *crack!* as a bullet flew through the metal. A mechanical whirring followed. As Carver sprang back, the mounted pistols, moving of their own accord, crawled from the shelf, spider-like. As they tumbled to the ground, another shot was fired.

Carver ducked behind a heavy table. As the whirring continued, he stuck his head out and watched in awe and fear as the pistols righted themselves and began crawling around the room. He pulled back, worried that they might somehow be able to see him.

For many breathless moments, the whirring continued, but no more shots were fired. What were they? Some sort of mechanical guns you could send in after the crooks? How would they know when to fire?

Ulp. He was about to find out. One rounded the table and crawled toward him, its little legs moving in sequence, like an insect. Carver squirmed back but didn't want to be in sight of the other guns, either. How many were there? Eight?

Closer and closer it crawled . . . and then stopped.

Soon, the whirring of the other spring-driven motors died down as well. He got behind the one nearest him and examined it. There was a timer on the back, this one set to zero. He reasoned you could set the timer, wind the spring engine, send the gun in to some dangerous spot, and it would fire when the timer reached zero.

At least that meant they couldn't see. Slowly, he checked them all. None of the timers were set. Jarring the cabinet had probably set off the first shot; the fall to the ground set off the other. Gingerly, he returned them all to the cabinet but left the door ajar. Praying they'd think the gun had gone off on its own (it practically had, hadn't it?), Carver decided that any further skulking around the headquarters was probably *not* the wisest thing to do.

Unless he wanted to get shot.

31

OUTSIDE, the sun made Carver wince. The air was warmer; the colors had returned. The sidewalk had a clear path, though each corner held a huge snow hill. The slick gray of the cobblestones already dominated the white on Broadway. People, wagons, carriages and streetcars all moved about as if there'd been no storm at all.

"Horrid murder!" a pleasant young voice called. "Savage mutilations! Body at the Tombs!"

People crowded around the newsboy. He held up a fresh copy of the *Daily Herald*, its headline reading **TOMBS KILLING**. The happy boy could barely keep up with sales.

Carver checked his money. He had more than enough for something decent to eat and the ferry ride back to Blackwell. He thought about getting a paper but felt he owed Delia some loyalty and should find a copy of the *Times*.

First, though, he bought himself a baked potato from one of the vendors lining City Hall Park. As the steam from its white center soothed his face, he listened in on passing conversations. Everyone was talking about the second murder.

Near the marble fountain at the park's center he found a newsboy selling the *Times*. Reaching an empty bench, he swatted the soggy snow off and sat down to finish breakfast and read the paper.

Not a usual *Times* reader, Carver was surprised it didn't have the same glaring headline as the *Herald*. The murder wasn't even front and center. It was on the first page but on the far right, next to a larger article about the storm, with a quiet headline—**SOCIALITE'S BODY DISCOVERED**—followed by, in smaller type, *Police Flummoxed by Killer's Daring*, then, in even smaller type, *by Jerrik Ribe*.

There was a photograph of the Echolses, posing with Finn, captioned with a note about the stalwart district attorney, well known for his strong hand in dealing with crime and his compassion toward the city's orphans. Finn looked good in his suit, if not particularly happy.

Carver already knew most of the murder details, having been there. The guard who'd found the body saw a set of footprints, but the storm covered them by the time the investigation was in full swing. That and a lack of blood led the police to believe the killer had murdered her elsewhere, then carried her body to the Tombs, just as Hawking said.

They also assumed he was "a singularly powerful man."

Carver's caped stalker certainly fit that bill. Then again, so did Carver's father and, as Hawking said, thousands of other men.

His father. He wanted to go back to Leonard Street to follow up the lead, but Hawking had forbidden that. Was this Raphael Trone really his father, or could he know how to find him? A violent man, strong. Wolfish, the cat lady had called him. Carver remembered the predatory sensation he felt in the presence of the stalker.

His mind stopped short. He'd been lost in thought so long, the potato was cold. It didn't matter; he wasn't hungry anymore. He looked up. The New York Times Building was right across the street. After it was first built, there'd been a competition. The *Tribune* had built a taller one, and then in 1889 the *Times* decided to top it. Eight at the time, Carver used to sneak out of Ellis to watch the construction. The giant printing presses were actually kept in place and the new thirteen-story building constructed as the old one was demolished.

He counted the windows to the fifth floor, where Delia worked. The thought of visiting tickled him, but he was filthy, his clothes crumpled, and he was still very much afraid of meeting her adoptive father, knowing he'd have to lie about the secret agency, not knowing if he could.

What should he do next? He could head back to headquarters, hope no one noticed the damage he'd done and try to find more Raphael Trones. Even if they caught him, Carver suspected Hawking wouldn't be very angry. As for Tudd, Carver found himself caring less and less what he thought. Maybe he could try to get his father's letter and signature back.

He crumpled the foil around his baked potato, tossed the remains in a trash can and made his way. He was practically at the fountain when he again had the sensation he was being followed. It wasn't as thick and heavy as it had been during the storm, but it was enough to make him pause and have a good look around.

Women in wool dresses and scarves, men in coats with fur collars and bowlers walked leisurely about, enjoying the early winter scene. Children threw clumps of snow. Vendors hawked food; street rats sold the papers. Nothing suspicious, but after yesterday, he really should pay more attention to his instincts.

He walked across Broadway backward, searching the park for anyone who might be watching him. After nearly being hit by a carriage, he decided to face the direction he was walking.

When he reached the brass pipe that unlocked the elevator, he hesitated, standing there awhile, hoping if someone were watching, they might dare come closer. If he waited for just the right moment and snapped around quickly, he might catch them. The feeling along his spine grew, as real as it ever had been.

He counted to himself, one . . . two . . .

And whirled.

He was right! These was someone there. "Delia?"

She wore the same hat as the night before, but the thick wool dress was green. A mismatched scarf was wrapped tightly around her neck. "Hello," she said, flustered.

"You're following me?" Carver said, stepping toward her.

"*Investigating* you. If you can practice being a detective, why can't I practice being a reporter?"

Carver narrowed his eyes.

"I'm joking, mostly," she said, coming nearer. "I saw you on the bench from the window, but by the time I got there, you were headed through the park."

"You could have called my name," Carver said.

"To be honest, I wasn't sure I wanted your attention."

Carver felt oddly hurt. "Why?"

She exhaled slowly. "There's something I found out . . . well, something *Jerrik* found out, and he told Anne and she told me, and I'm not supposed to tell anyone. Yet I really thought that you, of all people, should know."

"Delia, what are you talking about?"

She made a face as if deciding something. "Okay, then, here it is. This morning a letter was sent to Commissioner Roosevelt through the *Times*. They think it's from the killer."

His eyes went wide. "What did it say?"

"That's the reason I thought you should know. It was very short. Four words, but they reminded me of . . . well, they reminded me of the letter you found in the attic."

He frowned. That couldn't be. She wasn't making sense. "Reminded you? How? What did it say?"

She swallowed hard before answering. *"Dear Boss, Me again."*

"'Boss'? Like the letter from my father?"

She nodded.

Carver felt a sickly feeling come over him, as if he were trapped, a cleaver dangling over his head, ready to fall.

Only this was much, much worse.

32

CARVER was tumbling, down, down—so far down it seemed he'd always be falling. Was this the abyss Hawking had warned about?

He was barely aware of his legs buckling, barely aware of Delia grabbing his elbow, trying to guide him to a gentler landing on the sidewalk. "Carver! Carver!" she said over and over.

He blinked and looked at her. "My *father* is the library killer."

Her green wool skirt pooled on the concrete as she sat beside him. She looked as if she'd accidentally stabbed him to death. "No! It might not even *be* from the killer. It could just be a prank. Last week we received a lovely note from Abraham Lincoln, just writing to say hello. And, really, just because your father's letter used the word *boss* . . . doesn't mean anything by itself. A lot of people use the word. Most everyone *has* one, you know. I just thought . . . because of the coincidence . . . that I should tell you."

"It's not just the one word," Carver said. "The cat woman said he was violent, like a wolf. His letter talks about his knives. His work . . . is killing people. And I thought he was a butcher . . ."

He filled her in on what he'd learned.

"It still may not be true. I understand you're scared, but you're jumping to conclusions," she said, searching his eyes. She was trying to give him some hope. He wished she could. He furrowed his brow, scrunched his face and beat at his forehead with the palms of his hands.

Don't theorize until you have all the facts. But how many facts did he need?

"Are you thinking or just beating yourself?" she asked. "What are you thinking about? Carver?"

"Some way to know, some way to prove it, one way or another," he said miserably. "Delia, the letter, was it handwritten?"

"Yes."

"Did you see it?"

She shook her head. "It's locked in Mr. Overton's office. He's the news editor. There's a big fight going on about whether or not to publish it. Roosevelt's pressuring them not to, saying it will cause a needless panic. See? Even he doesn't think it's real."

"I've got to see it. I have to see if the handwriting matches."

"Why not bring your letter to Jerrik? I'm sure *he's* seen it," she offered.

Carver sighed. "I . . . don't have it anymore."

It was Delia's turn for brow-furrowing. "You'd never give up that letter."

He nearly explained, but caught himself before blurting out

that twenty-one feet below them lay the most sophisticated crime laboratory in the world. If only *they* could get their hands on the new letter.

Wait a minute. Tudd worked with Roosevelt. He might have already seen it. Carver's answer could already be waiting for him down below.

"I'm sorry. I can't tell you where it is."

She exhaled, exasperated. "One of the many secrets you keep for Mr. Hawking?"

"Yes. No. In a way. I'd tell you if I could!"

She moved closer. "I swear, Carver, I'd never tell a soul, not even Jerrik or Anne."

Considering it, he looked around. People were pausing to stare at the two youths plopped down in the middle of the sidewalk, atop an off-color patch of concrete. Carver stood, wiped his pants and offered Delia a shaky hand to help her to her feet.

"I *will* tell you all about it," he whispered. "I swear, but first I have to see that letter. Can you trust me? Can you help me?"

"Another deal, like back at Ellis, with you offering the bargain?" she said. She thought about it. "There's a gathering tonight at the *Times,* but it's really just an excuse for the editor to speak with Roosevelt informally. There'll be lots of people in the building. I could get you in. Even if we did get caught, we could say we were lost. But the office will be locked."

Thinking of the lock pick in his pocket, Carver smiled for the first time since she'd given him her news. "I never met a door I couldn't open."

"Then hope this isn't the first, and meet me at the side entrance at seven p.m."

He resisted a powerful urge to hug her. "Thank you, Delia.

Now, please. I've got to do something . . . alone. I'll see you tonight."

She looked about to object but frowned, nodded and walked back toward the park. Midway, she stopped and turned back to him.

"There is one more thing you should know," she called back.

"What's that?"

"Whatever turns out to be true, you'll still be Carver Young," she said.

Carver wished her comment had been uplifting, but instead it only made him wonder who Carver Young was to begin with.

33

IN THE headquarters, deserted only a few hours ago, Carver was surprised to find scores of agents scurrying about the open plaza as the train glided toward the platform. Tables were lined up, covered with the daily papers, files and photographs. The huge map from Tudd's office had been moved out here, mounted on twin easels, different-colored circles drawn on the city streets.

An exhausted Tudd stood in the center, holding a clipboard, waving his arms as if directing traffic. The subway was so well designed, Carver couldn't hear what he was shouting, but judging by the movement of his lips, it seemed to be something along the lines of, "Find it!" or, "Find *him*!"

Feeling their panic mix with his, he yanked open the oval door. The first word he heard from Tudd was a triumphant, "There!" He was pointing at Carver.

Good. It must mean Tudd had made the connection between his father's letter and the killer's note. Thinking he'd get some answers, Carver rushed across the platform to the plaza. Heart pounding, he called out, "Mr. Tudd! Mr. Tudd!"

"I'm sorry it had to come to this, son," Tudd said. He raised his hand and snapped his fingers. "Jackson! Emeril!" Then he stormed off in the opposite direction.

"Wait!" Carver cried. He tried to follow, only to find himself cut off by the muscular Jackson. Emeril rushed up behind him.

"Whoa, there!" Jackson said. Irritated, Carver tried to continue, but Jackson put his hands on his chest.

"I have to talk to Mr. Tudd," Carver said. "My father—"

"Can't now," Jackson said.

"He's insanely busy," Emeril said. "And doesn't have time to talk to a thief."

The word hit him like a bullet. They knew.

"Look, I'm sorry about that, but it's *incredibly* important," Carver said. "They've received a letter at the *Times*."

"We know," Jackson said, guiding him toward a corridor on the plaza's left side.

"It says *boss* like the letter from my father," he blurted.

"We know that, too," Emeril said. They hooked Carver's arms and dragged him along.

Carver looked back over his shoulder, glimpsing Tudd's back as he vanished.

"Please, just tell me if he's seen the handwriting on the letter to the *Times*. Has anyone?"

"Not yet," Jackson said. "The morning's been hectic, what with half of us scouring every block near the murder scene, looking for you."

"Me? Why?"

"Because Mr. Hawking told Tudd about your encounter last night," Emeril said. "Tudd's convinced you ran into the killer, and for the first time I know of, Hawking didn't disagree. When Tudd found you gone this morning, bullet holes in the lab and a certain device missing, he thought you were off looking for your father. And now we all know who he might be."

"I wasn't! I was just getting breakfast."

"Well, whether he is or isn't, if he lives in the neighborhood and spots you again, he might try to take care of any witnesses."

He held out his hand expectantly. Carver reached into his pocket and produced the lock pick.

Jackson coughed into his fist. Sighing, Carver was about to return the stun baton, but Jackson said, "There's also the touchy issue of your friend from the *Times.* Cute girl, but you practically brought her here."

"We're friends from the orphanage. She told me about the letter."

"Secrecy's a big thing with Tudd. And that chat with your girl did not look good. He's feeling a bit . . . betrayed."

Carver realized he'd been led to the hall that held the box-filled storage room he'd spent the night in.

"Between that and wanting to keep you alive . . ." Emeril waved Carver inside.

Vibrating with a mixture of guilt and agitation, he stepped in, wrinkling his nose at the slight septic odor. At least someone had put a lamp in the room so there was some light.

The agents remained at the door. Emeril's hand was on the knob, a key in the lock.

"You're keeping me prisoner?"

Jackson shrugged. "You're being protected, until we've more of a handle on the investigation."

"I can't stay here! I've got to . . ." His voice trailed off. They were already worried about Delia. How could he mention his meeting with her?

"A date?" Jackson said. "We'll have your secretary clear your social calendar."

The glib remark made Carver angry. "Take me to a phone. I want to call Blackwell."

Jackson looked at Emeril. "Didn't Tudd say that Mr. Hawking already knows about all this?"

"I think he *did* say that," Emeril said. "Either way, the phones are tied up. You'll have to sit tight."

"No!" Carver said. He rushed forward. His sudden speed startled Emeril, but Jackson grabbed him by the shoulders and gave Carver a steady look.

"We're not the enemy. We understand. We're sorry. But this is how it is. We'll try to get you a desk, some grub and something to read, but you *will* stay here until Mr. Tudd says otherwise. Understand?"

Gritting his teeth, Carver nodded and stepped back toward the cot.

"Be back as soon as we're allowed a breather. Promise," Emeril said as he pulled the door shut.

The clicking lock echoed in Carver's chest, but he knew he didn't need their little gadget to get out. He waited until their footsteps vanished, then slipped his trusty nails from his pocket. He unlocked the door in a heartbeat. But when he turned the handle and pushed, it still wouldn't move.

They'd *braced* it from the outside.

Carver slumped onto the cot. Unprepared for the sudden weight, the frame collapsed. Carver fell to the floor. It was cold, but at least the sewer odor was a little weaker.

How did they know about Delia? *Idiot!* They'd been right in front of the elevator, exactly where Tudd's viewing glass was. He'd seen them talking, seen Carver get upset.

And now he was a prisoner. A criminal.

34

CARVER paced, trying to plot his escape, if not from the room, at least from his own mind. He had to see that letter, he *had* to. After ten minutes, though, his only new revelation was that the sewer smell was stronger in one corner. More specifically, it came from the ceiling.

With nothing else to do, he piled some of the stronger-looking boxes for a better look. Standing on them, he pressed his hand against the smooth, hard-finished plaster. It was frigid and slightly damp. The sewer was probably right above that spot. His life was now literally lower than a sewer.

Was it possible to get in?

He pushed. The moist plaster gave a little and a fine powder drizzled around him. It was weak. Why? He put his hand in the air and felt a wave of rising warmth from the hissing radiator. The sewer above cooled the plaster. The radiator heated it. Between the two, they were constantly shrinking and expanding the plaster, weakening it.

He might be able to dig through, at least get past the ceiling. But the New Pinkertons wanted him here. Hawking, too, apparently. Escaping would be worse than "borrowing." How desperate was he? Hawking had promised him an incredible future. Was he willing to risk it for the sake of some answers? Yes.

He pounded his fist into the plaster. The first blow brought down a few thick chips. The next did little more. If he kept it up, they'd hear him. It'd be faster and quieter with a tool, but he didn't have any. Not exactly, anyway. He'd ruin his nails trying to scratch through.

Could he make something else?

He jumped down and snapped off a sharp piece of the broken cot frame. He set to work with it, stabbing, digging, prying off larger and larger chunks, until the plaster's whiteness mixed with dark earth. When he poked the sharp end of the stick up through the earth, half its length disappeared, but then it hit something flat and hard.

Abandoning the wood for his hands, Carver pulled away enough dirt and plaster to reveal a rough two-foot square of cold, moist bricks, slightly curved. It was the sewer's underbelly. All his effort had been ridiculous. He'd need a hammer and chisel to get through that.

But he was in a storage room, after all. Who knew what might be in all the boxes? Ransacking them, he found mostly office supplies, but, among them, were six pairs of scissors and an unassembled paper guillotine with a heavy iron handle. Not quite a hammer and chisel, but maybe close enough.

He placed a scissor blade into a crack between bricks and whacked it with the iron handle. The blade chipped a bit, but a few chunks of mortar fell. It was a start, at least.

After he'd pounded away awhile, a few drops of water seeped out. Of course there'd be water in the sewer, probably quite a bit. If it covered the floor and seeped under the door before the hole was big enough for him to escape, they'd catch him.

He rolled up the cot's canvas, pushed it against the doorsill and piled a few boxes on it to keep it in place. He went back to the bricks, working in earnest, chipping away at the mortar. More drops fell. Carver moved his efforts from brick to brick, hoping one would prove a weak link.

Soon, all but the last scissor blade had broken, and the iron handle held a series of gouges that threatened to crack it in half. Carver's clothes and skin were littered with sweat, dirt and flecks of mortar, but the bricks remained in place.

He shoved the last blade into the deepest crack and swung. The handle missed, slamming the blade sideways, snapping it in two.

No!

The only thing that kept him from screaming out loud as his last hope clattered to the floor was that someone might come in. Furious, he swung the broken handle at the brick, beating it, until the crack in the iron lengthened and it, like the blade, broke in half.

Carver barely ducked in time to avoid being clocked on the head. Hands on knees, head down, Carver panted. He was done. He gritted his teeth, closed his eyes and prayed that all of his life would simply *vanish*.

Something wet rolled down on his cheek. Was he crying? He

imagined Jackson and Emeril returning with some magazines only to discover their "junior" agent sobbing in the middle of the mess he'd made, like a toddler having a tantrum.

He felt another drop, thick and cold, then a little stream. A glistening line had appeared at the long end of one of the bricks. Water from above pooled and dripped.

Carver pushed at the brick. The little stream thickened. Thrilled, he grabbed the broken handle and used its jagged edge to claw at the loose brick. It lurched down and tilted. Icy water flowed from the gap as if from a spigot. Carver waited, expecting it to stop, but it didn't. It kept coming, thicker and faster, rolling off the boxes in a series of tiny waterfalls, carrying the mortar down to the floor.

Some water, he'd expected *some,* but . . .

In for a penny, in for a pound, Carver pushed the broken handle through the stream, hooked the edge of the loose brick and pulled. Six bricks, all loosened by his efforts, crashed down, followed by a torrent of water.

The freezing sensation forced him to inhale. The force knocked him backward. As his shoulders hit the floor, the gushing water pushed him sideways. By the time he struggled to his feet, the water was above his ankles and rising. If he didn't get out quickly, he'd drown. His feet and legs were already going numb.

For all his sharp thinking, it hadn't occurred to Carver that all the sewers in the city, even the one above him, would be full of melted snow.

35

THE WATER lapped up toward Carver's knees, the sensation more like burning than cold.

Could he make it through the hole? The flow from the ceiling wasn't quite as thick as when it began. It also had direction, pouring toward the door. There was a slight gap on one side, where the bricks seemed loose and eager to fall.

Carver sloshed toward the waterfall, unable to feel anything beneath his knees. Controlling his legs was like dragging dead wood. Teeth chattering, he pushed what soggy boxes he could into a new pile. As he worked, he noticed his fingers turning blue.

That was the last thing he saw.

Pop! The light went out, the lamp shorted by the water.

Clawing in the dark, he scrabbled up the wet cardboard. The boxes tore as he went. By the time he could touch the ceiling, the rising water still covered his feet. He tore at the bricks, hoping to pull himself up onto his knees, but instead only yanked more bricks free. The larger hole brought more rushing water.

An animal desperation kicked in. Widening the hole was his only hope. He pulled down as many bricks as he could. One scraped his side, another whacked him on the head, but he kept going. As the hole grew, so did the gap, but whenever he touched the icy stream, it felt as sharp as a killer's knife. The water was nearing the top of the piled boxes. There wasn't much time left.

Forcing his hands into the gap, Carver felt slick wet stones above. He wheedled his fingertips into the first narrow depression he could feel, put his back to the streaming water and lifted.

The thick flow of glacial sewer bit into his spine. A wild chill rode up into his head and skull. The bruise where the brick hit him throbbed, but he couldn't let go. His moaning lost in the rush of water, he pulled himself higher and finally felt the deadweight of his legs rise into the air.

He inched forward with his left hand, aching to find another hold. When he did, he pulled again, half-lifting himself into the sewer, where a stinging dampness drenched his chest.

He'd almost made it, but something pulled him back. He looked down. His legs were in the stream, being tugged by the water. They were so numb, he hadn't even realized it. He was so close now, he couldn't give up. It wasn't about his father anymore, his past or his future. It was about staying alive.

In the end the drag of the water was not enough to stop him from pulling himself fully into the sewer. Lying down, face half submerged, he yearned to rest, but a deathly feeling creeping up his legs told him he shouldn't, not yet. He crawled along the curved floor until he reached a drier spot, above the water, and lay there, just breathing.

In time, his eyes adjusted. It wasn't completely dark. Light drizzled in from grates above.

The sewer was a little like the brick sections of the subway tunnel, only taller. A river of water ran down the center, leaving the sides dank, but relatively dry. The smell, while not pleasant, was no worse than it was in the storage room, probably because most of the water was from melting snow.

In the gloom, he spotted a wide wooden board lying across the flowing water. It must be a bridge used by the workers who came down to check for leaks. With some effort, Carver crawled over and managed to drag it over the hole he'd made. Water rushed over it, holding it in place. Maybe the *entire* headquarters wouldn't be flooded now.

An image flashed in his head—the look on Emeril and Jackson's faces when they opened the door to see what was causing the leak. They'd be coming for him soon. He forced himself to stand and walk. As more feeling returned to his legs, he began to limp.

He came upon a ladder, climbed it and pushed the manhole cover at its top. As he slid the iron circle aside, some snow on it slopped off into his face. If he weren't freezing already, it might've bothered him. Dripping wet, he pulled himself out into the late-afternoon light, then slid the cover back into place.

He was on Newspaper Row, not as far from the New Pinkertons' headquarters as he'd like, but also not far from the *Times*. He was also soaked and freezing. A street clock told him it wasn't even four yet. Far too early to meet Delia. Nearby, he spotted a newsboy lodging. One of the poor quarters where he'd once considered living.

A few moments later, panting, he stood in its open doorway, eyeing the iron stove that sat against the wall. The younger boys played cards and dice. An older kid lay on a makeshift nest of old clothes, reading a dime novel whose cover Carver did not know.

Along with the others, he looked up at Carver, angry at first at the intrusion. When he saw how pathetic Carver was, how wet and shivering, the scowl faded. Not wanting to appear weak, the older boy snapped himself back into a grimace. "What do you want?"

"Just to warm myself for a few hours, dry my clothes."

"Where *you* been? The sewers?" a young voice sneered.

"Matter of fact, yes," Carver said. "I was escaping some kid-nappers. They were holding me in a basement room and I dug my way out."

A truth that's told with bad intent beats all the lies you can invent.

Trying to appear uninterested, the older boy said, "Make yourself at home, then."

36

MAYBE IT was because he'd nearly died, but hours later, when Delia met him at the side entrance to the New York Times Building, Carver had never seen her more striking. Her party dress, with stylishly wide sleeves over black, was tied in the center by a snug dark ribbon that showed off the shape of her body. He'd always thought she was pretty. Now she was beautiful.

He was about to tell her so when she wrinkled her nose. "What's that smell? Couldn't you have changed your clothes at least?"

He'd managed to dry them, but there'd been no way to clean them or him.

"I'll explain later," he said, sliding inside, trying not to touch her.

She pulled him into a stairwell. "It's always later with you. Tell me now!"

"Fine," he said. "I was kidnapped and had to crawl out through a sewer."

"Man alive, Carver, I feel sorry for you, but I'm not an idiot!" she answered, storming up the steps. It'd sounded better when he'd told the newsboys.

On each level, the stairs ended at a wide landing with an archway that faced the offices, leaving them exposed as they moved to the next set of stairs. The first few floors were mostly empty. The janitors mopping the floors didn't even look up as they passed.

When they came to the fourth floor, the sound of music and conversation reached them. Delia motioned for Carver to stop and went up the last few steps alone. Hiding behind a column of the archway, she peered out before waving for Carver to join her.

Unlike the other floors, this was a wide-open space, full of mustached men in three-piece suits and women in fancy dresses and flamboyant hats. They ate dainty sandwiches served on trays and drank from a tended bar. Alexander and Samantha Echols were among them. Finn, thankfully, was nowhere to be seen.

"You wouldn't know from the way they act," Delia whispered, "but half the city's in a panic over the Tombs murder. The *wealthy* half, since it's one of their own twice now."

Roosevelt was there, too, not directly at the center of things for a change. Delia's new family, Jerrik and Anne Ribe, were part of a small group deeply fascinated by the hushed conversation he was having with a gentle older fellow, whose white shirt and suspenders stood out sharply from the formally dressed crowd. For his part, Roosevelt looked ready to leap out of his three-piece suit and strangle the man.

As the partygoers shifted, Carver unhappily spotted Mr. Tudd standing quietly, but nervously, at Roosevelt's side. The leader of the New Pinkertons must know about his escape by now. Was that why he kept checking his watch? Was he eager to leave the party and hunt Carver down?

"I don't know how you got the impression this was open for debate, Gerald," Roosevelt said, unable to speak softly. "You *must* turn it over!"

Realizing he was nearly shouting, he put his hand on the man's shoulder and led him on a search for a less public spot. To his annoyance, the crowd followed.

"Roosevelt's trying to talk your editor out of printing the letter?" Carver asked.

"Oh, he succeeded. I don't know what they're discussing now. Mr. Overton is so staid some of his reporters think he passed away years ago. Jerrik doesn't want a panic either, but Anne says they're obligated to keep the public informed. Shh! They're coming!"

Carver and Delia leaned back as Roosevelt and Overton stepped by the arch.

"You know I respect the press, always have, but this is insupportable!" Roosevelt said.

Overton's voice was respectful and low. "As I've explained, Commissioner, I simply do not believe our police department is a safe place to keep something of such value."

Roosevelt was increasingly flustered. "I know better than any about the corruption, but even an officer who'll turn his back on a thief for a bribe wouldn't cover for this killer!"

"No, but that same officer might be tempted to sell it, say, to Mr. Hearst's *Journal,* or our other competition, for a hefty sum. *They* wouldn't hesitate to publish the contents. As I've said, any trusted experts you choose may examine the letter, but it will remain here."

"Balderdash, sir!" an exasperated Roosevelt said. "You have until morning to turn that letter over, or I shut this paper down!"

Overton's face was expressionless. "Sir, you may do as you wish. But if you shut us down, may I point out that the very information you wish to keep from the masses will then quickly become a matter of public record?"

Roosevelt opened his mouth as if to scream. Instead, he laughed.

"Well played, Overton. I suppose this *is* as good a place as any to examine the thing. I'll need twenty-four-hour access."

"I'll give you the building keys myself," Overton said. Arm in arm, they walked to the bar.

"You have to admire a man who loses graciously," Delia said.

"He does have style," Carver mumbled. "But that means we have to get to the letter soon, in case Roosevelt wants to see it tonight."

She nodded and took him to the opposite stairs. As they headed farther up the tall building, the landings were no longer open. Each floor was sealed by a windowed door.

After another three flights Delia stopped and tried the knob. "Locked," she said.

Carver removed a bent nail and opened it. It probably would have taken him longer with that gadget.

"What's so funny?" Delia asked.

"Oh. Uh . . . the locks at Ellis were tougher," he said, holding the door for her.

"Only because Miss Petty was on to you," Delia said.

They entered a wide, darkened space, full of cluttered rolltop desks, typewriters and pigeonhole files. Papers were hung on all manner of metal device, vertically, horizontally, wrapped on rollers. Even bereft of reporters, it seemed lively. Carver could practically see them rushing about, filing news stories, typing madly to make deadlines.

"Grand, don't you think?" Delia said proudly.

He swallowed hard and asked, "Where's the letter?"

She nodded at a windowed office. "Overton's office. In a wall safe."

Carver blanched. "A wall safe? How can I . . . ?"

"Oh, don't worry; it doesn't have a door. It's been out for repair for months. Mr. Overton is confident his solid mahogany office door is enough to keep it secure. Of course, he hasn't met Carver Young, master thief, yet."

Carver winced at the title but had no time to worry about it now. Dodging the clutter, they reached the door. Thief or not, picking locks was at least something he was good at. He confidently knelt, withdrew his nail and . . .

. . . stared in shock.

He'd never seen a keyhole like it. It was tiny, almost as if a rod more than a key would fit into it. He didn't even think the Pinkerton gadget would work. Heart sinking, he knew it was hopeless before he even tried. Just to be sure, he put his thinnest nail up to the hole. Too thick.

"What's the matter?" Delia said.

Carver sighed. "Any idea where he'd keep the key?"

Delia shook her head. "No. I thought this would be the easy part."

Too close now to give up, Carver pushed at the hardwood door. It barely budged. He shoved again, harder.

"Wait! What are you doing?" Delia said, her voice rising.

Instead of answering, Carver slammed himself into the door again.

"Stop it!" Delia said. "Stop it immediately! I can't let you smash down the editor's door!"

He looked at her. "*You* smashed a window at Ellis."

"That was different . . . it needed to be replaced and . . . and . . . oh, fine!"

He forced his shoulder into it again and again, until finally, he heard something crack. The sound hadn't come from the door or its frame, though. It had come from his shoulder.

He grabbed it in pain. "Ow! The thing must be reinforced with steel!"

"Forget it, Carver. We have to go. I can still sneak you down . . ."

"No, give me a minute. Let me think!" he pleaded. Think. But think of what?

And then he heard it, a steady sound that had been muffled by his insistent banging—footsteps climbing the stairs. Carver's eyes shot to the stairwell door. He'd stupidly left it wide open.

"Oh no, oh no, oh no," Delia said.

"Hide!" Carver hissed, but it was too late. A male-shaped silhouette stepped in. A streetlight shining through the window lit his red curls and made the edges of his expensive suit shine.

"Not you," Carver said.

Delia's expression changed from fear to befuddlement. For the life of her she couldn't recognize the newcomer, not until he spoke.

"Not very good at hiding, are you, Carver."

"Hello again, Finn."

37

"I'VE GOT you this time!"

Finn moved forward like a bull, not caring how many rolltop desks he bumped.

Carver, heart still pumping from trying to break down the door, mind seething from all that had happened, headed to meet him. "Come on, then, let's get it over with!"

Finn was briefly startled but then lowered his head and picked up speed. "Oh, it'll be over."

Racing through the darkened newsroom, dodging wastebaskets and desk corners, Carver growled, not just at Finn, but at everything. Finn, pulling off his jacket as he came, did likewise.

They stormed toward each other, floorboards shaking beneath their feet. Finn pulled back his fist, ready to strike. Carver reached into his pocket, ready to use the baton.

They were less than a yard apart when a flurry of cloth appeared between them. Delia had leapt into their midst from a desktop, her dress billowing as she landed.

"Stop it, both of you! Are you mad?" she hissed.

Carver halted dead in his tracks. Finn did the same, recognizing her for the first time. "Delia?"

"Whatever problems you *children* have," she said through gritted teeth, "the commissioner of the *police* is a few stories below us. Do you want to wind up in jail?"

"I wouldn't mind," Finn answered.

"*I* would, Phineas!" Delia said. "So, lower your fist and step back . . . *please*."

Finn's eyes locked on the metal cylinder in Carver's hand.

"Carver, whatever that is, put it away," Delia said.

When he put it back in his pocket, Finn lowered his fist.

The bully looked at them both and furrowed his brow. "Are you two . . . *together*?"

"Yes," Carver said.

Delia shot him a glance. "No." She turned to Finn. "It is nice to see you again. I've been seeing your face in the papers a lot. You look absolutely dashing. Are you here with your parents?"

"The upper-crust Echolses," Carver said snidely.

Finn winced. "They're not my parents."

"Your adoptive parents, then," Delia said. "You're set for life. How lucky!"

"That's what they keep telling me," Finn said. "I saw you both in the stairwell. What are *you* doing up here, Delia, with this thief?"

"*Me?*" Carver said.

Finn glared. Delia put her hand up. "Stop! Phineas is an old friend. I don't mind at all telling him why *I* asked *you* up here."

"Huh?" Carver said stupidly. A sharp glance from Delia silenced him.

She stepped closer to Finn, close enough to make Carver inexplicably grit his teeth. "There's something in that office," she said, pointing back toward the heavy door, "that I desperately want to see."

"You? Stealing?" Finn said dubiously.

"I don't want to *take* it, just look at it," she said. "I snuck old Carver in here to help me break in, but, well, he can't do it. It's too much for him."

The grin on Finn's face widened. "That scrawny sap? Why'd you even bother asking?"

Carver scowled, but, realizing what Delia was up to, he held his tongue.

"Because I didn't know you were here, Phineas. Maybe if you worked *together* . . . ?" she said.

Finn looked over her shoulder, past Carver. "That door? I could do it myself."

Delia nodded. "Possibly, but we're in a hurry . . ."

"Not possibly," Finn said. "I can do it."

He headed for it. Carver gave Delia a smile, but she ignored him.

"Be as quiet as you can, Phineas," Delia said, trotting up behind him.

The burly youth put his shoulder to the door, testing it.

"Okay," he began. "But there's something you have to do for me, too."

Delia shrugged. "What?"

He'd better not ask her for a kiss, Carver thought.

But the bully looked embarrassed. "Just . . . stop calling me Phineas. It's Finn."

She smiled warmly. "All right, Finn."

Finn nodded, braced his feet and pushed. For the longest time, the only sound was Finn's heavy breathing and the occasional shifting of his shoes as he adjusted his feet for better traction. In time, his face turned red. The veins along his temples bulged. Moist patches appeared under the arms of his silk shirt.

Delia glanced at the clock. "Finn, maybe if Carver . . ."

"I . . . don't . . . need . . . help!" Finn insisted.

Carver decided he could help just by reminding Finn he was there. "That orangutan can't do it. All he's good for is stealing necklaces from little kids."

"I didn't steal that necklace!" Finn growled. He clenched his jaw and shoved so hard that Carver and Delia thought for sure that either the door or his shoulder bone would have to give.

The expensive wood shuddered and gave off a single, distinct *crack*.

Finn, sweat dripping from his face, pulled back, panting. His face fell. "No good."

"Wait," Carver said. "That sound meant *something*."

Finn was so exhausted, he actually let Carver pull him back. Carver ran his fingers along the door, then around the plate surrounding the knob. Excited, he pulled a nail from his pocket, wedged it under the plate and wriggled it. Both plate and doorknob came away. Putting his fingers into the crack, he tugged. With a splintering sound, a jagged piece of mahogany came loose, revealing a metal bar beneath. The broken piece was large enough for Carver to ease the entire doorknob out from the frame.

Carver turned to Finn and smiled broadly. "You did it!"

Not knowing what to do with that reaction, Finn answered, "I knew *you* couldn't."

"There, now," Delia said, pushing the door open with one finger. "See what happens when you play together nicely?"

Carver stepped in. The only sound was a ticking wall clock. The office looked like a miniature version of the newsroom with all its papers and files. One enormous desk faced the door, a plush leather chair behind it. To the right was a covered birdcage. An electric fan, unplugged, sat on the center of the desk, used in the winter as a paperweight.

"What's so important?" Finn said, looking around curiously.

"A letter," Delia answered. She stepped over to an architect's drawing of the original New York Times Building on the wall near the birdcage. When she pulled, it swung open on hinges. A series of small shelves was set in the wall behind it.

Carver's heart pounded so hard, he could barely hear what Delia was saying.

"Overton's safe isn't much of a secret," she explained. "The lock was sent out for repair ages ago and hasn't come back. I can see why he trusts that door, though."

Carver hurried up beside her. As they pulled out files and scanned them, Finn, refusing to be forgotten, stood between them.

Delia stopped and looked at Carver. In her hand was a file labeled *Tombs Murder.* "Are you absolutely sure you want to do this?" she asked.

Carver nodded. "I have to know."

"Wait a minute. Why does *he* have to be sure about anything?" Finn huffed.

Delia handed Carver the file, then put her hand on Finn's shoulder. "It's a long story, Finn. I'll tell you sometime over a soda, if you'd like to buy me one."

Too concerned with what he had in his hands to be jealous, Carver put the file on the desk and opened it. There was a sheet of notes and a letter addressed to the *New York Times*. Carver snatched at the letter.

The moment he saw the heavy scrawled address, he knew, but he opened the envelope just to make sure. Four words, as Delia described, *Dear Boss, Me again,* were written on a single white sheet of paper. The handwriting was identical to his father's brutish scrawl.

Carver shook. He put his hands on the desk for support. No, no. No.

"Oh, Carver," Delia said. She tried to put her arm around him, but he pulled away and sank into Overton's chair.

"It's true," he muttered.

Delia knelt by his side, wrapped her hands around his and rubbed them. "I'm so, so sorry."

"Hey! What's going on?" Finn said.

Delia explained. "The *Times* received a letter from the Tombs Killer this morning. The handwriting matches a letter Carver believes is from his father."

The bully's face swam with a variety of expressions. "His . . . Carver's dad . . . that's . . ."

Delia turned back to Carver. "You have to tell Commissioner Roosevelt. It doesn't matter what sort of promises you made. Your letter is evidence. You should tell him right now."

Carver looked into her clear blue eyes, surprised how sad she seemed for his sake. He was about to agree, about to tell her all about the New Pinkertons, when his eyes fell on the sheet of notes accompanying the letter. A name popped out at him: Septimus Tudd.

Roosevelt had apparently shared some details of the investigation, mentioning Tudd had written to Scotland Yard in London back in August, regarding similar killings, but hadn't heard back yet. In any case, Roosevelt considered any connection to the London killings a long shot at best.

London? August? That was a week after Carver had written to the police. Tudd *knew* about the connection to his father. He knew all along!

38

"HEY, WHERE'RE you going?" Finn asked.

"Carver?" Delia called.

Swept away by feelings of shame and massive betrayal, he ignored them. Hawking was right, the world was a madhouse. He'd been nothing but a fool dazzled by gadgets. How could he think Tudd would pick an orphan to help Hawking just because he'd written a good letter? Now he knew exactly what Tudd saw in him—a clue, a lead in a case, a way to find a killer and save their failing agency.

By the time he reached the door, Finn blocked his way.

"Carver, wait!" Delia called.

Finn held up a single strong hand and warned, "Don't."

Wordless, Carver grabbed the sleek material of

Finn's shirt and shoved him aside. Finn, either exhausted from his effort at the door or, worse, feeling sorry for Carver, didn't put up any resistance.

Carver hit the stairs, where the only thing to glare at was the blur of his own feet.

Delia raced alongside him. "Carver Young, you promised you'd tell me what's going on if I helped you. I've helped you, so tell me."

"That's not even my real last name," Carver said.

"You promised. I took a terrific risk . . . ," she said, exasperated.

He stopped. "Septimus Tudd? The man whose name is on the letter? He only pretends he works for Roosevelt. He's actually the head of a secret group of detectives. Tudd snatched my letter from the police, then invited me in as a junior agent just to get my father's note." He looked heavenward but saw only the steel of the staircase above him. "He *had* to have made the connection to my father. He *used* me. And right now, he's downstairs at that party."

"You don't expect us to believe that cock and bull . . . ," Finn said.

Delia's face twisted, the way it sometimes did when she was puzzling something out. She seemed to be thinking deeply, wrestling with impossible ideas on a day full of them.

Coming out of her daze, Delia interrupted him. "No, Finn. He's not lying. It makes sense."

At the fourth floor, the sounds of the party murmured like river water. Carver slowed, thinking to warn his fellow orphans. He looked at both of them. "Don't follow me, understand? Get back to the party some other way. I'll say *I* broke into the office by myself."

"What are you going to do?" Delia said.

Carver didn't answer. Instead, he strode into the party.

As the filthy, foul-smelling boy invaded the soiree, all conversation ceased. He felt the stares of the rich and famous but kept his eyes dead ahead. He moved so quickly that by the time anyone thought to do something about him, he'd already reached Tudd.

Tudd still had his back to the teen and was talking to Roosevelt. It was the commissioner's ever-darting eyes that caught sight of Carver first. Not knowing what to make of Carver, Roosevelt adjusted his pince-nez glasses and narrowed his gaze.

Not caring, Carver grabbed the heavyset leader of the New Pinkertons by the elbow and spun him around. Taken fully by surprise, Tudd nearly fell. He quickly caught his balance, anchoring himself as if ready for a battle.

"You *knew*," Carver said, his gaze boring into the man. "You used me."

If Tudd was shocked, he didn't show it. He spoke carefully, softly, as if hoping to exclude all the watching partygoers, especially Roosevelt, from his words.

"If you care *anything* about your future," he said, "all the work you've done, the progress you've made, you will walk out of this party with me immediately."

The words puzzled Carver. He didn't think he *had* any future. Before he could respond, Roosevelt pushed his barrel chest between them.

"Who is this fierce indigent, Tudd? If he's hungry, give him some food and send him on his way. We're not done talking."

Tudd kept his eyes on Carver. "This is . . . my nephew, Commissioner. He's having some personal difficulties regarding his father but knows better than to come here to complain to me about it. I apologize for the interruption. He'll leave with me right now."

"Nephew?" Roosevelt said. "And you let him walk about in rags? No wonder he's so full of beans. You should be ashamed, Septimus, as should you, young man, for not showing yourself enough respect to . . ."

Moving quickly, Tudd dragged Carver back toward the stairs. Carver wanted to put up a fight, but he was confused now. What had Tudd meant?

The entire floor was watching, whispering. Roosevelt cried loudly, "I don't generally support corporal punishment for the young, Tudd, but in that boy's case, see to it you make an exception!"

Several partygoers laughed. A few applauded.

At the archway, Tudd tightened his grip. They passed a gaping Delia and Finn and walked down the steps wordlessly, until they reached the empty lobby.

There, Carver yanked his arm away.

"I *saw* the letter to the *Times*. I read the notes about your request to Scotland Yard in August, right after you saw my father's letter!"

Tudd straightened his jacket. "So I gathered. Hawking was right about you. Clearly I was wrong to underestimate you. The water damage proves that much. You should have heard Hawking cackle."

Carver ignored the comment. "You knew all along."

"I *suspected*," Tudd said, a bare hint of remorse in his voice. "From the moment your letter arrived at Mulberry Street. And what can I tell you now? Seven years ago, a certain killer in London wrote to the police. The tone, the grammar, all matched the letter from your father. The wounds from the library killing matched his method of operation. But when I summoned my friend, the brilliant Mr. Hawking, for support, he called me a fool in front of all my agents! What could I do then? Waltz you in and tell you I suspected your father was a monster? I wouldn't say that to my worst enemy without proof. And what would you have done? Run off? Given us away to the police? My hands were tied."

"And when you *saw* the letter from my father?"

Tudd shrugged guiltily. Briefly, the stout man seemed somehow smaller. "I should have gone straight to the police? I admit the thought of capturing the killer without them may have blinded me, but there were other concerns. *I* was convinced. Not Hawking. So, I chose to wait for Scotland Yard. When the letter arrived at the *Times,* of course I knew. But then, how could I explain to Roosevelt I'd stumbled on such explosive evidence without giving the New Pinkertons away? As for you, I'd hoped Hawking would arrive while you were in our custody and tell you all this himself."

"Hawking," Carver said, realizing it for the first time. "He knew, too?"

"Only that I was an idiot," Tudd said, softening further. "When he read your note . . . he *did* take an interest in you. We struck a deal. He'd take you under his wing while I waited to hear from Scotland Yard. I thought your little investigation was just a way to keep you busy. I never imagined you'd make progress."

"But you were happy to use the information I found," Carver said.

Tudd stiffened. "I wish things could be different, but here we are now. You don't even realize what we're up against. A savage killer like your father doesn't control his demons, he's *driven* by them. That, and his own self-loathing. At the same time, he's obviously interested in you, or he'd never have sent that letter. In fact, I suspect you *wouldn't* be making progress without your father's help. It's like some sort of game he's playing, and *you're* our only link."

"Why shouldn't *I* just go to the police?" Carver said.

Tudd's kindly demeanor faded slightly as he gritted his teeth. He was losing patience. "Putting aside my hopes for myself and the agency, the story would leak. The media circus could drive your father away from you and on to more killings. You must trust me. I can catch him, I need that chance, I *deserve* it!"

"Trust you? How?" Carver said.

Tudd started shouting. "You owe me more than trust! I've saved you from being a street rat, given you the best teacher in the world. In exchange you flood the headquarters and nearly ruin my life's work, all because you're ashamed of Daddy!"

If Tudd realized he'd gone too far, he didn't get the chance to say so.

Schick! Carver held the stun baton out, the copper tip humming with electrical energy.

"So you're a criminal," Tudd said, stiffening. "Stealing from us. I may have misjudged your heart, too. What else runs in your blood? How much more are you like your father?"

Carver jutted the tip forward, but, wet from the sewer water, it crackled and went dead.

Fuming at the sight of his broken prototype, Tudd shook his head. "Stupid child! You've no idea . . ."

The angry expression on his face was shattered by Carver's fist. As Tudd's jaw snapped to the right, Carver followed with a left to his gut.

The older man crumpled to the ground. Carver watched him drop. It was hard to say which of them was more surprised. Carver's hand, where it had connected with Tudd's jaw, was throbbing. His breath came in ragged gasps; his vision clouded with rage. He was suddenly ashamed, deeply embarrassed.

And worse, a familiar voice snapped him around. "C–Carver?"

It was Delia, staring at him, her eyes filled with disgust. She'd seen it then, seen his savage attack.

A moan from Tudd turned her toward his crumpled form. "You better go," Delia said, choking back a tear.

"Delia, I . . ."

"Go!" she shouted, eyes red.

Carver nodded. In a daze, he stumbled onto the streets and ran.

His head soon ached as badly as his hand. What had he done? Why? He'd never attacked anyone like that before. Tudd wasn't evil. In a way, he'd been trying to protect him. But when he'd said *Daddy,* Carver found himself filled with an alien fury. He'd wanted to kill him. And the way Delia looked at him.

Was he . . . like his father?

39

"YOU LIED," Carver said.

He stood in the center of the octagonal room. Hawking's old overcoat, far more beaten and muddied than it'd been two days ago, was slung over his arm.

"Hang the coat and pull up a chair," Hawking said. "You know where the door is, boy. I promise I won't lock you in."

Carver hesitated to let go of his rage, but from what Tudd said, Hawking *had* seen something worth molding in Carver. He put the coat on a hook and sat across from his mentor. On the table, the brass pieces, all polished now, were spread out between them like a massive picture puzzle. A whiskey glass held scores of tiny screws.

"I just didn't tell you everything. I didn't want you distracted by nonsense. I haven't made a secret of my opinion of Tudd's theory, have I? And I didn't lie about my plans for you."

It wasn't what Carver expected. "You can't *still* think Tudd's wrong, can you? You can't believe the killer *isn't* my father?"

Hawking sighed and pursed his lips. "No, but it was more a lucky guess than a theory, and the facts aren't all in yet. I assume if there'd been a response from Scotland Yard, Tudd wouldn't be keeping it to himself. If you weren't so wrapped up in yourself, you'd see that."

"But my father . . ."

Hawking held up his clawed hand. "I didn't say it was unreasonable for you to be wrapped up in yourself." Out of nowhere, he cackled. "*And* you brought the whole sewer down on them! Ha! The whole sewer!" When Carver failed to join him in the laugh, he stopped, but the smile didn't fade from his face. "It could be worse, you know."

Carver slammed his fist on the table so hard that two of the tiny screws flew from the glass and rolled off to the floor.

"How?" Carver shouted. "How could it be *worse*?"

Hawking didn't move, but his smile faded. "I'll let that go, but mind your tone. You say you want to be a detective. If your father is the killer, you're in a unique position to catch him. Who better to get in the mind of the father than the son?"

"You're saying I'm like him?" Carver asked.

"Of course you're like him, boy! He's your father!" Hawking barked. "Probably have the same hair color, eye color, gait . . . unless you take after your mother."

Carver's hands shook visibly. When Hawking saw this, he clamped them together with his own, pressing his strong hand into Carver's knuckles, bracing it with his wounded claw, making them still.

"Young men are so good at eating themselves up from the inside," his mentor said quietly. "I'd like to say the older are wiser, but the fact is, we just lack the energy to twist ourselves into such tight knots. I didn't say you were *exactly* like him."

"I don't want to be like him at all," Carver said.

"You don't want to breathe air or have two arms, two legs? First rule of detective work—be more specific. In what *ways* don't you want to be like him? I assume you're not worried about inheriting his grammar. You speak well enough."

Carver stated the painfully obvious. "I don't want to be a killer."

But of course that wasn't enough for Hawking. "Soldiers kill, police kill. Detectives sometimes kill, to protect themselves or others. A man who kills a killer is a hero. Wouldn't you kill someone who was threatening to kill a child?"

"Yes, but . . . the way I beat Tudd . . ."

"Beat Tudd? Ha! Well, I daresay he deserved it. He lied to you, used you, locked you up, and I'm sure, as night follows day, that he said something stupid to set you off. Are the killer's victims, as far as we know, people who used or hurt him?"

Carver shook his head. "No. He just . . . attacked them. They were innocent as far as anyone knows."

"Do *you* want to murder innocent women?"

"No!"

Hawking blew air from his lips, as if he didn't believe him. "Really? Never thought about it in your idle time? Chatting with your black-haired reporter girl, the idea never popped into your head?"

Carver was repulsed. "No! Never!"

Hawking let go of Carver's hands and opened his good palm triumphantly. "Then why on earth do you think it's something you'd ever do?"

"What if I can't help myself? Tudd said the killer can't control himself, that he's driven by demons and self-loathing."

Hawking snickered. "Say it with me, Tudd is an ass! You've read the letters. Does the author strike you as full of self-loathing?"

Carver furrowed his brow, recalling the terse phrasing, the energy behind the pen strokes. "No. I think he likes it. He likes it a lot."

Hawking rubbed the index finger and thumb of his good hand together, as if he rolled a tiny hard kernel of truth between them. "That's the key to him—and to you. He does, you don't. He enjoys himself immensely, every aspect, from the killing to the letters to the clues. He's not hiding behind some thin veneer of civilization. He's living his desires to the fullest, unadorned and unafraid. *Sooner murder an infant in its cradle than nurse unacted desires.* Remember? That's William Blake, boy, Proverbs of Hell. Study that one if you ever want to catch anything other than a cold."

Hawking's usually steady eyes scanned left and right, losing focus. "Your father is no simple driven beast. He dropped the second body exactly where it would cause the biggest stir, to be sure that everyone, especially *you,* would know about it. It's like some sort of intricate game. He's very cunning," Hawking said, as if admiring him. "Perhaps brilliant, strong, dedicated, all qualities one might be *proud* to possess."

"B-but . . . ," Carver stammered, "he's also evil."

Hawking turned his intense gaze on Carver. "And no one wants to hear good things about the devil, eh?"

40

AT FIRST Carver thought the scream was his own, left over from a nightmare he couldn't quite recall, but the muffled, pitiful wail came from below. Simpson was resisting his treatment again.

Carver showered, ate, and patched his overcoat, but still couldn't clear his head. Too many bad thoughts were colliding in his mind. He craved reassurance.

"Are you going to get involved in the case?" Carver asked his mentor.

"No."

"But . . ."

"No. I don't do that sort of thing anymore."

"What should I . . . ?"

"It's your life, not mine. You'll have to figure out what to do with yourself next."

Carver had no idea, not in the least. With Hawking constantly cursing as he fidgeted with the tiny screws, he felt as if he'd soon explode. Desperate, he begged to be allowed to go to the city.

"Why?"

"I have to get out of here. I feel like I'm going crazy."

"What better place for it? But I understand your point." Hawking grumbled slightly, then said, "If your father wanted to find you, he could have done so years ago. As long as you're not looking for him, you should be safe. And stay away from Tudd, too. For the moment at least. You will have to deal with both of them eventually, though."

"I know," Carver said.

By mid-afternoon, he found himself on the corner of 14th and Broadway, staring at his old home, Ellis Orphanage. At the time, his life there had seemed awful, mostly because of Finn. Yet in comparison, it had been carefree. Now the windows and doors were boarded up. A sign proudly announced that the new owners were preparing to demolish the eyesore and replace it with something new and wondrous. He wished he could do the same with his life. The look on Delia's face the last time she saw him still hovered in his head, gargoyle-like.

Delia. Finn. What had happened to them? Had they been found out? He had a responsibility, even if it was partly toward his former tormentor. Trying to live up to it would make him different from his father, wouldn't it?

It was Saturday. If they weren't in jail, they'd be home. Delia had mentioned her address only once, but he remembered it. 27 West Franklin Street was a good, long walk from Ellis, but the release of energy would do him good.

Along the way, he passed many newsboys shouting headlines,

but not one had a word to say about a break-in at the *Times*. That was a good sign. Finn's new parents were wealthy and influential; Delia's were employees. Roosevelt didn't want the letter's existence made public. A lot of people had an interest in keeping things quiet.

When he reached Franklin Street, his hopes faded. The block was full of town houses, newer and in better repair than those on Warren Street. None stood out more than the Victorian at number 27, with its nearly carrot-orange bricks and the gray-brown gables. Carver would've liked the place if it weren't for the carriage parked directly outside, marked *Metropolitan Police*.

Just when he thought he couldn't feel any worse, he did. Had Delia been arrested?

He wanted to know, but if he walked up, the carriage driver would spot him. Delia had mentioned an oak tree at her window. There weren't any out front. Could it be in the back?

He doubled back to Varick Street and snuck through the yard of the property abutting the Ribes' Victorian. There, a thick, majestic oak rose along the brickwork. Beyond the roof, white clouds glowed in a darkening sky, nearly as orange as the bricks. It seemed like such a . . . home. It brought an ache he couldn't place.

Shaking it off, he slipped to the base of the tree and peered through a first-floor window. Mostly, he saw an empty hallway, but a little of the front parlor was visible, as well as some people in it. The Ribes were seated, listening to a stocky man who paced around, gesticulating with familiar energy. Roosevelt. That wasn't good.

Seeing a light on at the third-floor window, Carver shinnied up the tree trunk. As he climbed, loose threads kept catching on the rough bark, forcing him to yank the coat free and undo his patching. Once among the branches, he almost slipped on the lingering snow.

Hadn't Delia said this was an easy climb? By the time he made it to the window, he was out of breath. The lamp glowed beyond a thin curtain that made everything inside blurry. Some shapes looked like furniture, but he was guessing. Only Delia was instantly recognizable, sitting near what looked like white drapes.

Carver rapped on the glass. Oddly, Delia gave the drapes a quick glance before coming over. When she parted the thin curtain and saw him, the relief that swept her face brought a smile to his lips.

She pulled open the window. "Carver!" she said in a strained hush. She took a step back, as if afraid of him, but then pulled herself together. "I was worried. Are you all right?"

"I'm . . . still here," he said. "And . . . Delia, when you saw me . . . I . . ."

He thought he was whispering, but she put a finger to her lips. "Shh! Roosevelt's here and . . ."

He nodded. "I know. Is he here for you?"

"Me? Of course not."

Carver breathed a sigh of relief. "What happened after I left?"

"Well, I tried to help that poor man up, but he pushed me away and raced into the street, trying to find you, I imagine."

"So then why—"

He was about to ask why Roosevelt was here when what Carver thought was a window drape appeared behind Delia, revealing itself to be a girl.

She was wearing a white coat and a feathered hat wider than

her shoulders. Despite the formal attire appropriate to a woman, she seemed younger than Delia.

"Do you often talk to windows?" the girl said with calm, practiced confidence. Seeing Carver, her smooth face filled with obvious pleasure. "Oh, a boy! Shouldn't we invite him in?"

41

"I JUST adore secret meetings," the girl said. "Though I'm far too young to have had any myself." Somewhere between child and young woman, she spoke and carried herself as if she were royalty. Carver couldn't take his eyes off her. Her bright manner was so different from his personal gloom.

Still tentative, Delia held his arm as he struggled to put a leg over the sill. "Where've you been all this time?"

"Home," he said.

"You mean the . . . ," she said, catching herself in mid-sentence.

"*The?* Where's *the?* Is *the* a pleasant place to live?" the girl asked cheerfully. "Is it near *a* or *an?*"

Who was she? A neighbor? The daughter of a wealthy family member? To answer Delia, he quickly said, "No, not there."

"Where, then?" Delia asked.

He nodded toward the girl in white.

She cleared her throat and announced, "It doesn't take much to see that you two have a lot to talk about, so if you'll excuse me, I'll listen in from back here."

She floated over to Delia's bed, pulling the length of her elegant white coat aside as she sat. "Do continue."

Delia pulled a little harder on him, as if trying to get his attention back.

"Blackwell Asylum," he said, in a low whisper.

"Asylum?" Delia repeated.

"It's where Mr. Hawking lives." He was about to explain how his mentor studied the criminally insane when he stumbled through the open window, his feet landing loudly on the floor.

"Quiet!" Delia hissed. "They'll hear you downstairs."

The girl spoke up again, smiling widely at Carver. "Pardon me, but I'm sure such a stealthy climber would have no concerns about evading mere policemen."

He wasn't sure how to react to her. Wanting to say something witty in response but having only Hawking to emulate, Carver grinned and said, "Roosevelt? That silk-stockinged cowboy?"

"Carver . . . ," Delia warned in a whisper.

"He's probably so busy listening to *himself* . . ."

"*Carver*," Delia hissed.

". . . he wouldn't hear an *elephant* stampeding behind him."

Delia sighed and swept her hand toward the girl. "Carver Young, meet Alice Roosevelt. The commissioner's eldest *daughter*."

"Oh. Uh . . . ," Carver said. "I . . ."

Her precocious smile remained. "Oh, it's all right. If you don't have anything nice to say about anyone, come sit next to me." She patted the bedcover beside her.

Carver was speechless. As far as he could tell, she was not at all offended and, if anything, delighted by his embarrassment.

"I *know* Daddy's a blowhard," Alice said in a conspiratorial whisper. "But if you're going to do anything, why not do it as hard as you're able? You're mistaken about that elephant, though. *Any* creature attempting to sneak up on him would be felled with a single shot, even if he were listening to himself at the time. I do promise I won't repeat a word of anything I've heard, or might hear, provided it remains entertaining."

"Oh," was all Carver could think to say.

Delia cleared her throat pointedly. "They're talking about the murders. When the *Times* agreed not to publish the letter, Jerrik was given a limited exclusive and—"

Alice interrupted. "I was brought along to make it look like a social visit. Wouldn't talk about such grisly things in front of a *child,* after all," she said, accenting the word with obvious derision. "I have, as you can see, been relegated to the upper floors."

Now Delia was the one staring at Alice, but with an expression more akin to dislike. She turned back to Carver and tried again. "The coroner report confirmed that the wounds on the new body were similar to those inflicted in the library killings, and . . ."

"London?" Carver added.

Delia shrugged somberly. "I'm sorry, that's all I heard before I was sent up here to keep an eye on . . ."

"Call me Alice!"

"Can we get closer?" Carver asked. "Listen in?"

Alice answered for Delia. "No need. When Father gets going, we'll hear him clearly enough."

A muffled bellow came from the hallway. "I shall raise an *army!*"

"See? There he is now," Alice said, pleased with her timing. "Shall we find better seats?"

Delia sighed and moved into the hall. "There's a floor vent we can use."

As Carver followed, Delia tried to get ahead of Alice, but the girl seemed unwilling to give up the lead. Finally, Delia pulled her back, saying, "It *is* my house."

Delia took them down into a large bedroom with a huge four-poster bed and wide, pleasant windows. Alice spun in the center, letting her white coat swirl. "Small for a guest room, isn't it?"

Pulling a cushioned chair away from the heating vent, Delia answered flatly, "It's the master bedroom."

"Oh, Delia," Alice responded. "I'm only teasing. Don't hate me for that!"

"I won't," Delia said, smiling back. "Not for that."

The vent exposed, the three gathered near. Alice, about to kneel, put her hand out toward Carver to hold for support. Without thinking, he took it, leaving Delia to let out an exasperated grunt as she picked up the end of her cotton dress and knelt on her own.

The first voice they heard was Jerrik Ribe's. "Were you in London during the murders, Commissioner?"

"No," Roosevelt responded. "Two years earlier, 1886, for my wedding. But I've certainly read all I can about that fiend since. I tell you, quite plainly, if he is here, there'll be no place for him to hide. I'll set out a net and draw it in so tightly, even the shadows will spit him out. Every officer is on alert; our patrols have been doubled. All we lack is a witness."

From the way he was talking, the killer sounded famous. Carver wondered if he'd ever heard of him.

"Don't you think," a female voice put in, "that the public would be more helpful if they knew *exactly* what was going on? That printing the letter would more likely prompt someone to come forward?"

"That's Anne," Delia said proudly.

"I like *her*," Alice said.

But her father apparently did not. "We've been through this! To even *suggest* he's in Manhattan would unleash a circus. Every crank will line up to give false witness or even confess to the crimes! And the panic! Backed into a corner, the poor can riot, but the rich can start a war." Roosevelt lowered his voice. "I detest subterfuge. The fact someone broke into that office while I was present shows how fragile this situation is."

"Overton's convinced it was the *Tribune* or the *Herald*," Jerrik said.

"If it was, wouldn't they have printed the contents of the letter by now?" Anne said.

"Let's stick to the issue at hand. The longer we operate without public attention, the better. Until the situation collapses of its own accord, any who come forward will be more reliable."

"*If* anyone comes forward, Commissioner," Anne said.

Delia eyed Carver meaningfully. "You have to tell him."

"I don't know," Carver said. "I'm not sure who to trust."

Alice scrutinized their faces. When she spoke, her whip-like wit was replaced by an equally well-spoken sincerity. "I don't know what Father's done to earn such a low opinion from you, but he is a man of incredible principle. I find it tedious. He's never, for instance, spoken to me about my own mother, his first wife, whom I never knew, and I'm certain it's because of some *principle*. But that's my problem as his daughter. As a confidant, or a friend, there is no one more reliable. If there is anything you can do to help him catch this murderer, of course you should do it."

Carver glanced from Alice's calm assurance to Delia's concerned face.

Hawking's words echoed in his head: *It's your life, not mine. You'll have to figure out what to do with yourself next.* Was that his way of giving permission? Maybe this was his only chance to prove to Delia, to himself, that he wasn't his father's son.

"Okay, I'll do it," he said. "I'll do it right now."

42

DELIA led Carver to the door. "It'd be better if someone they knew explained who you were."

"I'll stay here, then," Alice said. "But I *am* looking forward to hearing whatever it is you're going to say."

At the stairs, Delia slipped her arm into his. "Speak simply and plainly. Keep in mind you don't sound completely sane when you start talking about a secret detective base."

"How will I sound when I say I'm the killer's son?"

She frowned. "Take it from the beginning. Start with finding the letter."

When they arrived in the foyer, Jerrik came into view first. Fair hair neatly combed, a legal pad on his narrow lap, he was in mid-sentence when he saw them.

". . . Delia?"

Roosevelt turned his square head, his eyes zeroing in on Carver. "Tudd! Your nephew has the most disquieting habit of showing up in odd places."

Tudd? Carver jerked his head around. Alone in a deep cushioned love seat sat Mr. Tudd, a dark bruise on his face. Carver froze.

The fifty-something leader of the New Pinkertons rolled to his feet. "I'm glad he's here."

"Why *is* he here, Delia?" Jerrik said. "And who is he?"

"Carver Young," Anne said. "An old friend of Delia's from the orphanage."

"I made it clear this was to be a private interview!" Roosevelt said, rustling in his seat.

By now Tudd was at the entrance, facing Carver. "I have something of grave importance to tell you. It's about Mr. Hawking," he whispered.

"What?" Carver said. "Is he all right?"

"No."

The word hit Carver like a ton of bricks. The depth of his concern for the bristly man surprised him. "Not here," Tudd whispered. "Let's take a walk."

Tudd turned to the adults. "My deepest apologies again, Commissioner, Mr. and Mrs. Ribe. Would you excuse us a moment?"

"If you mean may you leave with your nephew, the answer is yes," Roosevelt said. "If you're asking me to forgive a second scene, I'll withhold judgment until given a full explanation."

Tudd nodded. "Of course," he said, then made for the door with Carver.

As Tudd opened the door, Roosevelt looked around. "How did he get in? We've been sitting here the whole time, the front door in view. Is there another entrance?" As he scanned the room, he glanced up at a vent directly above his head. His eyes narrowed and he shouted, "Alice! Move away from the vent at once!"

Whatever he said next to his daughter was muffled by the closing door.

On the stoop, Carver immediately asked, "What's happened?"

Tudd nodded toward the carriage driver, who was watching them curiously. "Just to the corner. Thanks to you, I no longer enjoy the Commissioner's complete confidence and I'd rather not have the situation deteriorate further."

They moved up along Franklin, toward Varick Street.

"What happened to Mr. Hawking?" Carver asked again.

"No apology for pummeling me and leaving me to bleed in a hallway? Do you realize I had to crawl into the street and *pretend* I'd been hit by a cab? Thank heavens your friend said nothing, though I suspect she's more interested in protecting *you*."

Part of Carver felt he should apologize, but something held him back, an unease in the air. Tudd looked back over his shoulder. The driver had stepped off the carriage and was now in the middle of the sidewalk, watching them. They were far enough away, though, for Tudd to speak. "Regardless of whether you share Hawking's attitude toward me and my gadgets, I am not a fool. The only reason for you to step into that parlor would be if you planned to tell Roosevelt everything."

Carver's hackles rose. He moved to put some distance between himself and Tudd. "The letter from my father is an important piece of evidence. They *have* to know."

"Would you have told him about the New Pinkertons as well?" Tudd said.

"I . . . ," Carver began. He shook his head, only now realizing it wasn't necessary. "No, they just have to know about the letter. Tell me about Mr. Hawking!"

They rounded the corner. "I am fully prepared to share everything we know with the police," he said.

The hairs on the back of Carver's neck tingled the way they always did when he felt he was being watched. "What about Mr. Hawking?" Carver demanded. "You still haven't told me . . ."

But Tudd was no longer looking at him. He was looking over Carver's shoulder, giving someone a curt nod.

Carver spun, but before he could see who was there, he was yanked forcefully backward. His arms were swiftly pinned. Something coarse and woolen was shoved in his mouth. It balled his tongue toward the back of his throat, making him gag.

He twisted and pulled, trying to fight, until a sudden kick took him off his feet. The world spun. He was on his back, Tudd towering over him. His facial bruise, made black by a streetlight, did not conceal his look of triumph. "I will tell them about you and that letter as soon as *I've* caught your father!"

43

HIS HANDS and feet bound, the gag fixed in place with a thick cord, Carver was thrown into an open two-seat carriage. An athletic figure with a thick mustache climbed in beside him. He propped Carver up to make room for himself, then pulled a hinged metal cover over their legs. The snug fit forced the figure to lean forward to click it into place, exposing him to the streetlight.

It was Jackson. Outraged, Carver struggled harder against the ropes. He writhed so violently, the little carriage shook.

"Don't," Jackson said. "Emeril used two interlocked handcuff knots. The more you pull, the tighter they get. Keep at it and you'll cut off the blood supply. You could lose a hand or foot."

He wasn't lying. The pressure around his wrists was vise-like.

Jackson called to an unseen driver up and behind them. "Let's get there tonight!"

Carver looked forward. There were no horses. How did they plan to get anywhere?

A steady electric hum erupted from behind him. The carriage lurched, then rolled along the cobblestones, maneuvering into the center of the street. Carver's eyes went wide.

"That's right, finally got the electric carriages in from Philly," Jackson said.

They rode north. As they moved along, pedestrians stopped and gaped to see them roll uphill, as if by magic.

Hudson Street held a crowded streetcar. The passengers nearly pushed each other out, pressing against the doors and windows to stare. One woman screamed, reminding Carver of the woman in Hawking's tale who saw the fire truck onstage.

Carver writhed and puffed at the gag, trying to draw attention to the fact he was being kidnapped. Jackson tossed a blanket over him.

"Some kidnappers we are," Jackson muttered. "Why not strap a portable light on the lad's head for the entire world to see?" He called back to the driver, "Emeril, can't it go any faster?"

"It can," the higher pitched voice responded. "Over thirty miles per hour since Tudd tweaked it. When we tried that yesterday, though, every horse we passed reared in panic!"

Jackson sighed. "It's a wonder the agency's been secret this long."

Emeril called again, "Did you tell Carver it's not us? It's Tudd's idea we catch the killer ourselves?"

"Speak for yourself," Jackson said, sounding uncharacteristically snippy. "I'm fine with it. We're better than the police, and it's about time we got some credit for it. And Carver here was ready to blab and have us all arrested."

Emeril maneuvered the carriage into a small garage on War- ren Street. There, the two removed Carver, covered the vehicle in old horse blankets and escorted him quickly to the side of Devlin's.

As the elevator descended noiselessly, Emeril pulled the gag out.

Carver spat and coughed a few times. With as much fury as he could muster, he said, "What if someone *dies* because of what you're doing?"

Jackson shrugged. "What if someone dies because of what *you're* doing?"

44

THERE WAS little left of the friendly
feeling Carver once shared with the two agents. They
grabbed his arms and pulled him through headquarters. Everyone picked up their heads to watch. Some
seemed horrified; others eyed Carver with contempt.
Here he was, the son of the killer, the thief who
flooded the place. Worst, the boy who attacked Septimus Tudd.

They brought him to an empty room, which
Emeril assured him was nowhere near the sewer line.
There, they replaced his ropes with handcuffs and
ankle braces, then checked his pockets.

"Where is it?" Jackson demanded. "The broken
stun baton."

Carver was surprised. Hadn't it been in his pocket
just hours earlier?

Carver glared at him. "It must have fallen out
when you attacked me."

"Right," Jackson said. They frisked him again but still couldn't find it.

Unwilling to repeat their mistakes, he was never left alone. They took turns sitting with him. Emeril busied himself studying files and newspapers. Jackson was content to leaf through magazines.

When Carver asked what they were waiting for, the answer was, "Tudd."

When he asked for some food, the answer was, "When Tudd gets back."

When he asked if he could lie down and get some sleep, the answer was, "We'll see what Tudd says."

There was nothing for him to do but sit and be ignored. In time his eyes drooped and he slumped forward, nodding off until some stray sound jolted him back awake.

Carver was so tired that Tudd's arrival was anticlimactic. He stood in the open door, clothes rumpled, his usually clean-shaven sheepdog face a forest of salt-and-pepper stubble.

"What time is it?" Carver asked.

Tudd pulled out his watch fob. "Almost ten in the morning. Roosevelt has us following every lead that comes in, no matter how ridiculous. I've barely enough time for a shower and a change of clothes before I'm due back at Mulberry Street. After your appearance at the Ribes', he made it quite clear that if the situation weren't so dire, he would have fired me on the spot."

Finding a grain of defiance left with him, Carver said, "You don't still expect an apology, do you?"

Tudd sighed. "No. Likewise, I trust you don't expect me to let the child of a maniac destroy all I've built?"

Carver thought for a second, then said, "No."

The older man clasped his hands behind his back. "This time, you forced me to tie more than your hands. Even if you do some-how get out again, the Commissioner won't believe a word you say. I've made it clear that you're a seriously troubled individual, burdened by morbid curiosity, afflicted by an inability to distin-guish reality from dime novels. Your own father threw you out because of your wild delusions, and you've since refused my offers to seek professional aid."

"You won't get away with it. I have proof," Carver said.

"The letter you gave me?"

"Delia . . . ," he began. He was about to announce she'd also seen the letter, but caught himself.

Mistaking his intent, Tudd shook his head. "Her hysterics only helped convince Roosevelt and the Ribes you'd manipu-lated her."

Carver shrugged. "My father will strike again. I should be helping."

"We agree on that much. You can help. That address you were hunting down before you arrived at the Tombs, give it to me."

Carver couldn't believe what he was asking. "You expect me to just tell you?"

"You want him caught, don't you?"

Of course he did, but something told him it would be the wrong move. "What if he sent that letter to Ellis because he wants *me* to find him? What if he's laying out all these clues *for me* alone? Who better to think like him than his own son?"

Tudd exhaled dismissively. "He's cunning, but ultimately little more than a tormented beast."

"No," Carver answered. "He enjoys what he's doing, and he's very good at it."

"Enjoys it? Good at it?" Tudd said, his face twisting. "That's repulsive."

Hawking was right; he couldn't even accept the possibility. *No one wants to hear good things about the devil.*

"Give me the address. If you don't, the next killing will be on your head."

"Roosevelt could say the same thing to you if he knew, couldn't he?"

"The commissioner is not here. You and I are. And much as you are his son, Carver, believe me, you don't realize the first thing about the killer. Let professionals handle it."

He didn't really have a choice, did he? He'd made the argument himself. Keeping the information from Tudd was as bad as Tudd's keeping it from the police.

"All right, it's—"

"Tudd!" A familiar voice thundered from the plaza, followed by the crack of a cane against the floor tiles. "Tudd! Come out here! I've dragged myself from Blackwell; you can crawl out of whatever rat's nest you're hiding in!"

Tudd rubbed his forehead. "Hawking."

Carver grinned. "You were lying to me about him, too."

45

WORDLESS, Tudd headed for the door. Carver tried to follow, but Jackson blocked his path. The door remained open, allowing Carver to hear the booming voices.

"You've something of mine, Septimus. I intend to have it back!" Hawking shouted. "Where's the boy?"

"He's fine; he's safe," Tudd said.

"I didn't ask his status, you bloated imbecile!" Though nasal, his voice was loud, commanding, geared to draw attention. He slammed the cane down again. "Bring him out, now!"

Tudd puffed himself up. "You don't give orders here. Who told you we had him?"

"Now!" Hawking said. The demand echoed up to the arched bricks of the roof.

After a brief silence, Tudd withered. "Jackson, Emeril. Bring him."

Jackson stepped aside to let Carver into the hall. He shook his head grimly. "How on earth Hawking got wind of this so soon is beyond me. He must have an informer here."

With Jackson's back briefly to them, Emeril winked at Carver. "He must."

Surprised, Carver smiled back. Maybe he did have *one* friend here. Once out of the room, Carver looked around. He'd never seen so many agents. The entirety of the organization had gathered on the plaza to watch.

Seeing Carver, Hawking cried, "Shackles, Tudd? What on earth were you thinking? Didn't you learn your lesson the first time? You're lucky the place is still standing."

"He was going to betray us to Roosevelt," Tudd answered.

"Betray us?" Hawking said. "We're not a religious order or a sovereign nation. Let him go at once, Septimus, or *I'll* go to Roosevelt!" He whirled his cane at the watching agents. "Unless, of course, you plan to order them to take *me* prisoner!"

Tudd blinked. His expression became more pleading. "The boy stole from us. He *assaulted* me."

Hawking kept screaming. "He was lied to and manipulated! And, really, is being beaten up by a fourteen-year-old something you want to brag about?"

Though they tried to hide it by covering their mouths, a few agents chuckled.

Tudd shot them all a look. "Silence! I am in charge here!"

Everyone except Hawking stiffened as if soldiers, but Carver sensed some damage had been done.

Trying to look in control, Tudd said, "If I release him to you, you'll swear to keep him in check?"

"This is not a negotiation," Hawking said flatly. "But what are you afraid of? You've already seen to it no one will believe him. *Morbid curiosity?* Tsk, tsk."

From Tudd's reaction, that was something else Hawking wasn't supposed to know. "The address he was investigating near the Tombs. I want it."

Hawking surveyed the crowd. "The head of the greatest detective agency in the world can't get any leads, so he resorts to extortion. Allan Pinkerton would turn over in his grave! You had only to ask me. I was there that night, remember? Number 42 Edgar Street. Satisfied?"

Tudd nodded for Emeril and Jackson to free Carver.

"Am I really the fool here, Albert?" Tudd said. "*You* never believed my theory was possible. Even now, instead of helping, you judge me. You never fully returned from that gun battle. Face it, the game has passed you by."

"Fine talk coming from someone who's never *been* to a gun battle. You've no idea what I lost that night, Tudd, because you've no idea what there *is* to lose!" Hawking snarled.

Rubbing his wrists, Carver straightened in front of Tudd. "Mr. Hawking's better than you, and you know it."

"We'll see who's better than whom when I catch your daddy," Tudd said, nearly spitting the words. "Best get back to the asylum, son."

"We'll do that, Septimus," Hawking said. "At least the people there make some sense."

As Carver pulled the door shut on the subway car, he heard Tudd shouting, "Why are you all standing around like Romans at the gladiator games? We have our lead! Edgar Street! Get to work!"

Carver and Hawking remained silent until they were several blocks away, along Broadway.

"You gave him the wrong address," Carver said with a smile.

"Of course," Hawking said. "Not because I didn't know the right answer. You did mention Leonard Street to me, but the number, 27, was something I learned by rubbing a pencil against the last sheet of paper you were writing on in the athenaeum. It's a handy trick. Here."

He tossed the crumpled sheet to Carver. He unfolded it and saw how the rubbing left his notes visible. "Not that Tudd would ever think of anything that didn't involve a *machine*," Hawking went on. "The game has passed *me* by? Ha. And try to get that broken gadget out of your coat lining. It must have fallen there a while ago. You might further damage the thing or electrocute yourself."

Being affronted seemed to have energized him. "*Were* you going to Roosevelt?" Hawking asked.

"Yes."

"I don't blame you for that, boy. As I've said, it's all baubles. The case is the important thing."

As he lifted the edge of his coat and pulled out the broken baton, Carver said, "I don't have to reveal the agency, just about the letter, the evidence. The New Pinkertons can survive. Why don't you take over? The agents would support you. We could go to Roosevelt together."

Hawking stopped short. "Not my preference, but if there's to be an agency left by the time you're ready to take over, it may be the only solution. The problem is, Tudd would have to be removed first."

"Removed?"

"His position with Roosevelt is precarious enough; shouldn't take much to tip things over the edge; maybe even use one of his precious gadgets against him."

Carver stared at his mentor until Hawking blew some air through his lips. "Well?"

"You'll take over and we'll bring the agency out into the open?"

Hawking shrugged. "Just Tudd, for now. You can bring Roosevelt the letter, though, and anything else you like. Any ideas?"

"Me?"

"Consider it a test, to see how much you've learned. Are you up to it? You like gadgets, don't you?" Hawking said mischievously.

46

ON A chill and dank Monday, Carver stood behind a pickle vendor in one of the city's worst tenement districts, staring at number 300 Mulberry Street. Though it housed the Board of Police Commissioners, the detective bureau and all the police captains and inspectors in the city, the marble-fronted four-story building was very plain. It looked more like Ellis Orphanage than, say, the New Pinkertons' headquarters or the exotic Tombs. The iron bars on the basement windows impressed him, though. The cells beyond were where he'd end up if he failed Mr. Hawking's "test."

Twinges of uncertainty and guilt nagged him. Was he interested in the best way to catch his father or out for revenge? And the plan: How much was Hawking's, how much his and how much remembered from an old *New York Detective's Weekly*? The old agent certainly cackled genuinely enough whenever Carver added a thought, and surely his gadget-hating mentor would never have thought to study the *Operating Guide for Your New Western Electric Switchboard*.

No looking back now, but there was so much to remember. "Roosevelt is called president, not commissioner," he reminded himself. There were actually three other commissioners, who'd unanimously elected Roosevelt their head.

He checked the small watch Hawking had loaned him.

It wasn't the only recent show of his mentor's largesse. Carver also wore all-new clothes, chestnut pants with a matching jacket and black shoes that actually fit. His haircut, given by a fat-fingered Octagon worker, was sloppy, but the deerstalker cap, like the one Sherlock Holmes wore, covered its flaws.

He didn't look wealthy, like Finn, but he no longer resembled a street rat, either. He felt, if not good, at least more in control.

It was time.

The package held carefully in front of him, he crossed the cobblestones and entered the building. The desk sergeant was a heavy, balding man, wisps of dark hair combed sideways across his forehead. His jacket was open, his hand shoved beneath, like Napoleon, but Carver doubted the French dictator ever scratched his belly so enthusiastically.

A quick movement of the man's chin told Carver to state his business.

"Delivery for Mrs. Tabitha Lupton."

The sergeant sucked at his back teeth. "*Miss* Lupton's inna telephone room, first floor, last door onna right," he said in a thick Brooklyn accent. "It her birthday?"

Carver shrugged. "I guess."

"She didn't say n'thin'." He nodded Carver through the gate.

So far, so good, but as he headed for the telephone room, Carver felt as if everyone he passed, police officers and support staff, could hear his racing heart.

The door open, he walked into the room. Only one person was there, seated at the Western Electric switchboard Carver recognized from the manual. She was short, with frizzy golden hair and eyes that had the innocent look of a much younger girl.

He held out the flowers. "Miss Lupton? These are for you."

"Oh!" she said, staring at them.

The bouquet was big and showy, as per Hawking's instructions. When the beady-eyed clerk at the florist told him the price, Carver tried not to balk, but he could have lived on it for weeks.

He nearly forgot his next line. "They're from an . . . anonymous admirer."

She smiled broadly, taking them. "Oh! Oh!"

Carver cleared his throat. "I don't think the outside air is good for them. You should get them into some water right away, to make them last."

"Oh, oh, oh!" Miss Lupton said. She rose and headed for the door.

Carver stuck his head out and watched. As she walked down the hall, a patrolman whistled his admiration. "Get a load of what Tab's got!"

A blushing Tabitha Lupton was shortly surrounded by her co-workers, insisting she'd no idea who the flowers were from.

He and Hawking had guessed this would give Carver about ten minutes alone in the room. He wouldn't need all of it if everything went as planned. He gently closed the door and sat at the switchboard. The device was built into an unassuming

wooden table, two feet wide with a high back full of holes arranged in a labeled grid. A bed of likewise labeled plugs lay before
him; weighted cables, one connected to each plug, dangled beneath the board.

Most large businesses and government buildings had their
own switchboard. Since Alexander Bell's patent had expired last
year, new phone companies had sprung up across the country, all
refusing to connect to one another. That forced the police to
subscribe to several, to have as wide a reach as possible.

Carver pulled a cable, connected it to the board and turned
the handle to ring an outside operator. A female voice crackled
from a speaker. "Party, please."

"Blackwell Island," Carver said.

"One moment."

It felt like an eternity before Hawking's voice floated through
the ether. "I'm here, boy."

"I'll patch you through."

"Speak a little higher. You have to sound at least a bit like a
woman."

Carver pulled another plug and turned the handle again.

He gritted his teeth when he heard Tudd say, "Yes, Miss
Lupton?"

He raised his voice an octave. "A Mr. Hawking at Blackwell
Island." He thought he sounded ridiculous. After a silence, Tudd
answered. "Put him through."

"One moment." Carver pushed the cable with Hawking's line
into place.

"Mr. Hawking, this is Septimus Tudd, how can I help you?"

"So formal, Tudd?" Hawking said, the usual sneer in his voice.

Even through the speaker, Carver heard Tudd's exasperated
sigh. "Miss Lupton, are you still on the line? . . . Miss Lupton?"

When Carver said nothing, Tudd was satisfied the call was private. "Are you *mad* calling me here? Is someone dead? The boy, I hope?"

"Just doing you a favor," Hawking said. "I have reason to believe Roosevelt suspects you."

Carver was surprised how easily Hawking lied. Was it something *all* adults did well? In any case, that was Carver's cue to move quickly. He connected another cable and cranked the handle so fast, he worried it might break.

"Yes, Tabitha?" a woman answered. It was Roosevelt's secretary, but all at once Carver couldn't remember her name. What was it? What was it? He snatched it from his mind at the last second.

"Miss Kelly, Mayor Strong for Commissioner Roosevelt."

As he waited, sweat beaded on his forehead. Seconds passed. He eyed the door, wondering how much time he had left.

"Roosevelt here, Mr. Mayor." The voice's forceful quality was unhindered by the tinny speaker.

"He's waiting. I'll connect you," Carver said, forgetting to raise his voice. He connected the commissioner's line to Tudd's.

The first words the man heard from his assistant were, "Roosevelt has no reason to suspect me of anything. I've been careful. He thinks I'm completely loyal. There isn't a shred of evidence to connect me . . ."

"Tudd?!" Roosevelt bellowed.

"Commissioner . . . ?"

"No need to come to my office, Tudd. I had a good strong extension wire put in last week so I could pace while on the phone. At this moment, I'm standing right outside your locked door. Open it at once!"

It was done.

A funny taste filled Carver's mouth as his body shed some anxiety. He pulled the lines free, leaving them as he found them, opened the door and walked out. The group still admiring Miss Lupton's flowers was large enough for him to have to squeeze past.

As he did, she recognized him. With yet another "Oh!" she forced a nickel into his hand, a tip, then smiled so widely, he felt he'd done at least one good thing today.

Hoping no one saw the sweat on his brow, he headed past the stomach-scratching desk sergeant, out the front entrance, down the steep stone steps and into the chill of the city, never happier to disappear.

47

AS HE ran along the fog-shrouded streets, Carver knew it was a dream. The buildings were too misshapen, the fog too thick. He reached out to touch it. He scooped some into his hand. It swirled like living smoke in his palm.

The screaming still disturbed him, high-pitched, pained. Knowing it was all unreal, he didn't run. Instead, he walked through the narrow alley. For some reason, it ended not in a filthy open area, but the phone room of Mulberry Street. The switching station was in the center, surrounded by flowers. There was a body on the floor, a top-hatted figure hovering above it. For a moment, the body was Delia's, but then, all of a sudden, it was Tudd's.

His blood-smeared belly quivered as his chest heaved, taking in its final breath.

Carver was no longer watching; he was participating. It was *he* who hovered over Tudd. He could feel the hat tight on his head, the folds of the black cape around his shoulders, the cool knife in his hand. The warm blood spattered on his fingers was so thick, it dripped.

But the thing that made it a nightmare wasn't the death or the body. It was the fact that Carver was happy about what he'd done. It was *so* much better, so much more satisfying than beating the man with his fists.

He woke with a start, sitting up in his bed, sweat on his brow. His right hand, the hand that, in the dream, held the killing knife, had fallen outside the protection of the blanket and grown cold.

The more his mind kicked in, the more nausea roiled his belly. A voice whispered in his head, mixing with the moaning of the patients, scratching at him like an insistent insect: *It was your idea. You are a killer's son.*

He looked around the octagonal room. Distant lights slapped at the dark, but the shadows held sway, thick as the dream fog. He *had* done the right thing, hadn't he?

He took some comfort that Hawking was near. *He* knew it was the right thing. Thorny as he was, there was something strong about his mentor's certainty, his conviction. It steadied Carver.

But . . . where was the sound of his snoring? He heard a thud from the floor below and assumed it was Simpson. More moans followed. The inmates were unusually active for so late. But if he could hear them, why not Hawking's breath?

A childish fear took him, probably because he was still so close to the dream. What if Hawking were dead? What if he had a weak heart or his old wounds had claimed him while he slept?

Carver rose, unsteady on his feet, and tried to peer into the nest of blankets across the room, the spot where his benefactor slept. It was hard to separate what might be blankets and what might be body, but everything seemed so still.

"Mr. Hawking, sir?" he whispered.

There was no answer, but he knew he was being silly. It was like when he was five years old and used to panic when Miss Petty was late coming back, fearing she'd died in some accident. But she always came back. He was surprised his mentor could evoke the same reaction.

But what if he had died? How could Carver be sure of *anything,* then?

More moans and thuds crept up from below. Fear seeped into his skin. He stepped closer. "Mr. Hawking?"

He was being ridiculous. The man would be furious if he woke him. But for some reason, even being yelled at would be comforting right now.

Carver hovered near Hawking's bed. He still couldn't make out his form. The pile seemed too flat. Heading for the window, he twisted a half-hung sheet, aiming the light from outside. The scant glow crept up the bed, over the rumpled blankets.

It was empty. Hawking was gone.

The sound came again from below. It wasn't Simpson. It was footsteps.

48

CARVER pushed open the door and peered down the asylum tower's spiral stairs. Faded light sliced the dark, but the tiled floor below remained cloaked in black.

The thuds came again, the moans and more. Scrapes and a crunch reached his ears, echoing through the halls. Carver held his breath and strained to hear just as the front doors squeaked open, followed by a whisper of wind.

And then, far below, one of the shadows *moved*.

It loped across the open area and made for the base of the stairs.

Someone was down there, but who? The possibilities flooded his mind. Was Tudd coming after him, looking for revenge? Was it a New Pinkerton agent, angry at the betrayal? But how would they

even know about it? Hawking was certain Tudd would never . . .
Where was Hawking?

The distant creak of a wooden stair. A gray blur with a glint
of silver slid along the railing, a hand. The hackles rose on Carver's back. His father? Had his father found him? The facts flashed
in his mind. His father knew he was at Ellis Orphanage; he'd sent
the letter there. They'd *met* on Leonard Street. How hard would
it be to stalk Carver, watch him and his mentor board the ferry,
ask the returning captain a few questions and learn his son was
here?

The steps creaked again, but the hand was gone. Carver had
no way of knowing which floor the figure had reached. Barefoot,
he padded down the steps, hoping to see before being seen. He
thought about the stun baton, remembered how sad Tudd looked
when he realized it was broken. Feeling naked without it, he
looked around for anything to defend himself with. Through the
windows, a pinkish ring hugging Manhattan told him dawn was
near. The dull light reflected a metal cart on the landing below.
A blade lay atop it. A scalpel. Well, it was something at least.

Staying close to the curved wall, he reached the landing,
grabbed the knife, then waited. He tried to listen, but the pounding of his heart flooded his ears. When nothing happened for a
time, it slowed and he had to wonder if he was imagining it all,
or maybe still dreaming.

Summoning his courage, he peered down the lonely hallway.
It seemed empty, nothing out of place.

Wait. There was. The narrow "mystery" door he'd seen
Hawking use once. Usually, it made such a neat line with the wall
it was practically invisible. Now it looked like it was jutting out,
ajar.

A bit of relief warmed Carver. His mentor could be in there, and at least his fear had given him an excuse to look inside. He headed for it, nearly reached it, but a cool wind from the open entrance blew it shut. With a click, its edge disappeared.

Worse, he realized he wasn't alone. The figure was there with him, on the same floor. At least his back was to Carver as he walked deeper down the hall. Its direction confused him. If it was his father, wouldn't he go straight up the stairs? No. Not knowing where his son slept, he'd have to search the building.

Carver pressed himself against the door until the figure slipped into a room. He heard papers rustling, a metal cabinet opening. The intruder was in a nurse's station, probably hoping to find some paperwork to lead him to Carver. He had to find Hawking.

Praying he was right about his mentor's location, he took the scalpel to the lock on the narrow door. It was unwieldy, thin but wide, more difficult to use than his nails, but it would have to do. With much wriggling, the latch pushed inward and the door came free, creaking as he pulled it. Beyond it was a steep set of tiny stairs, each step so small it seemed made for a child.

Terrified the creaking would alert the stalker, Carver left the door open as he crept up, trying not to slip. At the top, he reached a wider hall that ran the length of the patient rooms. One side had a series of angled windows, each looking down on a different patient. Must be some sort of observation area, for the doctors to spy on the inmates in secret.

It looked empty now, but there was an open area ahead, some sort of office. Perhaps Hawking was in there? Less worried about being seen or heard up here, he hurried along, only to freeze when he came upon the window that looked down into the nurse's station.

The glass reflected the dawning sunlight, making it difficult to see, but the stalker was definitely there, hunched over a file cabinet. This was no dream, no hallucination born out of fear.

Crouching, Carver moved past, then entered the office space. The clutter, mere chaos to some, had a kind of personality all its own that told him at once the space belonged to his teacher. There was a desk, half-buried in typewritten notes. A quick glance confirmed they were from Hawking. All, as far as he could tell, were either about various patients or the stupidity of particular doctors, *idiot* being the word that appeared most often.

There were a few recent train schedules in the pile, but before he could begin to puzzle over their presence, something else caught his eye, a *second* typewriter. Near as he could tell, it was identical to the one kept upstairs. An explanation was obvious enough. Hawking probably kept it there so he wouldn't have to lug the other around. But something about it still seemed odd to Carver, even if he couldn't say why. Maybe he was just disappointed at the *lack* of mystery. Otherwise, the space was empty.

Now what? The intruder was still below, and he was alone. Before Carver could decide his next step, a sudden pounding, less than a yard behind him, nearly made him scream.

"Got to get through!" a male voice said. "Got to get through!"

Carver whirled. Simpson. He'd somehow gotten out of his room and wandered up here. Now he was banging his head against the glass wall. *Thud! Thud! Thud!*

"Shh!" Carver hissed. He had to quiet him down.

Simpson, suddenly alerted to Carver's presence, banged his head faster and harder.

Thud! Thud! Thud!

"Got to get through! Got to get through!" he screamed. *Thud! Thud! Thud!*

If the figure below hadn't already heard him, it must have by now. Shoving past Simpson, Carver looked through the window in time to see the shadowy blur race from the nurse's station.

Footsteps rushed down the hall. The door creaked. He'd be here any second. There was no way out, no place to hide. Carver held out the scalpel and braced himself.

Black and terrifying, the figure appeared at the end of the hall and came forward.

"Go back to hell!" Carver screamed.

"Huh?" the figure said.

As it approached, Carver saw it was the wrong size and shape for his father. Beneath a heavy coat, a white uniform was visible. An attendant!

"What the devil?" he said. "Hawking's kid? What are you doing here screaming like a maniac?"

"It was Simpson. It sounded like you'd broken in," Carver said. "I'm sorry."

"Got to get through!" Simpson said. "Got to!"

The man scowled. "Some of the patients are on a new regimen, medicine every four hours, and I'm the lucky dope who has to give it to them. I'm so half-asleep, I must've forgotten to lock Simpson's cell. They could fire me for that. Would you mind keeping it quiet? I mean, no harm done."

"Sure," Carver said. "No harm done."

Making a quick exit, Carver could see that the pink ring outside had expanded. The dull light creeping through the windows did nothing to make the asylum seem less dismal, but it did make it seem less dangerous. By the time he made it back to the upper room, there was enough light for him to spot something he hadn't seen earlier.

Reading Hawking's words, as usual, made him feel even more foolish:

Had to get to NP. No news. Join
me after you've had breakfast.

"Sure," Carver repeated. "No harm done."

49

"IT'S m-madness, Carver," stammered a pale John Emeril on the subway platform. "Somehow, Tudd was found out and Roosevelt's tossed him in jail!"

"Jail?" Carver's jaw dropped.

Emeril tossed his hands up. "Thinks he's part of some street gang! Wants to make an example of him!"

As Hawking had instructed, Carver had returned to New Pinkerton headquarters. Of course, he was supposed to say nothing about what they'd done. To avoid looking Emeril in the eye, he looked around, surprised how quickly things had changed. Many of the open areas were empty.

Emeril went on. "We're losing people left and right. Jackson was one of the first to quit. He was loyal to Tudd, but others are worried that if he reveals our existence, we'll all be arrested, too."

"Everyone?" Carver said.

Emeril patted him on the shoulder. "Easy, there. I know Mr. Tudd. He won't talk. He spent years building this place. He won't give it up."

Carver felt a lump in his throat. "Is . . . is Mr. Hawking here?"

Emeril pointed to a lonely corner where the old detective sat at a desk with a typewriter, speaking somberly to an agent. "He's stepped in to keep things from devolving into total chaos. Technically, I'm in charge, but he's giving all the orders. Frankly, I'm relieved to have him."

Feeling too guilty to say another word to Emeril, Carver headed for Hawking.

"Don't worry," Emeril called after him. "Things will sort themselves out."

Poking one key at a time, the hunched detective cursed with great inventiveness. "Damn this infernal contraption!" he muttered as Carver neared. "I'm not used to it."

"Mr. Hawking, the place is . . ."

"Shedding deadweight," Hawking said. "Did you know Tudd had *three* of those electric carriages ordered? Thank heavens I was able to cancel the other two." He looked up from his work and scanned Carver's face. "What is it?"

Carver lowered his voice to a whisper. "Mr. Tudd in jail. And I feel like I've destroyed the place."

"Ridiculous. We've saved it, for the moment. And now you're free to tell Roosevelt all about the letter and your father. Isn't that what you wanted?"

"Yes, but . . ."

"Life isn't about easy choices. Even those who seek to do good do damage. Learn to live with it, or you won't survive the week."

"Yes, sir," Carver said. "Do you know where Mr. Tudd was keeping my father's letter and the immigration sheet?"

Hawking shook his head. "Another mystery. Mr. Tudd, thinking himself clever, decided to hide them."

"But Roosevelt thinks I'm his crazy nephew, or worse, a spy like Tudd!"

"Well, you are, aren't you?"

"Without that letter . . ."

"The only way to convince him would be to bring him down here," Hawking said. "Well, if that's what you decide, I won't stop you. I should warn the agents, though. Some of them, anyway." He cackled, amused.

"I have to stop my father," Carver said.

"Yes, yes. I detest repetition, but I'll say it again: life isn't about easy choices. What are your other options?"

"Look for the letter."

"Start with Tudd's office. We'll be staying the night later, I'm sure, so I've had a bed set up for you there. What else?"

Carver racked his brain, but nothing came to him.

"Come on, boy! Use that soggy melon on top of your neck."

"I don't know!" Carver snapped back. "It was a long day."

"Oh, the nights will get longer, even if winter nears. Trust me. Guilt is slowing you down. Get rid of it. Use the Pinkertons . . ."

"Follow leads," Carver said. "27 Leonard Street."

Hawking clapped slowly. "Yes. Speaking of, I had Emeril speak with the building owner by phone, a Mrs. Rowena Parker. She remembers Raphael Trone quite well. The woman's a night owl but agreed to meet us tomorrow, at what she called the 'unforgivable' hour of ten a.m. Emeril planned to go with several agents. You and I will now accompany them, Detective Young."

"Detective?"

"Oh yes," Hawking said. "We can do that now, too." He opened a drawer in the tiny desk, withdrew a leather billfold and tossed it to Carver. Inside was a gold badge with a number and his name. Carver's eyes went wide.

"Utterly useless," Hawking said. "Except to identify yourself to other agents, but I know how fond you are of shiny things. Good enough, Detective Young?"

Detective Young.

"Yes," Carver said. Then he added, "Thank you."

"You're welcome," Hawking grunted. He went back to his typing, pecking out a letter at a time. Carver eyed him a moment, realizing that despite his mentor's thorny exterior, he was actually growing fond of the man.

50

HOURS OF searching proved fruitless. Tudd's office had thousands of files and papers. All he'd have to do to hide the letter forever would be to slip it into the middle of a particular stack. He did manage to locate the lock-picking device he'd taken earlier and this time kept it, with Hawking's approval.

"Easier than making you a new set of keys," his mentor mused.

Carver used it to enter the area devoted to hand-writing analysis, but the space was even larger than Tudd's office, even more filled with papers. With the document expert nowhere in sight, it was a dead end.

During lunch, Carver had his one success. He'd brought along the stun baton, thinking he might somehow fix it. Though he couldn't make heads or tails of the thing and was too afraid of getting shocked to try to pry it apart, he did learn that the thick end had a little latch, and a short space behind it that had an oddly familiar shape.

On a hunch, he put the lock pick in it, thinking it might open the thing safely. Instead, it slipped into place with a loud *click*. Seconds later, the baton hummed. Carver had no idea how or why, maybe it'd just jarred a loose wire, but the lock pick had somehow fixed the thing. Who knew what else it might do?

By nine o'clock, the place was all but empty. His mentor was asleep on a cot on the plaza, to make his eventual exit easier. Carver was left alone in the dark of Tudd's office, surrounded by reminders of the man who'd betrayed him and the man he'd betrayed. At times, thinking of the badge in his pocket, he felt like he'd won something, at times he felt guilty, wondering what sort of cell the former agency head was sleeping in.

With the light off, Carver found he missed his asylum bed. The moans were unpleasant, but the total silence here was suffocating. Worse, the blackness kept shifting, first into something that looked like Tudd and then into the shape of a caped, top-hatted man. And to think, he'd once considered the darkness a friend.

Carver was exhausted. He dozed on and off, but each time he roused, his senses stretched into the void, hungry for something to see or listen to that wasn't his agitated imagination. Even a vague vibration in the mattress beneath him made him snap his eyes open and ask, "What was that?"

It was no use. He was too wound up to sleep. Thinking he might as well turn on the light and look for the letter again, he rolled from the bed and let his feet feel the cool oilcloth that covered the floor.

The vibration came again.

It was faint, but real. He remembered his stupid mistake at Blackwell, but this was no psychiatric hospital. It was a secret base, supposedly empty. Stilling his breath, he made out a slight, regular hum. It was the fan, the giant machine that powered the elevator and the subway.

Was someone using the train?

Slipping on his clothes, he crept into the hall. Pale moonlight dribbled from the high skylights, allowing him to make out the platform, the railing and the elegant curve of the car. It was still there, then, but the hum was louder. The fan was definitely on, and it shouldn't have been.

As he walked farther down the hall, Hawking's bed came into view. Empty. Suddenly worried, he picked up speed, but by the time he reached the platform, the car was silently receding into the tunnel.

Where was his mentor going at this hour?

He lowered himself onto the tracks and headed into the round tunnel. Compared to the sewers, the clean brickwork and constant tug of air was very pleasant. Ahead, the light from the receding car grew dimmer. As he walked in the gloom, every yard he stubbed his toe or nearly tripped on one of the rails. By the time he reached the frescoed walls and goldfish fountain at the other end, the car was empty.

Carver sprinted to the elevator, but it wouldn't respond to the call button. The air had gone still. The steady hum was gone. Hawking had turned off the fan. He didn't want to be followed.

Carver had never had to turn it on directly before. The pipes above switched it on automatically, as did the lever in the subway. If he returned to the car to start it up, the door would seal him in for the return trip.

He was losing precious time. Hawking already had a sizable

head start on him. He headed across the hall and examined the huge fan. A hand lever was mounted on the top half of the shaft's metal covering, but pulling and pushing it did nothing. He kept searching until he discovered a small bank of switches and metallic buttons. Of the largest two, a red one was depressed, and a green one sat above it. Thinking it the obvious choice, Carver pressed the green button.

After a click, the massive fan groaned into motion, pulling Carver's hair toward it. Across the way, the elevator door opened. He'd done it.

Minutes later, he was out on Broadway, searching the length of the street for his mentor's hobbling shape. He had to relax. He told himself Mr. Hawking knew what he was doing, but a sense of dread wouldn't let him go. When he again wondered where the detective would go, an unsettling answer came to mind: 27 Leonard Street.

Could he be heading there to meet the "night owl" who remembered Raphael Trone? Tudd wanted to catch the killer himself. Had the old detective lied for similar reasons? No. If anything, he'd be trying to protect Carver, in case the killer was watching. But who would protect Hawking?

Ignoring the cold, Carver ran the six blocks up Broadway, turned and rushed up the block. A bright light from the apothecary's second-floor windows told him he was right. Finding the door ajar, he pushed it open, causing a bell above the door frame to ring with an oddly cheerful sound.

"Hello?" he called. "Mr. Hawking? Sir?"

No response. He stepped along the aisles of tinctures and powders to the narrow staircase at the rear. The light was brighter above, and he trotted up the steps.

"Mr. Hawking?"

A door at the top of the stairs was open. Reaching the landing, he peered in. What he saw inside made him wonder if he'd ever woken up.

Hawking lay crumpled on the floor, like an old lion felled with a single shot. His head was twisted. A dark spot began on his forehead and extended past the hairline. Blood pooled near him, the edge of it just above his fingertips. It wasn't all Hawking's blood. Most belonged to the woman who lay lifeless on the center of an oval rug, the wounds around her neck and in her abdomen horrifically familiar.

Her expensive hat, once a delicate thing with ostrich feathers, had tumbled to the side, looking as if it had been crushed underfoot in a struggle. One of the huge feathers had come loose and floated in the blood.

Unlike at the Tombs, the colors weren't burned into unreality by arc lamps. The woman's wounds weren't blurred by wind and storm. It didn't look like a theater play.

"Help," Carver said. It came out as barely a whisper.

He stumbled out, down the stairs, crashing into shelves. Tinctures fell and crashed; powders scattered.

"Help," he said again, louder, but not nearly loud enough.

He fell into the door, nearly cracking the glass in it. He reached the street and sucked in the air. It filled every winding turn of his lungs with cold fire.

Now at last he had the breath he needed to scream, over and over again.

51

AS CARVER stood in the middle of Leonard Street, screaming, disturbed sleepers called from open windows.

"What's that racket?"

"Shut yer trap, street rat!"

A brawny woman, hair stuffed in a net, eyes half-open, hurled a milk bottle. Luckily her aim was so bad, the shattering glass came nowhere near him.

A policeman, compact, earnest, trotted down from the Tombs. When he saw the sweat on Carver's brow, the anger on his face vanished.

"Are ye sick, boyo?" he asked in a thick brogue.

Carver pointed to the apothecary. "In there."

"Closed, lad," the roundsman said. "Why not come inside with me now?"

Carver shook his head, trying to tear the words free from his throat. "Upstairs. M–m–murder."

The officer twisted his head as if he hadn't heard correctly. He looked and saw the light from the upstairs room spilling out the door and onto the sidewalk. He drew his billy club, though Carver wondered if his gun would be a better choice.

"Stay here," he said as he walked toward the door.

"What the devil's it about, Mike?" the brawny woman called.

"Don't know yet, Annie, but make sure this one doesn't leave."

She gave him a soldierly nod, then eyed Carver menacingly. "I only missed because I wanted to."

Seconds later, the policeman flew out the front door, face white. The screech of his whistle sounded like the death cry of some giant bird. A hawk.

Hawking. Carver was crazy to leave him alone up there. If he wasn't dead, he might be dying. Shivering, he took a few mechanical steps toward the store. "Mike" stopped whistling and blocked his path.

"My . . . father . . . ," Carver said. "Mr. Hawking needs my help."

"I'll see he gets it, but no one goes in there, boyo."

"My father," Carver said again.

"Yes, help's on the way for your dad."

"No, my *real* father . . . he did this."

Real father. He used the words, but was that really the case? It was Hawking who'd done so much for him, who'd believed in him.

The officer eyed him, decided that whatever was going on was beyond his ability to sort, then blew into his whistle again. More police streamed from the Tombs. In time, carriages arrived. The onlookers from the windows came into the streets, dressed in bathrobes. Carver still didn't move.

When the ambulance attendants brought Hawking out on a stretcher, he was ashen and limp. The side of his head was horribly swollen. Blood marred his scraggly hair. Carver had no idea if he was alive.

"Where are they taking him?"

"St. Vincent's," Patrolman Mike said, holding Carver back. "But you'll be staying here, boyo. A lot of people will want to talk to you."

"No!" Carver gasped. He couldn't talk to anyone now. He'd have to lie to preserve the secrets of the New Pinkertons, and he didn't think he'd be able. Yet, if Hawking were dead, what did any of that matter?

A quarter block from the scene, a hansom cab clattered to a halt and a bleary-eyed Jerrik Ribe clambered out. Still half-asleep, the narrow-faced man had trouble righting himself. Spotting Carver, he straightened. Even at the distance, Carver saw his reporter face ripple through several emotions: confusion, concern, opportunity.

Ribe strode toward him, his quick left and right glances again recalling the movements of a ferret. Thinking he'd rather speak to Jerrik Ribe than the police, Carver moved to meet him. A firm hand yanked him back.

"Orders are to keep you from the press," Patrolman Mike said.

"I know him," Carver said.

"He your father, too, then?"

Before Ribe could reach them, several officers interceded. "Get out of my way," Ribe said. "I know the boy. Is he under arrest? Is he a witness?"

A younger man in a trench coat stepped from the pack and moved toward Carver, blocking his view of Ribe. Carver was upset until he recognized Emeril's thin mustache. He was about to shout his name when a swift shake of the man's head indicated Carver should keep quiet.

Emeril took Carver by the elbow. "I've got him now . . . Jennings, isn't it?"

Patrolman Mike furrowed his brow. "Yes, sir. Found him screaming in the street. Says it's his father did this. *And* it's his father who was attacked and taken to the hospital. Next thing, he'll be calling *me* his father. Boy doesn't make much sense."

Emeril nodded. "Indeed he doesn't. Good work. Put it in your report and have it sent to me within an hour. I've got things covered here."

Mike Jennings's eyes narrowed even more. "Aren't you junior detective on staff . . . sir?"

Emeril nodded. "I'm also the only one awake. I'm sure someone suitably important will be here by the time everything's sorted out. For now, though, I'm in charge."

Satisfied, Jennings nodded. "Make it look like I'm being rough with you," Emeril whispered before pushing him toward a quieter spot.

Once a reasonable distance away, Emeril spoke quickly. "He took a bad blow to the head, a concussion. The ambulance attendants said there were no other wounds."

"But the blood . . ."

"None of it was his," Emeril said, clearly relieved himself. "Lucky for him, not so lucky for Mrs. Parker. Old Hawking must have stumbled onto the killer in the act. But the only thing that's really clear is that Hawking was holding out on me. What was he doing here to begin with?"

Carver's jaw dropped. "You didn't know? This was the last

address I found for my father. Mr. Hawking said he'd talked to you, that we'd all go in the morning."

Emeril scrunched his face. "He certainly didn't mention it to me. Tudd always thought he was half-mad. Dear Lord. Maybe the old lion wanted a final hunt for himself."

Seeing Carver's reaction to the word *final,* Emeril punched him on the shoulder. "Don't worry. Man with a skull that thick has got to pull through."

Someone called, "Detective," from the crowd. Emeril waved, indicating he'd be there soon, then turned back to Carver. "They want you at Mulberry Street, but I'll take you to the hospital. I can argue it would be inhumane to drag you from the side of your adoptive father. I will have to take your statement, though."

"I want to tell them everything," Carver said flatly.

Emeril winced. "Can't blame you for that, but the situation's sticky. Think about this: when Roosevelt sees you, he's likely to have you locked up like Mr. Tudd. Could be days before you get anyone to listen. Why not wait at least until we see how Hawking's doing?"

Something twisted in his gut. It sounded reasonable, yet another delay didn't feel right.

Emeril read his mind. "Carver, your statement will contain the truth, or most of it. You were adopted by a retired Pinkerton agent and studying the case as an exercise. Mr. Hawking took it on himself to visit an address he believed the killer may have lived at. You followed and saw what you saw. It is up to you."

With that, he hustled Carver into a police carriage. Hawking's words rattled in Carver's head in tune with the clattering wheels: *A truth that's told with bad intent beats all the lies you can invent.*

52

THE NEXT morning at St. Vincent's, newspapers lay in a staggered pile on a small metal table next to Hawking's bed. The headlines were visible at a glance.

The *New York Times* allowed itself an unusually sensational headline:

KILLER STRIKES AGAIN.

The *Sun* had the more poetic:

FEAR STALKS OUR STREETS.

The *Tribune,* the mysterious:

WHO IS THE LIBRARY KILLER?

But the *Journal* outdid them all with just three words that took up the entire page:

DEVIL IN MANHATTAN!

Hawking's clothes hung from a hook by the door, gray as his skin. A black wall clock signaled noon was near. The only color Carver saw was a fallen rose petal on the floor, looking like a splotch of blood.

The bouquet it was from belonged to an older woman, one of six patients moved when Emeril ordered the room be made private. Hawking's sudden fame as the only witness to the killer's work had also earned him police guards and a mob of reporters. Emeril explained he was also keenly worried about exposing Hawking to the cholera and typhoid common here. By and large, hospitals were charitable places serving the poor. Anyone who could afford it had physicians attend them at home.

The privacy and protection would soon end, though. The doctors made it clear Hawking could wake anytime over the next twenty-four hours. Since then, the senior detectives took to arguing over who'd question Carver first. Emeril would return soon to tell Carver who'd won.

While he waited, he stared at his unconscious mentor and the thick bandage wrapped around his forehead. He thought back to his first meeting with the gruff man, how his personality seemed as mangled as his body. A gnome, Carver considered him. But, *father*?

Hawking seemed to make what they owed each other feel like entries in an accounting ledger. Yet Carver was bereft imagining Hawking was hurt. The man had changed him, given him something solid to hold onto, something to replace his dime-novel fantasies. Almost like a . . . .

Like a real father.

The idea of not having him around felt suddenly unbearable.

The door opened and Emeril stepped back in. "Not good, I'm afraid," he said as he quickly closed the door, sealing off what seemed a crowded hallway. "Two detectives are to take you to a carriage out back, then to Mulberry Street. The commissioner has insisted on being present for questioning. They're trying to keep the press in the lobby, though your Mr. Ribe has already tried to sneak up the fire escape twice."

"Roosevelt will lock me up?" Carver said. "Unless I show him the agency?"

"Without that letter, most likely," Emeril said. "Eventually they'd add things up and realize Tudd knew more about the murders than he let on, but no telling how long that will take. Either way, I suppose that'll be that for the New Pinkertons, eh?"

Emeril gave Carver's shoulder a light punch. "Not your fault. There are three dead now. Keeping secrets always seemed silly to me; now it's downright dangerous. If anyone, Tudd ruined things by keeping your father's letter from them to begin with. I've got every agent looking, but we still can't find the thing."

Carver shook his head. "At least Mr. Hawking has a good excuse for his odd behavior."

"Well, don't be too hard on Tudd. The way I heard it, he was once in line for Roosevelt's position. Instead, he toiled in secret. Catching your dad himself might have made up for it, in his mind. Not an excuse, mind you . . . ," Emeril said.

Carver sighed. "At least once I bring the police down to the headquarters, Mr. Tudd will have no reason *not* to turn over the letter."

"Expect to find it empty. And keep in mind you really don't have to remember anyone's *name*. Bad enough that instead of heroes, we'll look like a bunch of bumbling fools blocking a police investigation into the crime of the century."

"I don't think you're fools, for what it's worth," Carver said. "Emeril, do you think by doing this, I'll actually help catch him?"

Emeril nodded. "We'll have a better shot. At last count, five people have confessed to the killings, one of whom has been on death row for a year. Men are lining up just to be the center of attention. They need the real story badly."

He headed to the door. "I've got to go help clear the floor. The detectives will be with you shortly. An officer has been stationed right outside the door if you need anything."

Emeril put out his hand. "It's been a pleasure, Carver Young. Just remember, even if you can't pick your parents, maybe you can pick your future."

"Thanks," Carver said.

"Nice to be running things for a few days anyway," Emeril said. He raised his eyebrows, inhaled and headed out the door.

Carver glanced at Hawking's still form, wondering what he'd have to say. On the wall, the clock's minute and hour hands lined up at twelve. The windows were closed, but Carver could clearly make out the bells from the nearby church. He counted the tolls.

Somewhere around the tenth, Albert Hawking opened his eyes.

53

CARVER yelped and nearly fell from his seat.

When Hawking tried to sit, Carver moved to stop him. "You should rest . . ."

Surprisingly strong, his mentor swatted him away. "Don't ever use the word *should* in the context of my behavior. Help me up, not down! I have to reach the lobby before the police realize I'm awake."

Carver's eyes narrowed. "You were awake all this time? Why didn't you tell Emeril?"

"He has enough problems; besides you heard what he said about secrets. Why complicate things for him?" Hawking rolled to the side and put his feet to the floor. "Get me my clothes!"

Carver didn't know whether to feel relieved or angry. "Are you planning to escape? You can't . . ."

"Not escaping," Hawking said with annoyance. "Taking charge. Don't dawdle." He motioned for the clothes hanging on hooks by the door. "*Obey,* boy. Obey! Once I'm out of this infernal hospital gown, you'll have White or whoever it is escort you to the bathroom for a pee. I'll do the rest."

"But, Mr. Hawking . . . ," Carver said as he moved to get his clothes.

"No questions," Hawking snapped. "There's no time."

Clothes in hand, Carver halted in his tracks. "No."

His mentor glared. "*What* did you say to me?"

Carver held his ground. "I've been sitting by your side like a mourner! I thought you were dead! I want to know what's going on. At least tell me what happened on Leonard Street. Was it my father who attacked you?"

Hawking pursed his lips as if struggling with himself. "You're lucky I'm in a hurry. I was at Leonard Street to protect you. I didn't see much of anything before I was knocked out."

Carver narrowed his gaze in disbelief. "Protect me? You said we were going together, with agents, but you hadn't even told Emeril."

Hawking waved his bad hand in the air. "Fine, I *lied* about Emeril because I didn't want you to suspect what I was up to. I was the one in touch with the late Mrs. Parker. She had business in the morning but was free that night. She agreed to meet with *me,* not a bunch of strange secret detectives, so I decided to go alone. I didn't want to put you at any risk, understand? There, you have your explanation. Clothes. Now!"

Barely satisfied, Carver handed them over. Once dressed, Hawking took his cane and tested his feet, wincing as he managed a small circle. "When they wheeled me in, I noticed the closest bathroom was under repair. White will have to take you down the hall, leaving the path to the stairs clear. Take your time about it, but keep an ear out for those two detectives Emeril named. Meet them in the hall if you can. If we're lucky, they won't even bother checking my room."

"What do I do then?"

"I'm getting to it! If things go as planned, in a few hours you'll be back at our gilded headquarters. But don't bother searching for your letter anymore. I think I know where it might be."

"Where?"

"I should have guessed sooner. Remember when Tudd asked if you'd brought the letter along and I told him you'd keep something so precious on your person?"

"So you think Tudd did the same?"

"Exactly. Probably sewed it into the lining of his coat, or they'd have found it when he put on his prison suit. The point is, for now, you may as well consider it lost, though I'm sure that won't stop you from going to Roosevelt. Once you're back, take the time to put your notes together and *then* go to him. I suspect, if you've the mind to do it that way, you can even set him on the right path *without* revealing the Pinkertons."

"How? Will you be there to help?"

"Unfortunately, no. I'll be very busy. But you'll need someone to keep your head focused. That reporter girl, do you trust her?"

"Delia?" Carver said. "She's never lied to me."

Hawking winced. "Fine, bring her with you. At least she'll keep your mind off your inner gloom long enough to focus on what you'll say to the silk cowboy. But if you're wrong, our headquarters will be on the front page of the *Times* tomorrow. I hope you appreciate how much I'm sacrificing for you, boy."

"I think I do," Carver said. It was the first sincere compliment he'd paid the man.

Hawking grumbled, not sure what to do with it. "Yes, well . . . you're welcome, I suppose. Now get going! I'm already late."

"Late?"

"Go!"

54

ANY JOY at seeing Hawking healthy swept away by a mix of adrenaline and confusion, Carver headed out, surprised how successfully Emeril had cleared the hall. It was empty except for the pudgy, deeply bored guard leaning against the wall, reading a copy of *Police Gazette*.

"I need a bathroom," Carver explained.

Grudgingly, he escorted Carver, as Hawking predicted, to the bathroom far down the hall. White remained by the sinks as Carver entered a stall. As the man talked about his back pains, Carver put an ear to the cold tile wall. He heard Hawking's distinct shuffling walk, a closing door, then a steadier, more distinct tromping. That would be the detectives.

Carver flushed and rushed out.

"Here's our boy," an enormous man with ash-blond hair and green eyes said. A second fellow, with

matted red hair, nodded gruffly. Both wore brown three-piece
suits and bowler hats, marking them as New York detectives.

They dismissed the police guard and escorted Carver to the
service elevator. Under the command of its white-haired operator, it crawled down with the speed and grace of a sleepy turtle,
making Carver sigh to recall the elegant pneumatic version.
Eventually, the doors opened on a small hall. An exit door opened
to a rear alley, a carriage visible outside. They were about to leave
when a hubbub arose from the lobby.

Curious, the detectives inched toward the commotion. Carver
followed, until they all had a view of the lobby. Scores of reporters were was fixed on a hatchet-faced man in an expensive black
suit—Alexander Echols, district attorney, the man Hawking had
once described as a lizard.

As Echols cleared his throat, among the crowd, Carver spotted
Emeril. At nearly the same time, Emeril spotted him. Eyes wide,
the junior detective made his way toward the rear hall.

Echols smiled, basking in the camera flashes. "I believe our
police commissioner is more concerned with investigating police
officers than murderers. Therefore, I have taken it upon myself to
use *my own funds* to hire the only man in this city who *has* shown
some success in hunting this savage killer . . ."

Echols motioned toward someone at his side, but Carver's
view was blocked. As he moved for a better view, Emeril reached
him and immediately tried to pull him back down the hall.

"What the devil's wrong with you? Get out of sight!" he
hissed.

Echols put his arm around his unseen companion. "He has a
singular reputation and was a star employee of Allan Pinkerton
himself."

Hearing the description snapped them both around. Standing beside Echols was a familiar figure, listing slightly as he supported himself on his cane and trying to shield his eyes from the flashbulbs.

"Mr. Albert Hawking."

"Well, he's full of surprises, isn't he?" Emeril muttered.

After a moment's silence, a torrent of questions filled the air.

"Did you see the killer?"

"Do you want Roosevelt fired?"

"Will you be working with the police?"

After straining to hear the wispy-voiced Echols, everyone moved back at the powerful sound that boomed from the hunched figure. "No! I did not see the killer. But he did see me. If you'll all kindly *shut up,* I'll save you some time and answer the obvious questions. I do *not* think Commissioner Roosevelt is incompetent. I simply do not believe he is as competent as I am."

A chuckle made its way through the crowd.

Jerrik Ribe called out, "What exactly did you see at 27 Leonard Street?"

As Hawking turned in Ribe's direction, he spotted Carver. Before answering, he whispered something to Echols, who nodded and snapped his fingers. "When I arrived, Mrs. Parker was already on the floor. From the nature and extent of the wounds, it was easy to see she was either dead or well beyond medical assistance. Moments later, I was struck from behind and would have almost certainly been killed had not my brilliant protégé taken it upon himself to follow me against my instructions—"

"Protégé? What's his name?"

"Carver Young. With a *c.*"

"The kid they're holding as a witness?"

Carver didn't hear the rest. An energetic man with a head of bushy chestnut hair and a trimmed goatee grabbed him and was rushing him back toward the service exit. Though also carrying a thin walking stick and a bundle of papers, the man moved so quickly, they were nearing the rear exit before Emeril and the detectives caught up.

"Hey, you!" one shouted. "He's in police custody."

The man pivoted gracefully, yanked off one white glove and extended his hand.

"Armando J. Sabatier, attorney. I've been retained by Mr. Echols to represent this young man. Are there charges against him?"

The detective was taken aback, as if by the brightness of the man's white teeth. "He's a witness and he's cooperating!" He turned to Carver. "You are cooperating, aren't you?"

The wiry man's smile vanished in a flash. He turned to Carver and shook his head, no. Though Carver had no idea what game Hawking was playing, he felt obliged to say, "I . . . guess not."

"You can't just take him. You'll have to wait for the commissioner."

"It's the other way round. *You* can't just hold him," Sabatier said plainly.

A white business card appeared in his hand as if by magic, and he handed it to Emeril. "The commissioner may contact me anytime to arrange a suitable time to discuss the case. We will cooperate fully, but I must insist on a far less conspicuous location than police headquarters. And I, of course, will be present during any questioning. Good day!"

Before another word could be uttered, Sabatier swept Carver into the alley.

55

CARVER and his new attorney shared a seat as the carriage wheels clacked east back toward Broadway. Sabatier remained pleasant, but not talkative. Carver wasn't quite sure what to say.

"Thanks," he ventured.

"You are welcome," Sabatier responded.

"So Commissioner Roosevelt will be in touch?"

"Of that, you can be certain."

"Can you tell me what's going on?"

"I'm afraid that beyond what I've already told the detectives, I do not know more. So, no, I cannot." He flashed his white smile. "I'm paid very well to know only what I am told."

Carver nodded and settled back in his seat. The leather was so much more comfortable than the steel hospital chair, he nearly fell asleep. Given what Hawking had promised, he wasn't surprised when the carriage stopped alongside Devlin's.

"I'm to drop you here," Sabatier said, tipping his hat. "And no, I do not know why."

"That's okay, I do," Carver said, exiting.

Once the carriage was out of view, he descended into the headquarters. If it'd seemed lonely when he was here last, now it felt utterly desolate. He walked along the plaza, eyeing Hawking's cot. It looked so comfortable, and Carver hadn't slept in at least a day. He wanted to call Delia and get started, but she'd be at work, unable to leave until later. Surely a little nap wouldn't hurt.

He tested the frame and lay down, thinking he'd close his eyes for a few minutes. Before he knew it, he'd drifted off to a deep, deep sleep, swallowed by the strangest dream.

Gone were all the buildings he loved so dearly, gone were the cobblestone streets, the asphalt sidewalks, the iron girders, the masses. Instead, he was all alone in an unrelenting field of dead, yellowed grass.

He shared the barren terrain with only one other living thing: a large, ugly-looking ostrich. After staring at Carver a moment, it thumped its heavy beak into his shoulder, over and over.

Thump! Thump! Thump!

He couldn't even raise his hands to block the blows.

Thump! Thump! Thump!

"Stop it!" Carver shouted. "Leave me alone! Leave me alone!"

The great bird reared back its head and hissed, "Wake up, boy!"

Carver opened his eyes. Hawking was standing by the cot, prodding his shoulder with his cane.

"I thought I'd have to draw blood to rouse you," he said.

"You said you wouldn't be here," Carver said, getting up. "That you'd be busy. Not that I'm unhappy to see you . . ."

Hawking slumped into chair, a strange expression on his face. Strange at least, for Hawking. He looked full of emotion, *sad.*

"There's been a change in plan," he said grimly.

"What sort of change?" Carver asked.

"Septimus . . . ," Hawking said. He was having trouble with the words. "Septimus Tudd. He's . . . dead."

Carver jumped to his feet. "Dead? But he was in jail!"

Hawking kept his steely eyes on the ground. "There's no law saying you can't die in a jail. Happens quite often. In this case, there was a riot. His body was found afterward. Strangled. My guess is he tried to help the police."

Guilt rattled Carver's body. "It's as good as if we'd killed him."

Hawking's cane slammed into Carver's shin.

"Ow!"

"No! Boy, it's *not*. I should know, *I've* killed. With guns, knives, even my own hands. *You* haven't, not yet, anyway. Believe me when I say I'm far more responsible for this than you. But Tudd made his own decisions, decided his own fate. He could have given Roosevelt that letter at *any* moment, stubborn old fool! And sorry as I am about what happened, this is *not* time to lose sight of our goals. Your father is still out there, remember? His next intended victim is still out there, too, *alive* as far as we know. *They* can be saved. That's where your energy must go. Understand?"

Carver rubbed his shin. "Yes, sir."

"Good." Hawking grimaced, getting himself together. "The question facing you now is, what are you willing to do about it?"

"What do you mean? The nap? I was so tired . . ."

"No, not the nap," Hawking said. He exhaled, then took another breath before explaining. "What did I tell you about your father's letter?"

"That Tudd probably kept it on him, maybe sewed into the lining of his coat . . . ?"

Hawking wiped his lips. "His body is in the prison morgue.

It's already wearing the clothes he was arrested in. That little device you have should handle all the doors."

Carver stopped rubbing his leg. "Excuse me, sir?"

Hawking twirled his cane, looking down, and muttered, "Steal to catch a thief, kill to catch a killer." He looked back up at Carver, sadness still in his eyes. "I never said it would be easy, but right now you have to ask yourself, how far, exactly, are you willing to go to catch your father?"

"You're asking me . . . to search Tudd's dead body?"

"The letter is evidence," Hawking said. "Keeping it from the police has been the real crime here. You said so yourself. Here's your chance."

"No!" Carver said. "Can't we just tell Roosevelt to look for it?"

"If I'm wrong, you'd lose your credibility with him forever. It's a body, boy, a hunk of flesh. My old partner is gone, enjoying whatever rewards the afterlife has to offer, if there is one." He looked at Carver. "Time to see what you're made of. Trust me, it's never a pleasant process for anyone."

56

OUTSIDE, it was still daylight. "Shouldn't we wait until nightfall?" Carver asked.

"There's no time for that," Hawking said, moving at a surprising clip. "The attendant has the next hour off. After that, they'll be transferring the body to a funeral home for cremation, and I don't know the address."

Carver, carrying a bundled stack of afternoon papers, struggled to keep up. "How do you know all that?"

"Emeril found out what he could."

"He's in on this? It doesn't bother him?"

"He knows it's necessary."

They paused on Varick Street and looked toward the Tombs. "Aside from all that," Hawking said, "we are close to your father's last murder, and I don't think he'd risk an attack in broad daylight."

The sight of the street put a chill in Carver's bones. The feeling grew as they passed where he'd seen his father, the apothecary where Hawking nearly died.

They crossed over to the Tombs, the air thick with sulfur, then walked past it to a smaller three-story building surrounded by an iron fence. Rows of curved half windows indicated the basement level. Hawking counted as they passed.

"Five . . . six . . . seven . . . there." He stopped and put his back to the fence. "Try not to make it seem that you're looking, but the morgue is right behind me. Tudd will be out on a slab, ready to be transported. I assume you remember what he looked like." He motioned with his cane down the block. "There's a side entrance twenty yards to my left. Once you're inside, you're a paperboy making a delivery who got lost."

"Mr. Hawking," Carver said. "I don't know if I can do this."

"Neither do I," said his mentor. "But we're about to find out."

Carver shifted his burden and walked off. He had the lock pick already out and under the newspapers, so when he walked down the two steps to a basement side door, he unlocked it so quickly, it looked as if it'd been left open for him.

Inside, he caught the door with the back of his heel so it wouldn't slam. After the police station and his earlier adventures, breaking into buildings was getting to be easy. The hard part lay ahead, beyond the double doors marked *Morgue*.

Exhaling, he pushed into them with the bundled newspapers. The wide room was cool, wide and lit by afternoon sun coming in through the half-circle windows. A chemical smell hit his nose. It was so strong, it made him want to retch. Embalming fluid. One wall held a series of small wooden doors with metal handles. The freezers where they kept the bodies.

At least he wouldn't have to go opening any of those. There he was, laid out on a metal gurney near the opposite wall, Septimus Tudd. Eyes closed, hands clasped over his belly, with his bowler hat lying askew on his chest. He looked as if he were napping.

Carver lowered the stack of newspapers against the door, then stepped closer. The more he looked, the more *dead* Tudd appeared. His chest wasn't moving, of course, but the skin on his sheepdog face drooped even more, in a horribly unnatural way, and his skin was a bluish shade of gray except for the dull purple bruise on his face where Carver had hit him.

"Sorry," he said softly.

Where should he begin? *How* should he begin?

He had to get ahold of himself, get this over with, just do it. He could get sick about it later. Forcing down some nausea from the chemical smell, he took Tudd's hat and put it aside. Starting slowly, he patted the left side of Tudd's jacket, disgusted by how cold the body beneath it felt, how much like a thing.

It got easier as he worked, but not very much. He carefully checked the jacket, the shirt, the sides of the pants, even the shoes. Nothing. Then he spotted the bowler.

He grabbed it. Running his hands along it, he felt an uneven bump beneath the brim. Excited, he worked his fingers into the gap and withdrew a folded envelope. Yes!

His excitement faded when he realized it wasn't the envelope his father's letter had been in. It was thicker, and the return address was Scotland Yard. Maybe Tudd had put it inside to better protect it?

Inside was a piece of thick slick paper. He opened it up. It was photographic paper, a facsimile, and on it, he saw another message in his father's hand.

25 Sept. 1888

Dear Boss,

I keep on hearing the police have caught me but they wont fix me just yet. I have laughed when they look so clever and talk about being on the right track. That joke about Leather Apron gave me real fits. I am down on whores and I shant quit ripping them till I do get buckled. Grand work the last job was. I gave the lady no time to squeal. How can they catch me now. I love my work and want to start again. You will soon hear of me with my funny little games. I saved some of the proper red stuff in a ginger beer bottle over the last job to write with but it went thick like glue and I cant use it. Red ink is fit enough I hope ha. ha. The next job I do I shall clip the ladys ears off and send to the police officers just for jolly wouldnt you. Keep this letter back till I do a bit more work, then give it out straight. My knife's so nice and sharp I want to get to work right away if I get a chance. Good luck.

Yours Truly,
Jack the Ripper

57

CARVER swooned. *Jack the Ripper?* His father was *Jack the Ripper?*

The abyss Hawking warned about opened wide. He felt himself ready to tumble in. The smell of embalming fluid was making him sick. The room began to spin.

A rapping came from the window. It was Hawking. Somehow, Carver dragged himself over and opened it a crack.

"What's going on?" Hawking whispered.

"My father . . . ," Carver began.

He staggered closer on wobbly legs. Risking discovery, Hawking turned and kneeled so Carver could see his face. "What did you find? Give it here."

Weakly, Carver handed him the letter. Hawking gritted his teeth. "The fool was hiding *this*? Did he really expect to catch the Ripper himself?"

"You knew what Tudd suspected? Why didn't you tell me?"

"Of course I knew Tudd's crazy theory. As for the similarities, I'm surprised you didn't suspect. A detective fan who'd never heard of the Whitechapel killings? You were seven at the time. Old enough to read the papers. Your father's letter was from London at the time of the killings. All you had to do was add."

Carver knew the name Jack the Ripper, of course. His horrible killing spree was the most famous unsolved case of all time. For four months in 1888, he'd butchered prostitutes in a London slum. At one point, he'd even sent the police a human kidney.

He was never caught. The killings simply stopped.

"Miss Petty wouldn't allow any newspapers in the orphanage during the killings," Carver said, remembering. "She thought it was too ghastly. I *tried* to read about it, but all I knew was what the cook told me."

Carver went to his knees. "My father."

"Boy!" Hawking hissed from the window. "Don't faint on me! I'll never get you out of there. Stand up! Stand up now! Get to the door. Get out of there. You need air. Move!"

Carver swayed but managed to numbly rise and follow Hawking's commands.

His mentor's voice kept guiding him. "That's it. Through the door, down the hall. I'll meet you."

The next thing Carver remembered was the fresh air hitting his face as he half-fell out the side door. A frantic Hawking grabbed him and quickly pulled him across the street.

"This isn't a story, boy," Hawking said as they walked. "It's life. It hasn't changed. You have. Welcome to the abyss. Now you have to decide whether to fall in or not. Shall I take you to Blackwell, have you set up in your own padded cell like that poor screaming woman who didn't care for the play?"

Carver exhaled. "Maybe you should."

Hawking shook him again, harder. "Don't be ridiculous. I won't have you ruining all my hard work. You'll continue, just as you did when you first suspected your father wasn't exactly as righteous as Sherlock Holmes. Remember what I said then?"

"I don't have to be like him."

Hawking nodded. "I also said you may have inherited some of his cunning. If he's the Ripper, you may well be brilliant. And, as I said before, the best suited to catch him. Understand that, boy? You wanted to be a detective? That was your dream? Well, here you are. A detective in the best crime lab in the world, in a position to catch the world's most famous murderer since Cain killed Abel. Now is not the time for weakness!"

But for all his grumpy talk, as they hobbled down the street together, for the first time it was Hawking who helped Carver stay on his feet.

58

BACK AT the headquarters, Carver sat slumped in a chair. Hawking stormed about, increasingly antsy. "I have to leave. Echols is expecting me."

"Why are you working for him, anyway?" Carver asked.

"Not now!" Hawking said. "I can't just leave you alone. In your mood, who knows what you'll . . . the girl! Call your reporter friend. Have her meet you outside. Tell her nothing over the phone."

"But . . ."

"Just do it."

Too weak to argue, Carver lifted the receiver of a candlestick phone. "New York Times Building, please."

As he waited, Hawking waved his good hand in the air. "The newsroom will be flooded with calls, fake leads, fake confessions. Ask for a different department. Where does she work? Say you have a complaint there."

When the operator answered, Carver said, "I . . . have a complaint about yesterday's Word Scramble."

"I'll connect you to that department, sir," a crackly voice said.

As he waited, he closed his eyes.

"Puzzle department," a poised young voice said.

"Delia?"

Her voice dropped to a whisper. "Carver, where are you? What's going on?"

He looked at Hawking. "Can you meet me in the park in about five minutes?"

"Five minutes? I don't have a lunch break for . . . Fine. I'll meet you."

No sooner did he hang up than Hawking hustled him back to the subway. "She can still help you with Roosevelt."

Carver sighed. "I didn't find the letter. I failed."

"You didn't fail," Hawking said. "If you couldn't find the letter, it wasn't there. You did well, just as you've done all along, by and large, and just as you'll do with what's to come."

Carver wanted to thank him for the compliment, but his shock had muted into numbness. The pair stayed silent until they were out on Broadway and Hawking hailed a cab.

"I'll be back as soon as I can," his mentor said as he climbed inside.

Minutes later, Carver was walking Delia through the park, hemming and hawing as he filled her in on the details of the last few days. Her face wrinkled as he spoke, and he feared he'd soon see that look of disgust in her eyes again.

"You had the man you punched put in jail and he *died*?" she said. "And it was your idea?"

Carver squirmed. "Delia, what was I *supposed* to do? You're the one who said it was wrong to withhold evidence! He told Roosevelt I was crazy! He was concealing the letter!"

She was unmoved. "What is this man training you for exactly, a life of crime detection or a life of crime?"

"Maybe this was a bad idea," Carver said grimly as they crossed Broadway. "I'd still be in chains if it wasn't for Mr. Hawking. He risked his *life* trying to catch my father."

"That just means he's crazy as well as underhanded. And now he's working for that . . . that . . . Echols."

Carver winced. "He must have a reason! Maybe it's the excuse he needed to work on the case. But . . . that's not even the worst I have to tell you."

He hesitated as they approached Devlin's, not knowing where to begin, fearing she would hate him forever. "Have you heard of Jack the Ripper?"

"So you've heard about the letters?"

"I've heard. And it seems there's little question. My father . . . the Tombs killer . . . and Jack the Ripper—they're all the same person. Maybe you're right to hate me. After all, I'm the son of the devil himself."

All at once, her displeasure melted into sympathy. "Oh, Carver, I'm so sorry. It's all over the newsroom. They're still fighting about whether to print the letters or not. I wanted to tell you, but I didn't know how to reach you. I can imagine what it must be like for you having . . . *him* for a father. Carver . . . I don't know what to say, I just feel so helpless, and I don't like feeling helpless. I want to *do* something. Wait, what are you doing?"

"There is something you can do." Carver got down on his knees beside one of the brass tubes. As she watched, fascinated, he twisted and pulled it in the proper combination. The door behind her popped open.

"That's spanking fine!" she said.

"Just wait," he said, motioning her toward the elevator.

Once they were inside the pneumatic subway, Delia was so thrilled she shook. Her excitement was so contagious, it took the edge off his gloom. "Is it the only one? When was it built? Why aren't they all over the city?"

He put his hands out, trying to stop the barrage. "I'll tell you whatever you want, but I want you to see something first," he said.

When they emerged, the look on her face, the rosy color of her cheeks and the twinkle in her eye made Carver feel almost proud.

"It looks better with people in it," he said.

"Well, *we're* here now. Carver, *why* are we here?"

He explained as simply as he could. "I don't want to reveal the New Pinkertons, but I want the police to know as much as I do. I'm their best link to the killer and I have to put it all together in a way that will convince Roosevelt. You're the writer, so I want your help. It'll be tough without my father's letter, but if it works, we can give the story to Jerrik first. Think that'll help his career?"

Delia beamed. "It'll do more than that! Thank you for asking me, really. I don't think I've ever done anything so important. How do we get started?"

He led her across the plaza and into the athenaeum. The cavernous space was empty, the massive rows of books daunting.

Even though there was no one to disturb, Carver whispered. "I guess we should start by finding out everything we can about Jack the Ripper."

59

HOURS LATER the oak table was full of notes, books and newspaper articles. They were piled so precariously, Carver imagined Mr. Beckley would explode if he saw it. With the librarian absent, he thought about trying the analytical engine, explaining the punch card system excitedly to Delia. But aside from the fact he didn't know how to use it, interesting as it was, neither could see how it would help.

Instead, Delia sat opposite him, fountain pen in hand, all business, and they began the same way Carver had when he first visited, listing what they knew: how Carver found the letter, where it was, the date. It was slow work. Each new question required flipping through dozens of pages, each revelation more horrifying than the last. Every fifteen minutes, Carver was ready to give up, but Delia kept pushing.

"Come on, you have to try." She repeated her last

question. "Your father's letter was dated July 18, 1889. Does that tally with the end of the Ripper killings, yes or no?"

Carver numbly nodded toward the collection of articles he'd just finished reading. "It depends on who you ask. The last of the five most famous victims, Mary Jane Kelly, was murdered on November 9, 1888, but there were more murders afterward that may or may not have been the Ripper. One of the last was named . . . McKenzie, I think. I remember because she was killed July 17, 1889, the day before the letter I found was written."

Delia made a note and then tapped her chin with the pen. "Any other connections between Whitechapel and what's happening here? Even the obvious ones?"

Carver stared into the dark.

"Carver?"

He shrugged. "They were all women."

"They say he hates women," Delia said.

"He certainly doesn't seem to like them very much" Carver said. "But maybe . . ."

"What?"

"Don't get offended, but maybe it was just *easier*. They were weaker. And the women in Whitechapel were poor, desperate, easy prey."

"Not here," Delia pointed out. "He's picked two wealthy socialites."

Why? He remembered Hawking's imperative, to think like a killer, like his father. Why would he make that sort of extreme change? Poor. Rich. It couldn't be a bigger difference.

Was that it? It was so different from Whitechapel, it was like the killer was pointing to it, the same way leaving the body at the Tombs pointed to it. Was it about getting attention? Carver frowned.

"What?" Delia asked.

"Something Hawking, Tudd and Roosevelt all said, and I haven't heard the three of *them* agree often. They all thought it felt like some kind of game. Poor women, now rich women, the body left at the Tombs, the letter to me and the *Times,* and the names leading me from one place to another."

"Names?"

"Jay Cusack and Raphael Trone," Carver said. "I got them trying to find my father, back when I thought that might be a good thing."

He watched as she wrote them down.

"One *s* in *Cusack,*" he corrected. "And *Trone* is . . . wait! Can I see that?"

He grabbed the sheet and stared at the first name, the extra *s* neatly slashed out. Jay Cusack. He'd said it to himself often enough, but now he felt as if he was looking at the individual letters for the first time.

"What do you call that puzzle thing you write with the scrambled letters?" he asked.

"An anagram?" Delia said.

"Yes! Look." Carver began scratching out letters. He'd barely found the word *Jack* when Delia blurted, "Saucy Jack! Jay Cusack is *Saucy Jack*!?"

Carver nodded. "The Ripper called himself that in one of his letters."

He pulled a newspaper archives from the pile and fanned through to a bookmarked page. "Here. It was a postcard sent to the Central News Agency. It doesn't show the handwriting, but this is what it said."

I was not codding dear old Boss when I gave you the tip, you'll hear about Saucy Jack's work tomorrow

double event this time number one squealed a bit couldn't finish straight off. Had not got time to get ears off for police thanks for keeping last letter back till I got to work again.   —Jack the Ripper

"Saucy Jack, and Boss again," Delia asked. "Who do you think Boss is?"

Carver shrugged. "He uses the word in the letters Scotland Yard thought might be real. It's also in both letters here. I thought it was someone he worked for, a real boss."

As Delia scanned the article, Carver looked at her notes again. *Raphael Trone.* He started crossing out letters again and this time, slumped back in the chair.

"*Raphael Trone.* Leather Apron. That's the first nickname the London newspapers gave the killer. It *is* a game."

"Between him and the police?"

Feeling sick, Carver shook his head. "Maybe it was in Whitechapel. Now I think it's between him and me."

"What do you mean?"

His voice grew distant. "Why send that first letter to the orphanage? Does he *want* me to know who he is, what he's done? Does he want to show off? You say I'm not like him, but look what I did to Mr. Tudd."

"You never killed anyone, Carver," she said, holding his gaze. She blinked and looked over his shoulder. "Oh, the clock. I'm so sorry, Carver, I have to get back. Do you think this is enough to go to Roosevelt with?"

"Without my father's letter? Do you think it's even enough to take to Jerrik Ribe?"

Delia shook her head. "We can go back to it tomorrow. Can

I at least hint something to Jerrik? It will make it easier to get here."

Carver shrugged. "Do what you think is right. Come on, I'll walk you out."

"I hate to leave you alone. Will you be all right? Do you have any idea when Mr. Hawking will be back?"

"He didn't say, but don't worry. There's no place safer than a secret headquarters, right?"

60

A FEW hours later, for the second time, Hawking shook Carver awake.

Carver blinked, rubbed his head and pulled himself to sitting.

"Did the girl help?"

"Yes, we found . . ."

"Not with the case, with *you*."

"Yes."

"Good. I've got some time away from Echols and his photographers. Tell me what you've learned and then ask your questions."

If Hawking was impressed with the clues Carver found, he didn't show it. He simply nodded. When Carver finished, Hawking said, "Your turn. Ask your questions."

"How long did you know about my father?"

"About as long as you *should* have."

"Why are you working for Echols?"

"Same reason everyone works. For money."

Carver narrowed his eyes. "You said he was a lizard. Do you need money so badly?"

Hawking lowered himself into a chair and looked around with an odd expression. "The money's not for me, you imbecile. It's for you."

"I don't need any money," Carver said. "I just want—"

"I know what *you* want. I'm talking about what I want *for* you," Hawking snapped back. "I don't have many plans left, and these last few days they've all come close to unraveling. Echols gave me a substantial retainer, enough to set you up even if the New Pinkertons are gone. Even after I've gone."

"Gone? Are you going somewhere?"

"Where I go and when I go is my business," Hawking said, looking even grimmer than usual. "But I suppose the rest isn't. Things have gotten darker than you know, and I'm not talking about your hobgoblin of a father. The *Times* decided to print their letter this evening, alongside the one from Scotland Yard. It came out a few hours ago, in their evening edition."

"The panic . . . ," Carver said.

"I told you the nights would get longer," he said. "Tudd was half-right when he said the game passed me by. It passed us *both* by. We're relics. Do you know what's going on out there? I've always said the city was a madhouse, and now it's beginning to show. Vigilante committees are forming." He eyed Carver. "I'm going to put you at the center of that storm. If it goes well, the winds will lift you above it all. If not, well, at least you'll have Echols's money to show for my efforts."

Carver shook his head. "But I don't want it," he said. "I don't want any of it. All I want is—"

"You're not being asked."

The phone rang. His mentor answered and listened intently.

"Of course," Hawking said. "Thank you, Mr. Echols. I'll head there immediately."

He put the speaker back on its cradle and looked at Carver, his face grim. "Do you want to lie down in case you feel faint before I tell you what he said?"

Carver shook his head. "I'm all right. Tell me."

"Another body's been found."

A fruit bowl sat on the desk beside the phone. Hawking grabbed an apple from it, buffed it on his jacket and then, thinking better of it, put it in his pocket for later.

61

AFTER THEY hailed a hansom cab clopping along Broadway, Carver asked, "Where was the body found?"

Hawking gave his answer to the driver, "Mulberry Street, number 300."

"Police headquarters?" Carver said as he helped the hunched man through the door. "You're taking us to police headquarters?"

Hawking waved off the question, settled back and closed his eyes. "I preferred it when you were more afraid of me, boy. Don't make me think about smashing something just to earn a respectful tone. I don't frustrate you without purpose. I simply don't want you prejudiced by anyone's half-assed theories, even my own. You've got eyes and you can put them to use soon enough."

Not so much mollified as stymied, Carver quieted. With the man's eyes closed, Carver took the opportunity to give his mentor a good look. He noticed it'd been harder to get him into the cab than usual. He was more unsteady. Was it the longer day? The blow to his head? How hard had Tudd's death hit him? Why was he talking about leaving?

One father at a time. The killer was still out there, more daring than ever. Another body—this one found at Mulberry Street. Had Tudd been right about a beast driving him? No, it was too reasoned, too complicated. It felt like another move in the game. But what was the point? Was his father showing off so Carver would want to be with him? If so, the effect was the opposite. More than ever, Carver wanted to catch him. Aside from stopping the murders, it would prove he wasn't anything like the man. It also felt like the only way to purge his own guilt, not only about Tudd, but also because he'd been so wrapped up in the killings, he felt somehow responsible.

As they neared their destination, the street was as dark as any other. The cab slowed, progress blocked by carriages jockeying for curb space and a growing crowd. He pressed against the window, looked around and up.

There was a white haze on the roof. The moving shadows told him it was full of activity.

"He left it up there," Carver said.

Hawking opened one eye. "Left it? You don't think he killed her there?"

The answer came with frightening ease. "No, he'd have been heard. He must have carried her up there, maybe left her in the snow."

Hawking rapped his cane on the roof. "Driver! Make a left at Mott and leave us at the Health Department." He pointed out the window. "Squint a bit and count the shadows, boy. The rooftops left and right are full of reporters. The Health Department abuts police headquarters from the rear, making it our best bet for a closer look. You'll have to help me manage the steps."

After navigating a U-turn, the carriage traveled around the corner, eventually depositing them at a large institutional building, its tan stones gray and black in the night. Finding an open side door, Carver helped Hawking inside. The detective grunted loudly with each step.

His mind was still sharp as ever, though. The darkened rooftop they soon reached gave them a perfect view of the light-washed 300 Mulberry Street. The slightly lower roof seemed again a crowded theater stage. Hidden by a wide brick chimney, they walked closer.

There were ten or so suited detectives at the scene. There were at least twenty uniforms and, of course, center stage, the square pacing figure of Theodore Roosevelt. All attention was focused on the new body. Again drained of color and humanity by the blaring light, it was wrapped in some sort of cloth. An arm and a pleasant round face jutted out at strange angles, the rest half-buried in a pile of snow.

The powder flashes from a police photographer's camera intensified the bright arc lamps.

"Confound it! Confound it! Right here all along!" Roosevelt cried.

Carver turned to Hawking and whispered, "All along?"

"Echols said they think this woman was killed the same night as Rowena Parker. A double event," Hawking said softly.

Double event. It sounded familiar. Carver grabbed Hawking's shoulder. "That was what the papers later called the Whitechapel murders of Elizabeth Stride and Catherine Eddowes, both killed on the same night."

His mentor nodded, either in acknowledgment or approval, then pointed back to the scene.

Roosevelt could barely contain himself. "We'd never have found her without that letter! I told you it was real! A newsboy could have identified that handwriting. A challenge to everything decent. Do we have the woman's name yet?"

"Another letter?" Carver asked.

"Hush! No need to repeat what you've just heard. I want to hear the name if they have it," Hawking said.

"Petko? Reza? Is it Russian? Locate the poor woman's relatives immediately," Roosevelt said. He stepped closer to the body and shook his head.

"Parker and Petko!" he declared, rounding on his detectives. "Both begin with *P*. Does that tell us anything? Eh?"

The detectives lowered their heads in unison. They continued to earn Roosevelt's expectant stare until he offered, "Could he be going through the social pages? Alphabetically?"

"It's a thought, at least," Roosevelt said. Raising his head, he spotted the moving shadows on the neighboring roofs. "It seems we're giving an interview to every paper in the city!" He waved. "Hello, Mr. Ribe! If I can spot a rhino in the brush, I can certainly see you! Go home along with the rest of you! You'll all have to wait for the official report! I *will* learn to speak softly one day, but when I do, I promise you, I will also be carrying a very big stick!"

He motioned all the detectives toward the rear of the roof, away from the reporters but nearer to where Carver and Hawking hid. He also made good on the promise to lower his voice. As they huddled, the last few words Carver could make out were, "And no one knows yet that the . . ."

If only he were a little closer. He stepped on the ledge, braced himself against the chimney and lifted himself. The move would've been silent if his shoe hadn't settled on a loose brick. It flew free and thudded loudly onto the roof less than two yards from Roosevelt.

62

WITH surprising force, Hawking yanked Carver behind the chimney and pulled himself up onto the ledge. "Boy!" he hissed. "Stay put!"

When the misshapen man appeared on a roof they thought vacant, twenty or so uniformed officers drew their pistols. Though his balance seemed precarious, Hawking didn't move.

"Excellent reflexes, men," Roosevelt said. Carver was close enough to see water vapor coming from his mouth. "But we'll have to work on your thinking. Guns down and turn a light on him."

With a metallic creak, an arc lamp spun toward Hawking. "Tilt it up. We don't want to blind anyone!"

The light dimmed slightly. Roosevelt's face registered recognition. "You, sir, are my nemesis, aren't you? Echols's great detective? Former Pinkerton?"

Hawking nodded, but barely.

The commissioner offered a toothy grin. "I know something of the work. In Medora, North Dakota, more than ten years ago I was a deputy sheriff. I hunted down the three outlaws who stole my boat. Caught them, could have hanged them, according to the law, but I guarded them for forty hours until assistance could arrive. Read Tolstoy to keep myself awake. I did it, because I put my faith in the system, not *vigilantism*. Do I make myself clear?"

"Tolstoy puts me to sleep," Hawking said, in an equally loud voice. "I prefer Dostoevsky's *Crime and Punishment*, especially the punishment."

He put his cane to the slightly lower ground of the Mulberry Street roof and, with difficulty, climbed down. "Oh, but to punish the *guilty*, you'd need to catch the criminal, wouldn't you? That's why Echols hired me."

Carver had seen Roosevelt angry, but never so stone-faced. He raised his index finger to Hawking. "In our great nation, Mr. Echols is free to say what he likes, both to the press and to his servants. Yet he is not free to act in contradiction to the law. I will not tolerate any interference in this investigation."

Hawking lowered his voice. "I've no such intention, Commissioner, none at all."

Roosevelt narrowed his eyes. "How, then, do you intend to fulfill your obligation to your employer?"

"As an asthmatic child, your doctor warned you against a strenuous life, did he not? You rejected that advice, with great results, so I'll assume you're familiar with the expression don't just sit there, do something?"

"It is a favorite," Roosevelt said.

"You may *not* have heard the dictum, since it is my own, don't just do something, sit there. That, sir, is my intention."

To Carver it sounded like the strangest thing his mentor ever said. It didn't make any sense.

Roosevelt's small eyes glowed as he scanned Hawking's face, taking his measure the way Carver had seen Hawking do dozens of times. All at once, as if he'd stumbled upon something unexpectedly vile, the commissioner took a step back. He wiped his mustache with his thick hand and then stiffened to attention.

"Sir, I misjudged you. You are not in the way of this investigation, you are *nothing* to it. There is no fire in your belly, none at all. You ask no questions, you provide no information. If I thought he'd listen, I'd instruct Echols to get his money back and spend it on a more useful tracker, like a bloodhound. Any animal at all, really."

It was the worst insult Carver could imagine. Roosevelt paused, waiting for a reaction, but none came. "Your attorney informed us that you and your ward will be at his office at nine a.m. sharp for a complete interrogation. If you do not appear, I will have you arrested. If you remain here now, I will also have you arrested, whereupon you may sit and do your great nothing in one of our fine prison cells."

Roosevelt spun back to the detectives. Hawking clambered back over the ledge.

"Time to head home, boy," Hawking whispered to Carver. "We'll have to hurry before the reporters make it around the block."

Carver was confused to say the least. "That's it? We barely looked at the murder scene. There must be a clue here from my father. And what was all that about doing nothing? Are you feeling all right?"

"What we need to know will be in the papers. It's far too crowded, the light too bright."

Hawking ambled toward the stairs. Carver followed. "You sounded as if you don't intend to find the killer at all."

"I *don't* intend to find the killer," Hawking said, not even slowing his descent.

Comfortable they were out of earshot, Carver said, "What? How can you stand there . . . how can you . . . say something like that as if it's obvious, as if it's adding two and two to get four? People are dying! Is this some kind of game for you, too?"

As if Carver weren't even there, Hawking calmly leaned against the wall and withdrew the apple from his pocket. He sliced off a piece and popped it into his mouth.

As he chewed, he said, "A game for *me*? No, boy, not at all. As you said yourself, it's a game for *you*. Apple?"

63

CARVER and Hawking barely exchanged words as they headed back to the abandoned New Pinkerton headquarters. Carver wanted to scream, to grab Hawking's cane and beat him with it until he made sense. Instead, he just felt nauseated. Had the blow to his head, Tudd's death, or both left the man completely insane? Carver couldn't do this *alone*. He needed help.

After a fitful night and equally wordless breakfast, they headed to the attorney Sabatier's office on Centre Street. Hawking hadn't even told Carver how to handle the questioning.

The tension on the streets was even more palpable. News of the fourth killing spread like wildfire. The fear seemed writ as large on people's faces as it was in the headlines. Pedestrians walked faster, rudely shoved one another, seemed ready to fight at the smallest slight. Newsboys shouted reminders, calling out every word of the letter sent not to some paper, but directly to the police:

Dear Boss—

Gave you a real two for one. Had not the time to get you the ears this go either. Thanks for keeping the letter back till I got my work again. Near the end now, but catch me if you can.

Yours truly,
Jack the Ripper

His father wasn't even bothering to conceal his identity anymore. From his reading, Carver knew the middle part of the letter was practically a quote from the "Saucy Jack" postcard the Ripper sent in London on October 1, 1888. He was too furious to even mention it to Hawking. He didn't want to disturb him while he was so busy "doing nothing."

Echols was waiting for them in the marble lobby of the law office. While he wasn't surrounded by photographers, as usual, he also wasn't alone. Finn was with him. It was an awkward surprise. Carver hadn't seen the powerful redhead since the night he'd helped him break into the editor's office. So much time had passed, so much had happened, he had no idea how to react to his old nemesis.

"I trust we have no worries here, Mr. Hawking?" Echols said, holding out his hand. Hawking balanced on his cane and put his good left hand forward.

"Not a care in the world," Hawking said.

They fell to whispering, their murmurs echoing in the gilded lobby. Carver wanted to try to hear what they were saying, but a sudden tug on his arm turned him toward Finn.

They grunted hellos, Finn seeming as uncomfortable as Carver. Delia said the bully had tried to lie to protect them, so Carver felt he owed him an apology for getting him in trouble in the first place, but the words wouldn't come.

With a sneer, Finn nodded toward Hawking. "So that's the best detective in the world? The only reason my . . . Mr. Echols . . . hired him was to get more photos of himself in the papers. He couldn't care less about catching your dad. So what's been going on?"

Though mad at Hawking himself, Carver did not care for Finn's tone. The last thing he wanted to do was confide in his former tormentor about Hawking's bizarre speech last night.

"Nothing," Carver said.

Finn looked confused. "Nothing? Did we break into that office for nothing?"

Many emotions fought for control over Carver. "We? It looked to me like *you* did it to impress Delia. Beside, when did you ever care what you might be stealing?"

Carver realized he was being ridiculous. He was trying to think of some way to say so when Finn moved to slam him in the shoulder. No longer a frightened little boy, Carver blocked his meaty hand.

If Finn was surprised, he didn't show it. "You're helping Echols and you're still lying about me being a thief?"

He shoved Carver with both hands. Carver shoved back. "You *did* steal that necklace. Why can't you just admit that much at least?"

"You *still* haven't told anyone about that letter from your old man, have you? What does that make you?"

Without thinking, Carver socked Finn in the jaw. As he did, a sharp pain traveled from his knuckles, along the back of his hand and up along his arm. But it was Finn's jaw that took most of the blow. The large youth's head snapped sideways, his eyes widening in disbelief and fury.

After that, things happened so quickly, it took time for the adults to react. In response, Finn reminded him exactly what *scrawny* meant. He grabbed the slighter boy by the belt and lapel, lifted and *threw* him three feet into the wall. Carver's back hit hard, winding him. He fell but scrambled to his feet, still ready to fight.

Finn came forward with his left. The meatier fist barely grazed his chin, but Finn followed up by forcing the top of his skull into Carver's abdomen. He wrapped his thick arms around Carver's waist, planning to slam him down onto the hard, expensive marble tiles.

Carver refused to go down easy. He dug his elbows into Finn's wide back, hitting his ribs below the shoulder blades, making them both fall sideways. On the floor, they pummeled each other.

Even a soft punch from Finn was nothing to be sneezed at. One landed on Carver's ear, filling his head with a dull ringing. He let fly with a decent shot to Finn's nose.

Above the throbbing came the muffled bark of adult voices. The next thing he knew, Finn was sliding away along the marble floor. Carver felt himself lifted by his shoulders.

"Cease this nonsense at once!" a voice bellowed. Carver twisted and saw he was being held by no less than Commissioner Roosevelt. Would there ever be a moment, he wondered, where he didn't look like a thief, liar or fool to the man he had to convince about his father?

Two detectives were holding Finn, the raging youth helpless against them. Echols rushed up. "Release him at once! Release my son!"

When they let go, the wealthy man pointed a bony finger into Finn's face. "How dare you cause this scene! You're lucky the press isn't here yet! I should throw you back into the gutter where we found you!"

Finn, flushed with rage and embarrassment, muttered, "You'd be doing me a favor."

"You can let him go now, Commissioner," Hawking said, trudging up on his cane. "There'll be no further trouble. Right, boy?"

Carver eyed his mentor. "Yes, sir."

But Roosevelt ignored Hawking. He kept his hold on Carver until the slight Echols had shoved Finn out the front door. When he did let go, Carver stepped away and straightened his clothes.

"I'm sorry," he said, still panting.

"You *are* sorry," Roosevelt said. "Sanity is in short supply lately. Hold on to what little you have." He turned to Hawking. "And you, sir, are as poor an example of a mentor as you are a detective!"

There was a barely perceptible twitch in Hawking's lip. "It won't happen again."

Roosevelt seemed oddly disappointed, as if he'd hoped Hawking would fight back. "Well, then, see that it doesn't."

They entered the elevator; the operator closed the door. Carver was close enough to Hawking to hear him say, softly, "We shall see how poor an example I am."

Whether he heard him or not, the commissioner struck a more respectful tone. "Hawking, I've been reading about you. It's a matter of record that you worked with Septimus Tudd at the Pinkertons'."

"Has the interrogation begun?" Hawking said.

"No," Roosevelt said. "I only wish to offer my condolences. As the man who had him arrested, I can't help but feel some responsibility for his fate. But I know what I heard him say on the phone. *He thinks I'm completely loyal. There isn't a shred of evidence to connect me . . .* Had he at least owned up to that much, he might be alive today."

Carver cringed.

This was not going to be easy.

64

"**THE KILLER** is your dad, and you're part of a secret detective organization?"

"Yes."

"In Devlin's department store?" a detective asked for the thousandth time.

Once inside the plush offices, Carver and Hawking had been separated. As he was led away, his mentor didn't offer so much as a meaningful glance. Carver decided to tell the truth, but it turned out to be more difficult than lying.

"Underneath. The headquarters was built as an extension to the Beach pneumatic subway," Carver said.

"Perhaps you rode on it as a boy?" Sabatier put in, his smile unwavering. "I know I did."

His green eyes darted from the detectives to

Carver to Roosevelt. "Surely two such great minds can at least come up with new questions?" the attorney prompted.

The detective gave the slight Sabatier a wicked stare.

Roosevelt exhaled. "He's right. This isn't getting anywhere. Sabatier, I want to speak with the boy alone a moment. Without all this . . . formality."

Sabatier shook his head. "I'm afraid I can't allow . . ."

"It's all right," Carver said. "Anything's better than just sitting here repeating myself."

The lawyer rose smoothly. "It's against my better judgment, but as long as you realize any private conversation will not be admissible in court?"

Roosevelt nodded. Sabatier turned to the detective. "Perhaps I can interest you in some scotch?"

"Not while I'm on duty," he grunted.

"Perhaps you'll enjoy watching me have some, then," Sabatier said, walking out with him. Before closing the door, he glanced back at Roosevelt and said, "Ten minutes. No more."

Roosevelt stepped closer to Carver. "The fellow you fought with before was much larger than you. Are you in the habit of challenging impossible forces, or did you know him?"

"Both," Carver answered. "I know Finn from Ellis Orphanage."

"You got in a few good shots. It was impressive, but not right."

"I said I was sorry."

"For hitting him?"

"No . . . for the circumstances."

Roosevelt allowed himself a chuckle. "Bully. So you'd rather do something than just sit there, unlike your Mr. Hawking, eh? No need to answer that. The purpose of having you repeat your story was to try to uncover inconsistencies. You know that, don't you?"

"Yes," Carver said.

"There weren't any, which means either the lies are well prepared or you believe what you're saying. The late Mr. Tudd wished me to believe you were deluded, but he also wished me to believe he was loyal to me. I know that wasn't true, and you sound fit to my ears. You interrupted the party at the *Times* because you'd found the letter upstairs and were convinced it was from your father?"

"Yes."

"At the Ribes' you were prepared to tell me the whole story, but Tudd stopped you?"

Carver nodded.

"Alice was impressed with you," Roosevelt said, narrowing his eyes. "I'm not, not completely, not yet. Being sane doesn't mean you're telling the truth. The anagrams you've uncovered are based on a trail that began with a letter you say has gone missing."

He clasped his hands behind his back and stalked around the office. "I make it my business to know my enemies well. Echols is a lizard. Would you agree?"

"Yes," Carver said, surprised Roosevelt used the same word as his mentor.

"He seeks to undermine me partly because he owes much to the corruption I'm fighting, partly because he loves the attention. Yet you'd have me believe that unlike Mr. Hawking, Tudd was *not* working for Echols. Instead, he remained silent to defend the existence of a wondrous organization. At the same time, a room away, your mentor has said nothing about them or about your relationship with the killer. Why?"

"I don't know," Carver said.

"Can you guess?"

He didn't want to say what he was thinking, that lately his mentor seemed increasingly unbalanced. "He's protecting . . . me? Wants me to be the one to show you? He sees a great future for me."

"Does he? Jail is not a great future, young man. You should consider your opportunities more carefully."

Carver scrunched his brow. "We don't all have the same opportunities, sir."

Roosevelt nodded. "True enough."

He leaned his square head and beady eyes forward. "I don't know what to make of you. You're intelligent, you seem principled, but there's something about you I can't place. You're like some new creature one might stumble across while hunting. But I've bigger game to hunt and can't be sidetracked. In the end, it's simple. My detectives will take you to Devlin's and you can show them this magical headquarters of yours, if it exists."

Carver exhaled and grinned. "Thank you."

"For more reasons than one, I hope it does," Roosevelt said. "Such an organization could be invaluable. If it does not, if you are trying to deceive me for any reason, as soon as we've caught the killer and I can spare the time, I will make sure charges are brought against you for interfering with a police investigation."

Though Roosevelt meant to frighten him, Carver kept smiling. "Don't worry. It's there."

Roosevelt gave him a sharp nod and exited.

Mysteriously, Hawking remained behind, but shortly, Carver, Sabatier, and two of Roosevelt's detectives stood on the side of Devlin's.

Thinking that Roosevelt's last words meant there might be a future for the New Pinkertons after all, an excited Carver knelt by the four curved brass posts. The detectives positioned themselves on either side of the off-color concrete rectangle. Sabatier busied himself by filing his nails.

"It's sort of like a combination lock," Carver said.

"Get on with it."

Grasping the tube with both hands, he twisted and . . . nothing.

It wouldn't budge. He grabbed and turned again, harder. Was it jammed? He tried a third time, twisting hard until his hands squeaked across the cold surface.

The detectives eyed each other.

"It's here!" Carver shouted.

"Just like a combination lock."

"It's right here! Don't you understand? Someone's changed the combination!" Carver kicked and pulled at all four tubes but couldn't get one to budge. It was only when a small crowd paused to stare that he finally stopped.

As one detective motioned for the onlookers to keep moving, the other turned to Sabatier. "We'll go tell the commissioner. He will make good on bringing those charges."

"Good thing the boy has an excellent lawyer, then, isn't it?" Sabatier said with his bright smile.

The two detectives climbed back into the police carriage and drove off.

"I don't understand," Carver said, tugging at the posts.

Sabatier waited until the detectives' carriage was out of view, then pulled a white envelope from his jacket pocket and handed it to Carver. "For you."

"What is it?"

"I do not know."

"Who is it from?"

With a tip of his bowler hat, he said, "Good day, Mr. Young," and melted into the midday crowd.

Furious, confused, ashamed, he tore open the envelope and unfolded the single sheet of paper inside. There, painstakingly typed, one letter at a time, was the new combination.

65

CARVER once enjoyed the elevator's pneumatic silence but this time wished for some noise to
drown out his pounding heart. He stormed the cor-
ridors, paced the subway car, then stood in the center
of the lonely plaza and screamed, letting the sound
echo along every hollow in the empty headquarters
of the finest crime lab in the world.

It's a game for you.

Now there was no way he could prove anything
to Roosevelt short of solving the case himself. Was
that what Hawking thought would make Carver rise
above the chaos? And where *was* the mad detective
now? Limping back to the Octagon to count Echols's
money? Was there anyone left in his entire life that he
could trust?

After another scream, he grabbed the phone and
dialed the *New York Times*.

"There's a rumor going round that you *lied* to Roosevelt?" Delia said in a hushed voice.

"Actually," Carver said, gritting his teeth, "I'm in trouble because I tried to tell him the truth. Can you come to Devlin's? I'm going stir-crazy; I could use some help . . . or even some company."

"Considering the fact that everyone is in the newsroom talking about the latest murder and I'm stuck here trying to make up puzzles, I'm dying to do *something.* Just give me fifteen minutes to finish today's anagram. Honestly, a monkey could do it."

The line went dead, but Carver felt some of the enormous weight he'd been carrying lift, just a little.

When he opened the elevator door to the street, she was already waiting.

"That was fast," Carver said.

She gave him a knowing smile and pushed in beside him. "I've got an hour, maybe two. Everyone's so distracted, I don't think anyone noticed when I said I was going for lunch. So what happened?"

Carver filled her in as quickly as he could.

The first thing she said was, "Poor Finn."

"Poor *Finn*?" he said, aghast. "He insulted Mr. Hawking!"

"He only said what *you* were thinking. Is that why you called me here, to feel sorry for you?"

He wanted to say *yes, of course.* "No . . . but . . . what do *you* think of Hawking?"

"Assuming you're not going to punch me for agreeing with you, you're probably right. The attack and losing Mr. Tudd may have shaken his brain loose. In a *very* weird and horribly *dangerous* way, he seems to be still trying to teach you."

"By making Roosevelt think I'm a liar?" Carver said as they entered the empty athenaeum.

"Well," Delia said, "he has left you with a nice library."

Originally, he'd only wanted to see her, but seeing their worktable made Carver eager to do something rather than "sit there." He pulled a chair out for her.

"Big deal. All the books in the world are useless unless you know what to do with them. My father's been leaving clues to his identity, anagrams of his names, but that's not exactly an address we can look up. We have no idea where he is or who his next victim might be . . . unless . . . he left a clue about that, too?"

Delia stared at him dubiously. "It'd have to be a *very* good clue. There are a million people in the city, at least."

Carver slumped into his seat. "Mr. Hawking taught me to narrow the list based on what I know. We know the Ripper attacks only women, right?"

"So that cuts it down to half a million," Delia said.

"But it's not just women, is it?" Carver went on. "In London he may have targeted prostitutes, but in New York he's gone after only socialites. That cuts it down a lot, doesn't it? What else do we know? Anything, even what's most obvious."

"Most obvious? He's fond of word clues and names, his at least."

"His name. That's good," Carver said. "What about the victims' names?"

He tugged at a bound newspaper volume from 1889 and opened to a bookmarked page. "This reporter tried to figure out where the Ripper lived. Assuming he had to be in Whitechapel somewhere, he made this list of the victims and where they were killed."

He pushed it near her and pointed to the list:

Mary Ann Nichols, Buck's Row
Annie Chapman, Hanbury Street
Elizabeth Stride, Dutfield's Yard
Catherine Eddowes, Mitre Square
Mary Kelly, Miller's Court

"Fine, but what are we looking for?" Delia asked.

"I don't know. You're the puzzle expert. Any kind of pattern in the names? The dates, the words, something . . . ?" Carver said.

"You mean, like maybe he's duplicating the original crimes somehow?" Delia said. "It's not an anniversary; the dates don't match . . ."

"There was a double murder," Carver said. "He even quoted the original letter. Stride and Eddowes were killed on the same day, like Parker and Petko. Roosevelt noticed that both their last names start with a *P*, but what could that mean?"

They stared at the list long and hard, coming up with nothing. Delia broke the silence. "Maybe we're doing this backward."

"Okay, I'll list the new victims," Carver said. He'd just finished writing when he made a face.

"What?" Delia said. He turned his pad toward her and pointed to the list of the victims' names:

Elizabeth B. Rowley
Jane H. Ingraham
Rowena D. Parker
Reza M. Petko

"I don't understand," Delia said, scanning the list. "I . . ."

Confident she'd see it any second now, he waited. Before another word could form, her eyes lit. "Oh my heavens! *RIPP*, the last names of the victims are spelling out *Ripper*. It's his name again!"

"All except an *e* and an *r*." Carver nodded. "Another stupid game. And two murders yet to come."

"I can't believe no one noticed this," she said.

Carver shrugged. "Maybe someone has; maybe the police are working on it right now. I told Roosevelt about the anagrams. He would have believed me if Hawking hadn't changed . . . Where are you going?"

Delia was rushing to the shelves. "If we're right," she said, "the next victim is going to be a wealthy woman whose last name starts with *E*."

She returned with a volume of a recent social directory, flipping the pages as she walked. She slowed and stopped, disappointed. "Edders, Egbert, Eldwin . . . there are *hundreds*."

Remembering his own daunted feeling when he started searching for his father, Carver said, "That's better than half a million."

"If we can't save her," Delia said, putting the open book flat on the table, "it's not better than anything at all, is it?

"Is there anything else? Some other kind of pattern?" Delia ventured.

"What about the locations?"

"The Lenox library, the Tombs, police headquarters," Carver said, shrugging. "City buildings."

Up against a dead end, they scanned the list of the dead, new and old, over and over. As they worked, Carver's tired mind drifted, but he enjoyed having Delia here so much, he didn't want to say. He found himself staring at her skin, her cheeks, especially when she pulled back from the table and stretched her neck.

She stopped stretching and noticed him. Their eyes met.

"I should get back," Delia said. "Maybe I can sneak out early and we can try again. At least I can tell Jerrik about how the names spell out *RIPP*. That's something they won't ignore."

As she rose, Carver felt a sudden urge to stop her. He nervously turned away, his eyes falling again on the list of new victims, Elizabeth B. Rowley at the top.

B. Rowley, B. Rowley. There was something familiar about that, but what?

"Buck's Row," he said aloud.

"What about it?"

"B. Rowley. B. Row. Buck's Row. It's where Mary Ann Nichols, the first victim, was killed. The *B* is part of Rowley's middle name, the first victim here."

Delia stiffened, then sat back down. "Not just her middle name. It's the custom for women to use the initial of their maiden name."

They hovered over the list. "Jane H. Ingraham. Can we find her maiden name?" Carver asked.

They pulled out the articles covering Ingraham's death, nearly ripping the pages in their haste to split them up.

"Here!" Delia shouted, her voice echoing in the empty space. "In the obituary. Jane *Hanbury* Ingraham!"

"Annie Chapman, second original Ripper victim, killed on Hanbury Street," Carver said. "So there's got to be more, right?"

Though they failed to find anything spelling out Reza M. Petko's middle name, Carver uncovered a social announcement listing Rowena Parker's father as John Dutfield. Elizabeth Stride had been killed in Dutfield's Yard.

"Which means," Delia announced, "the next victim would have a married name beginning with *E* and a maiden name beginning with *M,* for Miller's Court."

Carver slowly nodded. "Where Mary Kelly, the Ripper's final Whitechapel victim, was found. She was . . . she was the most brutally butchered of all. But we'd still have to go through each name beginning with an *E*. It would take hours, maybe *days*."

"We should get started, then," Delia said, grabbing the directory from the table.

"Wait," Carver said, snapping his fingers. "The analytical engine. Emeril said it contains most of the upper-class citizens in the city, and there's no one here to stop us from trying it out."

Delia made a face. "But you don't even know how to work it. And wouldn't we have to create our own punch card to ask the question in the first place?"

Carver headed for Beckley's desk. "I know where the instructions are. We could at least take a look. And you're good at puzzles! A monkey could do it, right? What's the worst that could happen?"

66

DESPITE Delia's protests, Carver handed her a thick manual explaining how to create a punch card. Apparently, it wasn't as difficult as she feared.

"Huh," she said. "The cards are a little like the patterns they use in an automatic loom. I saw one once in the Garment District. Instead of making a shape, each hole in the first two rows represents a letter. The rest of the rows tell you which bit of information it refers to, first name, last name, street, and so on . . ."

But Carver wasn't listening. He was too busy fretting over the second manual, the one explaining how to get the labyrinth of spindles, rods and dark gears moving.

In less than half an hour, Delia produced a card she was reasonably certain asked for any women with a last name starting with *E* and middle initial *M* and was eager to try it out. Carver was still busy reading, though.

"Can you do it or not?" she asked.

Carver frowned, stared, but then suddenly grinned and said, "Yes!"

"You're sure?"

"No," he said. "Not at all."

Taking Delia's card, he headed for one end of the huge machine. There, he carefully positioned the round holes in the thick cardboard over a set of matching metallic fingers. Before trying to start the engine, as the manual said, he checked to make sure the main gear wasn't engaged and the boiler had sufficient water.

As Delia looked on, he put paper and coal in a small furnace alongside the boiler and set a match to it. As the fire heated the water, the pressure gauges rose. In short order, the main gear began to turn.

"That's it!" Carver said, terribly pleased with himself.

"But it's not doing anything," Delia said, pointing to the rest of the machine.

"Not yet," Carver said. "I have to engage the gear."

When the needle on the gauge was in the green, Carver pulled a lever that lowered the turning gear. For a moment he was afraid nothing would happen, but the whole machine shuddered. Its pieces began to move. He understood at once why Beckley hated the sound. It was dreadful, as if they'd been locked in a closet with a locomotive, but still, amazing to watch.

Spindles, with steel wheels imprinted with numbers and letters, turned. Rounded metal fingers poked up and down, grabbing this and that. Within the frame, scores of punch cards shifted, faster and faster, almost like marbles rolling down a maze. Hyp-

notized by all the moving pieces, the cards that seemed to magi-
cally sort themselves, neither Delia nor Carver noticed for several
minutes that the athenaeum was filling with smoke.

Carver's eyes snapped toward the boiler. Cotton-thick clouds
rolled from beneath it.

"The fire's not vented!" he cried, rushing for it.

No sooner did he yank open the little iron door than a lungful
of smoke sent him staggering back. He'd only made things worse.
Now sparks flew from the fire as well. If one red ember should hit
a book or paper sheet, the whole place would go up. Perfect. First
he nearly destroyed the place with a flood, now he was on the
verge of completing the job with fire.

"Water! Get a bucket of water!" he called to Delia, but he
couldn't even see where she was.

Eyes tearing, he forced his way back toward the boiler. Wrapping his shirt around his hand, he managed to close the door.
Then, holding his breath as long as he could, he headed for the
back of the machine, hoping to find the equivalent of a chimney
flue.

But he could hold his breath only so long, and time was running out. There *had* to be a vent; there *had* to be. At last his teary
eyes spotted a tin cylinder leading up from the back of the furnace. There was a knob on its surface. He lunged for it, twisted it
and stepped back.

Above the din of meshing gears, he heard a small electric whir.
He staggered back into vaguely cleaner air, gasping and coughing
as Delia rushed up, water sloshing in the basin she carried.

Between gasps, he stopped her. "Wait . . . I think . . ."

As he spoke, the air already seemed clearer. Soon, while there
was still a substantial haze, most of the smoke had cleared.

"Whew," he said.

Delia seemed equally relieved, but then she pointed at the analytical engine. "The gears are still turning, but the cards aren't moving anymore. Is it broken?"

Carver walked up to the far end of the machine. "I think it means it's finished." He reached down and withdrew a piece of cardboard with several freshly drilled holes. "And this is our answer."

"One card?" Delia said.

He shrugged. After sorting through hundreds of Jay Cusacks, it did seem strange. "Maybe the list is incomplete. The machine could be broken, or maybe there really is only one possibility."

"What does it say?"

He handed her the card. "You'll have to tell me."

Delia seemed to have forgotten all about returning to the *Times* as she worked, checking through the codebook. A few minutes later, her face went white.

"What is it?" Carver asked.

"Samantha Miller Echols," she said hoarsely. "Finn's mother."

67

CARVER tried calling the Echolses, but their butler wouldn't put him through.

"I work with Mr. Hawking!" he said, frantic.

"We've received dozens of prank calls about the murders," came the dull response. "Why can't the operators show at least some judgment in who they patch through?" The line went dead.

Hoping he could get Hawking to call, Carver tried Blackwell, but his mentor wasn't there. Had the man abandoned him completely? *Now?* Carver stormed around, growing more and more agitated.

A worried Delia tried to calm him. "It might *not* be Mrs. Echols. You said yourself the machine could be broken."

"Of course it's her!" Carver snapped. "Don't you get it? He knew I was at Ellis. That's where he sent the letter. That means he'd know about Finn, too.

And thanks to Echols, Finn's face has been all over the papers. It's a connection to the press, to the wealthy, to the clues *and* to me! I've got to go there. They'll recognize my face at least."

"Then let's go," she said.

They emerged from Devlin's a little after five. The rush-hour streets were jammed, the waiting line for cabs as thick as the foot traffic. As Carver led Delia across Broadway, he nearly yanked her into the path of an oncoming streetcar.

"Carver!" Delia shrieked. "You've *got* to relax!"

"The Echolses are on Fifth and 84th," Carver said. "We can take the Third Avenue El at Fulton Street up and then walk over. That'll be fastest."

Delia eyed the Times Building. "Wait! I can tell Jerrik! *He* can call the Echolses."

Carver shook his head. "Echols won't *listen* to a reporter; he only likes talking to them."

"The police, then," Delia said.

"No! They've already passed judgment on me and my stories thanks to Mr. Hawking, remember?" He stopped and looked at her. "Delia, I don't want to lose you. You're . . . the only person I have left here, but you should do whatever you think is right. If you want to go tell Jerrik and see what he can do, fine. I have to go find Finn."

She shook her head. "Then I'm with you."

They dodged, ducked and, when a gap in the crowd allowed, ran. They crossed beneath the steel girders of the elevated tracks just as a squat locomotive and its four passenger cars came to a halt above them, sending flecks of rusted steel tumbling like burnt orange rain.

As they raced up the stairs, Carver said, "No time for tickets. We'll have to jump the gate. Ready?"

"It won't be the first time. I'm an orphan, too, remember?" Delia said with an odd pride.

The crowd made it easy. They made it onto the platform and boarded the most densely packed car. That way, there'd be no room for a conductor to move around, let alone check for tickets. The train's loud hiss and lurch as it pulled out reminded Carver of a fire-belching black dragon he'd once seen in a painting, being slain by some saint or another. And the black dragon reminded him of his father.

He was wedged against a businessman attempting to read the evening news. The car was a sea of open papers, all with loud headlines about Jack the Ripper and the body atop 300 Mulberry Street. The last time he'd been on a train, people read, but they also spoke to one another. Now the only sound was the *chuff-chuff* of steam escaping the valve cylinder as the piston pushed the wheels.

They'd be there soon enough, but how would he approach Finn? The last time they met, they'd beat each other senseless. The whole fight seemed so petty now. So what if Finn had stolen some necklace? He *had* been returning it. And Carver had done worse since. Delia was right.

She always did seem to side with Finn, though. Oh, what did it matter if she had feelings for him? Carver's own heart was such a muddle. It wasn't as if he had anything to offer beyond his hor-rifying lineage. Bodies flashed in his mind's eye, his father in the alley, the man's speed, his strength—Carver's scrawny hopeless-ness. He had to calm down, keep his head, or all would be lost.

As it was, he barely noticed the train coming to a halt at 84th Street. Delia had to pull him out to the platform, where the dis-embarking passengers scattered quickly, eager to get home.

It was fully dark now, overcoats melding with shadow, faces

tinted by electric streetlamp. Even so, it was easy to see they'd entered a different world. Delia and Carver weren't dressed badly, but not nearly well enough for this neighborhood, full of expensive hat and clothing stores, furriers, tobacconists, ritzy dining establishments and upper-class homes. Even the horses didn't smell as bad.

As they walked, their clothing was noticeable enough to attract attention, not from the police, but from a group of men in three-piece suits. They were marching along like they were soldiers, headed straight for them. Carver and Delia looked down at their feet and tried to walk past but had to stop when the barrel of a rifle appeared beneath Carver's chin.

The others formed a semicircle around the youths, some hitching their thumbs in their pleated pants to reveal holstered pistols. Carver put his hand around the stun baton, but there were so many of them.

"Do you have business on these streets?" said an earnest, unfriendly man with deep-set eyes.

"We're visiting a friend, if it's any concern of yours," Delia said.

"Delia," Carver cautioned. His eyes were on the rifle.

"You should be more careful about where you walk. Women have been turning up dead lately, in case you haven't been reading the papers."

"I not only *read* the papers," Delia said, glaring, "my father is Jerrik Ribe, the reporter covering the murders for the *Times*."

"Oh, is he?" the man said.

"Are you with the police?" she demanded. "And if not, what do you mean by interrogating us?"

He sneered. "The police? If they did their job, we wouldn't be out here, trying to keep our homes safe."

Before Delia could say anything that might agitate them, Carver said, "I work with Albert Hawking. He thinks the police are idiots, too."

The man's eyes opened wider. "Hawking? The detective Echols hired? What a famous pair, then. How lucky to run into you. I'm Abraham Lincoln's nephew!"

The men laughed. "My name is Carver Young," Carver said. "Check a newspaper if you like. I'm the one who found Hawking at the murder site on Leonard Street. We're heading to the Echolses' with a message from him."

The leader looked back at the others. A thin man with a paper under his arm nodded. "Okay, then. Give Mr. Echols our regards. And be careful."

"We will," Carver said. He took Delia by the elbow and hurried away.

She turned to him, exasperated. "Militia on the street? It's insane. They're more dangerous than the Ripper."

"If only that were true," Carver said.

68

WORRIED another group or the police might stop them, Delia and Carver rushed past homes that were each more lavish than the last. Servants peered from behind satin curtains, tall windows suddenly darkened. Neither had ever been to the Echolses', so they passed the large marble building front three times, both thinking something so large must be a museum or a gallery. At last recognizing the number, they mounted the wide steps, both adjusting their clothes to make themselves more presentable.

"What should we say?" Carver asked. "The butler didn't believe who I was on the phone."

Delia pushed ahead. "Let me do the talking. I can be more diplomatic."

"Like you were with the militia?" Carver said with a smile.

Ignoring him, she turned a golden knob that

caused a pleasant ringing sound. The wide black door opened a crack and a sour-faced butler peered at them. "Yes?"

Delia cleared her throat. "Good evening. We're friends of Phineas."

"Are you?" he asked dubiously. "You don't look like garbage shovelers."

"Why on earth should we?" Delia answered, already looking annoyed. "Is he in?"

Carver rolled his eyes.

Not caring for the tone, the man was about to turn them away when a voice called, "Delia!"

The butler looked as if he still wanted to close the door but, with an exaggerated sigh, pulled it open. A posh entry hall and an enormously wide staircase appeared behind him. Finn was on the fifth step, looking, if possible, even more out of place than Delia and Carver.

He galumphed down the stairs, his heavy footfalls echoing. Seeing Carver, he stopped short.

"I'm not here to fight," Carver said. He wanted that to be enough, but Delia nudged him. "I'm sorry . . . about all that," he added halfheartedly. "We have to talk to you about something important."

"*Very* important," Delia added.

Finn's glance moved between their faces, his expression changing depending on whom his eyes fell on. Looking at Delia, he nodded. "Fine. Come in, but be quiet. Mr. Echols is in the study."

They stepped onto the tiled marble floor and stared up, slack-jawed, at the crystal chandelier hanging from the high ceiling.

"It's from Europe or someplace," Finn grunted. After an annoyed look at the butler, who was obviously listening in, he nodded at a hall to the right of the stairs. "There's a garden. Cold, but private."

"You won't be requiring refreshments, then," the butler said with a sneer.

"He doesn't like me," Finn said as he marched them past a series of paintings, small statues and delicate vases. He eyed a particularly old vase as if he wanted to smash it. "He thinks I'm a rap . . . rap . . ."

"Rapscallion?" Carver offered. Finn looked at him the same way he looked at the vase.

In the center of the house, they reached a set of framed glass double doors. Finn didn't bother turning the finely wrought handle; he just pushed, nearly cracking the wood. He stalked into a courtyard with a garden. Its flower beds and fountains were covered up for the winter months.

Delia paused by the doors to close them quietly.

"You're lucky that giant pulled me off you," Finn said to Carver.

Carver felt himself tense. "*I'm* . . . ? I'm . . . sorry about all that." He still didn't sound like he meant it but thought it was an improvement.

Finn slumped into a chair, looking embarrassed. His face and bull-like body half in shadow, he said, "What do you want?"

"Maybe I should start," Delia said. Carver grunted.

As she spoke, Carver looked around. It was a cool night, but warmer and quieter in this protected space. Tall columns ran up to the full height of the three-story building, ending in a rectangle of sky. The window lights dimmed the pinprick stars but not the moon. It was out and bright, half-hiding behind a wide, oddly shaped chimney.

It was hard to tell what Finn was thinking as he listened to Delia. Carver thought he'd be upset, worried to hear of the threat, but he reacted so little. Delia, who knew him better, paused several times to ask, "You believe us, don't you?"

Numbly, he nodded.

Didn't he even care? Carver knew Finn was unhappy, but did he hate his adoptive parents so much that part of him might prefer to see them dead?

But when she finished, Finn rose, his head blocking Carver's view of the moon and chimney. "She's here. I'll tell her. I don't know if *she'll* believe *me,* though. Then again, they might think it'd be a great way to get some more photos in the papers."

"Phineas," Delia began. Remembering her promise, she corrected herself. "Finn, do you want us to go with you?"

"No," he said, eyeing Carver. "You should just go."

They stood awkwardly.

"Maybe we could help," Carver said. "They know I'm Hawking's student."

"No!" Finn barked, but he didn't look angry, he looked . . . ashamed. For the first time, Carver realized how stupid the Echolses made the bully feel. After years of being top dog at Ellis, he didn't like appearing weak. Carver felt the same way around Hawking, even more so lately. Were they so different?

"Finn, listen, back at the lawyer's office, you were trying to help. I was . . . being stupid."

"Wouldn't be the first time," Finn said.

Carver sighed. "I'm trying to say I really am sorry. I'm sorry for getting angry. I'm sorry for hitting you. I'm trying to tell you, I know how it feels, in a way. My real father aside, I've got my own problems with Mr. Hawking."

Finn recognized the peace offering but didn't know what to make of it. "I didn't steal the necklace."

Carver fought an urge to roll his eyes. Worried he'd say something that would get them fighting again, he looked up, then noticed the odd chimney. It wasn't just odd; its edges were wavering in the wind, as if it wasn't a chimney at all.

And then it vanished.

69

"THE RIPPER!" Carver said, pointing. "He's on the roof!" He raced for the glass doors. His father had been watching all along, listening, waiting to be seen.

"Where's your mother?" Delia asked Finn, voice tinged with panic.

"She's not my . . . Upstairs, in her bedroom." Finn sounded surprised by the sudden commotion, as if the danger hadn't dawned on him yet. Carver once made fun of the bully's slower thought process, but now he pitied him. Whatever the three of them did in the next few minutes could change all their lives forever.

His hand on the gilded knob, Carver realized he wasn't thinking fast enough himself. He turned back to Finn. "What's the fastest way up there?"

"Not that way," he answered. Picking up on their

urgent tone, he ran, not toward any door or window, but at one of the thirty-foot stone columns.

"What the . . . ?" Carver said.

Less than a yard away, Finn leapt, wrapping his arms and legs around the cold cylinder. Without so much as a beat, he began shinnying up to the roof.

"Finn, don't!" Carver warned. "Not alone!"

"Done it a hundred times," Finn called back. He was ten feet up and rising.

But Carver wasn't worried about him falling. Finn was strong, but the Ripper was beyond human. He wouldn't stand a chance.

Carver dashed for the nearest column. He pulled his chest into the cold surface and pushed at it with his feet. He wasn't nearly as fast as Finn, but he was moving.

At his back he heard a helpless cry from Delia. "I can't climb that!"

"Get help," Carver called. At least one of them should do the intelligent thing.

Hearing nothing else from her, he assumed she was doing as he asked. Now his attention was torn between climbing and watching Finn. By the time Carver was at the halfway mark, Finn was at the gutter, clambering over the ledge. He crawled across the roof's six feet of angled terra-cotta like a huge red-haired spider, then disappeared onto the flat middle.

It would take Carver less than a minute to get up there, but how long did it take to kill someone?

His hands reached the gutter, but when he pulled, it nearly tore free. He stretched his arm for a stronger handhold, found one and dragged himself onto the shingles. Somewhere above he heard scuffling and a groan.

He wanted to pick his head up to look but had to stay flat to keep from rolling off the roof. Quick as he could, he clawed and kicked, cracking the ceramic shingles, then heaved himself onto the flat black tar-pitch.

He rolled onto his feet, pulled out the baton and pressed the single button.

Schick!

The weighted feel of it humming in his hand might have made him more confident if he were facing anyone else. As it was, between the exertion and the fear, Carver was so out of breath he felt dizzy. His gaze darted around. Away from the window lights, the stars were brilliant, the moon bright. Everything else was shadow.

"Carver," Finn moaned from somewhere.

Holding the crackling copper tip out in front of him, he peered among the silhouettes. "Finn, are you all right? Did he cut you?"

"No," Finn said weakly. "But I think he broke my arm. I can't . . . can't move it. Hurts . . ."

"Where is he?" Carver said.

Hearing footsteps against the tar paper, he whipped the cane to the left and the right. "Finn," he said again. *"Where is he?"*

Two thick rectangles stood about four yards away, one on each side of the flat roof. Their brickwork glinting in the moonlight told him they were definitely chimneys.

A hunched shadow moved from behind one of the chimneys.

Before Carver could react, the killer appeared. A single step had brought his tall body within a single stride of the fallen bully. He faced Carver.

My father.

He was tall and straight, draped in a black cape, a top hat on his head. As if a magician performing a trick, he withdrew a long, sharp butcher's knife. It sang, like a sword drawn from a scabbard, and then seemed to float in the air, the only glowing thing in a world of blacks and grays.

Then he pivoted and lunged toward Finn.

"No!" Carver screamed. He raced ahead, stabbing the killer in the shoulder.

Kzt!

The man let loose a weird howl. Carver expected him to fall, but he didn't. Instead, he batted the stun baton out of Carver's hand. It went flying. He was weaponless. But knowing if he gave up now, Finn would die, Carver barreled forward and slammed into the killer's side. His father might as well have been made of stone for all the good Carver did. With a slight grunt, the killer wrapped his left arm around Carver's chest, then threw him.

Carver's right shoulder took the brunt of the fall, landing on a fallen chimney brick with a sickly crack. A rough hand flipped him on his back, sending waves of agony through him.

The figure towered over him. For the first time, Carver could clearly see his face, so gleeful, so hungry, so aflame. No nightmare could do it justice. It was long and strong, almost the way he'd imagined Sherlock Holmes would look but younger, with thicker, curly hair and a twisted demonic grin. His eyes were wide circles filled with a sort of joyful fury. Adding to the terror, Carver saw something hauntingly familiar in the visage, something he couldn't, or didn't want to, place, maybe because it reminded him of his own.

Finn moaned pitifully.

"Run!" Carver called. "Get out of here!"

The Ripper shook his head slowly and said, "No."

Carver knew what he meant. Finn would not be running. Not anymore.

Holding his blade high, the killer turned back to the helpless figure, the boy who'd once, long, long ago, been the thing Carver feared most in the world.

With no time to hunt the darkness for the baton, he used his good left hand to grab the brick he'd fallen on. Screaming loud and long, as if he were a beast himself, Carver rose and rammed the brick as hard as he could into the side of his father's skull.

WHACK!

"Aghhhh!"

The Ripper wasn't off his feet, not by any means. His grin replaced by fury, he staggered. He'd been hurt. A thick blob of glistening liquid made its way down from his dark hairline.

"What are you going to do now?" Carver asked. "Kill your own son?"

Carver would never find out. Finn, from the ground, unleashed a powerful kick at the Ripper's right knee. Carver swore he heard a bone crack, though it might have been the sound the dropped blade made when it hit the roof.

Favoring his other leg, the Ripper snatched up his weapon. By then, Finn was on his feet, stepping back but clenching his fist, ready to strike.

The figure looked from one boy to the other. He moved forward, testing the distance, but when his leg nearly buckled, he turned and seemed to leap off the roof.

Carver and Finn looked briefly at each other, then raced to the roof's edge in time to see the Ripper clamber down the outer wall. He'd been shocked, then wounded twice, but still climbed twice as fast as Finn. He even leapt the last five feet, scurried down the street and lost himself among the shadows.

When they were sure he was gone, when the only sound was their panting, Finn turned to Carver and said, "You saved my life."

"You saved mine," Carver answered.

70

UPON HEARING the story, Mrs. Echols looked more as if she'd had too much tea to drink rather than nearly faced death. Mr. Echols wanted to contact the press before the police, but after Carver pointed out how bad that would look, he had his butler call Mulberry Street. Neither expressed the slightest bit of gratitude toward the trio.

Instead of Emeril, only one detective was sent, a squat man with green-gray eyes that were glassy from either a lack of sleep or too much drink. As he and several officers tromped through, Mr. Echols did insist that any questioning take place as speedily as possible. Delia thought he was being kind until Finn assured her he only wanted to clear the house for the photographers. Carver was only glad he'd managed to find the stun baton.

From the tone and content of the detective's questions, Carver understood the damage Hawking had done by changing the agency's combination earlier. The detective clearly thought it was some sort of hoax, too. Delia wasn't even questioned. Instead, she had to content herself with trying to reach her parents on the busy phone lines, something she was allowed to do only after she told the Echolses they were with the *Times*.

In less than an hour, the detective flipped his notebook closed.

"That's it?" Carver asked.

The man raised a caterpillar eyebrow. "The reporters will be happy to talk to you. That's what you wanted, innit?"

"No! This was real!" Finn objected.

"Didn't say it wasn't, but it was dark, right? Could've been anyone, right? But he's gone now, isn't he? I've got another call, and the owner of the home wants us out fast, so . . ."

He headed for the door.

Then, with Carver's shoulder still aching and Finn's arm possibly broken, they posed for photographs as Mr. Echols answered questions from the few reporters he'd managed to summon. To Delia's chagrin, the *Times* wasn't even represented. She hadn't gotten through to the Ribes and the dispatch editor probably concluded, like the police, that it had been one of many hoaxes they were following up.

The press gone, the Echolses vanished. A weary Carver, feeling much older than fourteen, and a sullen Finn soon found themselves in a larger parlor, lying on matching pink chaise lounges, where their wounds were at last tended by a doctor. Finding nothing broken, he prescribed a pain reliever and left the boys alone.

After a lengthy silence, Finn asked, "What was that thing you stuck him with?"

Carver pulled the baton out and held it up. "Stun baton. It's got some kind of battery in it."

"Where'd you get it?"

"I . . . stole it," Carver said. Finn looked shocked for an instant, then started laughing. Carver laughed, too.

When they stopped, Finn's face grew serious. "I really didn't take the necklace."

"It doesn't matter."

"It was Bulldog."

Carver stared. "You were covering for Bulldog?"

Finn shrugged. "He nicked things all the time, mostly from stores. It was like he couldn't help himself. When I heard Madeline's necklace was gone, I knew it was him. The only way to get him to give it up was by promising to return it myself."

"Finn," Carver said, aghast, "that was . . . noble. I always thought . . ."

"I know what you thought. It's not like you ever shut up about what you think. Sticks and stones, yeah, but you've got a mouth like a *knife* and you don't even know it."

"Bulldog. Bulldog's a thief."

"Not anymore. Last week, while I was stuck here, he nicked the wrong man's wallet, had his jaw broken and then got thrown in jail. Mr. and Mrs. Echols won't help. They won't even let me visit."

"I'm sorry," Carver said.

Finn shrugged. "I barely saw him to begin with. It's not like they let me have the guys over. I don't have many friends anymore. Not since Ellis."

He dared a glance at Carver, who managed a stoic, "Me neither."

A girlish laugh turned them toward the door. Delia stood there. She'd been crying recently, her face stained with dried tears, but now she covered her mouth to keep from laughing.

"I'm so sorry. I know this is serious," she said, trying to contain herself. "I hope you're not hurt badly . . . It's just . . . the two of you . . . on those *pink* . . ."

Carver lifted an empty teacup, pinky extended, and pretended to sip daintily.

"One lump or two?" Finn said, raising the sugar bowl.

"Neither, please!"

Delia howled, until a loud voice outside made her stop to listen. The doors, open since her arrival, gave them a view of the entrance hall. There, a decidedly agitated Echols barked commands at an unseen assistant.

"Under no circumstances will Roosevelt be allowed on my property! I don't care if he has an arrest warrant," Echols said.

"Sir," a weaker voice responded. "He only wanted . . ."

"Enough. The man just wants his name in the papers next to mine. Where's Hawking?"

"There's still no answer at his residence."

Echols slapped himself on the head. "What am I paying him for? He should have been here to talk to the reporters. Did you see how they thought we were making this up? Those policemen were talking before they rushed off. I saw you listening in. What were they talking about?"

When the assistant lowered his voice to a whisper, the three orphans craned their heads to hear.

"Another body was found."

Echols's eyes widened with excitement. "Why didn't you tell me at once? Get the press back here! I'll have to prepare a statement . . ."

"Sir, the victim was Amelia Edwin. She was . . . butchered, like the others."

Echols's demeanor suddenly changed. He stiffened, then reached for something to steady himself with. "We play bridge with the Edwins . . . I saw Millie just yesterday . . ."

Seeing the open doors, a decidedly pale Echols closed them. The last words they heard were, "I . . . don't want Samantha to know yet. My wife . . . she *could* have been killed?"

The news drained all joy from the trio.

Carver spoke first. "He found himself another *E*. Amelia Edwin probably has some connection to Miller's Court as well."

"I already know what it is," Delia said. "He called her *Millie*. It's a little different, but he probably had to improvise after you drove him away."

"But it's over now, isn't it?" Finn said. "He's done. You said there were five original Ripper victims, right? Amelia Edwin makes five."

"You're forgetting something," Delia said, her voice almost a whisper. "Something very important."

"What's that?"

"He still needs an *R*."

71

THE SOUR-FACED butler who'd tried to turn them away informed Delia and Carver they were to stay the night, "In case the press returns."

Carver was taken to a room the size of an Ellis Orphanage classroom, with a four-poster bed and a small fireplace. He wanted to stay awake, to sort the night's details, but after a few hazy thoughts about the Ripper's most recent letter, the next thing he knew, bright sunlight warmed his face. A yawn brought the smell of eggs and toast. A silver breakfast tray was laid out on a table.

He rolled out of bed, but when he tried to stretch, a sharp pain in his shoulder reminded him of the worst of his sprains. It didn't keep him from eating greedily. The Echolses weren't the kindest people, but the food was great.

Halfway through the meal, a knock came at the door. "Come in," he said.

It was the butler, holding a tray. Carver hoped it was more food, but it held a phone.

"Good to see you awake, young master," the butler said. "Your friends are eating breakfast in their rooms. Your clothing is being cleaned, but I've left some of Master Phineas's things in the wardrobe closet, the smallest I could find. Meanwhile, the master of the house has a request."

Carver shrugged. "Mr. Echols? What is it?"

"He's having difficulty reaching your . . . Mr. Hawking." He stepped over, placed the tray on an end table and plugged the phone's cord into a wall socket. "He would appreciate it if you'd inform him in no uncertain terms that he should speak with Mr. Echols immediately."

"I'll do what I can," Carver said. He had a few things to say to Hawking himself.

The butler spun and exited. Carver picked up the phone and asked for Blackwell Asylum. After a few moments, an unfamiliar female voice said, "Yes?"

"This is Carver Young. Could you please bring Mr. Hawking to the phone?"

There was no pause before the response. "Carver Young?"

"Yes. Who is this, please?"

"My name is Thomasine Bond," she said in an English accent. "It's my first day. Mr. Hawking isn't here, but he left a message for you. I'm sorry, but first, he's asked that I make *sure* it's really you. It's just a question he's written. A moment . . . Who is . . . no, wait, I'm sorry, the typing is smudged; who *should* be your favorite detective?"

Carver smirked. Maybe his mentor hadn't deserted him completely. "Auguste Dupin. What's the message?"

"You're on your own."

Carver's face dropped. "That's it?"

The man he'd begun to think of as a father really meant to do it, then, really meant to leave the city at stake so his pupil could solve the case. He'd been abandoned all over again. Carver hung up, gnashed his teeth and thought of asking Finn to teach him some new swearwords. He opened the wardrobe and found a tailored shirt and pants, both so oversized he had to roll the cuffs just to keep from tripping over them.

It took fifteen minutes to find the den. There, Finn, in a three-piece suit that made him look like some sort of businessman in training, paced. Delia, in a too-large dress doubtless borrowed from Mrs. Echols, sat at a desk, poring over the morning newspapers.

"You look as ridiculous as I feel," Finn said, not unpleasantly.

Delia picked her head up. "Not much new."

"Do the Ribes know you're here?"

"Yes," she said with some satisfaction. "They still believe you and Echols are not to be trusted, but they think it's safer here than anywhere *and* they want me to keep an eye out for anything newsworthy. Delia Stephens Ribe, crime reporter. I like the . . ."

Her face darkened.

"What is it?" Carver asked.

"*Ribe*. I know they're not rich, but it does begin with an *R*. And if he went after Finn's mother because she was connected to you, why not mine?"

She jumped up.

"Easy, Delia," Carver said. "Call, but I don't think they're in danger. Like you already said, they're not rich, and everyone else has been. We're not talking well-off, either, we're talking wealthy." He swept his hands at the huge room. "Like this. I was thinking about his last letter, where he says he's closer to *you* and *the end*. The end is the end of his name, right? It also sounds like he's planning to reach the *Boss*. Whoever that is, I don't think it's a reporter."

After briefly relaxing, Delia said, "There is another obvious *R* that fits the description."

"Who?" Finn asked.

But Carver knew instantly who Delia was thinking of. "And he is a boss," Carver said grimly. "The biggest boss in all this. He's wealthy, influential and a hunter himself. The man who he's been taunting, *insulting* by making the bodies so easy to find."

"Who?" Finn asked again.

"How can we warn him?" Delia said. "He's the last person on earth who'd believe any of us!"

"Warn *who*?" Finn shouted.

"Roosevelt," Carver said.

"But he only kills women," Finn said. "You mean he'll go after his wife?"

"His second wife, Edith," Delia said. "There must be some connection between her and the Whitechapel victims."

It hit Carver so hard, he flew to his feet, nearly tripping on the too-large clothing. "No! Finn had the right idea. He's past the five most famous Whitechapel victims, but there were others after Mary Kelly, remember? One of them was *Alice* McKenzie. Alice is the name of Roosevelt's first wife."

Carver's every intuition was screaming that he'd unwrapped the final clue. "She's dead. But Roosevelt's daughter Alice Lee is very much alive. For now, at least."

72

KNOWING the police would laugh and hang up before hearing the complicated clues, Delia tried Jerrik Ribe. It was only after she screamed and nearly burst into tears that the harried *New York Times* operator put her through to her adoptive father.

"Of *course* I'm certain; I'd never waste anyone's time without . . . But you see it, don't you? I already explained about the list of victims' names. Forget about Carver and look! It's so obvious! If you could make *someone* listen . . . But . . . I'm fine here. I want to stay."

At last she hung up. "He believes me, but since the *Times* printed that letter, they've been persona non grata with the commissioner. He'll try to get past the commissioner but expects his pleas to be ignored. There's a party tonight at City Hall. Mr. Overton and Roosevelt will both be there; so will Alice. Jerrik will ask to approach the commissioner personally."

"How can they have a party with everything going on?" Carver asked.

Delia shrugged. "Safety in numbers? Life goes on?"

"The Echolses are going to that shindig," Finn said.

Carver looked at him. "Then . . . maybe . . . Mr. Echols could warn Roosevelt?"

"Echols won't even let Roosevelt in his home," Delia said. "Add to that the fact that the police think the attack here was a publicity hoax."

"Exactly," Carver said. "Roosevelt thinks Echols is publicity hungry. But if he warned him privately and promised *not* to tell the press . . ."

"Why would he promise that?" Finn said.

"Because it's the right thing?" Delia offered.

Finn snorted.

"Isn't it worth a shot?" Carver prodded. "I don't think it would take much. If there were the *slightest* chance his family could be harmed, I have to think Roosevelt would protect them. Can you just try it, Finn?"

Finn nodded. "I've banged my head against walls before."

Knowing Finn wasn't exactly well spoken, they rehearsed what he'd say until he knew it by heart. In the meantime, their clothes had been returned, so they took a break to change back.

The butler looked suspicious when asked, but informed them Mr. Echols was in the study. At the door, Finn grew pale. Carver was shocked by how timid he'd grown. Delia rubbed his wide back while Carver gritted his teeth at the sight and struggled to say encouraging things.

Finn knocked, but there was no answer. Carver nodded for him to try the door. When Finn refused, Carver turned the knob himself and pushed. It swung open.

Behind an enormous desk covered with phones, Echols, always frail, looked like a sickly child. His face ashen, he slowly turned his eyes up toward them. He looked as if he were dreaming or ill.

"Phineas," he said.

"There's something important I have to ask you," Finn began, but Echols barely seemed to register their presence.

"I was convinced you were lying," Echols said slowly. "I thought Hawking put his boy up to it, to frighten me into paying him more money. I thought you were in on it, too, same orphanage, after all. But I went along with it, for the press. Then Millie . . . was killed . . . cut up, just a few blocks away. Edwin, the same last initial, just like you told the police. Samantha, your mother, she could have *died*."

Shaky, Echols rose to his feet and stiffly embraced an utterly bewildered Finn. "You *saved* her."

Forgetting his prepared speech, all Finn could manage was, "Uh . . . thanks?" as he pulled back and, with extreme awkwardness, patted his adoptive father on the shoulders.

Carver was about to bring up the party when Echols waved weakly at the phones. "I tried calling Roosevelt, to make sure he believed the Ripper was here, but they wouldn't take my call. The police think I'm a liar, and it turned out I was telling the truth."

Echols wouldn't be able to help them convince anyone. Hawking was right. They were on their own.

73

BY SIX o'clock it was impossible to reach the City Hall entrance. Mobs in the park and on the sidewalk spilled into the street. Cabs and private carriages lined up, blocking Broadway. The upper-crust gathering had become a lightning rod for the city's fear, bringing people from every walk who believed they could somehow be part of the gathering by watching through the windows. About the only advantage to being stuck among so many people was that they blocked the wind and near-freezing drizzle.

Finn had taken the lead, pushing forward, head down, like the bull Carver always imagined him to be. Delia held Finn's overcoat with one hand and clutched Carver's arm with the other. A swell in the crowd, caused by the mayor's arriving carriage, pushed the trio into the wooden barricades surrounding the hall. Carver felt his back crushed into the wood, the sprain in his shoulder throbbing.

"Down!" Delia called. She vanished among a press of faceless coats.

Carver went to his knees. People rushed into the seeming gap, forcing him sideways under the barricade. Delia and Finn were waiting. Severed from the crowd, they got down on all fours and crawled toward the back of the building, where the fine marble gave way to rougher sandstone.

A lone tree grew along the first-story windows. There, they stood and caught their breath.

"It's impossible," Delia said. "The police are back here, too. There's no way we'll reach a door."

"But if we can't get in, neither can the Ripper, right?" Finn said.

Carver shook his head. "If he's planning to attack tonight, he's already inside."

Finn looked up at the nearest window. Parted drapes revealed a wide office full of file cabinets. "That room's empty. Why don't we climb in there?"

Delia shook her head. "Nice idea, but I'm sure it's locked."

"So?" Finn said.

"You're a lock picker now, too?" Carver asked.

"Don't have to be." He lumbered up, braced himself against the stone and pushed the frame. After a quick, loud metallic snap, the window slid open.

"Easier than that newspaper door," Finn said, climbing in. "That's two for me and none for you, Carver."

"But . . . never mind."

With a boost from Carver, Delia went next. Struggling to hold on to the sill, he climbed in himself, annoyed to find Delia tenderly adjusting Finn's tie and straightening his suit.

Seeing how Carver stared, Delia said, "It's a party. We have to look presentable. Your turn."

But when she came over to him, she frowned. "It's easier with tailored clothes," she said, tugging at his jacket. "Weren't these just cleaned?"

"I've just been crawling!" he objected. She yanked the deer-stalker cap from his head and shoved it into his pocket, brushed his shoulders and ran her fingers through his hair. The last part was the most pleasant.

She stood and stepped back. "Now me, how do I look?"

He leaned in and removed a single black hair that'd been clinging to her cheek. "Perfect."

She seemed embarrassed. "You'd better be right. And we'd better get going."

They made their way into the hall and headed for the party. The central pavilion's rotunda was a soaring space with a grand marble stairway that rose to the second floor. There, ten columns held up a coffered dome. It reminded Carver of the Octagon, only twenty times larger.

The crowd was equally grand. The women wore odd, flamboyant hats, fine jewelry and flowing gowns. The men, dressed in far less colorful variations of black and white, looked as if it were their job to keep things in order. Carver had to wonder if the wealthy *owned* any simpler clothing.

Even Roosevelt was dressed to the nines, sporting a gold-headed walking stick, recently trimmed side-whiskers, a tall silk hat and fashionably tight trousers that flared over his shoes. Standing near the hall's center, surrounded by a crowd, his booming voice, as usual, was easily heard.

"A sheriff I once worked for in the Dakota Territory had once been a member of the Bismarck police force. When I asked why he left, he explained it was because he'd hit the mayor on the head with a gun. The mayor forgave him, but the chief of police insisted he resign. That, in short, is politics."

There was also no shortage of Roosevelt's detectives, their cheaper suits and bowlers easy to spot. Carver even recognized a few faces from the New Pinkertons.

"Let's split up," Carver said. "If they catch one of us, the others can keep trying."

"What should I say to Roosevelt?" a worried Finn asked.

"Forget Roosevelt," Carver said. "Try to find Alice."

"Easy enough," Delia said. "Look at her dress!"

Carver turned his eyes to where Delia was pointing. There, indeed, standing next to a grand piano, was the girl he'd met at the Ribes'. Her dark hair was freshly curled and had a bow that matched her flowing white and yellow gown.

"Wow," Carver said. "She looks so . . . adult."

Delia's eyes hardened. "Well, she's *not*," she said.

Carver Young, junior detective, completely missed her accusing tone.

74

ALICE Roosevelt wore a wicked look on her face as she whispered excitedly to the pianist. He protested, but apparently Alice won, because a new song soon filled the hall. It was a popular tune among the middle and lower class, highly inappropriate for the wealthy crowd. Looking a little nervous, the man sang.

Sweet Lorraine gets right inside your mind.
Sweet Lorraine puts you down and leaves you far behind.

Alice scanned the crowd, amused by the shocked reactions. Her eyes found Carver's. She smiled and waved him over.

"I'll go alone," Carver said to the others.

"And what are *we* supposed to do?" Delia said. "Stand back in admiration?"

As he neared, Alice swayed to the music.

Carver would have to talk fast. While he was trying to remain hidden, she was intent on attracting attention. Her father in particular kept glancing over.

"Girls are supposed to love thieves and liars, you know," she said pleasantly.

The comment brought Carver up short. "But I'm not a thief or a liar."

"Pity," she said. Carver briefly speechless, she patted him on the arm. "Don't look so serious! I'm just practicing my flirting. Have to start sometime, you know, and you seem like a nice safe person, despite all I've heard."

"Of course . . . I . . . knew that . . . but, Alice . . . I have to tell you . . ." He leaned closer to whisper. "I think you're in danger."

Her smile had yet to vanish. "From what? Boredom? A consequence of wealth, I'm afraid . . ."

"No. The killer . . . it's a long story . . . I . . ."

She stiffened. Her lively eyes revealed a sharp spark that reminded Carver of her father. "Does this have to do with your fantasy about a secret detective agency?"

Before he could explain, a small woman with a brittle smile motioned for the pianist to stop. Forgetting Carver, Alice wheeled on her. "Excuse me, I requested that song!"

"And your *father* requested I stop it," the woman responded. "And that I bring you to the food table for something to eat."

The commissioner was right near the food table. Carver wouldn't have a chance to start, let alone finish his story.

Alice motioned toward Carver. "But this young gentleman was about to tell me something fascinating."

The woman pulled her away. "Young girls always think young gentlemen have something fascinating to say."

Alice put on a wide smile, speaking loudly as the woman dragged her away. "Perhaps we should meet again? Say, in about four years?"

Carver winced. People were looking at him. He backed away, trying to hide himself. He'd just about reached one of the columns when a hand grabbed his shoulder.

"Say nothing," a familiar voice intoned.

Carver turned. "Emeril!"

"Sh! Keep your back to me and I shall do likewise."

Carver did as asked, positioning himself behind the column.

"Let's make this quick," Emeril whispered. "Hawking left a typewritten note under the mat at my apartment this morning that said you'd be here, but it didn't mention why."

"Then he's talking to you more often than he is to me," Carver whispered back. "Honestly, I think he's gone crazy." In hushed tones, Carver explained what had happened and why he'd come.

At first Emeril made a show of nonchalantly scanning the crowd. Halfway through Carver's story, he was shocked enough to give up on concealing their conversation.

He faced Carver with a grave expression. "The senior detectives explored the initials, of course, but I don't believe they figured out clues in the victims' names! A game inside a game. Goes to show why the New Pinkertons were needed. Follow me, quickly."

Feeling as if he might finally get somewhere, Carver followed Emeril up the winding stairs. On the way, he scanned the crowd for Delia and Finn but couldn't see them. On the second floor, the junior detective opened the door to the first room and waved Carver inside. He said only, "Wait here," before hurrying off.

Suddenly alone, Carver paced, too nervous to pay much attention to his surroundings. Impatient, he opened the door to see what was keeping Emeril. His jaw dropped. Two city detectives stood outside. Had Emeril turned him in?

No. Far from it. Moments later, Commissioner Roosevelt marched in. He closed the door, removed his top hat and gloves and laid them on a side table. This was it. Emeril had given Carver the chance he'd needed to make his case.

"Young men," Roosevelt said, "are often very good at unexpectedly sneaking into places where they are not welcome. But you appear to have made a profession of it."

Carver froze, not sure where to begin. Roosevelt closed the distance between them. "You believe the killer will target my Alice."

"Yes."

"Why should I put any stock in a fellow who believes in underground detective headquarters?"

"The last names of the victims . . ."

"Emeril told me about all that. If any man adds two and two and gets four, I don't doubt his arithmetic. We figured out the same word game this morning. We did not, however, make the key connection with the unfortunate Alice McKenzie, since she is generally not considered a Ripper victim. For that I am deeply in your debt. As we speak, my men are attempting to discreetly remove my daughter from the party. As you've met her, you can imagine how difficult that task may be."

Hearing Alice was being protected, Carver exhaled. Roosevelt pulled a high-back chair from a desk and put it in front of Carver. "Sit."

As Carver complied, Roosevelt unbuttoned his jacket and put his hands on his hips. "What I am asking you is something different. I want to know why I should believe *in* you. I knew you first as a deluded street waif with a treacherous uncle, then as protégé to a poser. Today, you're a valiant rescuer who knows more about this case than my own detectives. That's a lot of identities for one person. It doesn't breed trust."

When Carver said nothing, Roosevelt added, "I'm not unsympathetic. I've had many identities myself."

Carver choked. "I . . . don't know how to answer, sir."

"I see," Roosevelt said. He pulled out another high-back chair, placed it in front of Carver and sat down in it himself. "Men know each other through their words and deeds. You've come to warn me, a fine deed. Now I want words. We'll start off simple. What do you think of . . . Mr. Albert Hawking?"

"That's a simple question?" Carver asked, shaking his head. "I don't know. Sometimes he seems brilliant, sometimes . . . insane."

"The Ripper, the man you believe is your father, what do you make of him?"

Carver reared back in the chair. "He sickens me. My life's been a nightmare since I found out who he was. And all these clues seem as if they were left to taunt me."

"Something we have in common. He sickens and taunts me as well," Roosevelt said. "This threat on Alice, any idea how soon?"

Carver shook his head again.

"Do you think he might strike tonight?"

Carver thought about it, tried to imagine how his father was thinking. "We hurt him on the roof. He's angry. I don't think he'll wait long."

Roosevelt slapped Carver on the knee. "Bully! That flash in your eyes when you were thinking. I see you in there. You have a storm going on in your head, son, but your gut is good. Your father, my heavens, I've no idea how I'd deal with a devil's blood in my veins."

Carver looked at him helplessly. "Neither do I."

Roosevelt nodded. "How could you? A young man needs someone to instill him with ideals, pride and courage. That kind of gap isn't easily repaired." He seemed to ponder the question a moment, then said, "I can't give you a new father, but perhaps I can loan you mine. Hasn't been a decision I've made where I don't ask myself what he'd have done. My own childhood was often dismal, for very different reasons than yours. I suffered from asthma, dreamt of a werewolf attacking me in my bedroom. Life felt like a nightmare for me then, too. And my father said to me, don't dwell on the darkness within, reach out and *act*. That's how I've tried to lead my life ever since."

Carver was stunned. "You're giving me *advice*?"

"Yes. How do you like it?" Roosevelt said.

"It's . . . good," Carver answered.

Roosevelt gave him a toothy grin. "Of course!"

A knock came at the door. One of the detectives leaned in and nodded.

The commissioner rose. "Alice is ready to be taken home. I have to go."

Carver was relieved to think his job was done, but Roosevelt waved him along. "I'd like you to join us. Time to stop lurking in the shadows and come out into the light, don't you think, Young?"

"Yes, sir," Carver said, rising. "Thank you, sir."

"Don't thank me yet. I'm going to have *you* sit next to Alice!"

75

THE EARLIER drizzle had turned to fog. It was so gray that the great lights of the city, electric and gas, were visible only as blurry patches. It was so thick, it swirled as men strode through it. The world looked enough like a dream to fill Carver with dread.

Alice, terribly nonplussed, sat in a fine carriage at the rear of City Hall. Her ride was flanked by two large police carriages each full of armed detectives and uniformed buttons.

Roosevelt marched toward her, pausing to take in the gloomy scene. "This," he said, putting his boot on the carriage step, "is what they call *suicide weather*. Mr. Young, get in on the other side."

"But, Father, I don't want to . . . ," a surprisingly meek voice said from within the carriage.

"It's been decided, Alice. Edith, your brothers and

sisters are already on their way to meet us. You'll be free to wreak as much havoc as you like at Sagamore Hill." He climbed in and pulled the door shut.

Carver hurried to the other side, but the seat was made only for two. With Roosevelt a wide man and Alice in a flowing gown, there was much shifting and shuffling to squeeze him in.

Alice blinked and sighed. His shoulders at an odd angle, Roosevelt said in a fatherly tone, "Thank the young man for possibly saving your life, Alice."

"Thank you for possibly saving my life," Alice intoned.

"Now, I suggest we all try to enjoy the fog."

He rapped his hand on the roof and the three carriages rolled onto Broadway. With the party in full swing, the crowd had thinned, and the traffic was moving again. Roosevelt tried to settle but only managed to look more uncomfortable.

They'd traveled barely half a block when the cab rattled as if something heavy had hit it. Roosevelt snapped forward to see what had happened, in the process knocking Alice into Carver. At once, the carriage picked up speed, throwing them all backward.

"What the devil?" He looked out the window. "Where's the escort? There should be police on either side of us!"

Roosevelt had no intention of waiting for an answer. Despite their increasing speed, he pushed open the carriage door and leaned out into the cold gray air.

"Are you drunk, you fool? Pull this carriage over at once!" he shouted.

The carriage twisted side to side as the driver wove through the traffic. Roosevelt looked up at the driver and then shouted to Carver.

"Young, get Alice out of here, now!"

Carver was about to grab Alice, but his attention snapped back to the open door. In a flash, Roosevelt, for all his courage and strength, was gone, kicked off by powerful legs that swung down from the roof.

Alice screamed.

"The Ripper," Carver said.

Praying he could move fast enough, he hooked one arm under Alice's shoulder and tried to throw open his door. Before he could, a shadow appeared in the space Roosevelt had occupied and slipped in next to them. His hair, peeking from beneath his hat, was dark as a panther, his black eyes more monstrous than any werewolf.

This time Alice didn't scream. Using Carver, who held her, as a brace, she kicked the heels of her fine shoes into the intruder over and over again, her feet flailing wildly. One blow caught the Ripper's tall hat and sent it flying out into the night. There was a wide bruise on his forehead where Carver had hit him with the brick.

"His right knee! Kick it!" Carver shouted, recalling where Finn had kicked him.

But when she took a moment to aim, the Ripper grabbed her calves and growled.

Feeling the tug as the Ripper pulled Alice, Carver finally pushed his door open. The murky ground whizzed by. The Ripper must have tied the reins and left the horses to run dead ahead. Carver knew he had no choice. He pulled on Alice as hard as he could, trying to drag them both into the blur of fog and cobblestones.

The killer had Alice's legs, and for a time they were locked in a bizarre tug-of-war. When Alice screamed again, Carver didn't know if it was terror or if all the yanking was hurting her.

He pulled again, surprised how easily she came forward. Had she kicked herself free from the killer? They were halfway out. He had only to jump and they'd both be on the street.

But then Alice was yanked back and thrust forward so quickly, Carver lost his grip. He flew from the carriage, alone. As he slammed into the cobblestones, he realized his father had used her body to shove him out.

Galloping horse hooves directly behind him, Carver pushed himself onto his knees and barely ducked the first of the pursuing police carriages. Instead of chasing after Alice, it turned and came to a halt.

A horrified Theodore Roosevelt was half a block away but coming up quickly. He ran full tilt down the middle of the street, traffic veering to avoid him.

"Alice! Alice!" Roosevelt cried.

But even his booming voice was muffled by the fog as the carriage with his daughter and the killer disappeared into the thick gray wall of the night.

THE SECOND police carriage careened after the Ripper. Roosevelt wheeled toward the first. Rather than climbing aboard, he frantically undid the harness.

"Call ahead! Block the street! I want this city shut down, do you hear me?" he shouted.

"Commissioner, what are you doing, sir?" the driver asked.

"Getting myself a horse, man!" Roosevelt said. He pulled the chestnut-brown mare away from the carriage, stripped off his overcoat and jacket and tossed them to the ground. "I've ridden bareback a thousand times. It'll be the only way to catch that fiend!"

Hearing those words, Carver thought of *another* way. He raced toward Warren Street.

"Hyahh!" he heard Roosevelt cry. His horse reared and galloped forward.

Carver, meanwhile, ran to the garage alongside Devlin's, where Emeril and Jackson had left the electric carriage. Excited to see it still there, he threw off the horse blankets and climbed into the driver's seat. His hand on the bar he'd seen Emeril steer with, he flipped switches and pressed buttons until one produced a hum and a lurch. The electric carriage rolled forward, pushed the gates open and barreled onto the street.

Emeril *had* driven it slowly. Carver was already moving fast, but the vehicle still picked up speed. He'd have to be even faster to catch up, but when he moved the steering stick to make the turn onto Broadway, the carriage nearly flipped.

Pulling back one of the levers slowed him in mid-turn. He could see the stares of the city detectives, stranded by their own horseless carriage.

Once moving straight again, he pushed the lever as far as it would go. His chest lurched backward. The cold fog rushed by at a dizzying rate. He easily passed hansom cabs, the pursuing police carriage and even a streetcar. Ahead, he saw the silhouette of a man on horseback.

He came up alongside Roosevelt. Despite his visible panic, the commissioner gave him a huge grin.

"Splendid!" he called.

Carver waved him over. "Climb on!"

Roosevelt tried to bring his horse closer, but the frightened mare kept veering away.

"Forget it! I'll move ahead!" Carver said.

"The devil you will!" Roosevelt answered. Bringing the chestnut horse as near as it would go, he leapt the remaining distance, landing in the passenger seat. The electric carriage wobbled, but Carver managed to right it.

"I think I'm beginning to believe in your underground detective agency!" Roosevelt called as he leaned forward to peer into the fog. "Can we catch that devil?"

"Not only that, it'll scare the hell out of his horses!"

Carver pushed the lever all the way again, making the carriage zoom forward.

"Yii-hiie!" Roosevelt cried. "We're coming, Alice!"

Carver realized at once he was being too optimistic. All the Ripper had to do to lose them was turn down a side street. As they sped past Prince Street, though, Roosevelt pointed east and cried, "There!"

Without questioning, Carver slowed for the turn. As he did, down the wide avenue he saw it, first in fog-shrouded wisps and then in its entirety, a dark carriage, bobbing madly as its tall driver tried to control both the horses and a struggling figure by his side.

"Hurry!" Roosevelt said. It seemed more a plea than a command.

Carver pushed the lever down.

As they sped up, Roosevelt stood. "Just get close enough; I'll jump for it."

"Wait!" Carver said. He wanted to explain he could *pass* the Ripper and drive the horses to the sidewalk, but Roosevelt had already climbed to the front of the electric taxi.

Once they were within a yard, Roosevelt leapt again, this time grabbing the back of the fine carriage with one hand. Without much of a hold, the force of his jump threatened to throw him.

As Roosevelt struggled, Carver came up alongside. His seat wasn't quite as high as his father's, but they were close enough to exchange glances. The wild grin and flared, fearsome eyes were no less terrifying, but his missing top hat made him seem vulnerable. Again Carver sensed something familiar about that face.

Alice struggled mightily, but the Ripper held her firmly in one arm, the other grasping the reins. His flapping cape revealed his long butcher blade. Carver realized with a gulp that if the Ripper didn't have to steer, Alice would be dead by now.

He turned the steering stick, bringing his carriage forward and nearer, not to the Ripper, but the horses. At the sight of the weird, unnatural vehicle, they whinnied and lurched.

The wicked grin vanished from the Ripper's face. He kept control, but barely.

Roosevelt, meanwhile, was atop the carriage now, crawling across its roof. He'd pried off one of the storage holds and prepared to use it as a club.

Again, Carver edged his carriage near the horses. Again, the mares shivered and shifted. Their pounding hooves and frightened snorts almost drowned the sounds of the Ripper's curses.

Roosevelt was on his knees, ready to swing, but the Ripper spotted him, reached deftly for his knife and swung. Carver veered again, this time striking the carriage. The horses whinnied and rushed onto the sidewalk, taking the carriage with them. The rear axle snapped, throwing Roosevelt backward.

Carver couldn't slow down in time to keep from hurtling past the scene. By the time he'd stopped the vehicle and executed a U-turn, the Ripper had lifted Alice, climbed from the broken carriage and limped into an alleyway. His right knee, it seemed, was still hurting.

Roosevelt, bruised from his fall, grabbed a long wooden shard from the broken wagon and rushed after him. Carver, back in pursuit, rode to the head of the alley. There stood the Ripper, his long knife held to Alice's throat.

Roosevelt advanced, holding his piece of wood as if it were a sword. "Let her go!" he commanded.

"I don't want *you*," the killer bellowed in his impossibly deep voice.

"You won't have Alice!" Roosevelt snarled.

"I don't want her either! I want the boy!"

In that moment, Alice put her mouth forward and bit deeply into the Ripper's wrist. When he cried out, she pulled away and raced behind her father.

"Stand back, Alice," Roosevelt said. He came forward, swinging the wood.

The Ripper parried, using his knife like a sword. It sliced a neat piece from the timber, but not enough to render it useless. He limped deeper into the alley.

Roosevelt pressed his advantage, swinging, pushing the Ripper until the killer's back hit a brick wall beneath a fire escape. Roosevelt straightened, thinking he'd won.

But then the Ripper laughed.

As Carver watched, his father reached up and grabbed the fire escape's lowest rung. Lifting himself, he kicked Roosevelt square in the chest. With a loud thud, his back hit the ground.

Roosevelt down, the Ripper raised his knife to stab.

"Stop!" Carver cried from his perch on the carriage.

The Ripper looked up. They both knew that by the time he climbed off the carriage, Roosevelt would be dead. Instinctively, Carver drew the baton.

Schick!

The Ripper eyed its tip, remembering the shock he'd received. "That's a child's weapon," he said, shaking his head. "Can't even kill."

"It doesn't have to," Carver said. When his father moved to

strike, Carver hurled it like a javelin, aiming for the flat of the blade. The two metals made contact. There was a small *bamf* and a flash. The Ripper howled, dropping the blade, grabbing his wrist.

But again, somehow shaking off the charge, he snatched up the still-smoking knife and glared at Carver.

"Now what?" the Ripper said. "Anything left to throw? No?"

The Ripper dove for the prone commissioner. With no other choice, Carver pushed the lever as far down as it would go. The vehicle flew forward. Carver prayed the carriage wheels were high enough to avoid hitting Roosevelt.

At the moment he hit, he couldn't quite see what happened but knew he'd caught his father in the torso and slammed him into the brick wall. Then he felt himself flying, out of the carriage, through the air and into the same brick wall.

After that, there was nothing at all.

77

THERE WERE flashes of light, hums, hollow rumbles, as if Carver had been forced inside the electric carriage's mysterious engine. At first nothing hurt, but when the pain came, that's all there was. It felt like the pieces of his chest no longer fit together. Something sharp, like the end of a broken stick, stabbed into his lungs.

He woke to the smell of flowers and the feel of a wintry wind. Opening his eyes, he decided he was dreaming. How else could he be in Hawking's hospital room, lying in his bed, surrounded by tables full of flowers and piled newspapers?

Head hurting too much to move, Carver strained his eyes to make out a headline:

**YOUNGEST PINKERTON SAVES
COMMISSIONER'S DAUGHTER.**

So, it *was* a dream. No one knew about the New Pinkertons. Besides, it was too cold for a hospital. Was he still in the alley? Was Alice all right?

The coarse sheets felt real, and damp, too, soaked with sweat. Even his hair felt wet. Turning his eyes toward the breeze, he saw the cause: an electric fan by an open window. On the ledge it looked like . . . snow?

"You're awake!"

The voice came from a spare, cheerful man in a white doctor's coat. The warm palm he put to Carver's forehead sent a sickly shiver down his spine. Carver felt like he was dying.

The doctor seemed pleased. "Fever's broken. Wonderful." He unplugged the fan and closed the window. "You were near 106. Another hour, I'd have used an ice bath. Had to break that temperature somehow."

Carver managed only a dry moan in response.

"Don't try to speak. You broke two ribs. One splintered, so I had to operate to remove the shards. And, well, there was an infection. There'll still be pain for a few weeks, but you'll feel much more alert in a few hours," the doctor said. "I'll tell the Roosevelts at once that our newest hero will pull through."

Carver pointed weakly at the newspaper headline. "Alice?"

"She's fine. Rest. All is well." Then he exited.

It was good to hear about Alice, but he also wanted to know what happened to his father. It would have to wait. As if obeying the doctor, a wave of exhaustion took his body. He fell asleep again.

The next thing Carver felt was a soft caress against his cheek. He opened his eyes and saw Delia's freckled face above him. She moved her fingers across his forehead, brushing some hair away, just as she had in City Hall. Half-asleep, he grabbed her hand, feeling her soft knuckles against his palm. Moving didn't hurt as much anymore, and the sheets, he noticed, were soft and dry.

Delia, who hadn't bothered taking off her winter coat, sat sideways on the bed.

"Carver," she said. "I thought you were going to die . . . They said you might, but you're not, are you? I feel so . . . so . . ."

She leaned forward impulsively and pressed her lips into his. While the doctor's touch had brought shivers, the kiss made his whole body warm. After lingering briefly, she pulled back, but Carver, finding more energy, raised his head to keep their lips together. She obliged. They stayed that way until a cough from deeper in the room stopped them.

Delia sat up, smiling. "Finn wants to say hello, too."

"Just a handshake, though," he said, stepping up behind Delia. "How are you?"

Carver had to think about it. There was a thick bandage wrapped around his rib cage, but the twinges weren't too bad. The doctor was right: most of his discomfort was from the fever. A rumbling in his stomach gave him the short answer: "Hungry."

"You must be starving," Delia said. "You've been out a week."

Finn looked around. "I think there's a food tray here some-where."

"A week?" Carver pulled himself up higher onto the pillows. "What happened?"

"Depends on which paper you read," Delia said with a wry smile. "According to the *Sun*, Roosevelt chased Jack the Ripper riding bareback and you cornered him in an alley using some sort of electric carriage!"

"Uh . . . actually . . . that's true," Carver said.

Delia made a face, uncertain if he were kidding. "Well, they all say you're a hero. Drove off the killer, rescued the damsel."

But Carver wasn't thinking about Alice. "My father. Did they catch him? Is he . . . ?"

Delia frowned. "There was a lot of blood, but no body."

Carver's thudding heart pressed against his bandages. "Has there been another killing? A different *R*?"

"That's the thing. There hasn't been," Delia said quickly. "They think he either crawled off somewhere and died or is so wounded he can't hurt anyone anymore."

Carver shook his head. "He's strong, Delia."

Finn nodded. "You haven't seen him. He's just licking his wounds."

Delia rolled her eyes. "He's *not* a bogeyman, and you *did* hurt him badly. The entire city is different; you can feel the relief in the air. That's why the papers are playing up your story so much, with Roosevelt's blessing."

Finn found a tray with fresh fruit and a sandwich. Carver grabbed the apple while Finn took the sandwich and nodded at the papers. "How do you like being famous?" Finn asked. "I know I never did."

"I don't know yet," Carver said with a shrug. "I've been unconscious. But what's this about me being a Pinkerton?"

"Because you're Hawking's assistant," Delia said. "He worked with Pinkerton and the press picked up on it."

"Mr. Hawking. Where's he? Has he been here?"

"I don't know," Delia said. "The doctor said you've had a few visitors. Maybe he was one."

"Finn, has Echols seen him?" Carver asked. The thought of how his onetime mentor had abandoned him still hurt, somehow deeper than his splintered rib.

"No, and he's furious. Said he'd have to hire a detective to find his detective."

"Should we check the get-well notes?" Delia suggested.

Carver frowned. "He was never exactly the sentimental type. Unless there's a one-word typewritten note in there somewhere."

The three spent the rest of their visit sorting through the well-wishes. Most were from people Carver didn't even know. He was pleased to see a package of books from Miss Petty, but nothing from his mentor. Might he be off hunting the Ripper, or had his eccentric behavior grown so extreme he'd become one of the asylum's patients?

Still weak, he had Delia call the Octagon. Thomasine Bond assured her Hawking still wasn't there.

"As soon as I'm released, I'm heading over there. He must have left a clue, a note, something!" Carver said.

"We'll go with you," Delia said.

In a day, Carver was on his feet; in two, he felt almost completely his old self despite the pain in his ribs. But the doctor still wouldn't release him. As more days passed, in addition to frequent visits from Delia and Finn, Emeril dropped by, telling him he'd "taken care" of the electric carriage. Carver gave Jerrik Ribe a lengthy, exclusive interview, during which he made no mention of the New Pinkertons and insisted the horseless carriage was just someone's wild imagination, born of reading too many dime novels.

It was easier to lie than he'd thought.

Very early one morning, to avoid the press, Commissioner Roosevelt appeared. His gratitude seemed boundless. With the same boyish enthusiasm he brought to all the facets of his life, he talked about sending Carver to college, setting him up in politics, or, "If you insist, as a detective. You seem to have the knack."

He presented Carver with freshly typed pages from a book he'd been writing and a handwritten letter from Alice complaining about how bored she was and hoping he'd come visit soon. Recalling Carver's fondness for gadgets, he'd even brought along a prototype for a new type of handcuff, from Bean Manufacturers. He'd intended only to show them but, seeing how much Carver liked them, decided to let him keep them.

As Carver tested the lock and the strength of the cuffs, Roosevelt rubbed his hands in an uncharacteristically self-conscious fashion. "Mr. Young, if you're willing to show it to me, I'm eager to see this headquarters of yours. Mr. Tudd died to protect its secrets, so I give you my word that despite my position, I will guard them as well."

"You're not . . . angry? After what you said about vigilantism?"

"Angry? I'm furious, furious that the corruption in this city ran so deep Allan Pinkerton felt a secret force was necessary. But he was right. My work is far from done, and I can't help but feel regret about Tudd. I don't know how I could have done different. I wish the man had trusted me. I could've used the help. Still can. Perhaps in time *you* can revive the organization."

"Me?"

"Of course. I'm striving to make our police a more organized force, like the army. When we hire now, we seek men of resolute temper, sober, self-respecting and self-reliant, with a strong wish to improve themselves. You fit all that and more. In addition, you are bright, eager and possess a secure moral compass. Who better?"

It seemed Carver's dream, and Hawking's plans might be fulfilled after all.

The next morning, the bandage was removed and his ribs

didn't hurt at all. Tomorrow, the doctor told him, he could go. Carver was feeling so good that when Delia was ready to leave after her afternoon visit, he dared to take her in his arms and squeeze until she laughed and pushed him away.

"I can't breathe!" she said. Her cheeks blushed as bright a red as the day he saw her in the Ellis laundry room so long ago. Embarrassed by her feelings, she rushed for the door. "I'll see you in the morning, with Finn," she said. "He's taking us to some fancy restaurant, courtesy of the Echolses. Maybe Delmonico's!"

"After we go to Blackwell," Carver said.

"Of course."

Long after the door closed, the feel of her body against his tingled in his memory.

There'd been no further word from the Ripper. Maybe his father really had crawled off to die; maybe the nightmare was over.

As night fell, he settled down with Roosevelt's manuscript. Carver had so much energy, he read for hours before finally turning off the light and falling into a peaceful, dreamless sleep.

He'd no way of knowing how long he'd been out when the faint click of the door stirred him. Drowsy, he turned to his side and saw a dark figure by the door, a familiar hunched shape, wavering slightly as he supported himself on his cane.

"So what do you think of my lessons, boy?" Albert Hawking said.

78

"MR. HAWKING!" Carver said. At first he was pleased and relieved, but then, realizing his mentor looked as healthy as ever, his anger returned. "You abandoned me."

The old detective moved closer, stepping into a streetlight glow from the window. "Nonsense. I taught you to fly, something you'd never do if I were there to hold you up."

"There were lives at stake," Carver said grimly. "Mrs. Echols's, Alice's . . . *mine.*"

"They're both fine, no? As for you, sometimes scars make the man. I know you find it difficult to admire him, but you have your father's stamina to thank, I think, and your own resourcefulness. Even used a few gadgets, from what I understand. You did well. So, are they taking better care of you in this cesspool? Are you well?"

Carver felt a swirl of pride and his anger fade. Hawking cared about him after all. He nodded. "They're releasing me in the morning."

Hawking grunted. "That fool surgeon almost killed you. Now, no doubt, he'll try to take credit for your body's own ability to heal."

It was another surprise. "You've been keeping track."

Nearer now, he looked at Carver. His gaze didn't seem quite as cold as it usually did. Putting his clawed hand on his cane, he reached over with his left and touched Carver's forehead. "Every move."

Carver had no idea how to react. Hawking patted him, leaned back and, with difficulty, carefully poured some water from a pitcher into the glass.

"Where have you been?" Carver asked.

Holding the glass in his clawed right hand, he offered it to Carver. "Drink, you sound hoarse."

Though half-full, the glass trembled so much, the water threatened to spill. Obediently, Carver took the glass, put it to his lips and swallowed. His throat *was* dry.

"I still want an answer," Carver said.

"So, *you're* the master now?" Hawking said with a chuckle. He put the pitcher down, maneuvered himself sideways and half-fell into the steel chair.

"My student," he said, half to the air, "is now as famous a detective as any dime-novel hero. He has an extremely powerful family in his debt and knows the combination to the finest crime lab in the world. But is he grateful? No. He still wants more."

"Of course I'm grateful, but . . ."

"There *is* more. Echols's money is now in an account in your name. You'll find the papers back at Blackwell. Not me, though. I'll be taking my leave for real this time."

Carver's mind grew dizzy. He had trouble trying to sort his words. "I don't understand. Where are you going? You still haven't said where you've been."

"And you still have a habit of asking questions right before you're about to hear the answer! I've been checking loose ends, making sure everything works to its best advantage. Now I'm all but done, and there's something else I have to do. My business, not yours. The lessons are over, so I'll ask again, what did you think of them, boy?"

Carver felt the prick of tears behind his eyes, but he held them back. Instead, he glared. "You showed up just to run off again?"

"Don't give me such a look, boy, or that tone. Are you some babe in swaddling clothes that needs me to change his diapers?"

Hawking put his cane against the floor and stood. He wavered more than usual, and for the first time, Carver realized his face looked even more ragged. "I *am* proud. And I'm glad to have seen you again."

His unusually emotional tone filled Carver with worry. "Are you all right, Mr. Hawking? Won't you please tell me where you're going?"

Hawking hesitated. "I've had some news. Someone I thought was dead may still be alive. I have to find out one way or another. It will require some traveling."

"My father?" Carver asked. "Are you hunting my father?"

Hawking eyed him. "Don't worry. There will be no further Ripper slayings in New York City. I'll make sure of it."

What did he mean? Was Hawking planning to *kill* the Ripper? But he seemed so weak. Something was wrong, insanely wrong.

The room was spinning. He put his hand out to the table to steady himself.

"I don't feel well," Carver said.

"That will be the chloral hydrate I put in your water," Hawking said. "Knockout drops. Maybe I'm getting sentimental, but I wanted to see you before I left and had to make sure you didn't follow. You'll never catch me saying this again, but I may have taught you *too* well, and this was the only way."

79

"CARVER! Carver!"

The back of his head ached as if he'd been smacked with a blackjack. Someone shook him by the shoulders, trying to wake him, but the movement only made the pain worse.

He flailed with his hands. "Stop!"

Delia and Finn were in front of him. Early-morning light came through the windows.

"Were you having a nightmare?" Delia asked.

Carver sprang up. "It was Hawking! He drugged me."

"Why?" Finn asked.

"I think he's found my father," Carver said. He stood and started pacing. "I think he's going to kill him."

"What?" Delia said. "That's mad!"

The doctor stepped in. "Everything okay in here?"

"I'm fine," Carver said. "Really. Just a bad dream."

The doctor studied him. "Good. It's almost time to check out. There'll be some papers to sign, and I'll walk you to the door."

Once the doctor was gone, Carver began ripping off his hospital gown, pausing only long enough for Delia to turn her back while he dressed. "The doctor will want to march me in front of the press, but I've got to get to Blackwell Asylum. There must be some clue there, some research. What time is it? When's the next ferry?"

Delia grabbed a newspaper. "I'll check the schedule."

Finn rushed for the door. "I'll get a cab and meet you out back."

Almost as an afterthought, Carver snatched the handcuffs Roosevelt had given him.

Before the doctor could return, Delia and Carver headed down a side stairwell, found the service corridor and emerged in the rear alley. Finn had the cab waiting.

As they rode to the ferry, Carver kept talking. "He's going to face him himself, I know it. Maybe he sees this as his last great battle. Even if no one else knows, *he'll* know he was the one who caught Jack the Ripper."

"I thought *my* parents were strange," Finn said.

In his rush to dress, Carver brought the stun baton and his lock pick, but forgot his new overcoat. It wasn't terribly cold in the cab, but as the wind whipped off the East River onto the bobbing ferry, he thought he'd freeze. He huddled with Delia, but it didn't help as much as he'd hoped.

At the Octagon, a guard warned them to slow down, but when Carver ignored him, the man didn't seem interested in making any effort to stop them. Carver rushed for the circular stairs, pulling himself along with the railing. Strangely, the door at the top was locked. Carver had never been given a key; there was no need. His pick made quick work of it.

The large octagonal room was a mess, almost a photograph of what it looked like before Hawking forced Carver to clean it. Carver's bed was barely visible beneath the fallen boxes and books. The desk was littered with refuse. He knew in a flash that Hawking *had* been here, working all along.

Delia and Finn came up from behind, panting, as Carver scanned the room. He tried to sense what had gone on here. How could he find the man's trail? He had to put himself in Hawking's place. What was important to his mentor?

The typewriter was gone. The brass railway gadget also came to mind. Carver rushed over to the table and spotted a few small screws on the floor. It was gone, too. So were Hawking's clothes.

"He's moved out," Carver said. "Delia, head downstairs and see if you can find a woman named Thomasine Bond. She's English, probably one of the nurses."

Still panting, she said, "You want me to run *down* the stairs now?"

"Please. Remind her we spoke on the phone. Tell her I know he was up here these last few weeks. Ask what his tone was like when he talked to her, if he went out often. It's important. Hurry."

Delia nodded, then headed back down the stairs.

"What can I do?" Finn asked.

Carver paced. "Make piles. Get the furniture back in place. Put the papers together. If you find a book open to a page, don't close it. Stack it with the binding open."

"Okay. What am I looking for?"

Carver shrugged. "I don't know. Notes about Jack the Ripper. Notes about . . . traveling."

Finn set to work, moving the heaviest boxes into place with ease. Carver kept pacing, glancing at an open book or two. He saw the old overcoat Hawking had loaned him, hanging lonely on the coatrack, watched his bed slowly uncovered as Finn worked.

"Carver," Finn said, holding up a long piece of paper. "You said travel."

It was a map of Manhattan's elevated railway lines, including the suburban trains that led out of the city from Grand Central. There was a schedule attached. He'd seen it once before but didn't remember where.

"Any good?" Finn asked.

"I don't know," Carver said. "Maybe the Ripper fled the city and Hawking figured out where he was going. Where'd you find this?"

Finn nodded toward a pile of papers half-covering a broken machine. Carver was wrong; the typewriter was still here, unrecognizable because it was in shambles. It looked as if Hawking had smashed it in a rage. Carver plopped himself on the floor and stared at the mangled keys.

Delia appeared at the door, gasping so hard she looked ready to collapse. "Carver, there *is* no Thomasine Bond, and no one else remembers giving you any messages. They did say Hawking left early this morning, on the ferry before ours."

"Then who did I talk to?" He flashed on the moment he'd broken into the telephone switchboard, his mentor telling him to use a higher voice to sound more feminine. "How did I miss that? Thomasine Bond *was* Hawking. The ferry before ours? That gives him a head start, but if he's planning to take a train out of the city, we could still catch up, if we knew where he was going. Keep looking!"

Finn, still clearing the refuse, grabbed the typewriter by the chassis. When he lifted, the carriage came loose and clattered to the ground. "He's going to need another typewriter."

"Another . . . Finn!" Carver yelled.

"What? I'm sorry . . . I . . ."

"No, you're a *genius,*" Carver said. He handed Delia the schedule, then raced downstairs to the narrow door that led to the observation room. He'd remembered *where* he'd seen that schedule before. There, in the small, cluttered office space, the second typewriter remained intact. The notes, however, all seemed to be about the patients. The roller.

He swept a space free on the table and was hunting for paper and pencil as his friends arrived.

"Please, please, no more stairs," Delia said. "And what are you doing, anyway?"

"Hawking read my notes at the athenaeum by rubbing a pencil against the next blank sheet of paper on the pad. He *pounded* these typewriter keys. The most recent impressions would be deepest, so maybe the same thing would work with the roller here."

His first few efforts yielded some stray words, like *idiots,* but when he rotated the roller and tried again, some numbers appeared. "10:10 and 870. Delia, anything match that on the train schedule?"

Her eyes darted along. "Yes! 870 is a locomotive number on the New York Central Line. And there's a 10:10 out of the city."

"An elevated train at the 34th Street Ferry pier goes to Grand Central," Carver said. "We can make it by ten easily."

"That el's mostly for tourists getting to and from Brooklyn and Long Island. It only runs every hour," Delia said. "He might even still be waiting on the platform."

As Carver ran for the door, he saw that Delia was already holding his mentor's old coat. "You'll want this," she said. "It's cold out there."

As he glanced at his friends, for the first time, Carver didn't feel like much of an orphan.

80

THE FERRY made good time. Thanks to Hawking's old coat, Carver was able to stand on the upper deck with Delia and Finn and watch as the landing came into view.

Even if they did catch his mentor, what would he do, short of handcuffing him to a pole? But he couldn't let him face the Ripper alone. Even wounded and cornered, his father had survived a head-on crash. And his mentor was looking weaker by the day.

"That must be the train," Finn said, pointing at a rising plume. It wasn't moving yet, but it would be soon. The captain screamed at them as they jumped the last three feet to the dock and ran for the stairs. As they reached the platform, the engine gave off a sharp whistle. The doors were sealed, locked for safety's sake. With a pant of steam, the train pulled out.

"Too late," Finn said, slowing. "But if I tip a cabdriver enough, we could beat it to Grand Central."

Carver scanned the passengers through the moving windows. "Okay, let's . . ." In mid-sentence, he spied a familiar slouched figure. Before Carver could think to duck, Hawking looked up and saw him. His mentor grimaced unhappily and shook his head.

"No!" Carver said. "He saw me! He'll get off at the next stop and find some other way out of the city. We'll never find him. We've *got* to get on that train."

"How?" Delia said. "You can't just jump on it."

He looked up at the sheet metal roof overhanging the platform and said, "Why not?"

Climbing up on a railing, he managed to pull himself to the roof. As he got his bearings, he heard Delia call his name in exasperation, then the heavy thuds of Finn following him.

The train was still slowly gathering momentum as it strove to leave the station. He could make it. Feet pounding, Carver raced faster than he ever had in his life. At the edge of the roof, he took a wild leap and landed flat atop the second of the five passenger cars. His ribs ached, but after a brief roll he was able to stop himself and get to his feet. Behind him, Finn jumped as well, the crash of his heavier body leaving a dent in the top of the train.

Before either could focus on what to do next, they saw Delia on the station roof. She was racing along, one hand holding her wool cap tightly on her head. The train was picking up speed. She wouldn't make it.

"Don't!" Carver shouted. "Stop!"

But by then she'd jumped. Carver held his breath as she flew into the air, exhaling only when she landed dead center on the fifth and last car. She rose, still holding her cap, wobbled slightly, then came resolutely forward. Carver and Finn eyed each other, impressed and relieved.

The relief was short-lived. An abrupt bump in the tracks

nearly shook them off the train. Carver knew it wouldn't be the last bump. The tracks would take the train sharply right onto Third Avenue and then again onto 42nd before the final stop at Grand Central Station.

"We have to get inside!" He waved to Delia and pointed down.

Ignoring him, she trotted up to the edge of her car and jumped to the next.

"I don't think she likes to be left out," Finn said.

Carver shook his head. Getting down on all fours for better balance, he made his way to the front of the car he'd landed on, thinking it should be an easy matter to climb down and enter.

Below, he saw a stream of frenetic businessmen and workers pushing and shoving their way out of the first car and back into the second. Finn squatted beside Carver and frowned.

"What's going on?" he wondered aloud.

"Wait for me!" Delia called from behind. She was on the third car now. Sensing something wrong was going on, he tried to wave her back, but she just scowled.

He looked ahead. "We're coming to the Second Avenue stop. When the train slows, we can climb down and try to cut off Hawking," Carver said to Finn.

But the train sped up, making the people waiting at the station a confused and annoyed blur. Something was definitely wrong.

As the last few riders dashed from the first to the second car, Carver tensed, readying for the climb down. Before he could, a tall figure in black cape and top hat appeared at the first car's rear door, hurrying the passengers along.

His father. The Ripper.

He must have realized Hawking was after him and decided to

return the favor. Carver gritted his teeth. Instead of fear, he felt rage. He had to end this, once and for all. He had to.

A rattle shook the train. The killer winced as his right leg nearly buckled. He was still wounded, at least. With Finn here and Hawking below, the three of them might be able to capture him.

The moment the last passenger fled into the second car, the Ripper withdrew something long and gleaming from the folds of his cloak. Carver furrowed his brow. It wasn't his blade; it was the brass gadget Hawking had worked so hard to assemble. He choked. How did he get it? Was Hawking already dead?

Despite the huffing of the train and the rattle of the wheels, it was as though the Ripper heard Carver's gasp. He looked up and, with a feral grin, thrust the pole into the space between cars and twisted. With a wink and a tip of his hat, he vanished back into the car.

Carver felt a lurch as his car slowed. The first car, along with the locomotive, did not. The Ripper had uncoupled the cars. The gap between them was increasing. His father was getting away.

Carver stood shakily. The space widened by one foot, then two . . .

"My father's on that car! I have to jump!" Carver said.

"Are you crazy?" Finn said, rising beside him.

"You'll never make it!" Delia shouted as she caught up. "And if you do, you'll be alone with him!"

Three feet. Four.

Carver turned to Finn. "Throw me!"

"What?"

"Like you did in the attorney's office! On three, I jump, you throw!"

"Finn, don't do it!" Delia shouted.

"Whether you do or not, I'm jumping!" Carver said. "One . . . two . . ."

"No!" Delia called.

Finn grabbed Carver's coat at the neck and his belt at the waist.

"Three!"

Carver leapt. Finn's powerful arms lifted. The pants dug deeply into his crotch. The back of the old coat tore, but the moment his legs were fully stretched, Finn let go, and Carver was air bound.

81

CARVER landed flat on his belly. For a second he thought he'd made it, but the train was traveling much faster than it had been as it left the station. Unable to stop himself, he rolled backward off the roof. Snagging a metal pole, he held on for dear life, then swung onto the small space at the back of the car.

His father was inside. Hawking, too, unless he was already . . .

The speeding car jangled violently. Panting, steadying himself, Carver tried to find even a small drop of calm in the ocean of rage and fear inside him. There was none. There was nothing left to think or do but push the door open.

At the opposite end of the car sat Albert Hawking, his hunched form blurred by the staccato movement of light and dark as the train hurtled past buildings and sky. An old blanket covered his chest and shoulders.

He was as motionless as a corpse.

Slowing his breath, Carver scanned the space between them. On the seats he saw coats, briefcases and lunch pails, all left by the fleeing passengers. Snacks and drinks were set out on some of the tables that sat between the seats, many spilled or spilling from the jarring car. Otherwise the car seemed vacant.

Carver ached to reach Hawking but knew any mistake he made now could be his last. He took a tentative step, then halted. The floor space under the tables seemed too small to hide anything bigger than a small child, but the Ripper had to be hiding somewhere.

"Don't stop now, boy. You've come this far."

Hawking, suddenly animate, raised his clawed hand and motioned him forward.

Carver walked up, glancing nervously between the seats. "Is he here? Are you all right?"

Hawking muttered to himself. "Serves me right. The papers said you were fine, but I had to see for myself. Found the second typewriter, did you? Well, don't expect a pat on the back for it."

A covered teapot sat on the table before his mentor, wobbling before an empty cup. Hawking unfurled the fingers of his clawed hand, straightened them completely. Despite the train's bouncing, he lifted the pot with perfect poise and held it steady.

"Some poor fellow left this behind," he said, pouring himself a cup. "No sense letting it go to waste."

Once the cup was full, Hawking sat up. Briefly, he was at the hunched height Carver was used to seeing. Then came a sharp, bony pop as his back straightened further, adding half a foot to his stature. He paused to wipe some white powder from his hair, revealing how black it was beneath.

Carver tried to make sense of what he was seeing, but sense was the one thing that wouldn't come.

Hawking twisted again and rose further. The covering blanket fell away, revealing his cape and dark formal attire.

"You've no idea how difficult it is to stay in that position," he said, his voice gaining resonance and depth. "Especially after your thuggish friend wrecked my knee and my own blood smacked me with a brick, shocked me twice with that infernal baton and ran me over with an electric carriage!"

Wide-eyed, slack-jawed, Carver managed to say, "It can't be."

His mentor seemed annoyed. *"Can't?* No fire trucks on a stage? Really, boy, unless you're ready to deal with the monster, you shouldn't go looking under the bed. "

He lowered his head, pressed two strips of black hair along his cheeks, and stretched his jaw. When he looked back up, instead of Hawking's ragged face, Carver saw the leering wide-eyed grin of Jack the Ripper.

Quickly as it came, the demonic visage vanished, leaving Hawking looking more like his narrow-eyed self, save for the muttonchops and darker hair.

He ran his fingers along his black cape and suit. "You know, I didn't even dress like this in London. This is how a bunch of lurid artists rendered me. A dime-novel character for dime-novel mentalities. A costume," he said with obvious distaste. He pulled a top hat from beneath the table and held it out. "Care to try it on?"

Carver didn't know whether to scream or sob. "I saw you knocked out at the apartment on Leonard Street!" he said, as if reason could somehow make the image before him vanish.

His father bristled. "Surely you can guess *some,* now that you have the answer? The fact I used the typewriter so no one would recognize my handwriting? Then again, you wouldn't know it was different before I was wounded. As for Leonard Street, Rowena Parker was more worried about her ostrich hat than she was about dying. *She* clocked me on the head. I almost passed out before I killed her."

"You did it. You killed those women . . . ," Carver said.

"And Mr. Tudd. Don't forget dear Septimus."

"Him, too?"

Hawking seemed briefly regretful. "That was harder than I'd imagined. Not technically. You'd be surprised how easy it is to start a riot once you've snuck inside a prison. Easier still to strangle someone in the middle of all that delightful chaos. He never even knew it was me. Better that way, don't you think?"

"Your own partner," Carver said.

"Interesting fact: most murder victims are done in by people they know. Tudd made the luckiest guess of his career, but I couldn't have him figuring out the rest before *you*. You did help there, though, didn't you? Set him up? Even rifled through the corpse." He smiled. "You *are* my blood."

Carver hesitated. "I'm nothing like you."

"We've been through that. Of course you are. Still a bit raw, though. And I am far more entertaining." He raised the pitch of his voice and sounded like Thomasine Bond. "Sorry, Mr. Hawking isn't here." He twisted his head. "Thomas Bond was the only examining pathologist convinced Alice McKenzie was another victim of the Ripper. Never caught that clue, did you?"

"Why? Why did you do this?"

"We've been through that, too. It was a game, for *you*. Planned it from the moment I learned you were alive. After Whitechapel, I couldn't be the detective I'd wanted to be anymore, but my *son* could. Why not let *him* catch the greatest killer in the world? Pretended I was English born; when the boat docked, signed my name Jay Cusack, became Raphael Trone, sent that last letter to Ellis, then waited until you were ready to find me. And here you are, at the brink of greatness. Could have stayed there, too, if you hadn't followed me."

The train lurched sideways. They were turning onto Third.

"You were a great detective!" Carver shouted. "You helped stop an assassination attempt on the president! What could have been so horrible that it changed you into this?"

Hawking slammed his hand onto the table, rattling the teacup. "You've no idea, boy, *no* idea. I thought you and your mother were dead, mutilated worse than anything the Ripper's ever done, and they made me believe *I* did it. That was *my* abyss. I lived through it, or thought I did, until that last gunfight. Finest doctors in London worked on me after that. I got stronger, grew smarter, but they couldn't heal my soul. That, I had to do myself. Killing was the only way I had of crawling back! But you couldn't possibly understand that. Not *yet,* at least."

82

CARVER staggered back in disgust. He'd seen the abyss now, fully. It was standing right in front of him.

His father grew somber. "I was going to die for you, die *as* the Ripper, let Albert Hawking disappear a misunderstood hero. But that was before. Now, well, as I said, I've something else to do. The game is over, Carver. Just let me go; I won't come back. You have my word as your father."

"I can't," Carver said.

Hawking rose. "Why not? It's just one more step. I'm prepared to let *you* go."

"I'm not a killer."

"But you'd have to kill me to stop me."

"No. I don't think so."

Schick! The baton expanded to its full size, the copper tip crackling.

"That again? Very well." The long butcher knife slipped from a fold in his cloak into his hand. "Go on, boy. Stop me."

Hoping to end things quickly, Carver snapped the baton up, pointing the tip toward his father's face. He lunged, but Hawking ducked. He swatted the center of the baton with the flat of the blade so hard it nearly flew from Carver's hand. Tightening his grip, Carver tried again.

Swack! Ping! Clack!

Both swung, dodged, parried. Hawking not only knew something about fencing, he was also faster and considerably stronger. Try as he might, Carver couldn't get the copper tip near his father. But . . . he didn't have to touch him, did he? Last time, Carver only had to touch the blade. The electric shock had carried through the metal, forcing him to drop it.

Hoping to surprise his father again, Carver aimed for the knife. With blinding speed, the Ripper raised his blade and let the point of the baton slip by. At the last instant, he sliced downward.

Sssp! Crackle.

Carver gasped. The baton had been sliced as neatly as if it'd been made of paper. The copper tip fell. Smoke curled from the severed end.

"See that? You made me break your little toy. What a shame."

Carver looked from the knife up to his father's eyes. "Are you going to kill me?"

"No, but I can't have you follow me. So, one last game. Your appearance here forced me to improvise it, but I think I've done well." He pointed his knife toward the locomotive behind them. "The engineer's unconscious. Aside from being handy at uncoupling cars, my device is now keeping the throttle down. It's a nice metaphor for life. *No one's driving the train.* It *will* stop when it hits

Grand Central, but then our poor engineer will be crushed by tons of exploding steel and burning coal, not to mention what will happen to anyone in *front* of the train."

Nonchalantly, he tossed the blade from one hand to the other. "So here's what you can do: pass by, save the engineer and the train or keep trying to fight me, in which case, we'll *all* die."

"You just said you wouldn't kill me."

"I never said I'd keep you from killing yourself. Some things are nearly impossible to stop. A little like . . ." He briefly twisted his face back into the berserk visage of the Ripper. "A runaway train?"

Carver gritted his teeth. The cuffs Roosevelt gave him jangled in his pocket. He clapped his hand over them to stop the sound.

"Here, I'll stand aside to let you through." He lowered his blade and shifted, making room. "If you are different from me, as you like to think, there's only one choice."

Carver stood motionless, his thoughts a jumbled blur.

"Come on, boy, there isn't *all* that much time left! Decide . . . decide . . . decide!"

Carver put his eyes on the door and, trying not to look at the dark figure, walked. He passed Hawking, put his left hand on the door and opened it, letting winter air and hot steam rush in. His father looked relieved.

"You will make a great detective," he said. "Second best, next to me."

Carver opened his mouth as if to answer. Instead, he pulled the cuffs out and slammed one end around Hawking's wrist. Even off guard, his father's reflexes were phenomenal. He pulled away rapidly, but a sudden rattle from the train forced him to shift his weight to his bad leg. As he winced, the blade fell from his hand.

With his father slightly off balance, Carver clamped the other end of the cuffs to the seat's metal arm.

The only thing left was to get out of his reach. Carver threw himself backward through the open door, trying to stay on his feet as he reached the small space between the car and the locomotive. Furious, Hawking lurched forward. Steam billowed around them, fanning the dark man's cape.

Carver kept backing up, slamming into the rear of the coal bay. Hawking's long strong fingers nearly grabbed him but were stopped dead by the steel cuffs. Caught, the killer yanked as if he were willing to rip the hand off. He snapped his arm, gnashed his teeth and let loose a feral scream that seemed louder than the thrumming engine, louder than the wheels screeching against the steel tracks.

But then, he started cackling. "Excellent, boy! You've chained the devil! Now what are you going to do with him?"

83

HIS FATHER'S laughter loud behind him, Carver climbed atop the coal bay. Sooty smoke covered his eyes, filling his mouth like a vile liquid. Having made its last turn, the train barreled along 42nd Street. He could see the rounded tops of the three Grand Central towers visible in the distance, marking the end of the track.

He lowered himself to the open cabin door. The coal smoke let up, and he tried to spit the grit and foul taste from his mouth. Once inside, blasted by the heat, he was amazed how quickly his father managed to wreak such havoc.

The engineer, a compact, older man whose au– burn hair and sideburns mixed with the blackish smears on his face, lay in a heap, lolling dangerously as the train swayed. A bright swelling rose on the side of his forehead, but his fitful breathing told Carver he was still alive.

He turned to the controls, a series of unfamiliar levers and a panel of gauges, the dials all pointing into the red zone. Carver didn't need to know much to realize the boiler could explode before the train even crashed. He searched the cabin, at first not even recognizing Hawking's curious brass instrument because it fit so seamlessly with the design.

He wrapped his hands around it and pulled. It wouldn't budge. Finding a crowbar, he swung at the device. Still nothing. He wedged the flat end of the crowbar into it and yanked with all his might. His grip snapped. The brass pole didn't move.

On a straightway now, the train stopped rocking and picked up speed. Below the elevated track, pedestrians gaped up in wonder. Calling to them would be useless, but he did need help.

He turned to the prone engineer and shook him. "Wake up! Wake up!"

The man's head rolled as if it was barely connected to his neck. There was a lunch pail on the floor, a drinking bottle jutting from the top. Carver grabbed it, opened it and poured the contents on the man's head, realizing too late that it was whiskey.

As it splashed against the man's ruddy nose and mouth, the sparks flying from the boiler threatened to set him aflame. Frantic, Carve tried to mop the liquid with his shirt. As he did, the man sputtered. Seeing Carver, he screamed and withdrew a pistol from the thick pocket of his overalls.

Carver winced. "It wasn't me! I didn't attack you! You've got to help me stop the train!"

The man looked highly dubious until Carver pointed to the brass pole wedged against the throttle. Together, they grabbed and pulled. The engineer was short, but his arms were thick and powerful. As he strained, his eyes grew so wide it seemed they'd pop out of his head.

With a gasp they both let go. The brass pole still hadn't budged.

"Forget it!" the engineer said. He looked out the door at the blur of tracks and then ahead. The great terminal building grew larger every second. "We'll have to jump!"

Carver nodded and then remembered his trapped father. He was a vile, crazed killer, but he'd also been his mentor and, in some sick, twisted way, tried to care for him. Leaving him to die, handcuffed to a speeding train, sounded more like something the Ripper might do.

"I left someone behind!" Carver shouted.

"Get 'em fast!" the engineer said, aiming himself at the door.

Carver pulled him back. "Can I have your gun?"

The engineer shrugged and then handed him the pistol. An instant later, his small, thick body was rolling and bouncing along the tracks. Carver had no idea if the man even survived. He didn't have time to wonder now. Grand Central was less than four blocks away.

He climbed out of the heated cabin, back into the chill and smoky air. Pistol in hand, cocked and ready to fire, he made his way back to the passenger car.

He formed a plan. He'd toss his father the keys. He could unlock himself, and they'd make the leap together. It wasn't a great plan, but it was all he had.

But the doorway was empty. So was the rest of the car. His father was gone, the door at the far end of the car still open. Only the handcuffs remained, one end connected to the seat arm, the other jangling free, a thick ring of dark blood marring the steel.

Had he broken his own hand to escape?

Ahead, the track tunnel that would bring the train into Grand

Central swelled like a monster's gaping maw. Small blurs of motion that Carver took for people were scurrying and leaping out of the way. He made his way to the door his father had left open. The moment the train careened into darkness, he leapt out, having no idea where he would land.

84

CARVER didn't hit the tracks so much as skimmed them, skipping back into the air like a stone on a pond. He rose once, twice, and then a third time before settling into a sideways roll. He heard a crash as the locomotive hit the end of the track, tore the concrete stop from its foundations and kept going.

It was the first of several ear-shattering sounds he would hear.

Carver raised his head in time to see the locomotive dive off the end of the track, pulling the passenger car behind it. Then came the second, louder crash, a sound like thunder, as the locomotive's prow slammed into the marble floor of the terminal below.

By the time the passenger car rolled over the track edge, people were screaming. The car didn't completely disappear from view. Instead, after a third, lesser crash, it halted, remaining tilted at the track's end. Carver could only imagine it had somehow hit the rear of the fallen locomotive.

The fourth and final sound was the most terrible. The locomotive's boiler, weakened first by the pressure, then by the crash and lastly by the passenger car, exploded. It was a huge rolling boom, a single beat on a vast drum, followed by a rush of hot air and billowing smoke and flame.

To Carver it looked as if his father, in a final act of spite, had opened up the mouth of hell.

85

THERE WERE forty-seven wounded but, miraculously, no deaths. Carver earned several gashes and colorful bruises, but nothing that required bed rest. Timothy Walsh, the hapless train engineer, suffered only a broken wrist. When Carver visited him to return his pistol, he cheerily said he'd gained more than he lost. Now he had a grand adventure story he could tell again and again.

A week later Carver sat with Delia, Finn and Commissioner Roosevelt on the plaza of the vacant New Pinkertons headquarters. The smell from the analytical engine's smoke had long cleared, the air relatively fresh. It was Roosevelt and Finn's first visit, and even now, an hour after arriving, they both kept glancing back at the pneumatic subway car that sat quietly at the platform.

Carver had pulled Tudd's plush, comfortable chair

onto the plaza for Roosevelt, but the commissioner preferred to strut around, jacket open, thumbs hooked in his pants. "It *is* a good place, Mr. Young, quite fine and very quiet," Roosevelt said. "Even now, though, I still hear the rumble of Mulberry Street, much the way one hears the ocean roar when putting a shell to the ear. Duty calls, and we should get to it."

He tapped a file on the table and pushed it toward Carver. "As I told you, I got in touch with the Pinkerton Agency to see what they could tell us about Mr. Hawking. I did not, as you requested, mention the money Allan Pinkerton bequeathed to found this place."

Carver grabbed the file and flipped eagerly through the pages. Delia wanted to peer over his shoulder but instead asked the commissioner, "What did you find out?"

Roosevelt shrugged. "Hints, Miss Stephens, echoes. Hawking was no stranger to the double life. The Pinkertons used undercover agents in the Civil War, against outlaw gangs and, as the agency spread, against criminal gangs in New York. In the late 1870s Hawking was asked to infiltrate one such group responsible for kidnappings and violence to women. He was in deep for years, living among them, acting like one of them, tipping off the agency to the worst of their crimes. As time passed, against the advice of Pinkerton himself, he married. In 1881, the leader of the gang discovered Hawking's identity."

Carver tensed. "The year I was born."

Roosevelt softened his tone. "According to the file it was also the same year Hawking's wife was brutally murdered. She was pregnant at the time."

"My mother," Carver said. "Hawking said they somehow convinced him *he'd* done it."

"If he believed himself the murderer, he did not confess. The record does show that he became erratic, eccentric, but still remained a brilliant detective. Other than what you've told me about his founding the New Pinkertons and the final gunfight that left him wounded, that is all we know." Roosevelt paused to think a moment. "Were I a betting man, I'd guess the death of his wife nearly destroyed him, but that final battle pushed him over the edge and turned him into a callous killer." He looked at Carver purposefully. "But when dealing with something so important as the identity of the world's most hated murderer, it is not appropriate to bet."

"No, it's not," Carver agreed. "There has to be more to it."

Hoping he'd see something new, Carver quickly scrawled a time line:

1881	I'm born. Hawking, undercover, thinks my mother and I dead.
1885	Tudd and Hawking establish New Pinkertons in NYC
1888	Hawking wounded in battle, travels to Europe/London to heal
1888 Aug/Nov	Ripper Whitechapel murders
1889 July	Hawking finds out I'm alive, writes letter I found. Starts plan
1895 May	First NYC murder

He stared at what he'd written, but unlike the clues his father had left for him, nothing sprang immediately to mind.

"We'll have to content ourselves with this for now. His purpose accomplished, perhaps Hawking will vanish as promised. But my people tell me that this sort of savagery cannot contain itself for long. He will eventually find reason to kill again. But should he do so within this city, we will be here to stop him, armed with courage, allies and information."

"I have to track him down," Carver said.

"I understand the desire, but I don't see how to manage it. Seeing as we have no inkling to his whereabouts, the next move, I'm afraid, is his. Until he makes it, I advise you stay put, learn and grow," Roosevelt said. He looked admiringly at Carver. "You may be young, but there is much of a man in you already."

He pulled out his pocket watch. "I must be getting back. Once I've left, you may begin contacting any of the people who worked here that you deem trustworthy. Though their identities can and should remain secret from me, you will keep me apprised of their activities."

"Yes, sir." Carver nodded.

"Bully!" Roosevelt said. He shook Carver's hand firmly. "It will be good to be able to call upon such a force. Mr. Hawking aside, the corruption in this city remains vast, varied and as determined to destroy us as we are to destroy it. Now I say with greater confidence than ever, it is fighting the losing battle!"

With that, the thick-shouldered commissioner strutted over to the subway. "Remember, Mr. Young. Do not dwell on the darkness within. Act!"

With a wave, he stepped inside the car and closed the door.

A few moments later, the door opened again. Roosevelt stuck his square head back out. "I just press that lever under the seat and it takes me back?"

"Yes, sir," Carver said with a smile.

"Excellent! Alice sends her regards," Roosevelt said. Delia winced at the sound of the name.

Moments later the car moved off into the round tunnel, silent as the gentle air that propelled it.

"He should run for president," Finn said. He turned back to Carver. "Sorry about your mother."

Carver shrugged. "I don't even know how to feel about that. I never knew her."

When Carver fell into a silent brood, Delia nodded for Finn to do something.

Obliging, the larger youth punched him on the arm.

"Ow!" Carver said. "What was that for?"

"Nothing. How's it feel being in charge?"

Carver looked around. "I won't really be in charge. I'll be more of a liaison between the new Pinkertons and Roosevelt. I'd have no idea how to run this place."

"Yet," Delia added. Sitting next to him, she began idly running her hands over the worn coat Carver had left hanging on the back of his chair.

Carver shook himself back into the moment. "Let's start with Emeril. *He's* the one who should be in charge. Then Mr. Beckley. *Someone* has to clean the athenaeum."

He shuddered to think of the mess he and Delia had left it in.

Delia ran her fingers along the tears in the old coat. "I'm still not sure how I feel about lying to the Ribes about all this. But it *is* important." Her index finger found a large hole. "Carver, why *are* you still wearing this old thing?"

"It was his," Carver said. "It's a reminder."

She rolled the fabric through her hands. "It's falling apart. It stinks of coal. Do you want me to mend some of the . . ." She stopped and looked up at Carver.

"What?" he said.

"There's something in the lining."

He grabbed it and spread it out on the table. As he pressed against the cloth, a rectangular outline became visible. Unwilling to wait for a knife or scissors, Carver ripped at the seam and withdrew a wrapped package.

"I don't believe it," Carver said.

"Should we check it for fingerprints?" Delia asked, but by then Carver had torn it open. Inside was *The Memoirs of Sherlock Holmes,* by Arthur Conan Doyle.

"The newest collection," Carver said, puzzled. "He left me a present?"

As he flipped idly through the pages, three sheets fell out. One was the letter Carver had found at Ellis. Another was a facsimile of the *Dear Boss* letter from London, but this copy seemed to have been ripped from a book. The third was new, but written in the same scrawl.

Finn and Delia crowded near as he read.

From the Abyss

Three souvenirs. The first I'd writ in London when I planned the game. Second snatched from a library book. Wicked of me.

Did lie a bit, but can you blame me? Your mother would never forgive me if I went to the gallows without a hello. Turns out she may be alive.

Yours truly,
. . . you know

Carver took a long look. "My father."

". . . is totally crazy," Finn said.

Delia nodded toward the file Roosevelt left. "At least now you know he was a good man once."

"I think that's what worries me most of all," Carver said. "If he can change so much, what's to say I can't?"

"Because you won't," Delia said. "No matter what else happens, you'll still be Carver Young."

EDITOR'S NOTE

The following article was in fact printed by
The New York Times
on January 20, 1889:

"JACK THE RIPPER" KINDLY WRITES THAT HE IS READY FOR BUSINESS IN GOTHAM

The following communication, written in a poor hand, was received by Capt. Ryan of the East Thirty-fifth Street station yesterday afternoon:

Capt. Ryan:
You think that "Jack the Ripper" is in England, but he is not. I am right here, and I expect to kill somebody by Thursday next, and so get ready for me with your pistols, but I have a knife that has done more than your pistols. Next thing you will hear of some woman dead. Yours truly,
Jack The Ripper

The captain received the letter about two o'clock yesterday afternoon. It came by mail, and the envelope bore two stamps. There was also two cents due on the letter. Capt. Ryan did not notice where the letter was postmarked and, after taking a copy of it, sent it to police headquarters.

CHARACTER & GADGET GLOSSARY

Hey, *lots* of fiction authors take liberties with history for the sake of an exciting story. We'll change details about famous people, invent new technologies, imagine wars, aliens, monsters or whatever, all to keep the reader glued to the page.

And while your humble author is guilty as charged, in researching *Ripper,* more often than not, I found the truth pretty fascinating in its own right. As a result, many of the gadgets, as well as details regarding the historical people appearing in the novel, are historically accurate. What was real and what wasn't? Some of the answers may surprise you!

Jack the Ripper

Yep, the world's first internationally famous serial killer did indeed exist, was never caught, and his identity remains a mystery that has fueled many books, novels and films. The details regarding his heinous crimes in London are all true, including the theoretical sixth victim, Alice McKenzie. Two of the letters the killer supposedly wrote appear in the novel verbatim. The New York City murders are entirely fictitious, but in 1895 Jack was still very much on everyone's mind. More than one newspaper article from the period wonders if some grisly killing was actually old Jack in action, and the July 20, 1889, letter published by the *New York Times* did, in fact, exist. As far as anyone knows, however, he did not have a son, and given his attitude toward women, I think it unlikely. Was the Ripper ever in New York? Maybe. One suspect, Francis Tumblety, returned there after the Whitechapel murders, and, at Scotland Yard's request, the police kept him under surveillance.

Allan Pinkerton

The exciting career of America's first private detective is much as Mr. Hawking describes, including his debilitating stroke, his remarkable recovery and his battles with his sons for control of the agency he created. And the Pinkerton Detective Agency really is credited with coining the term "private eye." Past that, I did make up the stuff about Mr. Pinkerton leaving copious cash to the fictional agents Hawking and Tudd to establish the New Pinkertons, but I like to think he'd have been fond of the idea.

Teddy Roosevelt

Having seen this boisterous gap-toothed man whom the Teddy Bear was named after portrayed in films like *Night at the Museum*, I always figured all the shouting and derring-do were an exaggeration. Nope. The real-life Teddy Roosevelt is the most exciting figure I've ever had the pleasure to read about. I've kept the details about him and his life accurate, even quoting him when feasible. He did indeed serve as New York City police commissioner, and actually did lean out the window of the Mulberry Street headquarters and scream *Yieee!* to attract the attention of the press. He later became assistant secretary of the navy, vice president, and, when President McKinley was assassinated, president of the United States. Even all that is only half his story. A big-game hunter, he actually went on an expedition to find a *monster*.

Alice Roosevelt

A flamboyant figure and trouble for her dad throughout her life, Teddy Roosevelt's eldest daughter is often quoted as saying, "If you can't say anything good about someone, sit right here by me." I think the quote sums her up nicely, though I doubt she originally said it at the young age she does in this book. It is possible such a lively gal might've practiced the line on someone like Carver. She's also known for saying, "I have a simple philosophy. Fill what's empty. Empty what's full. And scratch where it itches."

Sarah Edwards and the Midnight Band of Mercy

The creepy cat-killer Carver meets while searching for his lost father is another of those things that are simply too strange to have been made up. The Midnight Band of Mercy was made up of thirty or so middle and upper class women who spent their evenings putting cats to death, often unconcerned with whether they were pets or not. When Mrs. Edwards was found with a basket full of chloroform and dead cats, she was arrested. When asked what right she had to be killing cats, she replied, "I found the cats out after eight o'clock last evening, and they haven't any right to be." Charges were brought in 1893, and the group officially disbanded.

Alfred Beach Pneumatic Subway

The New Pinkertons' headquarters is a complete fabrication.
Not so the amazing train leading to it. The Beach Pneumatic
Transit System existed exactly as described. In 1870, it could
indeed be entered from Devlin's Department Store on the
corner of Broadway and Warren Street. In its first year, over
400,000 passengers rode the short dead-end track. It was
rumored Beach never acquired funding to continue the system
because he failed to bribe the corrupt government, but more
reliable sources say he couldn't get the financial backing due in
part to a stock market crash. America's first subway was
immortalized in the Beatles-esque tune "Sub-Rosa Subway," by
Klaatu, as well as enjoying a brief appearance in *Ghostbusters II*.
Though it no longer exists, in 1912 the station and track were
excavated to make room for a new subway. With a little
hunting, photos of the cylindrical car can be found on the Web.

Pneumatic Elevator

I *thought* I'd made this up. But it seemed such a reasonable
enough extension of the pneumatic subway, I couldn't be sure.
So, as I was fact-checking for this glossary, I checked the Web
and came upon a few current companies that actually build
these machines. They're more properly called *vacuum elevators,*
but the principle is the same. They're generally used in private
homes for a single passenger. There is no record of them being
around in 1895, though.

Speaking Tube

The speaking tube used in Tudd's New Pinkerton office was a
popular means of communicating on ships and in offices as early
as the 1700s. They were made from metal, rubber or even linen
and remained in widespread use during the early twentieth
century.

Office Periscope

Carver is wowed by a peek at the street through a dim mirror
that Tudd describes as a periscope. While the view mirror, the
curved tubes described, and the distance involved are all literary
license, periscopes, consisting of angled mirrors in an enclosure,
have been around for ages. Johannes Gutenberg, better known
for his printing press, sold them way back in the 1430s to pilgrims
so they could see over the heads of crowds at religious festivals.

Pneumatic Tube

The idea of delivering something by using air to suck it through
a tube was invented by William Murdoch, around 1799.
Everyone loved it, but it wasn't very useful until the capsule was
invented in the mid-1800s. Then you had something.
Pneumatic tubes quickly became popular in businesses and
remained in popular use until around 1960.

Phonograph

There were a few fascinating early precursors, but Edison's
successful device for recording and playing back sounds dates to

1877. Fairly widespread by 1895, and used by businessmen to record dictation, the general public saw them mostly in the parlors described by Carver, where people would listen to music recorded on a cylinder for a nickel.

Stun Baton

In terms of available technology, Carver's stun baton is the only real anachronism. To stun a man, approximately two million volts are required, and the batteries to handle such a load did not exist at the time of this story. For comparison, the zinc-carbon cell, first marketed in 1896, produced a mere 1.5 volts. It wasn't until the 1970s that stun batons appeared. But hey, secret lab with a lot of funding? Who knows what you can do.

Auto-Lock Pick

Lock-picking is as old as locks (four thousand years plus), but as far as I know, I made up Carver's handy-dandy auto–lock pick. Today there are electric lock picks available that speed the process, so there's no reason a mechanical version wouldn't be feasible, but if it came in a kit, I'd hate to be the one to assemble it.

Electric Taxi

While it may well be the way of the future, the electric car was also the way of the past. Not many realize it, but there was a thirty-year competition between the noisy, smelly gas engines and their quieter, battery-driven counterparts. The battle lasted from the 1890s through the 1920s. After some fine-tuning, the gas engine provided such greater range and speed, it won out. The electric taxis that appear in the book first appeared in New York City a mere two years later, in 1897, but if a secret detective agency can't get a few advance models, who can?

Hawking's Train Device

The brass device of many pieces and screws that Albert Hawking spends hours diligently cleaning and assembling is, sadly, completely fictitious. That said, it doesn't strike me as impossible. In the early days, train operators changed tracks by whacking the switcher's lever with any old stick as they passed, and there's no reason I know of why the cars couldn't be decoupled with the correctly shaped tool.

Automatic Guns

A bit of fancy. The motors and other mechanics required to build the weapons certainly existed at the time, but a windup gun strikes me as an oddly *dangerous* thing to have around.

Police Headquarters Phone Switch

As the book mentions, once Alexander Bell's patent on the telephone ran out, there was a mad rush of companies providing service, kind of like cell phones today. The big difference was that you needed *wires* to connect all the phones. Larger offices like police headquarters went crazy trying to keep up and always had their own phone switch. The version Carver uses is an early model from the time, described in an old catalog I discovered during my research.

Analytical Engine

While I take liberties by imagining it manipulating a large database, the analytical engine, the world's first general-use, steam-powered computer, is real, on paper anyway. It was designed in 1837 by English mathematician Charles Babbage, but sadly never built during his lifetime. According to his plans, the program would be input through thick cardboard punch cards (used at the time to automate looms, like the roller on a player piano). For the output, the machine would have a printer and a little bell to indicate when it was finished. Babbage assembled small parts of it before his death in 1871. In 1910, his son, Henry, built a larger piece and used it to print out an (incorrect) answer to a mathematical problem. It wasn't until 1991 that the London Museum of Science built a fully working version. Pictures are available online, and if I may editorialize for a moment, it's the coolest-looking thing ever—putting the steam in steampunk.

ACKNOWLEDGMENTS

Ripper has been a wild and wonderful trip through time and myth, my ticket provided by three equally wild and wonderful people. Joe Veltre's done a great job repping my books for many years now and did me a particular solid by putting me in touch with the intrepid and eternally enthusiastic Pete Harris and quint-essentially savvy Philomel editor Michael Green. Pete's support and Michael's guidance made working on this book extremely gratifying.

Scouring through history and nineteenth-century technology also put me in touch with some terrific reference works. I studied old maps, train schedules, telephone-switching manuals and more too numerous to name. I do want to make special note of four particular works. In terms of reality, there's the exhaustive *Complete History of Jack the Ripper* by Philip Sugden (Constable & Robinson, 1994) and the wonderfully evocative *Commissioner Roosevelt* by H. Paul Jeffers (Wiley & Sons, 1994). On the fiction side, I greatly enjoyed two novels set in 1890s NYC, *The Alienist* by Caleb Carr (Random House, 2006) and the lesser-known but no less worthy read *The Midnight Band of Mercy* by Michael Blaine (Soho Press, 2004).